MAKING OUT WITH MERMAIDS

HAVEN EVER AFTER - BOOK SEVEN

HAZEL MACK

COPYRIGHT

© Hazel Mack Author 2025

EBOOK ISBN: 978-1-957873-60-2

PAPERBACK ISBN: 978-1-957873-61-9

All rights reserved. No part of this publication may be reproduced, stored or transmitted in any form or by any means, electronic, mechanical, photocopying, recording, scanning, or otherwise without written permission from the publisher. It is illegal to copy this book, post it to a website, or distribute it by any other means without permission.

This novel is entirely a work of fiction. The names, characters and incidents portrayed in it are the work of the author's imagination. Any resemblance to actual persons, living or dead, events or localities is entirely coincidental. However, if I get the chance to become Ever's newest resident, I'll take it!

I don't support the use of AI in book, book cover or book graphic creation. If you love human generated books, please feel free to learn more at my website at www.annafury.com/ai. I do not approve the creation of derivative works based on this book or series without consent.

Editing - Krista Venero at Mountains Wanted

Cover - Anna Fury Author

Cover Art - Linda Noeran (@linda.noeran)

❀ Created with Vellum

THIS BOOK WAS WRITTEN BY A HUMAN
HUMAN GENERATED
I DON'T SUPPORT AI BOOKS OR ART

AUTHORS ARE NOW FACING AN UNPRECEDENTED CHALLENGE - ARTIFICIAL INTELLIGENCE (AI).

AI-based "books", which are computer written, rather than human, are flooding the market and reducing our ability to earn a living wage writing books for you, our amazing readers.

The problem with AI as it stands today? It's not capable of thinking on its own. It ingests data and mimics someone else's style, often plagiarizing art and books without the original creator or author's consent.

There's a very real chance human authors will be forced out of the market as AI-written works take over. Yet your favorite authors bring magical worlds, experiences and emotions to life in a way that a computer can't. If you want to save that, then we need your help.

LEARN MORE ABOUT THE HARMFUL EFFECTS OF AI-WRITTEN BOOKS AND AI-GENERATED ART ON MY WEBSITE AT WWW.ANNAFURY.COM/AI

SYNOPSIS

Betmal

Starting over in the hidden monster town of Ever was meant to begin the next phase of my life—freedom from an unfortunate romantic entanglement and with plenty of time to spend with my son and his mate. But all of that changes when I scent *her* in the coffee shop…a kindred soul, an artist, like me…Amatheia.

My obsession with the hauntingly beautiful mermaid is immediate and complete. But when I introduce myself, she holds me at arms' length. That won't do. It won't do at all. So I cook up a plan. I'll redesign Ever's welcome packet and hire her to do the art. That will give us plenty of time alone together, time I can use to get to know her better…in my boardroom *and* my bedroom.

Yet the closer we get, the more obvious it becomes that my immediate draw to her isn't a passing lustful fancy. It's something deep, primal, and irrefutable—she is my fated female, and I have waited for her for thousands of years.

But the fates have a sense of humor when her uncle, the king, tells Amatheia she's to be wed to a merman of his choosing. He claims he's simply fulfilling her mother's dying wish. I suspect darker motives.

One thing is clear, I can't guarantee Ama's freedom from her uncle's political maneuvering without bringing a fight into Ever, something she is desperate not to do. I lost my heart to her when we met. Now, I'll have to fight to keep it…

Making Out With Mermaids is a spicy MF monster romance. Come for the charm but stay for the happily ever after.

GET THE FREEBIES

WANT SPICY EPILOGUES?

Sign up for my newsletter to access the FREE bonus epilogues to every Hazel Mack book I write.

www.annafury.com/subscribe

CONTENT NOTICE

While this book is very sweet and lighthearted, there are a couple heavy themes to mention. In particular, there's a cruel family member, reference to past parental death and resulting limb loss, shark attacks, and if you're wondering how those things connect together, it's probably exactly what you're thinking!

If you have any particular questions, feel free to reach out to me at author@annafury.com!

DEDICATION

For Leah, whose obsession with merfolk led me to beg her to write the beautiful poem in this book. You have a way with words, my friend…

PS If you want to read her book where the part-god merman with double you-know-whats claims his maybe-human mate, you can do that here.

CHAPTER ONE
BETMAL

Smiling, I straighten my fitted navy vest and step through the glittering green portal surface, into the translucent hallway that'll take me straight to Ever. It's the last of many trips, I hope, as I leave the hidden monster haven that's been my home for centuries.

The reality is that I won't miss much about Hearth Headquarters. I lived here only because my mates lived and worked here.

If I can even call them mates. I certainly don't think of them that way, not after everything that's happened over the last thousand or so years.

Focusing to relax the automatic tension in my jaw when I think of Evenia and Aberen, I release the agitation and stride confidently through the portal hall, emerging on the other side in Ever haven's portal station, in the American state of Massachusetts.

The first two monsters I see are my son, Abemet, and his mate, Morgan.

"Betmal!" she shouts, lurching forward to fling herself into my arms. She squeezes my neck until I can barely breathe, laughing and making happy noises as my son watches silently. A tiny smile tips his lips upward.

I return Morgan's hug, but eventually I set the pretty, red-haired witch down.

She steps back and grins at me. "Please tell me Evenia caused some sort of scene on the way out, and you got to verbally bitch slap her in front of all of HQ? Please tell me it happened because I've been having dreams about it."

A laugh bubbles from my throat, but I shake my head. "Sorry to disappoint, darling girl, but she did not show up for my departure." I glance at Abemet, trying to decide if I should speak ill of his mother and other father. Ultimately, I decide it's fine. We all know whose son Abe truly is.

I return Morgan's feral grin. "Aberen did see fit to send me a gorgeous bouquet of poisoned blood roses on the eve of my departure."

Morgan gasps, and Abe snorts out an amused laugh.

His mate crosses her arms, gray eyes narrowing as one foot taps on the tiled floor of Ever's beautiful portal station. "He tried to *poison* you?"

"Purely symbolic," I assure her. "A last 'fuck you,' if you will. He would never expect me to fall for the trick."

"I swear to gods," she huffs, "if either of them shows their face in Ever, I'm gonna get Lou to run them through with her blue magic. She could do it, too. She could spin them up and like, I don't know, rip their skins off or something."

"But a blue witch never would," I remind my daughter-in-law. "Spiteful as your aunt might feel on my behalf, she's born to protect."

The noise that erupts from Morgan is half irritated and half conniving. I've gotten the chance to know my son's witchy mate well, and if I've learned one thing, it's that she will hold a grudge until the day she dies, especially in regards to protecting someone she loves.

Abe clears his throat. "I've already made it clear to Mother that she and Aberen are not welcome in Ever, not for any reason." He shrugs and reaches for my bag. "It won't stop her from coming if she sees something to meddle in, but barring that, they're not likely to show up anytime soon." He tosses my bag over his muscular shoulder and jerks his head toward the exit. "Shall we? A lovely cottage popped up on the edge of town with your name on it."

Morgan's fierce look morphs into a smile as she tosses auburn hair over her shoulder. "It's adorable, too. We hope you love it! We're just so glad you're finally here for good." She glances up at me, batting her lashes coyly. "Maybe now that you're here and…unencumbered, you might find a lovely monstress to date who likes you for you."

I chuckle as she slips her arm through mine, holding on to my biceps as I guide her to follow Abe. "I'm not worried about that in the slightest, darling. Entanglements happen when and where they want to, but it's not my focus. Not to mention divorce paperwork and visiting a warlock to undo the magic of dual mating bites were…physically painful."

Resting my hand over the one she has wrapped around my arm, I grin more broadly. "I want to spend time with you two and reconnect with friends who live here. I couldn't be more excited for that."

She squeezes me tighter as we exit the cavernous portal station and emerge deep inside the forest in what's known as Shifter Hollow, the part of Ever reserved for shifters, centaurs and pegasi. For the next half hour, Morgan regales me with tales of the shifter queen and her mate who rule from the Hollow. Apparently, the queen is now on a musical tour—a literal as well as figurative rock star.

"She's the coolest monster I've ever met," Morgan gushes, glancing at Abe with a quick nip of her lower lip. "Besides Abe, of course."

I look at my son as he strides confidently up the street a pace ahead of us. My intuitive gift pings. Abe's happy. More than happy. He's at peace. He's got Morgan after hundreds of years of wanting her. He waited for so long. I love that the read I get on him now is peaceful comfort.

We approach Downtown Ever's Main Street crossroads, the Galloping Green Bean diner to our left and the vampire-owned Higher Grounds coffee shop to our right. Main Street stretches long with nearly a dozen adorable businesses, red-and-white-striped awnings fluttering on a cool breeze. I'm excited to visit Ever's shops and restaurants, to explore, once I get my things settled.

Crossing over Main, we continue up Sycamore past the Community Garden and the beautiful pink and white Annabelle Inn, Ever's singular B&B. Ah, I need to pop in and catch up with my friend Catherine, the proprietress. I make a mental note to come back within a day or so.

We walk in silence for another quarter hour, enjoying the beautiful fall-feeling weather—a pattern Ever haven opted to keep year-round, no matter what's going on in the human world outside the protective wards.

"The house is just ahead." Abe points toward a curve in Sycamore Street. At the edge of the street's curve, a gravel driveway is clearly visible.

I bring my hand to my forehead, shading my eyes from Ever's bright sun as I focus up the road a bit. I'm accustomed to Hearth Headquarters' permanently pitch-black sky. This sunshine will take some getting used to.

Abe pauses as Morgan and I stop next to him. He looks at me with all his characteristic seriousness. "I think you'll be pleased, Father. The home is gorgeous. Gothic yet modern. I had a hand in a bit of the design, although Ever does what she wants when homes pop up, as you know."

Ah, that little bit of magic is something I insisted on when monster leadership designed the haven system all those centuries ago. It's a compatibility spell of sorts, ensuring those who belong in specific havens are given every reason to stay. Magical houses popping up out of nowhere certainly does make one feel welcome.

Excitement warms me and I clap my son on the shoulder. "Thank you, Abemet. I can't wait to see what you and Ever have cooked up."

His lips tilt upward. It's been a long time since he worked as an architect, and these days he's all but retired. Yet I know my son, and it won't be long until he gets the itch to work again. Or maybe not. Now that he's mated, his priorities have undoubtedly shifted to put her first. Perhaps keeping up with his brilliant, fierce mate is all he has time and desire for.

He takes off again, leading us to the curve in the road. Once we arrive at the driveway, I see my new home for the first time. Pride rushes through me, knowing the town itself built this home for me, but Abe had a hand in her design.

Morgan jogs ahead to catch up with her mate, clinging to his arm as they walk peacefully up the driveway with my luggage. I follow, admiring the bones of the home.

Wide black stone steps lead to a curved arch with a recessed front door. The entryway section of the house is built of pale gray stone with black-trimmed windows and doors. To the right of the entryway, two giant sections arch like church windows. Intricately scrolled details give the entire house a gothic yet modern vibe. Even the roof tiles are black. Through expansive windows across the home's front, interior lights shine pale yellow light on modern furnishings.

"It's beautiful," I murmur, knowing my son can hear the praise even from far away, good as vampire hearing is.

Abe spins and walks slowly backward, opening his arms wide. "I've imported quite a few furnishings for you, but the house is well aware that you might choose to change some things. And I left the entire backyard alone, although I get the sense she might try to put a workshop of sorts back there." His smile grows bigger. "I suppose that'll be up to you."

A workshop. He knows I love having a separate working space from my home. My workshop in the castle he grew up in was our little hideaway. When he was a child, he often joined me in seeking solace from Evenia and Aberen. I'd grown apart from them by the time Abemet was born, and he was my only bright light in remaining in a loveless triad. Most of my fond memories from his childhood are times we spent together playing, working magic, learning about our innate vampiric abilities.

He flew for the first time by jumping off the workshop roof with me.

I absolutely must have a workshop here. But he's right…it's best if I create it in partnership with the house.

Abe and Morgan swing matching glossy black doors open.

"Welcome home, Betmal," Morgan says quietly, her smile soft as I enter.

"Home indeed," I murmur, turning to stroke the matte black wallpaper covering every inch of the front entryway. Nearly all of the furnishings are dark, the entryway punctuated by a singular modern concrete entry table. Glittering ornate lamps sit on either end, a giant bowl in the middle full of stones.

I turn to Abe with a surprised look, pointing to the bowl. "Good luck stones from home? However did you manage that? You know Evenia will notice if a few are missing."

When Morgan looks between us in apparent confusion, Abe chuckles and waves a hand at the bowl of flat gray stones.

"Upon death, most vampires elect to be cremated and pressed into these river stones. It's a long-held tradition and our castle had hundreds of them in a little display in a side courtyard near Betmal's workshop."

Morgan's brows rise in seeming delight. "And you stole them?"

For the first time, his grin is as feral as his mate's can be. "They're meant to bring you good luck and guidance. The more you have, the better. Turns out the castle workshop still holds me in high regard, though, so I was able to snatch these from the display while Evenia and Aberen were at work one day. Mother counts them somewhat regularly. She'll notice they're gone and be unable to do anything about it."

A laugh bubbles out of my throat. Our former home was notoriously prickly and always loved my mates far more than it loved me. I always assumed that's why the workshop popped up for Abe and me—that was *our* home, our place, our sanctuary away from them.

I'd never have stayed in that relationship so long, but Abemet came along—the happiest of surprises—and I stayed while he grew up. I suppose I could have taken him and left, but I'd have given up my role in monster headquarters leadership. It was far easier for me to put up with them to keep my job, than to leave and not be able to affect policy change.

Now, I don't care. I've kept Evenia's secrets for so long, she'd be a fool to cross me.

"Now listen," Morgan starts, striding into the entryway as she jerks her head toward the back of the home. "We thought it might be nice to cook you dinner, but I also recognize that you might want time to yourself. Please kick us out if you'd rather be al—"

"Alone?" I cut in. "Never. I moved here to spend time with the two of you, and I have no other priorities. I don't even have a job anymore now that I extricated myself from my former partnership. But allow me to do the cooking, please."

She laughs. "As long as it's not Abe. Cooking is not his forté."

Abe pinches her side playfully. "You've never complained all that much about my cooking."

"It's awful, honey," she says with a teasing laugh. "Did you think I took over just 'cause I love it?"

I clear my throat, drawing my daughter-in-law's attention. "Do you have a dish in mind for tonight?"

She nods. "Yeah, I was going to test a lemon peel pesto on you. And then, of course, we stocked the fridge with imported blood from a place Abe says you like." She falls silent.

It's an awkward topic. I should have sustained myself on my mates' blood. But it's been nearly a thousand years since I touched or drank from them. Still, I would never betray our bond, either, so I've been purchasing donated blood for that whole time, unwilling to hunt as my ancestors once did.

Purchased sustenance is often considered uncouth, and if I had any other family still alive, they'd abhor it. But as they're mostly all dead or so far removed that we never speak, I'm not fussed over the habit.

Evenia and Aberen certainly hated the idea of anyone finding out I didn't partake of them. Not that the topic came up all that often.

"That was generous, thank you," I offer.

Pink tinges Morgan's cheeks. She tucks a bit of hair behind her ear. "Do you think you'll miss them at all, or maybe even just miss your job? You had a lot of power at headquarters. I'm a little surprised you were willing to retire."

Laughing, I sling an arm around her waist as we stride down the hall. "No, darling girl. I stayed because being in that position of power allowed me to keep an eye on Abe, to help him where needed, to push policies through for monsterkind and to have some oversight into what Evenia and Aberen were doing. But now Abe has you, the fiercest of creatures, and I no longer feel the need to babysit those two."

She smiles and squeezes me back.

Pacing past her, I tuck my hands at my belt and admire room after room of gorgeous, angular architecture with modern touches. Abe gets his love of this style from me, and over all the years I've lived, gothic modern remains my favorite type of design.

Eventually, we make our way to the kitchen, which sits at the back of the house. Black plated windows line the back wall and half of the ceiling, bringing in an incredible view of a clearing. Dense forest lies beyond that. A stack of wooden planks sits in the clearing, a singular box of nails and a hammer on top of it.

Turning to Abe, I chuckle. "I see what you mean about the workshop. She's ready to add on, clearly."

He pats the countertop in a friendly way, and the house creaks, making her agreement known.

Morgan gets to work on dinner as Abe crafts cocktails from a gorgeous bar built into one wall of the kitchen. When he selects beautifully etched glasses from the bar, I sigh at his attention to detail.

"You've thought of everything, darling."

He fills my glass, then slides it across the black concrete bar to me. "Well, I learned from the best. Preparation is key, is it not?"

"Just so," I agree, clinking my glass to his.

Dinner is delightful. Morgan has me in stitches, and Abe even laughs a time or two. It's not in his nature to be outright joyful—his career training stole that from him—but he finds obvious pleasure in Morgan's exuberance.

The meal is over far too soon, and my guests retire for the evening. If they're anything like I was when I was newly mated, they can't wait to get home and rip one another's clothes off.

I'd be lying if I didn't admit to missing those days, when my mates and I seemed to live perpetually in a tangle of limbs, blood splattered across the sheets, our bodies reduced to live wires of pleasure. It's been so long since then, I can scarcely remember what it feels like to be in love.

No. I fell out of love as quickly as I fell into it. If not for Abe and my desire to protect him from a harsh mother and an absentee second father, I wouldn't have stayed as long as I did. Even then, I wasn't able to fully protect him as Evenia became the most powerful monster in our world. I wasn't there when she forced Abe to go through Keeper training and the painful ritual that stripped him of much of his innate personality, rewiring his brain to think in terms of pure logic.

I'll never forgive myself for not seeing that coming, for not being there to save him from her. Even so, it worked out alright for him eventually. I have the gods to thank for that.

Night falls, and I sit in front of the pale stone fireplace in my room, thinking back to Morgan's comment about dating. Arches soar up and cross the ceiling, giving the entire bedroom a vaguely churchlike feel. I've been alive since before the first church was ever built, but there's something absolutely titillating about the idea of fucking in one.

Not that I moved to Ever to find physical pleasure. But I'm old enough to know that, sometimes, the moments you're *not* looking for it are the perfect moments to find it.

∼

Days pass before I leave the house. I take my time getting to know every nook and cranny and what my new home's personality is. Like me, she enjoys fine things and the juxtaposition between light and dark. She'll ensconce my bedroom in darkness just to fling a sheer curtain over the window, enough to let soft rays of moonlight through.

She's elegant and timeless and absolutely perfect.

And we need a workshop. She and I have already established that through regular conversation. She shimmies the pipes in a certain way when she's in agreement with me. When she's not, the creaks and groans of the floorboards are so loud, I have to cover my ears. Very quickly, we've come to find a common language.

As I don't yet *have* a workshop, I'll need to *design* one. On the fourth day after moving to Ever, I dress casually in slacks, my shirt unbuttoned at the collar, and a matching vest. Wingtip shoes lend the entire ensemble the casual look I'm going for. I will always be a fan of beautifully tailored clothing.

I consider donning a hat but decide it's too formal. Heading for the front door, I wave to the house. "I'll be back later, darling. Be a dear and consider the workshop. I'm hoping to return with sketches, but I'm open to ideas!"

As I walk out the door, a rack by the front entryway shimmies, and she tosses a black scarf at me. Chuckling, I wrap it loosely around my neck, draping it over my shirt and vest.

A beautiful quarter-hour walk later, I arrive at the intersection of Main and Sycamore Streets in Downtown Ever. I've been to Ever dozens of times over the centuries, but it seems more charming every time I come here.

Ah, beautiful Ever. The Massachusetts-based monster haven is fashioned after American towns of the fifties, replete with red-and-white-striped awnings and flower boxes overflowing to the nines. Monsters walk up and down wide sidewalks on either side of the main drag.

Twitching my ears, I catch snippets of dozens of conversations. Forcing myself to unfocus, I cross Main Street toward Higher Grounds, Ever's singular coffee shop. It's run by vampires as well. Recently mated, if I remember correctly. Entering through the coffee shop's wood and glass door, I smile at how quaint it is. The style inside reminds me of the coffee shops of Azuro, the Italian monster haven. This one is all exposed brick except for a wood and concrete bar with a handwritten menu hanging above it.

Moving to the back, I order a Type A latte before finding a seat in the window near the door. Withdrawing my notepad and sketch pens, I arrange them as I await my drink. Once the barista calls my name, I stand and cross the busy café.

At the pickup counter, a handsome vampire smiles at me, revealing twin fangs. "Betmal? Type A latte for you." He pushes the drink carefully toward me, then crosses both arms. "If the rumors are to be believed, you're Abemet's father?"

I notice how he doesn't mention my mates first, which is what most monsters would do—the blessing and curse of being mated to the monster haven system's primary leader.

News travels fast, I suppose.

"I am," I confirm. "I've just relocated to Ever."

"Ah," he lifts a brow, "now that we've got the Grand Portal Station, it should be easy to go back and forth, if you need to."

I don't bother to respond that there's nothing at Hearth HQ for me to return to. I closed that door and burnt all the bridges when I delivered divorce and bond dissolution paperwork to Evenia at her office.

"Betmal, is that you?" a female voice floats from behind the male. When she emerges, I recognize her—Valentina, Hearth HQ's Chief Haven Designer. Surprised to see her, I lean in and kiss both her cheeks in the traditional way.

She laughs as we part, looping one arm through the big vampire male's. "Betmal, this is my mate Alessandro. Alé, this is Betmal, from headquarters."

"So it is," he says smoothly, a friendly smile on his face.

"You were always so kind to me when I saw you at HQ," Valentina continues. "So Alé and I will not be poking into your private life even though I can feel him vibrating with the need to question why you're in town. Let me just say that I'm thrilled to see you."

The male nudges her hip with a playful wink. "He's just relocated to Ever."

She shoots me a surprised look. "Oh my, Evenia didn't

mention that in our last one-on-one. Well, welcome to Ever. If you need anything, don't hesitate to let us know."

"Thank you, darling girl," I say with a laugh. "I don't know how you manage being her direct report, but good on you for not throttling her. For the time being, coffee is all I need."

She smiles, clasping her hands together as she avoids speaking ill of her work superior. "Of course, Betmal. Coffee we can easily do."

I return to my spot in the window, ready to luxuriate in the sun like a cat. Sipping at the delectable latte, I muse over several ideas for a workshop behind the new house. It's always fun to have a blank canvas of sorts. It's been a long time since I moved and had the chance to design and build from scratch. Not since before Abemet was born.

Lost in thought, I sketch and draw, covering the notebook's pages all the way to the edges. I draw and draw, letting my imagination run wild as I consider what I'll need from the new space. Truth be told, I'm a blank canvas as well, having no job and no real plan other than to spend time with my son and his wife.

Still, I've never been one for idle hands, I'll find new work quickly. So the ideas flow from me like water, until I've covered nearly twenty pages with bits and bobs of what I imagine the perfect workshop could look like.

I sketch a big flat desk space with an ornate, grandiose chandelier above it. Droplet-shaped crystals drip down like rain, casting sunlight in shards all around the space. Yessss, I think I love that. I file the idea away in my "to keep" pile. Rainy days are my favorite. Ever never rains, so I add a weather-overlay window to the list of must-haves for my new workspace. That way I can pick and choose when I'm able to enjoy a good downpour.

The sound of someone clearing their throat pulls me from my work. Looking up, I see Arkan, Ever's centaur Keeper, standing there with his arms tucked at his back. He grins at me, the expression curving his black lips upward.

"Sorry to interrupt, Betmal, but Abe let me know you arrived, and I thought I'd take a moment to formally welcome you to Ever."

I rise from my chair and shake his hand. The handsome centaur replaced Abemet in this role, and I've heard his approach is...different. But different can be good. I'm excited to see Arkan in action.

He grabs a long, curved centaur bench from the table behind us and drops gracefully into it, shoving a manila envelope across the table to me. "I'm only going to steal a few minutes from you. I wanted to give you the official Ever welcome packet. I'm guessing you've seen one or two of these, but I'd be remiss not to provide you with ours, since you're our newest resident."

I'd laugh, but I've rarely looked at a haven welcome packet. Aberen designed them all centuries ago. I've honestly got no idea whose responsibility they are at this point. Probably no one's...

"Thank you," I confirm. "I'll dig into that when I return home."

Arkan crosses his arms. "I'm going to assume you've seen Abe and Morgan, since he let me know you're here, but is there anything I can do for you as you get settled? I've seen the new house; she's beautiful."

Pride fills me, and I smile at him. "Ah, yes. My darling boy had a hand in her design, he says."

Arkan's grin grows big. "Abe's a design whiz. I've got him working on some plans for an upcoming expansion I think we'll need, now that the Grand Portal Station is open."

I nod. "I came through it, and it's truly remarkable. No traveling through fifteen or twenty or thirty portals to get to your desired haven. It'll be so much more efficient to get around now."

Arkan nods. "And that travel means tourism. I'm trying to get ahead of the infrastructure needs for that as we speak." He waves a hand around. "Anyhow, I don't need to get into my inner thoughts, but *welcome*." With another bright smile, he rises gracefully from the bench and turns to go.

Just then, a new scent fills my sensitive nose. Flaring my nostrils, I glance up from my work. The coffee shop is full, but there are just a few monsters in line. No, it's none of them. A giant minotaur stands at the line to order. Not him. Much as I enjoy minotaur blood, this is different in a way I can't quite place.

But as he steps aside, I notice there's a woman in front of him. She must have just ordered, because she turns and ducks her head respectfully, averting her eyes from the big monster. He steps aside as she rounds him. I can't stop staring. She's merfolk, but in her human form. Long, frilled aqua and rust-colored ears frame an angular face with a dimpled chin and plump, turquoise lips. Even in human form, her hair falls in cylindrical waves around her shoulders, trailing all the way to her waist.

I suck in a ragged breath, masking it under a clearing of my throat.

Pure sea, wild and furious and depthless, fills my senses, clearing my brain of rational thought. The scent is tantalizing, intoxicating, and without really meaning to, I listen for the rapid thud of her heart. Blood sings through her veins, the purest of symphonies tinged by the crash of waves on a black sand shore.

"My gods," I murmur to myself, staring longer than I ought to.

She walks toward the closest chair and sits gracefully. It's then I notice, in human form, one of her legs stops just below the knee. Attached to it is a crudely shaped peg like a pirate from a human fantasy might wear. She winces as she stretches her leg long, staring at the wooden bit with what looks like hatred in her eyes.

I can't pull my gaze from her as she reaches into a small bag around her waist and retrieves a tiny notebook and pencil. She lays the notebook open and begins to draw.

An artist.

A kindred soul.

And just like that, I resolve to introduce myself because, if I know anything, it's that I need to know her.

I need to know her—immediately.

CHAPTER TWO
AMATHEIA

I'm lost in thought, sketching out what I think the fancy new Grand Portal Station might look like, when Alessandro appears by my side. The handsome vampire smiles as he gently sets my oat milk seafoam latte to one side of my notebook.

He thrums his fingers on the picture I just started. "Looks like the new portal station. Am I right?"

Smiling, I look up and nod. He's always so kind to me. And this is a little game we play. I draw things from the world I'm not allowed to explore, and he tells me if I got them right or not.

"Yep!" I grin up at him. "What am I missing?"

"Well," he taps on the center of the drawing, "there should be a seating area here, and here. And don't forget the gargoyle protectors above every haven portal door. They sit on tiny stone shelves and they're so still, it's almost as if they're stone sleeping."

Scoffing, I laugh and sketch a small notch in the brick for a gargoyle to sit and watch. Alessandro smiles and pats my shoulder in a friendly way.

"Catch my eye if you need a refill. I'll bring it to you."

Because it's hard for you to walk.

Those are the words he doesn't say. He doesn't need to. Everyone knows I'm the peg-legged mermaid with the ill-fitting prosthetic. Uncle Caralorn won't allow me a new one, although his reasons are complicated. My reasons for not fighting him on that topic are even more so.

Glaring down at the wooden leg that brings me so much pain, I force myself to refocus on the recent opening of the new Grand Portal Station. It's a technical marvel, allowing monsters from any of the fifty-plus havens to visit any other without traveling through multiple portals to get there, which is how it used to be. As long as I can remember, every monster haven was connected to only one other. It was a security initiative.

No longer.

Bam. Take a quick trip to Santa Alaya to lounge on the beach or see the shifter queen play guitar.

Bam. Step through another portal to visit Rainbow, hidden in the human state of New York.

Bam. Bam. Another step or two and you can visit Arcadia, deep in the wilderness, home to shifters and trolls and giants.

So many places to visit. So many monsters to learn about. And I'll never get the chance to see any of it. Uncle Caralorn's unspoken rule is that I should be present but unseen—he'd rather his daughters be in the spotlight—and honestly, that's fine. If I up and disappeared, he'd possibly be fine with it. But disappearing takes a lot of money, and I don't have that.

Since I can't see any of those places in real life, I resolve myself to drinking coffee and daydreaming about them. My daily coffee visits are the one thing Caralorn doesn't begrudge me. He doesn't agree with my time spent on land, but he doesn't care as long as I complete my other royal duties.

The barista's mate, Valentina, appears from a back room to clear the drop station of dirty cups and plates. She gathers them, but as she turns, Alessandro is there, waiting for her. His crimson eyes drop to her mouth, and he licks his lips. He says something low, under his breath, something only she can hear. I wish I had hearing like a vampire's. He's probably saying something deliciously erotic.

I want to hear that, to know what it would be like for a male to put that sort of attention on me. But it'll never happen because mermaid society is too rigid for that, especially for the king's eldest niece. Caralorn's probably known who he planned to marry me off to since I became his ward, not that we ever discuss it. I pray we never do. I'd much rather fly under the radar than be shipped off to some far kingdom away from my cousins…well, one cousin in particular.

Alessandro gathers the dishes from his mate's hands and guides her toward the kitchen. A second vampire appears in the doorway, eating them up with his gaze. Pietro, their mate. And if I'm right, there's a dark elf, Diavolo, who's been living upstairs with them recently, too.

Goddess Thalassa, I can scarcely imagine one mate, much less three hulking beasts such as those. Still, it doesn't stop me from dreaming about it.

Returning my focus to my notebook, I sketch and draw for the better part of an hour, losing myself in the beauty of the art. If I had my way, I'd spend all day drawing or painting, and I'd travel nonstop. I don't think I'd even settle in one haven. I'd bounce between them, creating art for the masses. Unfortunately, I don't have the funds for that. I barely have enough money to come to Higher Grounds, so I budget what little I do have to ensure I get this time at my favorite place.

Eventually, Alessandro appears by my side, dropping to one knee so our faces are at the same height. "Friend, you look lost in thought. I figured I should remind you of the time?"

Ugh. The time. I never allow myself more than a few hours at Higher Grounds. Any longer, and Caralorn will send his eldest daughter, Malakat, or one of his guards to find me.

They'll be assholes and make a scene, and I definitely do not want that. Especially after recent events. I was attacked and spent days catatonic in a tub at Doc Slade's. My disappearance caused quite the mess when I eventually returned home.

Thanking Alessandro, I gather my things into my bag and stand to leave. Hobbling quickly across the beautiful café, I halt when a big figure stops my progress toward the door.

I look up into eyes the color of twin rubies. An elegant nose turns up at the end. Short, tapered ears and slicked-back blond hair remind me of our former Keeper, Abemet. In fact, if I added a little gray to Abe's temples, this could be him. A hotter, slighter older version.

Curious.

That damned curiosity draws my eyes to his formal outfit. He wears slacks, a navy vest, and an unbuttoned collared shirt. Vampiric familial tattoos cover every inch of his neck and chest, disappearing beneath the fabric. It's a struggle to pull my gaze back up to his face, but when I do, he smiles enough to show me both pointy fangs.

He grabs the door handle, turns it, and swings the door open, gesturing for me to move through.

"Please, allow me," he croons, his voice lower than I would have thought. It's smooth and silky, manly and yet elegant. His voice is sex, if pure sex and sin could be wrapped up into monster form.

"Thank you," I manage as I exit the coffee shop, my cheeks flaming hot.

No sooner have I turned to head up the sidewalk than the handsome vampire appears by my side, offering his arm. "May I walk you to your destination…?" He pauses, suggesting he's asking for my name.

"Amatheia," I offer, "and no. That won't be necessary." *Caralorn would shit a brick if he saw us together, given his hatred for all things land.*

He laughs. "Ah, but some of the most fun things aren't necessary at all. Another time, perhaps?"

I tuck a strand of hair behind my ear, trying to figure out if he's being serious. "Perhaps." I can't commit to any more than that. It seems like he's being nice, possibly even a bit flirtatious. But I don't have dalliances. And I've got to get home. So I turn to go, surprised when cool fingers gently grip my elbow.

The vampire appears in front of me again. "You didn't ask my name."

Any other monster saying this would make it sound like a threat. But this male? It sounds like a promise. His lips tilt up at the corners, his second eyelid flashing white over his red irises.

"Oh?" I lift my chin. "What is it, then?"

His eyes sparkle as he smiles big enough for me to see his fangs again. They're so much longer than mine.

"Betmal. My name is Betmal."

I clear my throat. "Alright, Betmal. Nice to meet you. I really must be going."

He steps aside so I can pass. "It was a pleasure meeting *you*, Amatheia," he says quietly, so quietly I almost don't hear.

I can't find anything to say as I hobble up the street and away from the handsome male. I'm not free to pursue him, or anyone. I'm a political pawn, trapped here, and the coffee shop is my only short-lived escape.

I wish things were different, but it is what it is.

CHAPTER THREE
BETMAL

Later that night, my dear friend Catherine slides a cocktail across her small kitchen island toward me. "How are you finding Ever, Betmal? Have you had a chance to see Abe and Morgan?"

"The day I arrived, yes." I take the cocktail and sip happily, looking at my lovely friend. "Morgan cooked for us, and I've been busy unpacking and getting to know the house. You must come by for dinner soon; the home is absolutely lovely. Abe outdid himself."

Catherine grins, blue eyes crinkling at the corners. She glances up, looking around the Annabelle Inn, her home and Ever's only bed and breakfast. "Ah, I remember what it's like when you find a home that feels like *the* home to end all homes. That's what I found when I came here and moved to the Annabelle. I can't imagine being anywhere else."

We share understanding looks as I nod. "Hearth HQ was certainly not the homiest of places to raise a child, or to remain after that child was long grown." I drum my fingers on the countertop, considering the reason I came here and knocked on Catherine's door tonight, apart from a general desire to catch up. "Tell me what you know of a mermaid called Amatheia. I met her earlier today at the coffee shop."

Catherine sighs. "Ah, that's a bit of a sad story, to tell you the truth. I've known Amatheia since her clan relocated to Ever from the sea. She's a lovely, lovely woman…an artist like you."

I sip quietly at the cocktail as she continues.

"As I understand it, she and her parents were in some sort of accident. That's how she lost her fin. Her uncle, King Caralorn, moved them here afterward, but he's…well, I've only met him once at their welcome ceremony. He's extremely prickly, and as you know, merfolk societal structure is quite rigid."

"What else?" I rise without meaning to, concern brewing in my stomach at the idea of such a delicate-seeming being under the thumb of a prickly, shut-in king.

"Well…" Catherine pauses, gray brows furrowing as she sips her martini. "The merfolk mostly keep to the lake, but Amatheia likes to visit Higher Grounds almost daily. I don't think she means to be a troublemaker, but I do think she likes escaping up here, honestly. Well, as much as she's able to, given her royal duties. And, of course, there was the recent attack, too."

The blood freezes in my veins, and I grab the stem of my glass so hard, it cracks. "The *what* now?"

Catherine nods, glancing at the cracked glass. "She was the victim of an attack by a revenant. It's quite a long story, but suffice to say she was rendered catatonic. Unharmed otherwise, but she did not wake until the revenant was released by Lou, the Hector triplets' aunt. She's a blue witch…have you met Lou yet? Or the other two triplets? Surely you heard about her from Evenia, or perhaps Aberen."

I shake my head. "No, I haven't. Of the Hectors, I've only met Morgan. So… when was this?"

Catherine purses her pink-painted lips. "Oh, about a month ago? It's fairly recent. I haven't seen Amatheia as much since then. I suspect she was shaken up by what happened. Or perhaps Caralorn finally took issue with her daily visits to Higher Grounds. Truly, the merfolk very, very rarely leave the lake. I've always assumed that was Caralorn's doing."

I fall silent, lost to the idea that anyone could attack such an exquisite soul.

"On a happier note," Catherine says. "She did some paintings for me last year, and they are stunning. Would you like to see?" She stands with her drink in hand and turns for the formal sitting room next to the inn's entrance.

I follow, still musing over how it's possible for Amatheia to become a victim like that. I can't imagine how terrified she must have been. Did she try to run? Was she unable to get away? Is her leg perhaps the reason she didn't escape? My heart halts and stutters in my chest at the idea of her being afraid.

Catherine slips one hand through my arm, resting it along my forearm. "See that painting there? The rose garden in the back? Amatheia did it."

My mouth drops open. The painting is whimsical and chaotic and inspired. It's easy to see it's a rose garden, but the way she splashed the color across the canvas gives the garden a sort of modern fairytale vibe.

Catherine points at the painting next to it, which appears done in the same style. "I commissioned this entire wall of paintings from her after seeing her paint on the lakeshore one day. She was hiding from Caralorn after some fight, and I thought perhaps I could offer her a reprieve." Catherine's expression grows sorrowful. "It took a while; it was hard for her to leave the lake for long periods of time. But she'd come here and paint, and she told me quite a bit more about her life in the merkingdom. Eventually, Caralorn found out she was painting for me and put a stop to it. Now I see her at Higher Grounds on occasion, but that's it."

"What a sad story," I murmur, staring at the wall of incredible paintings. The mermaid has talent, the kind that can't be taught. She's a natural.

Thinking back to the welcome packet Arkan gave me, an idea begins to brew in my mind. I took a look at it, and it was atrociously done.

Catherine turns and plants a hand on her hip. "Betmal, what is that look on your face? I've known you for a long time, and you're planning something. Why are you asking about Amatheia?"

I turn to find Catherine's blue eyes narrowed playfully as she gives me a saucy, expectant look.

"Well." I clear my throat. "I think we both know I'm not the type to formally retire. But I did leave behind a job I enjoyed when I separated from Evenia and Aberen. I need to do something with my time. I can't spend it all with Abemet and Morgan."

She winks at me. "Not planning to attend any of their parties, I suppose?"

I laugh at that. Vampires are famous for our orgies.

"No, I don't think so," I manage. "Between you and me, I haven't attended an orgy in centuries."

Catherine huffs out a wry laugh, tossing beautiful gray waves over her shoulder. "Sounds like we're both out of dating practice."

But there's something different about her that I've been noticing tonight. An extra sensuality I haven't seen from my succubus friend in decades.

"Oh." I laugh and point an accusatory finger in her direction. "You've identified a partner, haven't you? You're exuding pheromones, Catherine."

Her lips pull into a devious smile. "Perhaps I have, after all this time."

"And?" I cross my arms, fully expecting to be told the entire story about this new development. "Who's the lucky bastard?"

She beams. "The last monster on earth you'd think. I've just started my pursuit, but I'll be sure to let you know how it goes." She clinks her cocktail glass gently against mine. "To new adventures, Betmal." Her expression goes wry. "You didn't answer my question, by the way."

"Santé," I say pleasantly, falling into the French mother tongue. Of all the languages I've learned to speak over the thousands of years I've been alive, French is my favorite. "Another time, old friend."

She cocks her head sideways and smirks, but takes another sip and does not press the issue.

Eventually I take leave of Catherine and walk, lost in thought, back to my new house. When I arrive, she swings the front doors wide, revealing candles lit all the way through the main hall toward the kitchen in the back.

"Lovely girl, thank you." I stride through, setting my bag down on the kitchen countertop. "So," I begin, withdrawing my notebook. "I've got quite a few ideas for the workshop out back. Shall we look through them together? I'd like your opinion."

A loud groan of the pipes overhead tells me yes.

"Most excellent." With a smile, I walk to the fridge and withdraw one of the blood bags Abemet so thoughtfully imported for me. Slicing the top open, I pour the donated blood into a crystal goblet. That done, I return to the island and take a seat, bringing the cup to my nose. I swirl it in the glass.

Ah, minotaur blood. A male, based on the pheromone-rich tang that underlays the scent. Minotaurs are regular givers of blood. The money's good, and they're so big, they can give more than many smaller monsters. Minotaur blood is my dinner at least three or four nights out of the week. Not that I need to even eat that regularly, at my age, but I enjoy it. And I figure if I've denied myself bedroom play with a partner for as long as I have, I deserve good food.

Still, donated blood doesn't hold a candle to the intense and all-consuming pleasure of drinking directly from a willing partner.

Amatheia's face flashes into my mind, those wide, beautiful eyes. Her plump lips. I'd like to taste them, to nibble my way playfully down her neck and make her squirm. Then I'd strike and bring her ecstasy while drinking from her vein. I'll bet she tastes of the sea, pure, blissful inky water and tangy salt. My second eyelid flashes over my eyes, coating the world in a whitewashed haze as my lust runs high.

I card my hands through my hair, brushing back the stray strand that loves to fall out of place. I haven't been interested in a monster romantically in a very long time. This is new for me. Unbidden and unexpected, but delicious.

Am I thinking of pursuing something for the first time in thousands of years? Will she even be interested, given everything that's gone on in her life of late? Will she even consider me, given what Catherine shared about the merfolk?

I'll need to tread carefully because the circumstances surrounding her are going to present a challenge. But she's the right person for the job I'm considering creating, and if she accepts, it'll give me a chance to get to know her a little better. I've known other merfolk in the past, and they haven't all been as unpleasant as Caralorn sounds.

The house creaks and groans, expressing her displeasure that we haven't gotten started. With a quick apology, I take a sip of my dinner and open the notebook to the first page. Immediately, the house lets out a hideous clank of the pipes below my feet.

"Okay, that's a no," I murmur, grabbing my pencil to slash across the drawing.

Ten minutes later, we've been through the entire notebook, and it's clear my home has distinct preferences. Of everything I drew, her favorite options are a secondary cottage in the backyard with a loft for my office, and a backyard that's just one giant pool.

Obviously, I need a workspace, though, so I resolve to expand on the backyard cottage idea.

Next, I lift the watch at my wrist, directing it to call Abemet. He answers immediately, "Father, is everything alright?"

I wave away his worry even though he can't see me. "Fine, darling. I've got an idea I want to work on, but I thought I'd get your take on it." I take a few minutes to outline the project that formed in my mind over the last few hours—reworking the haven welcome packets.

By the time I'm done explaining what I'd like to do, Abemet is fully on board.

Morgan chimes in, having apparently overheard our conversation. "Yes, please, Betmal! The welcome packets are so dry, and when we came here, it turned out we were missing like, half of the pages. Being human and discovering a hidden monster town for the first time, it was…hard. I mean, it was helpful, but there's room for improvement, to be sure."

"Exactly!" Her excitement tells me I'm on the right path. "I'd like to hire a painter to do some haven-specific artwork and then bind everything into a beautiful coffee table-style book. Almost a collectible, if you will. Something to truly highlight each haven's beauty and characteristics. They're each so different."

"Don't I know it," Morgan mutters. "That sounds like quite the project. You're an artist yourself, aren't you?"

Oh, I am. But when it comes to the artwork for my new project, I know exactly who I want to hire.

CHAPTER FOUR
AMATHEIA

I move the pencil in quick, short slashes over the page, adding shading to the outline of the gargoyle brothers sitting at the table next to mine. Shepherd is the more openly joyful of the two, always smiling and making jokes when he does security rounds through the lake.

Alo's the more classically handsome, but he's a quieter, more intense presence. Although, being recently mated seems to have softened the harsh edges of his gaze. Not to mention, having a six-year-old will keep one young. Or turn your hair gray. Or perhaps both.

Character sketches are a personal favorite of mine to draw. When I look back on them later, it almost feels like I'm drawing friends. The fact is, I know many of the Evertons, but I don't know any of them *well*. Drawing them almost makes it seem like they're *my* friends, if I had time for friendships outside of the lake.

When someone clears their throat next to me, it pulls me from my trance-like state. Glancing up, I'm surprised to see the handsome vampire from yesterday standing beside my table. Today, he wears emerald green slacks and a white collared shirt, open to his navel. Both sleeves are rolled up to his elbows, revealing more tattoos. A half-dozen chunky necklaces, including a cross, drape over his chest. They pull my eye to stacked abdominal muscles and the faintest sprinkling of pale hair on his pecs.

Oh my gods, he's too hot. Thalassa below, why don't they make mermen like this? Or maybe it's just that mermen are always so focused on showing off their strength or bragging about the size of their fins. It is so *tiresome* to me.

Forcing my gaze up, I smile. It's the same smile I wear at home all the time. It's a mask, my armor to protect me from the snidest of my uncle's comments.

You're just like your mother, head in the clouds.
Why must you look at me like that?
I can't stand to look at you. Leave me.
If it wasn't for you, they'd both still be here.
Why are you such a burden, Niece?

The vampire cocks his head to the side, examining my expression for a long moment that quickly turns awkward for me. And probably him too.

"Let me guess," I blurt out, trying to brush away the weirdness. "You've come to try to walk me home again?"

He laughs, and like yesterday, the sound is sinful and rich. It's the laugh of someone who does it easily and often, someone full of joy. Someone unlike me. Someone *free*. I don't remember the last time I laughed for real, except with my cousin, Thatraeia. It's been ages, though.

"Not quite, Amatheia. May I sit?"

Goddess, he remembered my name. And the way he says it…

Speechless, I ensure my mouth is closed as I jerk my head toward the singular seat across from mine. Instead of taking it, he grabs the back and swings it effortlessly to my side of the table. When he sinks down into it, our legs nearly tangle together. He's close, so close I can smell him.

He's wearing cologne, I'm sure of it, because nobody smells this good. It's light, manly. Like if you took the forest and fresh soap and something burnt like one of the caramel candies from Miriam's Sweets Shop up the street.

"I've been thinking," he begins, leaning back in the chair as he crosses one leg over the other. "I'm working on a project, and I require the services of a painter. My friend Catherine tells me you did some work for her."

Ah.

"That was a long time ago," I confirm. "I don't paint anymore."

"And yet I've seen your work." He flashes a broad, toothy smile at me. "You're exactly what I need for this particular project. I'd like to discuss the specifics. Will you come to my home for dinner tomorrow to discuss it?"

Hope wells immediately inside me. Hope and the fervent desire to have enough money to escape the prison of the lake, even if just for short stints of time. But Caralorn keeps tight control over my meager dowry, and the only reason I even have money for coffee is because of my occasional shift at Sovereign Sip, the merkingdom's singular bar.

Caralorn would hate this, if he found out, because he'd lose some of his control over me. But, if this is a paying gig, I can add it to the money Catherine paid me for those paintings, money I've kept secreted away. Perhaps I'll be able to save up enough to move somewhere quiet. The key would be in doing that before Caralorn finds out what I'm trying to do.

I hate how a plan is already forming in my mind.

It's also true that I haven't painted in a while.

"Amatheia?" Betmal's voice breaks through my train of thought. "Say yes." He uncrosses his legs and leans forward, an elbow on each knee and his hands clasped. "Say you'll come."

"I'll hear you out," I say before I can stop myself. "I can't promise I'll agree, given my other...responsibilities to the king. But I'll listen."

"Excellent." He grins at me like that cat who got the cream. It sends consternation running rampant through my guts as I think about how to keep Caralorn or my cousins from finding out about this. This is probably a really bad idea.

"I require discretion," I say softly. "My coming on land isn't favored by my family, not when they think it interferes with my duties. If I do this, can we keep it between us until I decide if I can help or not?"

"A secret tryst?" His smile grows wide, fangs poking out from his upper lip. "I love secrets. I'm fine with that"—he gives me a seductive look—"for now. And I can promise this will be far more fun than any princessly duties you may have."

"That's fine," I say in a rush. "I might not even be able to *help*. But I'm willing to listen to what you need. Can I assume this is a paid gig?"

He inclines his head. "Naturally. Well paying. But we can discuss those details tomorrow over dinner. What do you like to eat?"

I shake my head. "There's no need to feed me. I'll eat before I come."

"Nonsense." He waves away my comment. "It would be highly rude of me to invite you to my home and not offer sustenance. Do you have any specific likes or dislikes when it comes to dinner?"

I can't think of any, not when his piercing eyes seem to drive shards of heat low into my belly. "I'm...I'll eat whatever."

"Ah, an adventurous female, then. Carte blanche, love that." He winks, and the heat swirling in my stomach turns into a raging bonfire. He's just being nice. I know that. Vampires are pure sex, or so I've heard other monsters say. He's probably like this with everyone. I just have no experience with single vampire males. And he must be single. Right?

After grabbing my notebook, I shove it in my bag and stand, desperate to get away from his probing gaze and ridiculously attractive smile. When pain lances through my knee, I falter and grip the edge of the table.

Before I see him move, Betmal grabs me by the waist, holding me tightly to his body. Red eyes flash and narrow, his nostrils flaring as he grits a muscle in his jaw.

"I'm sorry," I mutter, pushing away from him as I struggle around shooting pains that zip up my thigh to clash around my hip bones.

"For what?" His voice is low, deadly, the tone of a predator.

"Falling on you," I answer with a laugh.

"A beautiful woman falling into my arms hardly calls for an apology," he says roughly, his hand moving higher up my waist. His fingers curl into my skin, and everywhere he touches sends waves of heat radiating through my core.

"Well then," I offer with a smirk, "you're welcome."

His eyes crinkle in the corners as he stares at me in silence. It's like he's looking right through me, enjoying our little exchange. Nostrils flaring, he leans slightly forward.

Is he scenting me? Trying to decide how good my blood smells? Oh depths, I've got to get out of here.

I clear my throat. "Well, I'm headed home, but I'll see you tomorrow, I suppose."

"Tomorrow, Amatheia." He smirks as he slips a hand into his pocket. "I'll pick you up at the lake."

I beg my leave and scuttle out of Higher Grounds as fast as my legs will take me. It was foolish to agree to meet him. I can't possibly take this job and keep it hidden. Caralorn would stop me simply because he can.

But still, a tiny flare of hope burns bright inside me, and despite myself, I smile all the way back home.

By the time I reach the lake, my hip throbs, and my head has begun to join it. My heartbeat pulses painfully in my ears as I stumble to the log that serves as lockers for the merfolk the rare times we come on land. Sitting on the large fallen log, I move a piece of bark to the side. A rectangular section flips open, revealing a tiny locker. Pulling my human clothes and prosthetic off, I dump them in the locker with a sigh.

What I'm doing tomorrow is foolish. *So* foolish. I've never been allowed to replace the prosthetic because Caralorn says I shouldn't need it, that merfolk don't belong on land anyhow. I know my parents never would have agreed with him, but they're long gone. There's nobody left to protect me, aside from the warden who's very much *not* in my corner.

I always imagined there would come a day when I wouldn't feel so guilty about the accident that robbed me of my leg and my parents' of their lives. And on that Thalassa-blessed day, I'd miraculously have money, somehow get a new leg, and escape being under Caralorn's thumb.

The plan that took root in my mind earlier expands by the minute as I consider how merfolk rarely come out of the lake. I can likely milk this project for a while before anyone notices I'm not around as much. Maybe I can even save up enough to grab my cousin Thatraeia and take her with me.

I hop to the edge of the water, praying to the goddess Thalassa for the chilly lake to ease the pain quickly. As I hobble into the water, I shift and fall forward into the clear blue depths. Every shift into my natural form is painful, but on the days my leg pain flares up, it's nigh unbearable. I cry out as the shift overtakes me, gritting my teeth as my legs pin together and change into a long, scaled turquoise and rust-colored tail. Gills pop open beneath my ears, opening wide to pull oxygen from the water.

I shudder as the shift completes. Like always, I look down at the end of my tail where there should be two long fins to propel me through the water. Instead, there's just the one. It's long and beautiful and perfect, but it's had to do all the work for twenty-two years now. Poor thing is tired.

A sigh leaves my lips as the familiar pain shoots through my remaining fin, traveling up the muscles of my tail to stab at my lower back. Gritting my teeth, I push through the hurt as I glide slowly through the water. It turns from turquoise to royal to navy blue the deeper I get, although it's easy for me to see clearly. Heading to the northern side of the lake where there's a series of caves, I look for an outcropping where Sea Julienne grows. It's not natural to lake water, but we're able to make it grow here by injecting salt into the weed's roots every few months.

Technically there are many of us who have Sea Julienne duty, but I swear I'm the only one who ever actually does it.

It's a pain reliever, so caring for the hearty seaweed is usually top of mind.

Finding the wavy seaweed, I grab a few leaves and yank them from the stalk, stuffing them in my mouth. I chew around the bitter taste, sighing as the pain in my back and fin swirl and eddy away. I cut a few extra leaves to bring back to the castle. I'm working a shift tonight at the bar, and I'll need it.

Glancing at my comm watch, I realize it's actually later in the afternoon than I thought. I head past the Sea Julienne field and make my way through the other gardens outside our city.

I glide around a rock just in time to see a large figure hunched on top of an outcropping, his long green tail curled over the edge, fins twirling the sand into tiny tornadoes along the lake floor. He turns and looks up as I glide into view. Immediately, I tuck the Sea Julienne behind my back.

"It's you." Caralorn's emerald eyes—the same eyes as my eldest cousin Malakat—glitter in the faded afternoon light.

"What are you doing out here?" His eyes follow my hands, and I know he knows *exactly* what I was doing.

"Just a little bit of farming," I lie. "The fields are looking amazing, but—"

"That's fine," he interrupts, eyes narrowing before he looks away. "For a moment you looked like"—he glances at me then looks away again, pain evident in his eyes—"someone else."

My mother, he means. Merfolk don't take photographs like land monsters do, but I've seen drawings of her. We could be twins, with the same dark eyes and aqua scales. My rust-hued fin tips come from Father, though. I've always suspected that part of why Caralorn hates me so much is that he and Father fought over my mother, and my father won her heart. But when she died, Caralorn grieved her even though she wasn't his. Seeing me reminds him of that.

His eyes narrow. "What are you holding?"

Knowing I can never deny him here underwater, I bring the Sea Julienne from behind my back.

He blanches, lips pursing as he stiffens, rising from the rock to back away from me. After a quiet moment where he stares, and it feels like he's looking into my soul, he sighs. "Leave me, Niece."

"Thank you... Goodbye, Uncle," I say quietly, swimming slowly around him with the Sea Julienne tucked behind my back again. He says nothing as I glide away. I don't relax my gills until I'm safely over the ridge and nearing the edge of an underwater cliff with the merkingdom below. I almost felt like he could take one look at me and know I made plans tomorrow with a vampire.

It's not like it's expressly forbidden to have friendships or work outside the merkingdom. It's just considered distasteful. Especially for the king's eldest niece. If he had his way all of the time, I'd do nothing but prepare for being some distant royal's future wife. It was a fight to even get him to let me work at the bar. But working there is the only time I feel remotely peaceful, and I can masquerade as being of service to my people by literally serving them.

Sighing, I swim over the ledge and down into the cavernous valley the kingdom is built into. Tall spires punctuated by hole-like entrances dot the valley floor. Every so often, a glass bubble indicates an air-filled section of the city, not that any of the surface dwellers visit often. The gargoyles sometimes do while on their rounds, but that's about it. I truly think the bubble sections are a mere formality, because Caralorn never built any sort of transportation system to allow landers to access them.

My destination is a pink coral tower covered with ornately scrolled shell decorations, glittering tall from the middle of the city. Gritting my teeth against a fresh wave of pain, I pass the giant gates at the city's edge. Twin statues of my uncle holding a trident greet me, but like always, I feel nothing but frustration.

Swimming through the city, I force a smile and wave when other merfolk greet me with cautious looks and reverential dips of their heads.

By the time I make it to the suite I share with my cousins, I'm exhausted and the pain's nearly unbearable. The moment I glide through one of the big round openings into our suite, my cousin Thatraeia grabs my arm and yanks me to her side. Pale coral eyes flash and narrow, and she crosses her arms.

Sighing, I look away before she can start in on me. Not that it stops her.

"The surface again? Must you go every day, Ama?"

I return my focus to her. Where my scales and hair are all the shades of the lake, she's all pink and coral, like the castle come to life. We're opposites in so many ways, but of my bevy of cousins, she's the only one I'm close to. Their mother left after producing six girls—I think she couldn't bear living with the fact that Caralorn loved someone else—so I've become Thatraeia's surrogate mother in many ways.

"Yes, my sweet cousin. It's my one joy. Let me have it, please? I'm not bothering anyone by disappearing for a few hours."

It's the age-old conversation between us, and we only have it when we're alone. I'm certain my other five cousins know I go to Ever, but we don't speak of it, and they leave the lake infrequently.

But Thatraeia and I have always been the closest, even though she's the youngest of us seven. Now she twitches her ears and huffs out a bubbly, irritated noise.

"It's just coffee. We have coffee here. I hate it when you leave... The others are mean."

I thump the tipped-up end of her nose playfully. "Our coffee is served cold in bubbles. It's sludge. I'm not built like the other merfolk. I like my coffee hot and dark. Not gelatinous."

She rolls peachy-rose eyes at me but plants both hands on her hips. "Well, did you have fun, at least?"

I debate telling her about Betmal. I shouldn't. But she's always had a way of knowing when I'm hiding something. So, despite my reticence, the entire story comes out. She gasps at my plan to meet him tomorrow for dinner.

"How are you going to get out of work?"

I grin. "I'm off tomorrow."

"Ooooookay." She draws out the word with a skeptical look. "But what if Father finds ou—"

"He won't," I assure her. "This probably won't lead anywhere anyway, but what if it does, and I could save up enough money to start over somewhere else? You know that's always been my dream. And Caralorn probably wouldn't care if I disappeared. I wouldn't be a burden anymore."

Her concerned look morphs into one of sadness, the wispy coral tips of her ears drooping. "I'll be so lonely if you leave," she whispers.

"Then come with me," I encourage for the millionth time. "We've talked about this so many times. The only reason I don't go is because I can't afford to, and Thalassa knows, Caralorn would never *help* me leave and dishonor his promise to raise me. But if we could because of this..."

She purses pink lips together and shakes her head. In her mind, her father is still a giant figure of power. And he is, literally and figuratively. But I'm also not so naïve I don't realize there's a bigger world out there that doesn't include him or any of my other cousins.

Thatraeia and I just need money to access it and get far enough away that it won't matter what he does. I'm hoping we'd be out of sight, out of mind, especially given he has five other daughters who seem perfectly content living under his thumb.

I'm stuck in the meantime, and for the foreseeable future, but if there's any chance at all of eventually saving enough to leave, I have to take it.

When she shakes her head again, I sigh and swim across the room to my wardrobe. After pulling it open, I don a red coral bra and add a few red necklaces to my outfit. Merfolk aren't fussed about clothing in general, but I feel like dressing up.

Thatraeia gives me the silent treatment until it's time to leave, then she takes my hand and brings it to her chest, her gaze imploring.

"Please be careful, Ama. Vampires are dangerous. The entire *world* is dangerous, and you're delicate."

I pull my hand from hers. I know what she means. That I'm not strong, not tough.

When I yank my hand away, she pouts. "Don't be mad. But you being attacked and frozen by the revenant scared all of us. If you weren't so insistent on going up to the surface, if you could have run awa—"

"Stop." I put both hands up to halt her stream of consciousness. She doesn't mean to throw my disability in my face, but she does it nonetheless. I back slightly away from her. "If I didn't go to the surface, I'd be miserable. And nobody could have outrun the revenant. What happened wasn't my fault, and nothing could have changed the outcome. I wasn't the *only* victim, if you remember."

She lifts her chin but doesn't respond. She's right that if I never went above at all, I probably wouldn't have been attacked by the detached soul of a recently deceased Everton. I don't remember his attack, actually, and I don't remember much of what followed. I just remember pain and waking up in a saltwater tub at Doc Slade's, wondering what the depths happened.

When I got home, Caralorn was just furious I left the city at all. He forbade me to in the future, but I have to be true to some part of myself, if only for a few hours each day. Over the years, he's decided to adopt a "don't ask" policy on my coffee trips, as long as I keep them short.

The reality is that merfolk aren't meant for lakes—we're meant for the open sea. It's not natural to live in Ever…and Caralorn loves to remind me how it's my fault we're living in an environment that's not entirely suited to us. If I'm honest with myself, it's another reason I tend so thoroughly to the Sea Julienne—I don't even disagree with Caralorn's assessment of blame.

Leaving my cousin in stony silence, I swim out of the suite and through the city to Sovereign Sip, the swanky cocktail bar at the very edge of the Depthless Cliffs. Beyond that, the lake is so deep, it's said that nobody's ever seen the bottom. Sometimes I like to imagine that Caralorn leaves my little dowry down there, simply because it's his responsibility to safeguard it for me. And one day, I'll venture to the bottom, look for it, and scoop it up. I'll drag Thatraeia to another haven, and maybe get the new leg I know my parents would have wanted for me.

Working here at the bar is my second joy, something I fought tooth and nail for. I don't really earn any money for the work—Uncle sees to that—but I do it all the same. It's a chance to see my people under fun conditions. And when my boss

Rikard can, he slips me a little bit of cash under the table. It's enough for my coffee trips, but that's about it.

As I float through the bar's tan coral entryway, Rikard catches my eye from behind the bar. Purple lips curve into a genuine smile as he grabs a glass globe with a small hole in the top. He turns and slips it onto a tube that deposits gelatinous martini mix into the glass. That done, he sticks a sprig of seaweed into the opening and hands it to a merman hovering in front of the bar.

I join him, slipping up over the coral surface and smiling at the nearest patron. The Sip isn't super busy this time of day, but in about half an hour, it'll be filled with the King's Guard and merfolk getting off work.

"There she is."

My blood freezes as I turn, glass in hand, to see my cousin Malakat glide through the front arch with several of the King's Guard at her back.

I force a smile. "Hello, Cousin. Can I get you something to drink?" I make purposeful eye contact with the other three guards. "And what about you three?"

One of them opens his mouth to say something, but zips it shut when Malakat shoots him a dirty look. Technically, she's head of the guard, so they report to her even though she's far younger than the rest of us.

Not that you'd know it by looking at her. She's every inch the guard captain with long, glittering green nails and her emerald hair twisted into an intricate series of braids that give her a distinctly warlike appearance. She's closest in age to me, and being my uncle's eldest gives her a very fuck-off vibe.

"Mead, girl. Get it quickly," she snaps, drumming her fingers on the sea-leather straps crisscrossing her chest.

Resisting the urge to snap at her, I turn and get the drink. When I hand it to her, she takes it roughly, and the sludge sloshes slowly around in the glass, threatening to dribble out of the small hole.

I take the other guards' orders. They're terse and direct when she's around. But I know them all well. We're the same age, and all older than Malakat. But since she's here, they won't say a kind word to me. Not and risk her wrath.

"I looked for you this morning," Malakat says in a cruel tone, leaning over the bar to bring her face close to mine. "You weren't around. Where were you?"

I shrug. I don't owe her a minute-by-minute update about my day, and she knows I go to the coffee shop. Avoiding the topic is my usual tactic because she's always shitty about it.

When she sneers, I level her with an irritated look. "I was working in the Sea Julienne fields, among other duties."

She snorts and sips at the gelatinized mead we import from the General Store in Downtown Ever. "Farming. What a life. It's a shame you're not part of the guard, although I suppose with that fin, how could you be?"

It's hard not to remind her that even *having* a King's Guard is pointless since we live isolated in a lake. There are no other clans to protect Caralorn from. Mentioning that would just anger her and I'm already over this interaction.

I don't blanch or show any visible signs of irritation. It's exactly what she wants. The reality is that the only reason she's the head of the guard and *not* me is because of my half-fin. But in a way, it's a blessing. I'm not cut out for that work, nor do I have any interest at all in doing it.

And one day, when Caralorn matches her to some merman guard she's been the captain over for decades…things are gonna be awkward for her.

I wouldn't want that.

Rikard calls for me, saving me from having to talk any longer to my least favorite cousin. I join him in the back room, and he assigns me a task that doesn't need doing at all but will keep me out of Malakat's braids for an hour or so.

The moment he heads to the bar to take my place, that little flame of determination that started burning when Betmal made his proposal flares bright inside me.

I can't live like this forever, under the thumb of a king and a cousin who are, at best, dismissive and, at worst, downright cruel. Whatever it takes, I've got to get out of here.

∼

The following morning, I wake to someone violently shaking my shoulder. Blinking my eyes open, I flare my gills to pull oxygenated water into my lungs.

Malakat glares down at me. "Rise, girl. Father wishes to see you."

I sit upright and swing my tail over the edge of the coral bed.

Malakat's emerald eyes flick to the missing fin, and she smirks, but says nothing.

Goddess, she's mean.

The clamshell lights on the walls glow the palest of pinks. It's still early, the castle thoughtfully telling us it'll be time to wake a few hours from now.

Malakat lays her spear over her shoulder and sighs. "Get *up*, Ama."

Hissing at her rudeness, I slide, irritated, from the bed and wave at the door. "Well, go on. Lead the way."

She snorts and spins, shooting across the room and through the door.

My fin aches, but I don't take the time to stretch it, even though I usually do that in the morning before I leave the royal suite. I don't like to do it once I'm out in the city, so I have to do it here. I've had enough judgmental looks to last me a lifetime.

Grabbing my little pile of Sea Julienne, I stuff a huge handful in my mouth before following Malakat through the door and along a still-dark coral-hued hallway. We wind through the castle toward my uncle's suite. When we hook a right toward the grand ballroom, I sigh. Not his suite, I guess…his secondary meeting room.

Business meetings at this time of day? That does not bode well. It occurs to me that perhaps he's somehow found out about my dinner with Betmal, and he's going to put a stop to my escape plan right now. Caralorn doesn't want me around, but he doesn't want to give me the means to leave, either. He's insufferable.

Shoving concern down, I follow Malakat through a white clamshell-encrusted door into my uncle's private conference room. He floats at the giant arched window on the far side, staring out over the kingdom with his arms crossed.

When we enter the room, he spins in place, eyes narrowed as he takes me in. Every time he looks at me, I see the disdain and blame he has for me. It makes me feel so small, even smaller than I make myself feel.

"I'll be blunt," he says, floating to a flat coral table that takes up most of the center of the room. "I've arranged a suitor for you, Amatheia, from a clan I've known since I was a merminnow. They will be here in a few days to officially meet you and make an offer on what's left of your dowry, in the customary way. You will be on your best behavior for Prince Stefan, or so help me…" His voice trails off as he glares.

I can barely pull water through my gills fast enough.

A suitor?

It can't be.

I float toward him, desperate to find some reason why this won't work.

"Stop, Cousin," Malakat snarls. "Father sent me to arrange this with Stefan's clan. He's handsome, brilliant, and rich. This is good for our family, and Thalassa knows, you owe us."

I choke at the accusation. It's been so long since she reminded me that most of my cousins *also* blame me for my parents' deaths and our resulting relocation. It's why we're not close. It's—

I look from her to my uncle. "I don't want this. You have six daughters, and Malakat is *your* eldest. Give her to him. Sounds like she thinks he's great."

Caralorn's eyes widen, and he glides over the table to get right in my face. "And yet I'm stuck with you, and you are the eldest female under my care, Amatheia. Do what you must to your fin to ensure you don't seem weak when Stefan arrives. The prince brings money to our clan, and that is reason enough to accept him. You should be grateful I'm honoring your parents' wishes by providing a permanent place for you in the future, just as I have for the past years."

I cross my arms; I'm livid. "Why don't you just let me leave this Thalassa-forsaken castle and move somewhere else? My parents would rather me forge ahead on my own than be married off to a male I do not love. You *know* that's true. Why do you insist I remain here?" I narrow my eyes at him. "Is it just so you can continue to torture me about how their deaths were my fault? Because I can assure you, there's not a day I don't hate myself for it."

Caralorn snarls and lurches forward, gripping my throat and shoving me against the nearest wall. "I will not rehash their deaths yet another time with you. She died in my *arms*, or have you conveniently forgotten that? You will accept Stefan, or else I cannot guarantee your safety with this clan."

Eyes popping wide, I scan the king's face, but he looks serious as a heart attack.

"Just let me go," I whisper, begging him with my expression to stop being such an asshole.

"Never," he hisses. "I won't dishonor her memory by not

ensuring a successful future for you, despite my personal feelings on the topic."

Fuck that. I'm done.

So I smile up into my uncle's angular face, focused on his flashing green eyes. "As you wish, Caralorn," I say in a simpering tone, not bothering to use his title.

I shove out of his grip, and without waiting for him to say anything else, I spin in place—fin throbbing—and glide for the door. I lift my chin as merfolk begin to fill the halls to begin their day. I don't stop or drop the smile from my face until I reach the royal suite.

Everyone but Thatraeia is gone, and she comes to me immediately as I push the door closed and sink down to the ground, splaying my aching tail to one side.

"Ama!" Thatraeia drops down next to me, wrapping her arms around my neck. "What happened? I awoke, and you were gone!"

The tears don't come, not here underwater. But the rage builds. Rage at what happened to me, how Caralorn's clan treated me because of it, and the expectations of being the unwanted firstborn of a dead king and queen.

That same rage fills me until I'm ready to rip something to pieces.

Thatraeia pulls away from me, peachy eyes scanning my face. "Ama?"

"I'm taking that job," I say with conviction. "I'm taking that job and getting that money. And then I'm out of here, Cousin." I lift my eyes to hers. "And I'm taking you with me."

CHAPTER FIVE
BETMAL

"Perfect, darling," I tell the house as I light the final candles in the kitchen. She's set the light low. It could almost be considered romantic, although I haven't put out nearly enough candles for true romance. Tonight's dinner with Amatheia is about convincing her to work with me on this project. Secondary to that, I'd like her to get to know me. And I'd like to get to know her.

A scent hasn't intoxicated me like hers in more than a thousand years. Not even my mates' scents.

That's something. It *means* something. And I've learned over my long life to listen to my instinct.

Just then, the front doors swing wide. When I twitch an ear to listen, soft breathing reaches me.

She can't be here yet. I was planning to meet her at the lake and fly her here. It's a long walk, and it can't possibly be comfortable with her leg.

Horrified, I stalk to the front of the house. And there she is, standing in the doorway, gripping the frame with a trembling hand. The muscles of her partial leg twitch and shudder, but she forces a bright smile.

"You're early," I manage, swooping to the door and resisting the urge to cradle her in my arms, carry her to the kitchen, and feed her grapes from my hand.

She blanches a little. "Thalassa below, I hope that's okay. I wasn't sure how long it would take me to walk."

"Gods no," I offer by way of apology. "I planned to pick you up shortly, there was no need to bring yourself."

She waves my apology away, but she looks tense and tired at the same time.

I reach a hand out, opening my palm. "May I carry you into the kitchen?"

She laughs and shakes her head. "No, thank you. I'll be fine. Lead the way, please."

Stepping aside, I offer my arm instead. "I must insist on you taking my arm, at the very least."

She slides her hand around my elbow, resting it on my forearm. I rolled my sleeves up a little while ago, and the feel of her cool, textured skin on mine has my fangs throbbing.

Walking slowly to the kitchen, I give her a quick tour of the entryway and the formal dining room. She stares wide-eyed at everything, seeming enraptured by the house. The house herself shimmies and shakes with excitement, pushing a bar stool out for Amatheia when we reach the kitchen. I settle her onto it, then clasp my hands together.

"Can I get you a drink?"

She nods. "Surprise me? I don't drink terribly often, but something tells me you know your way around a bar."

Laughing, I agree. "I'm thousands of years old, ma siréne, I've made a drink or two."

She winks at me. "You don't look a day over forty-five."

Ah, there's a playful woman there under her initial reticence. Good. I love playful banter.

She stares for a moment longer. "What does ma siréne mean?"

I smile as I work up a gin and tonic.

"Mermaid, in French." That's not entirely true as it's a possessive version of the word, but we don't have to get into that now.

When I slide it over the concrete island, she takes it with an appreciative sniff. Does she know the wavy tips of her ears twitch and move when she bends to take a sip? I'm entranced, watching her delicate features as she samples the drink with a happy little sigh.

"It's excellent," she murmurs, dark aqua eyes flashing to me.

"Good." I lean over the bar, well aware that I left my shirt open to the waist once again, hoping to draw her attention. On cue, she drops those fascinating eyes to my chest, her gaze roaming my upper body and down my arms.

Everything about the way I dressed tonight is designed to attract her without being overtly sexual. Before my mates and I grew apart, I was the romantic one. I was the one to spend days seducing them before we made love. I adore the long, playful tease and build of seduction. True seduction starts before you ever touch the other person.

She brings her focus back to my face, her pale cheeks blushing a darker shade of blue. "I work at the bar in the merkingdom, so I've made a fair few cocktails myself."

I grin. "Oh? And do you make them differently?"

She takes another sip and tilts her head to one side, seeming to consider the answer. Finally, she levels me with a serious look. "I garnish mine with seaweed."

Roaring out a laugh, I straighten and plant my palms on the countertop. "Naturally, Amatheia. Up here, lemon is more common."

She returns the smile, though hers is softer. "I've managed to take a few cocktail recipe books from the historical society. It's fascinating to me what twists surface dwellers put on the same drinks. Although, we've also got a host of wildly different drinks based on the plants we grow at home."

I gesture to a saucepan on the stove. "Speaking of differences, since you mentioned being an adventurous eater, I started a chicken piccata with garlic mashed potatoes. Is that alright?"

Her smile grows broad, and she leans over the countertop, eyeing the bubbling pan on the stove. "Smells delicious. But… forgive me if this is a rude question. Don't you, you know…" Her voice trails off, and she points to her neck.

"Drink blood?" My nostrils flare, and I round the island, putting a finger under her chin. I make a show of perusing her throat as if I'm looking for the perfect spot. She freezes, but her lips tip into a smile. She's unafraid.

"Yes, ma siréne," I murmur. "If that were on the table, I'd accept the gift of your blood. But given we're here to discuss a business proposition, perhaps we'd better stick to business?"

The edges of her smile tip farther upward. "I wasn't offering, Betmal."

"Good." I drop my hold on her chin and return to the pot. "Just as well. If the bloodletting begins, I will find it difficult to concentrate, and I'm anxious to discuss this project with you."

She returns to her drink as I plate dinner and bring it to the already set dining table. Dozens of candles placed haphazardly down the center of its surface lend a romantic feel, but I left the overhead lights on low to keep it from feeling too over the top.

"Your home is beautiful," she says softly, hobbling off the stool and joining me.

Smiling, I round the end and pull a chair out for her, offering my hand.

She takes it and grips my fingers carefully as she lowers into the seat. It's easy to see she's trying to do it gracefully, but her leg buckles, and she falls the last few inches, landing with a hard thud.

"Are you alright, ma siréne?" I grab a puffy pillow from the side table and drop to my knee, carefully grabbing her ankle to rest her foot on it. She stiffens when I touch her, but I'm making a wild guess that she'll allow me to. And she does.

Her skin is cool to the touch, even by vampire standards. Just like before, she smells of the sea, of depthless wonders and inky blue deep. I resist the urge to bring her foot—and adorable toes—to my lips to nip and play.

Releasing her ankle, I rise and reach for a plate, setting it in front of her. "Please eat before it's cold." Pulling my chair close to the one she selected, I grab my fork and knife and lay my napkin over my lap. I don't need food like this, but I can enjoy a well-cooked meal.

Amatheia picks up her utensils and cuts the chicken. She eats the first bite with gusto, an appreciative hum rumbling softly from her delicate throat.

"So," I scoot my chair back enough to cross one leg over the other, "have you had occasion to see the Ever welcome packet? Or the welcome packet for any haven in our system?"

She shakes her head. "We moved here from outside the system, and I vaguely remember Abemet offering us packets when we arrived." Her lips curve downward. "Unfortunately, they weren't waterproof."

I frown. "That's unfortunate. I wondered why your uncle chose to bring your clan to Ever. Lake living isn't typical for mer, in my experience."

She sighs. "No, it's not. We have to do a lot of things to the lake to make it livable like an ocean location would be. I was born in the sea, but the open ocean is a dangerous place, and my family..." her voice trails off. "We were attacked, and..."

I shift forward, on the edge of my seat.

She squirms in her chair, picking at her napkin. "Another clan attacked us while my mother and father were playing chase with me around our Sea Julienne fields. We escaped, but they wounded my parents, and a school of sharks…umm. Well, they didn't survive, and I lost my fin, as you can see."

Grief strikes me to the core for her loss. "I'm sorry to have asked," I offer. "Are you an only child, then?"

She frowns. "Yes. Caralorn took me in when they died, so I've got six cousins. We're all a year or so apart. After the attack, he brought us all here. It was Mother's dying wish, despite merfolk not being all that suited to haven living. Caralorn found us just after the attack, and she begged him to take me somewhere safer. So, basically, he uprooted the entire clan for me."

She sounds *devastated*.

I reach out to place my hand over hers. "I've heard he's a bit prickly."

A fake smile comes to her face. "He hates me for their deaths and having to spend my once substantial dowry to bring us here. But truthfully, he can't hate me any more than I hate myself for wandering off and putting us in that position." She hisses in a breath, dark eyes widening. "Thalassa below, that was an awful lot to unload during a business meeting. Right up front, too."

She moves her hand from beneath mine, spearing a piece of chicken. It's clear she wants to move on. But one day, we are going to revisit this topic of self-loathing because, while I understand it, it's clear she doesn't see herself as the victim in that story.

"Family can be a blessing." I attempt to offer an understanding smile. "Or sometimes a curse, depending. I'm very close with my son and his mate, but gods know I ignore my extended family as much as possible."

"So you don't travel the world to visit them?" Her lips quirk upward into a soft smile.

"Not when I can avoid it," I say with a laugh. "The benefit to being quite old is that I'm rarely expected to." I glance at the table and the welcome packet sitting there. "Actually, that brings me back to the welcome packet. I have the advantage of centuries dealing with the haven system, but as the system grows, it's become more common for monsters and humans from the outside world to become residents."

I grab an envelope from the chair next to mine and slide it toward her. "Whenever a haven receives a new resident, it's customary to give them a welcome packet that's been approved by Hearth HQ. Each packet is customized to the haven and includes information on the layout and amenities, etcetera. For any non-monster residents, there's a secondary version on monster traditions that can be useful if they're new to our world."

Amatheia takes the envelope and opens it, pulling out the loose sheets that make up a sample welcome packet for Ever.

Sighing, I gesture at the pages. "What you have there is both the monster and human version of the packets. To me, the packet is an opportunity to impress new residents, but our current offering is short and direct and often missing pages. For example," I lean in a bit closer to her, "when my daughter-in-law received hers, nearly half the packet was forgotten, and it led to unnecessary confusion as she navigated a world she previously knew nothing about." I smile at her. "And, as you mentioned, the packets are obviously not waterproof, which is something we *should* be considering."

Amatheia flips through the pages, eyes eating up the small-print text. She frowns and glances at me. "The information seems useful, though, doesn't it?"

I shrug. "Assuming you get it all. But, yes, the information contained therein has its uses, but it's my intention to revamp the welcome packets into coffee table-style books. I'd like them to be beautiful, to highlight the unique charms of each haven. In short, I'd like them to be collectible, something new residents can be proud of."

I glance at my plate, then back at my guest. "This is the type of project my former colleagues never prioritized. In their minds, other efforts had greater importance. But I believe there is only one chance for a first impression."

Amatheia sets the pages down and takes another bite of chicken, chewing slowly. After a moment, she smiles over at me. "And how do I fit into this beautiful new collectible book idea?"

"Well," I say, "I need art. A lot of art. Sketches and paintings, and they need to be cohesive throughout each book. Then I'll need books for every haven, all fifty-something-plus of them."

"Depths below," she murmurs, looking thoughtful. "That sounds like quite the undertaking."

I'm certain she's thinking it sounds daunting, and I mean to reassure her.

Reaching over, I pat the back of her hand softly. "I'd like to start with Ever and gauge the project's success. Hearth HQ never wanted to spend the time and money to do this, but I can't imagine them objecting to me doing this on my own dime."

She looks carefully at me. "And do you know these leaders? What happens if they don't agree to pursue your project?"

I debate how much to get into this with her now, opting for the simplest version of the truth. "The vampire who leads Hearth HQ and her husband are my former mates." I level Amatheia with a serious look. "We separated, but they will give me this, if I demand it. Which I plan to do."

"Uh-huh." She looks skeptical, taking another bite of her food. I want to reassure her that this project is happening because I *will* it to be so. But I sense she needs a moment to absorb what I shared.

After a moment, she looks up at me, the tips of her ears twitching slightly. "Is there a chance this project won't see the light of day?"

"None at all," I promise. "I have quite a few tricks up my

sleeve to ensure they sign off on it. There is not a single doubt in my mind that it will be rubber-stamped when I request it."

She takes another delicate bite of chicken, chewing slowly as her eyes rove over the pages laid out on the table. Setting her fork down, she gathers up the papers and tucks them back into the manila envelope. "I shouldn't do this, but I'll admit to being intrigued."

I lean back in my chair, lifting my chin as I stare at her, wondering how long she'll hold the gaze. She does for a moment, then looks away at the envelope, setting it carefully down in the center of the table.

I chuckle. "Sometimes, the worst ideas have the most pleasurable outcomes, Amatheia. Don't you think?" I swirl my drink in the glass as she looks up at me, the aqua shade of her cheeks darkening.

"I wouldn't know, Betmal. Why don't you share a little more, and I'll decide if your bad ideas have merit or not." Her lips curl into a smile as she picks up the fork and spears another bite of green bean.

Laughing again, I take a sip of my drink.

She's hooked. Good.

CHAPTER SIX
AMATHEIA

For the next half hour, Betmal shares his vision for the coffee table book, going so far as to bring out sketches and a notebook. His vision is clear. The book should be beautiful but functional, full of stunning art with a high-end feel. Having seen his house, it doesn't surprise me. The entire home feels like a designer spent a very large amount of money making every nook and cranny perfect.

Somehow, his home is luxurious but cozy. It's not so fancy that it doesn't look lived in. But it's not casual, either. That's how he seems to me as well. The few times I've seen him, he always seems so comfortable, but he's always dressed impeccably.

After dinner, he produces a crème brûlée that I splurge and eat two of. When he insists so kindly, I can't help myself. Dessert isn't common in the merkingdom, but I love it. Just another way I'm not like everyone else. Not that I care terribly much about that as I stuff my face with sugary deliciousness.

Dessert finished, Betmal offers to show me what he's working on in the backyard. I debate how far I can walk with my leg throbbing from the earlier trek, but the truth is, if he's doing a project...I want to see it. He's so creative and expressive, whatever it is will probably be beautiful.

He offers me his arm, and I take it despite warning bells blaring in my mind. I'm attracted to him. I think any female *alive* would probably be attracted to him. And that is a conflict of interest I should consider before I agree to do this project. Although, the project itself is intriguing. I love the idea of making something beautiful that's also highly practical. Plus, I'm certain I can be professional if this project—and the money I earn from it—get me closer to my goal of leaving the lake.

Betmal opens an arched glass-paned door that leads into his backyard, pointing at a shed-like structure that rises two stories high. A gabled roof rises nearly to the branches of the giant trees surrounding it. It's *gorgeous*.

He smirks as he joins me in staring at the building. "My new workshop. The interior's not finished yet, but the second story will be an open loft that serves as my office. It takes up just half of the second story so I can look down below." His smirk grows into a full on grin. "That way it'll be easy to spy as you paint."

Chuckling, I turn to look up at him. "*This* giant home doesn't have an office space for you?"

He returns the soft laugh. "Ma siréne, I prefer to keep work and play a bit separate. It's a favorite custom of mine to take my morning espresso, walk across the yard and do my work in my office. At dinnertime, I return to this quiet space, and I do not bring work with me." He waves at the house behind us. "My home is all about pleasure, sweet girl. Good food, good time spent with people I care for. I don't bring work there if I can help it."

"Sounds amazing," I admit. While my workspace isn't in the castle, just being home in the suite shared by all my cousins is chaotic at the best of times.

He gestures toward the backyard cottage again. "That first floor is one giant sitting area, windows on all four walls. It would be a perfect place to paint, sketch, or draw. If you agree to do this project with me, I'd like you to work here so we can stay in touch as we progress."

"Oh." I move to let go of his arm, but he grabs my hand gently and curls my fingers around his firm biceps.

"Say yes to me," he says. "Say yes to this project. I have seen your work, and you're the only one I want for it."

I shouldn't. I really shouldn't.

"It's hard for me to get away," I finally admit. "It's embarrassing, but merfolk don't often mix with the rest of Ever. You've probably seen that in your short time here. I'm one of the only mer who comes out of the lake, well, at all." I glance up, frowning. "It might take me a while to do this. I'd like to, but you'd be better off having me paint one or two things and finding another artist for the rest."

If he has to wait on me to do all of the art, it'll take ages.

"Has to be you," he says with a smile that lights up his elegant features. "So, we will work on whatever timeframe you're able to manage. And the gig pays a million dollars per haven."

That silly offer makes me smile. "Sounds like I've got carte blanche, and I'm overcharging you by an arm and a fin."

His nostrils flare as he leans closer. "Whatever it takes to get a yes. Two million? Three?"

"Yes," I say as I stare at the adorable cottage in his beautifully designed backyard oasis. "Three million seems excessive, Betmal. A million dollars is quite sufficient." It's a joke, it must be. That number is ludicrous.

A spark of hope flares bright in my chest. I should squash it down, I really should, but the way he levels me with a devious smile serves as oxygen to that flame.

Crimson eyes flash. "If that's what you want, Amatheia, that is what you shall have."

I snort out a laugh. A million dollars for a few paintings is absolutely ridiculous. Even so, I'm certain we can figure out a number that makes sense. I'll bring it up again later.

CHAPTER SEVEN
BETMAL

It's been three days since I convinced Amatheia to work with me on the welcome packet project. In that time, the house and I have worked nonstop to finish building and decorating the backyard cottage. Today, it's finally complete and ready for my guest.

Striding across my lofted office space, I descend the stairs to the first floor, marveling at the beautiful sunlight filtering through the walls of windows. One of them slides open and shut several times, bringing a smile to my face.

"That's right, darling," I croon, reaching out to pat the wall lovingly. "She'll be here shortly. I'm planning to pick her up at the lake in half an hour, and then we'll be back so she can work. Exciting, isn't it?"

This time, all of the windows open and shut with loud, creaky squeaks. She's excited, and I love that.

"I'm going to head over a little early," I say more to myself than anything. I'd rather be early to pick Amatheia up than late and have her walk again. The last thing I want is for her to feel pain at my expense. Leaving the cottage, I head to the main house and find the keys to a gorgeous vintage Corvette, courtesy of Abemet.

After sliding into the black leather seat, I start the beautiful car up, marveling at the throaty purr of a perfectly tuned engine. I set off with a smile. Things couldn't possibly be working out any better.

Twenty minutes later, I pull off the road and park the car. A thin dirt path leads to the lake, which is where Amatheia is meeting me in ten minutes. Looking in the rearview mirror, I run both hands through my hair, slicking it back. As always, a tiny chunk falls over my eyes.

Feminine voices drift through the forest toward me. Twitching an ear, I listen as they rise. Amatheia's shouting at someone, and she sounds frustrated, almost angry. I don't recognize the other voice.

I'm out of the car quickly, jogging along the path to get to her. I don't stop until I reach the lakeshore, where I find Amatheia and another mermaid in the water, only their heads peeking above the surface. When I appear, Amatheia notices me and blushes, looking upset.

"Betmal, you're early. I was just—"

"Don't do this," the other mermaid hisses. "When Father finds out, he'll—"

"He won't find out if you don't tell him," Amatheia snaps. "Which you aren't going to do…right?"

The other female looks over at me and shudders. "Oh depths, I thought you were kidding. A vampire?" She looks back at Amatheia. "A vampire, Ama? For real? They're *dangerous*, you know that! And what about—" She stops talking and looks my way again.

Slipping both hands into my pockets, I stalk toward them until I'm knee-deep in the lake, pulling the other mermaid's focus to me. "I'm only vicious when I need to be, darling.

Amatheia is in no danger from me. I simply need a job done, and she's the woman to do it."

I wonder if this is one of the cousins she previously mentioned?

The other female's features twist into an expression somewhere between disgust and discomfort, and she looks back at Amatheia. "Please don't *do* this, Ama. I've kept a lot of secrets for you, but this is too much. When Father finds out, he'll raise hells and forbid you from continuing."

I remain watchful, curious to see how Amatheia will handle this.

She drags her fingers along the water's surface. "I'm going, Thatraeia. And you have to keep this secret for me, for us. I have a chance to not only help Betmal with an important project, but do something I love at the same time. Those chances come so rarely. Assuming Betmal still wants my help after this outburst, I'm going with him."

"It's got to be you," I confirm with a smile.

For a long, tense moment, neither female says anything else. Eventually, the pink-finned mermaid sighs and backs toward the deeper water. "I hope you know what you're doing, Ama. This isn't going to work out well." Without sparing either of us another glance, she flips backward, curling into a ball before shooting toward the middle of the lake.

Amatheia looks over at me. "Depths, I am *so* sorry, Betmal. She means well; she's my favorite cousin, but damn." She stares up at me from beneath impossibly long inky-blue lashes. "Today has been a *week*. Are you sure you want me to do this for you? Because you're probably going to have to deal with more merfolk nonsense if this takes longer than a session or two. My uncle hates for me to have anything of my own."

Oh, my sweet girl has no idea. Not only will this take ages and ages, but once we're done with the Ever book, I have every intention of hiring her to paint for all the havens, all fifty-plus of them. We'll be working on this project for a very, very long time.

"Absolutely certain." I wave her apology away. "I'm not concerned over anyone's opinion but yours."

She smiles and glides closer to shore, her upper body appearing out of the water. Long turquoise-green hair drips wet down her chest, completely covering round, pert breasts. Still, it's enough of a hint to make my fangs throb with need.

She waves a hand toward a giant fallen tree on the edge of the beach. "I need to hop over to the lockers and grab my clothes."

"Allow me," I offer, reaching for her. I've never known merfolks to be concerned with nudity, but it still surprises me when she takes my hand and hops toward me in human form. It takes a considerable amount of self-control not to let my gaze drop and stare at her body. Water sluices down her skin as her scales fade mostly away, revealing a taut, smooth stomach.

I force my eyes to hers. "May I carry you to the lockers?"

She nips her lower lip and nods. "I wouldn't want to impose, but it'll be quicker if you do." Her laugh is meant to take away the awkwardness of the moment, I expect. But for me, it's *not* awkward. Not at all. I want to put my hands on her, even if it's just to help.

I don't want her experiencing a moment of pain. Bending slightly, I slip an arm around the backs of her knees and another around her shoulders. She's light as a feather as I carry her out of the lake and toward the giant fallen tree that serves as lockers for the merfolks. It's a nice bit of haven design, thoughtful and unique. Most merfolk don't venture from their bodies of water that often, so many havens don't incorporate something like lockers, as they'd go relatively unused.

This'll be Abemet's doing, my brilliant son. He has an eye for detail.

He got that from me.

"Which locker, darling?" I pause in front of the moss-covered tree.

She wiggles out of my arms and takes a seat on the log, patting a patch next to her thigh. Her beautiful, very toned thigh. As she opens the locker and withdraws clothing, I take a moment to absorb how hauntingly stunning she is. Females are such glorious creatures—strong yet delicate. Hard but soft. Givers of life and rulers of kingdoms.

Amatheia pulls a navy tee over her head. I resist the urge to suggest she paint nude. One day. One day we'll get there.

Her prosthetic goes on next. She nestles the uppermost part of her leg into the cupped wooden cap, then wraps the straps around her knee, hissing as she does so.

Next she pulls jeans up her wet legs, but that's difficult to do without drying oneself. I drop to my knee and pull her foot through, helping her to inch the jeans up her legs. I'm being forward, more forward than I should be. But the need to care for her, to do *everything* for her, eats me alive as she struggles to get the jeans up her wet thighs.

When she hops to a stand, shimmying the jeans over round, muscular hips, I grit my teeth to stop myself from leaning in and burying them in her throat.

My reaction to this female is the strongest sentiment I've experienced in a very long time. I wasn't even this enthralled when I met Evenia and Aberen. There was immediate sensuality —it was fun, but eventually that fun ran its course. By then, we had Abemet, and I stayed to give him some stability.

Amatheia and I exchange wry looks. Reaching down, I grab the waistband of her pants and yank them quickly the rest of the way up. Dark azure eyes rove my face as I zip and button them, then place my hand on her hip. Her eyes are wide, bright, her cheeks flushed a darker shade of aqua, plump lips slightly parted. She looks ready to be kissed. That mouth is in desperate need of it.

But not yet. Taking a step back, I smile and offer her my arm. "Shall we, darling?"

She takes it with one hand then bends down, arranging her jeans around the prosthesis. I grimace inwardly as she winces. It's obviously ill-fitting. Clearly too small. I can't imagine how she's gotten around with it for so long. I'm going to fix this problem as quickly as I can. She deserves better, and I will make it so.

CHAPTER EIGHT
AMATHEIA

Depths below, I couldn't be any more embarrassed. Betmal should never have seen Thatraeia's hissy fit. I'm going to lose this job before I ever get a chance to paint a stroke. But now that I know Uncle Caralorn plans to pawn me off to some other clan, I'm fully determined to help myself out of the lake and an unwanted arrangement.

Betmal keeps reassuring me that it has to be me who does the art, but damn, I hope he really means it. Because as much as I love my cousin, she won't be able to keep this secret forever. Once Malakat or my uncle find out, all hells will break loose. I can only hope I've got enough money saved up by then to leave and start fresh somewhere else. Maybe somewhere that has no merfolk at all. Somewhere I can fully be myself. Perhaps I'll even try to heal the guilt that's part of why I don't just *fix* my prosthetic issue. I'm aware I need to do work on that.

But the pain is a good reminder to be careful and cautious in my decisions. Except for this one, because I truly believe my happiness depends on it. I can't go into a loveless marriage and foreign clan out in the sea. I won't.

"I'm sorry you had to see that," I apologize again as Betmal leads me along the forest path toward Sycamore Street.

"Never apologize for family insanity," he says kindly, holding me steady as we step over a large log.

"Tell me more about *your* family." I squeeze his arm as we slowly round a bend in the trail.

He flashes me a bright smile, twin fangs peeking out from his upper lip. "My son Abemet lives here. You probably know him as this haven's Keeper, although he doesn't serve in that role anymore."

"Wait," I blurt out. "The Keeper's your son? Truly?"

Betmal smiles. He looks proud, eyes crinkling in the corners as he beams. "Not the current Keeper. You might have noticed *he's* a centaur. But your former Keeper, yes."

"I saw the resemblance when we met, but I didn't realize…" I stare at his pale skin, those high cheekbones and thin but lush lips. Our former Keeper is very handsome, too. He must get it from his father.

"Definitely my son," he says. "When I was mated, there were two of us males. We never had any testing done to see who actually sired Abemet, but we always knew he was mine. He's like me in so very many ways, even apart from his good looks."

I laugh. "You're charming, though. I know Abemet relatively well, and he's not much of a joke cracker."

Betmal's smile falls a little, growing thoughtful. "He used to be. The Keeper training stole that from him, as it used to do all Keepers. After he went through the program, I forced HQ to make…well, let's call them updates. The training is far gentler now."

He falls silent, still carefully guiding me down the path toward the street. I sense he's slightly upset about the Keeper topic. That's not a surprise. Becoming a haven keeper is an incredible honor, but the training that zaps them of their emotional nature, forcing them to be highly logical, also seems to zap most keepers of their empathy and good-naturedness. Abemet was an incredible leader, but very dry and serious. I respect him greatly, but he doesn't get jokes.

We round a corner to find a beautiful old convertible with its top down parked by the side of the road. Betmal opens a door, helping me in. "I hope you like car rides, ma siréne. We're going home the long way."

"I've only been in a car once or twice," I admit. Actually, the last time I was in a car, Abemet drove me from Doc Slade's back to this very path, helping me to the lake so I could return home after the revenant attack.

But we don't need to talk about that and ruin a peaceful moment.

Betmal slides gracefully into his seat, putting the car in gear.

I reach over and pat the back of his hand. "Tell me something I don't know about vampires."

He smirks. "What *do* you know of my kind, darling?" He glances over, grinning, then pulls the car into the street.

As we head toward Downtown Ever, I consider that. Finally, I laugh. "You're dangerous, according to my cousin Thatraeia. You drink blood. And…honestly, that's about it." I'm not about to mention the sex bit. That's the only other thing I've heard whispered about from time to time.

He chuckles. "Your cousin is right. I can be dangerous. *Any* monster can be under the right circumstances. But vampires can be beautiful too. For example, did you know we all have wings?"

I stare at his wingless back, wondering if there's something I'm not seeing.

"Hidden, ma siréne," he says with a playful wink. He leans slightly forward in his seat. "Watch."

My mouth drops open as giant, shadowy black wings appear to grow from his back, lifting over the back of the seat. They twist and turn like smoke until they hang high above his head, fluttering in the wind. He flares them wide and curls the right one around me until I'm completely cloaked in darkness.

They're stunning. Fucking beautiful.

"I had no idea," I manage as I resist the urge to pluck at feathers that look so real one moment, then like smoke the next.

"You can touch, if you like." He smiles, eyes on the road as his left wing flutters and folds behind him, resting over the back seat of the car and trailing in the wind.

"I've never read about this in a book." Reaching up, I stroke my fingers along the feathers closest to me. They're cool and soft but rigid in the center just like bird feathers. "What else can you tell me?"

He tucks his wing tighter so it drapes over my door and down across my thighs. I touch the feathers absentmindedly. He's like a cat, resting in my lap to be petted.

"We are a highly sensual species." He glances over at me with a big smile. "Vampires own most of the kink clubs in the haven system, and even in the broader human world beyond our borders. Sex and blood are deeply intertwined for us."

Oh gods, he doesn't seem to feel awkward at all bringing up the topic of sex. I can't even fathom being that casual about it. Merfolk society is not like that at all.

"I can't really understand that," I admit. I've never even had sex. Aside from some rough, awkward fumbling when I was a teenager, I've barely even dated. I cast away the sour feelings that dredges up, determined to focus on Betmal and this incredible opportunity to learn more about the world outside of our lake.

I play with the feathers at the very tip of his giant wing, anxious to switch to a subject I might have an opinion about. "Have you ever met another monster with a prosthetic limb?"

He nods. "Yes, ma siréne, many over the centuries."

I suck in a breath. I suspected as much, although Caralorn

loves to make it sound like I'm the first monster in the history of monsterhood to be missing part of a leg.

I tug on a wing feather without thinking. "I wonder if they all have similar experiences to mine."

"Some, yes."

Silence falls between us as we drive along dappled roads and through beautiful forest along the outer edge of Ever. To my right, the glowing green ward is barely visible through the trees. Wind rustles my hair as I play absentmindedly with Betmal's feathers.

When I risk a glance over at him, one side of his mouth is curved up into a partial smile. The silence is sort of nice, even though it seems like it should be awkward after my question. I let the quiet stretch long until we round a bend in the road, and I realize we're already at his place. He pulls the car in the driveway. The house waves both front doors in greeting. I wave back, laughing as he puts the car in park.

When he hurries to open my door, I blush. He's so thoughtful. I'm not accustomed to that.

"Darling, there are plenty of monsters with prosthetics who manage to get along without much pain. They run; they play sports; they live a full and normal life." He taps my knee where the cup for my leg sits. "Shall we explore finding you a leg that fits better and allows you to move without pain?"

I rise, realizing we're standing so close to one another. I don't want to make this awkward. My leg is not his problem.

"It's fine." I force brightness into my voice. "Don't worry about me."

I deserve this pain, and I keep it around as a reminder.

Those are the words I don't say, and they're the truth.

"Ah." He grins and swoops me into his arms for the second time today. "We are not done talking about this, woman."

He carries me inside and straight to the kitchen, setting me on a barstool. Then he rounds the big concrete bar to the fridge.

When he withdraws a platter covered in plastic wrap, I grin. The scents of cheese and something tangy like tomato drift to me. Licking my lips, I watch as he sets the tray down and removes the plastic covering.

"Let us eat something before you get started." He pushes the offering across the island toward me. I was right about the tomatoes and cheese, but the large plate holds a few types of crackers, some dried fruit, smoked salmon and even seaweed kimchi, which shocks me because it's a merfolk delicacy that I've never seen in Ever.

I raise a brow. "Seaweed kimchi?"

He smirks. "I've been around a long time, darling. This comes from a good friend of mine in the beautiful coastal haven of Renitar, which is half on land but takes up a giant section of sea, too. He assures me this is the best of the best, but I hope you like it."

Grabbing a pinch of kimchi, I plop it on top of a cracker. The first bite fills my senses with the salt, sugar and the unique taste of truly excellent, perfectly harvested seaweed. Not the junk we're able to grow in the lake.

Another thing that's my fault.

"Depths, that's good," I murmur around a mouthful, even as I reach for another cracker. "My uncle insists on importing seaweed kimchi from a friend in an ocean-based haven because our crops don't taste the same. This is *just* like that. Sometimes I think we should have just moved there, but merfolk are so predatory, we'd have to attack and take it over. I suppose he wasn't willing to do that."

Betmal's crimson eyes drop to my mouth, narrowing even as his smile grows broad. His fangs peek over the edge of his lips.

I'm feeling playful, though, because this food is so delicious. And because, despite Thatraeia's warning about how dangerous he is, I don't feel that way around him. He's been nothing but kind and charming. Perhaps he's a spider, luring me into his web. But at the end of the day, that's a chance I'm willing to take.

"Are all vampires as charming as you?"

He snorts. "Not hardly, darling. I've honed this charm over several thousand years of existence and quite a few business dinners. Plus, I was born with a certain amount of it."

"Bunch of humility too," I tease.

He shrugs. "When you've been around as long as I have, you learn that humility isn't all it's cracked up to be. Why be humble if I can be this?" He gestures at himself, drawing my gaze to his upper body. Like always, he wears a collared shirt that's open to reveal his chest and all those incredible tattoos. A low-cut vest highlights his trim waist, a chain leading to a front pocket hinting that he's probably carrying a watch.

"What are you thinking about, Amatheia?" His voice goes low, deadly. It's the croon of a predator about to pounce, and it raises the soft scales along the back of my neck.

"Wondering if I should have taken this job," I say. "Because, as far as I can tell, you're paying me to eat your food."

He laughs and pushes the plate closer to me. "Why *did* you take the job, aside from my obvious charms and excellent negotiation skills?"

I grab another cracker and pile kimchi high on top of it, considering how much to tell him. Eventually, I decide I feel comfortable around Betmal. I don't think he'd do anything to ruin my plan.

"I want to leave the lake." I set the cracker down and fumble with my hands in my lap. "I want to live independently, away from Caralorn. I love most of my people, but I've never felt that I fit in." I'm not sure I'm ready to tell him about the Prince Stefan development. That's my issue to deal with.

Betmal cocks his head to the side. "If I can ask the blunt question, is it because of your leg that you feel this way?"

It's a question I've asked myself many times. Do I feel

different because of my fin? Or does that just exacerbate how I already felt anyway, an orphan thrust into a rigid society, displacing Caralorn's eldest in many ways?

"I suspect it's all interconnected." I bring one leg up, planting my foot on the chair seat and tucking my knee to my chest as I look down at my half leg. "I'd like to see the world. I've never been content to remain in one place. Taking this job means I might have a chance to do that."

Betmal reaches across the table, placing a hand on my knee, his expression serious. "If that's what you want, ma siréne, that's what you shall have."

CHAPTER NINE
BETMAL

Turquoise lashes flutter against aqua-dusted cheeks as she brings her focus to my mouth. For just a moment, she seems lost in staring at it. Then, she looks up into my eyes and waves a hand at me as the corners of her lips twitch.

"Coming back to your earlier comment, perhaps this just seems charming because I don't get out much."

I hold back the laughter that threatens to roar out of me at her dry humor. Instead, I take a step closer, close enough to slot myself between her thighs. Placing one hand on the counter and the other at her waist, I lean down until my mouth nearly brushes the shell of her frilled ear.

"This is a professional business meeting amount of charm, ma siréne," I whisper. "Imagine if I were courting you. It's unfathomable how much charm I can muster when the occasion calls for it."

Her scent melts at the edges, taking on that burnt caramel hint again. Straightening, I bring my gaze to hers, nipping my lower lip as I wait for her to say something.

If she's ruffled by my teasing, she doesn't show it other than a hint of dark aqua color on her cheeks.

She rises, taking a step closer to me, so close her breasts nearly brush against my chest. Her gaze wanders again, down to my waist and then back up until her focus is fully on mine.

"What a shame I won't see that extra charm, then, given we are here in a strictly professional capacity. You did offer me a job. That would be quite the power imbalance, don't you think?"

Oh, we are dancing on dangerous turf. She's being playful, but there's an undercurrent of true worry to the way she phrased that comment. Given that she just told me she wishes to escape the lake, and needs money to do it, that's not surprising.

I remove my hand from her waist and take a step backward. Grabbing the tray of snacks in one hand, I offer her my other arm. "Absolutely nothing is coming between me and this art, ma siréne, I can promise you that."

She takes my arm with a soft smile, silent as I guide her around the island. Silence reigns as we cross the backyard, but when we enter the first floor of the workshop, she gasps aloud. Dropping her hold on my arm, she spins in a slow circle, mouth dropped open as she takes in the changes.

"We've been hard at work these last few days." I point toward the front corner, which gets the most sunlight. "Stacks of canvases are there, any size you like. Paint wherever you want to. I can move the canvas stand around per your instructions."

As if on cue, the cottage shimmies the walls, and the pile of canvases shakes and rattles, making itself known. The cottage is so proud to be ready to use, and I love that.

I walk across the open-concept room, past plush twin sofas to deposit the snacks on a small kitchenette island. When I return to her, Amatheia is still staring at the entire room like it's a dream come true.

"What do you think?" I drum my fingers on her side, recalling her attention.

"It's beautiful," she murmurs.

"You sound shocked," I tease.

"I couldn't quite see your vision a few days ago." She smiles up at me. "But you and the cottage created something truly unique. It's the perfect workspace. But..." Her voice trails off, and she looks up at me in apparent worry. "How will I keep it clean? Painting is inherently messy, and this place is picture-perfect."

"Oh, I bought a cleaning spell for that," I say with a laugh. "But in all reality, I suspect she'd like to get a little mussed with paints. While we're lovers of beautiful surroundings, we want them to be and feel lived in."

"Perfect," Amatheia murmurs, clasping her hands as her gaze roves over the area where I stacked the canvases. She glances up at me. "I was thinking of painting Town Hall first. What do you think?"

I hand her a notebook with all the ideas I've been doodling over the last week or so. "My ideas, ma siréne. Take from it what you will. Use or don't use it as you please."

She takes the leatherbound notebook and clutches it to her chest. "Done."

I point toward a black leather cabinet next to the paint stand. "Inside that tall chest are all the paints and brushes I have, but please let me know if you require anything else."

With a big smile, she walks over to the chest cabinet and opens it. Immediately, her face lights up as she examines each big jar of paint and the variety of brushes I purchased.

The moment stretches long and silent between us. I don't force it. I let the tension build, knowing she'll say something first. Knowing when to remain quiet is a skill I developed at a very young age.

On cue, she runs a hand through her long dark hair. "I'll get started now, I guess. Are you going to watch, or…"

I shake my head, jerking a thumb toward the open staircase leading upstairs. "No, darling. I'll be upstairs working on designing the typography and interior formatting. I can do nearly all of that without the art, but I'm here if you need anything."

When she nods, I reach out and rub my hand up the back of her arm.

"Shout for me if you require anything, anything at all. Even snacks, ma siréne."

She laughs. "I'm not calling you down here for snacks, Betmal."

Oh, sweet girl, I think to myself. One day you will.

~

A week. It's been a blissful week of Amatheia coming to the house to paint. In that time, she's managed to come three days and completed a painting of Town Hall and another of Downtown Ever's Main Street. They're whimsical but elegant, exactly what I wanted for the welcome book. She works at a near feverish pace, to the point of me wondering just how desperate she is to leave the lake.

I've already photographed the art and begun to combine it with everything else, printed out and laid out on the kitchenette island for now. I don't want her to have to come up to my office to see the book starting to take shape.

I scan a few pages of typography for the welcome letter as I head to the main house—Ama needs more snacks. When I reach the fridge and grab the handle, the front doors swing open, and Morgan's voice floats to me from the front of the house. "Betmal? Can I come in? I brought you some dinner!"

Smiling, I head for the entryway. My daughter-in-law walks down the long hallway toward me, her auburn hair piled into a bun high up on her head.

When we meet, she leans in with a feral grin. "Is she here right now?"

"Yes, darling." I take the casserole dish from her and gesture to the kitchen. "Shall we put this in the oven to stay warm and go say hello?"

"Oh, I'd love that." She claps her hands excitedly. "You don't think she'll mind being interrupted, do you?"

I head for the kitchen, where I put the casserole into the oven and turn it on low.

"No, darling, I don't think so." I stand and plant both palms on the island. "If I've learned anything this week about Amatheia, it's that she's happy to talk about the process and her work. I'm sure she'd love to show it to you."

Morgan smiles and leans over the island, looking at a printed copy of the typography page I'd been holding. After a quiet moment, she looks up at me. "This is looking really beautiful, Betmal. You have quite the eye for design."

I cross my arms and lean against the oven. "Where do you think Abemet gets it from?"

"Noted," she says with a laugh, glancing out the back window toward the garden cottage. "Gods, that's cute as hell. You built that cottage pretty fast."

The kitchen windows open and shut in rapid succession, the house happy our guest noticed the new addition.

"We were highly motivated." I gesture toward the lush backyard garden. "Shall we find Amatheia?"

Morgan follows me across the simple backyard. Amatheia's outlined in the window, sunlight illuminating her dark hair as she bends over the canvas, lost to her work.

When Morgan and I enter, Amatheia looks up, a paintbrush

in her mouth and another in her hand. She removes it and puts them both in a jar of water on the window ledge. The cottage rumbles happily beneath our feet.

Morgan waves. "Hey, I don't know if you remember me. I'm Morgan, Abe's mate."

"Of course," Amatheia says with a tender smile. "You were there when I was injured. You tried to heal me, Doc Slade said." She blushes. "I know it turned out to be complicated, but thank you for giving it a whirl."

"That's right." Morgan frowns. "Pissed me right off that I couldn't help. Turns out black magic can't heal everything. Revenants and very old wounds are nearly impossible. I'm sorry for that, and what you went through."

Amatheia shrugs, glancing between us. We haven't talked about the attack. I only know because of Catherine, but perhaps she assumes I've already learned about it.

My intuitive sense pings, suggesting the girls could use a few moments alone. I love that Morgan's here and that she and Amatheia can have time together.

"Alright, my darlings," I point toward my second-story office, "I'm going to head upstairs for a bit, but shout once you're hungry, and we'll eat."

Morgan winks at Amatheia. "I brought casserole."

Leaving them in the front room, I head up the elegant open staircase to my loft office. It takes up nearly the entire second floor, with a railing on one side that opens into the space below. Sighing, I drop into my new, bloodred leather chair, rolling to the expansive desk where I've been working all day. Loose sheets of paper litter the top of it, dozens of sketches from this morning and the coffee shop earlier this week. I set down the sheets I'd carried to the main house while I was lost in thought.

I've got so very many ideas for the book's interior. That's what I'd like to focus on today. But as Amatheia talks to Morgan about her in progress paintings, I lose my ability to focus on my work.

I quietly roll my chair to the edge of the second floor, just far enough that I can see them down below. Amatheia sits on a tall stool, sketching on a large canvas. It's fascinating, watching her work. She hums and speaks quietly to herself. Does she know she does that? Morgan asks questions about the process, and Amatheia answers with gusto.

Her ears flex, stretch and flare while she traces the outline of Higher Grounds onto the canvas. Even upstairs, I hear every move she makes. Her sultry scent drifts up to me, washing against my senses like a cool morning tide.

She's intoxicating.

Having her in my home, watching her with my daughter-in-law, it feels right. Seeing the beginnings of a potential friendship between them makes my long-cold heart warm. I was never like this with Evenia and Aberen, never obsessed with watching over them. We were pure physical attraction in the beginning, and then I stayed to have political power and help others, namely Abemet. My mates were ruthless to the point of insanity. Still are, which is one of the many reasons I couldn't stay any longer. Some of the things they've done… eesh.

And so I allow myself to watch in utter silence as Ama paints with Morgan looking on. First she splashes a bright, cheerful red over the entire canvas. Then she goes back over it, filling the major shapes of her outline. I set up a fan to help the paint dry quickly, if she wanted it. She mixes paint colors together as she hums.

Fascinated, I watch as she begins to paint over the larger shapes, laying in extra detail until Higher Grounds begins to take form. It takes her half an hour to get the base layer done. She hums and twitches her ears the whole time, painting broad strokes. The afternoon's fading light plays over her hair, casting warm tones through navy, turquoise, sky, and every other shade of her beautiful locks.

Morgan sits on a chair in the living area, watching as Amatheia paints. Now and again, ma siréne explains what she plans to do next. She looks happy, lost in her element, her blood singing with pleasure as it courses through her body.

I lick my lips, fangs throbbing as I stare at the beautiful mermaid below me. I should be working too. Gods know I have plenty to do, but somehow I can't pull my focus from her as she paints. If I stare long enough, will that niggling sensation travel down her neck and let her know I'm here? What would happen if she turned around to find me observing her?

But she doesn't. Not for hours. Not even when Morgan asks if she's hungry and wants to take a break. Yet it's clear she's lost to the art. Morgan takes the hint and comes upstairs to kiss me on the cheek and say she's returning home. I walk her out, and then it's back to the office to pretend I'm working but stare at Amatheia instead.

It's not until twilight fades to the black of night that she slows down at all. She sets the brush down and glances out the window, seeming to just now notice how dark it's gotten outside. The tips of her ears twitch as she makes a concerned-sounding noise in the back of her throat.

"Everything all right, darling?" I rise and place both hands on the banister, curling my fingers over the edge as I look at her.

She spins slowly in place and smiles up at me, although it looks pained. "Just thinking I should probably head home—I've got some things to take care of. I got a lot done, though. Would you like to see?"

Beaming, I head for the stairs and descend quickly. Halfway down, I hear a crash and a shout. Breaking into a sprint, I rush down the rest of the stairs and across the living room.

Amatheia's on the ground with the canvas in one hand, sitting up with a dismayed expression.

She blushes when I drop to both knees to examine her. "I'm fine, I'm fine! Depths, that's embarrassing. I was just grabbing the canvas to show you, but I lost my balance for a second." Her brows scrunch together, and she turns to me, looking horrified. "I ruined it. All that work and look at the canvas!"

I'm far more worried for her, but I look dutifully to see the tip of a paintbrush has pierced the canvas completely, and is hanging out of the back side.

I give her a stern look. "We fix you first. The canvas comes later. Agreed?"

She nods, dark lashes fluttering against cool blue cheeks. "You're going to try to carry me again, aren't you?"

"Of course." I grab the canvas and set it back on the stand. Then, I swoop her into my arms and carry her out of the cottage and across the yard, entering the back of the main house. I carefully deposit her on the kitchen island and grab a first aid kit I put together yesterday.

She plants both hands on the counter's edge and slumps, as if she can take my attention off her leg.

I straighten, rolling my shoulders. "Show me, darling."

She scrunches her nose. "You don't need to fix this, Betmal. I just lost my footing."

"Show me."

After a moment, then two, where we stand off and I think she might refuse my command, she acquiesces. Straightening her leg, she points to the prosthetic, which is attached to her knee with a series of ill-fitting straps. Her knee is swollen and puffy, and her muscles quiver as they flex.

I step closer. "May I remove your prosthetic for a moment?"

She blushes. "Why?"

"I'd like to examine your leg. I've got several ointments meant for pain relief. I knew you might be standing quite a bit for this project, and I wanted to be sure to have them handy."

Her mouth drops open as she searches my face with bright, wide eyes. After a moment, she nods.

Looking down at the medley of straps, I see they're intricately woven together to create a cap that fits around her knee. But this design is old. No one has made prosthetics like this in a very long time.

"How long have you had this?" I reach down and undo the largest of the straps.

She hisses and grabs at my arm. "Sorry, it's just a little sore. Umm, since just after the accident?"

I resist the urge to fly to the lake and shake her uncle by the braids. She was ten years old. And now, as a grown woman, she has the same prosthetic leg. I'm not going to help her by becoming visibly angry, though, so I file that bit of information away.

There's a reason she hasn't chosen to fix this herself beyond her uncle's resistance. Anyone in Ever would have offered help, but I suspect she has turned it down...for some reason. I simply need to gain her trust to find out why that is. Knowing what I do about her accident, I'd guess it's related. Quietly, I undo the rest of the straps and slide the leather piece off her knee.

Her entire knee is swollen, lines crisscrossing aqua skin from where the straps dug in. Beneath her knee, the leg stops abruptly. She has maybe a few inches of her lower leg, but that's all that remains.

Grabbing the ointments I purchased, I look through them quickly. Several of them can be used in conjunction with one another. Glancing up at her, I show her the tins.

"One of these is a coolant, something to ease swelling. The other is topical pain relief. I'd like to apply them, if you're okay with it?"

I suspect she'll tell me she wants to do it herself, but it shocks me when she nods, nipping at her plump lower lip as she stares at me. Does some part of her sense that I'm drawn to care for her? Does some small part of her simply trust me, even though her cousin said she shouldn't?

Satisfaction swirls with the concern in my chest. Grabbing the first tin, I spin the cap off and set it aside. Inside, a smelly yellow goop fills it to the very top. Dipping my fingers into it, I gather a glop and reach down. As I smooth the gel onto her knee, I watch her face for signs of discomfort. The lid above her right eye twitches as I massage the cool gel into her skin. She grips the countertop harder, her knuckles turning pale blue.

"This hurts?" I continue slow, gentle circles over her puffy knee.

She bites her lip and nods, glancing over at me. "Yeah, but the coolness feels nice. It reminds me of the lake water."

When I gather more gel and place it on the front of her stump, she yips and grabs my arm, trembling. I immediately pause and wait, but she lets out a hard breath.

"You can keep going. It's just so tender."

"I don't like hurting you," I murmur, "but I want you to feel relief."

The wavy, elegant tips of her ears twitch and flex as she stares at me, allowing me to rub the ointment over her entire leg. When I'm done, she lets out a breath and glances at her knee. Cheeks flushed, she flexes her leg. The swelling's already going down. This ointment is expensive, from an amazing healer at HQ, but I'd pay hand over fist for Amatheia not to endure a second of pain.

"That's remarkable," she whispers. "The swelling's actually going down. I'm almost terrified to put my prosthetic back on."

And here's where I'm going to overstep. Because taking charge of her medical care is not my job. But I can't sit back and watch her when there's an easy fix.

"I know someone who can craft you a prosthetic that will fit and not hurt." I stare at her as I open the second tin and begin slathering the pain relief cream on her knee. I keep my gaze locked to hers so she can see how serious I am. "He doesn't travel to see patients, so I'd need to take you there. But he works quickly. He could make you something new within a week."

She stares deeply into my eyes. "Why are you doing this, Betmal? I'm not a medical mystery for you to solve. This is not your problem."

I glop more of the cream onto her leg and continue rubbing gentle, repetitive circles.

"You're a friend in pain. Morgan would help, too, if black magic worked on this sort of old injury. Anyone who could help, would." I lock eyes with her. "I want to help you because I can, and because you deserve a prosthetic that doesn't hurt. Care to explain to me why you've never gotten one?"

When she says nothing but grits her jaw, I worry that even offering feels like an overstep to her. So, I stay silent and wait to see how this plays out.

Eventually, she lifts her chin and looks into my eyes. "My uncle would hate this."

It's a struggle not to visibly bristle. This, meaning my offer? This, meaning everything she and I are doing together?

I shrug. "And so? You said he doesn't even come ashore. Why should you live in pain to soothe his emotions? You're his niece and the heir to his kingdom, right? You deserve better. I want to take you to my friend as soon as you'll let me." I place a finger beneath her chin, holding her brilliant gaze. "You'd get to see Grand Portal Station and another haven."

Her eyes seem to light from within. She nips at her lip. "To be very blunt with you, part of me thinks I deserve this pain for the pain I've brought others. Not to mention, Caralorn just told me he's arranged a suitor for me. He won't want me doing anything that makes it seem like I'm leaving." She shakes her head and looks away from me for a moment, her expression stricken. When she returns her focus to mine, her jaw muscles flex tensely. "I'm desperate not to be trapped in another clan, far from my cousin. So, I'm motivated to get the depths out of the lake. My leg pain seems secondary to that, to be honest."

She just unloaded so much information on me, I scarcely know where to start.

I want to start at the suitor bit, but that's not what's most important.

"Ama," I say, "there is no reason in this entire world for you to be in pain; you're right about that. Fuck your uncle and whatever archaic notions he has that would allow him to see you suffer, no matter the reason." I put my finger under her chin and lift so she's forced to look into my eyes. "I'm taking you unless you absolutely refuse to go."

She bites at her lip again, drawing my eyes to her mouth.

I smile, forcing my focus to the navy depths of her gaze. "Ma siréne, I will bind you to me and drag you through that portal if I must, but we are fixing this. Together, okay?"

She laughs, but it sounds nervous. "We'd have to be careful, Betmal, and let me know the cost, because I'll bring my—"

"Absolutely not." I brace my hands on either side of her hips, standing closer than any friend should. Our mouths are close, too, close enough that it would be easy to lean in and give her a kiss. But it's too soon, and during this conversation is not the time. "I can tell you're anxious over this. If any of your people see you and cause trouble, tell me, darling, and I will handle it."

She smirks. "Are you going to knock heads together for me, Betmal? That's awfully kind of my *business* partner."

Shifting forward until my lips hover over hers, I drop my eyes to her mouth, taking in the plump curve of her lower lip. Her upper lip is thinner, with a tiny scar on one side.

"I can, and I will. What happened there?" I reach up and brush a finger over the scar.

She shudders, chest rising and falling quickly as blood thrums through her veins. It calls me, stoking my lustful nature until the flames of need roar through my mind, demanding I do something, anything with that fucking blood of hers.

"The attack. But, Betmal..." Her voice is soft, a plea. She knows she wants...something.

I bring my eyes back to hers. "Yes, Amatheia?" Even to my ears, my voice has gone growly and predatory, roughshod and hungry.

I've never waited this long to taste someone I wanted.

"Are all vampires this sensual?"

For a moment, I'm shocked that she called me sensual to my face. It's unexpectedly delightful. Taking a step back, I laugh. "Yes, darling, I suppose we are. It's in our nature."

Navy lashes flutter against her cheeks. "I thought so. It's... overwhelming."

Good.

But I want to play.

Leaning into her space again, I hover my mouth over hers until our lips barely touch. "Is this overwhelming too?"

She shoots me an offended look. "You're teasing me."

I brush my mouth over hers, nipping playfully at her mouth. "Am I?"

Her lips part, and a soft moan tumbles out. Immediately, she blushes, and I know she'll say something or try to scramble away.

"Show me your neck."

My command hits her, and she gasps, but on cue, she leans back onto her hands and cocks her head slowly to the side, exposing her throat to me. "What are we doing?" she whispers, watching as I lean forward.

"Being friendly," I murmur, dragging the tip of my nose along her collarbone. Her blood sings in her veins, screaming for my attention as her chest heaves. When I bring my focus to her neck, nuzzling my way up it, she squirms on the countertop. "You smell delicious. Want a little bite?"

She huffs out a laugh. "Wouldn't that hurt? Or are you just trying to tell me you're hungry? We should have eaten hours ago."

I hold back a groan because I *am* hungry. For her, and I'll tell her soon. I want her to *want* it. Because when she gets me for the first time, we'll shatter worlds together.

I bring my mouth just below her ear and bite softly. "I'm always hungry, ma siréne. Beneath my very polished exterior, I'm still a predator." Mouth pressed to her skin, I whisper, "You haven't answered my question. Would you like a little bite?"

I'm pushing, perhaps harder than I should. There's still a power imbalance between us—technically—but I'll go out on a limb that she doesn't feel that way. She feels comfortable and drawn to me because there's an obvious connection between us. A week together has been plenty of time for me to figure that out.

"No." She sits up and stares me straight in the eyes. "I've read enough about vampires to know how being bitten is supposed to make you feel. And I'm woman enough to admit I'm not sure I'd be able to control myself, and I don't want to jeopardize this"—she glances at me with a wry look—"friendship."

Licking my lips, I take a step back and smile, slipping both hands into my pockets. "You're a smart woman, darling. It's true, if I bit you, you'd feel intense pleasure. Perhaps it's better that I don't make a sopping mess of you on the countertop right now."

Her prior blush roars into a full-on blue, and the scent of her blood buckles my knees. Fangs descended, I stare at the needy little female before me.

She lifts her chin. "You might be the most presumptuous male I've ever met."

I smirk. "Guilty as charged, darling." I jerk my head toward her leg. "How's it feeling?"

She straightens her leg several times. "Depths, it's...honestly, it feels fine. There's no pain. That cream is amazing."

I remove my hands from my pockets and grab both tins, tucking them into her bag on the counter behind her. "Take them. I don't think they'll work underwater, but any time you leave the lake, you can use these."

She leans into me when I straighten. Does she even realize she did that? That she's staring up at me with wondrous blue eyes filled with interest?

"Tell me when we can visit my friend." I resist the urge to drag my knuckles along her jawline. "What's the soonest you can get away?"

When she looks torn, I wait. I'd love to remind her that this is her life, her happiness, her decision. I've learned through the centuries that you can't force someone to change something about their life. They have to be ready. They have to want it.

Eventually, she straightens her shoulders. "I don't know, I mean, this is such a generous offer but—"

"How about tomorrow?"

She blinks rapidly, mouth dropping open. "So soon?"

I lift my chin. "Why not?"

"Well..." Her voice trails off as she looks around, presumably for a reason to put off my suggestion. She surprises me when she turns with a tentative smile. "Okay. How long do you think it'll take?"

This is momentous. She *agreed.*

"Overnight, darling. Maybe even two nights. You'll need to pack a bag. But I can have you back within two days, if you've got things to do."

She nips at her lower lip. "Two days, gosh. Depths, I...if you think you can have me back the next afternoon, I'll figure it out. The suitor's coming soon, and I need to figure out how to extricate myself from that."

"I promise I can, if that's what you need." I keep my tone

light. I'm a little shocked she agreed to this so easily. And dismayed that she's even got to consider this suitor bullshit. I don't know who the male is, but he's not going to lay a hand on Amatheia.

She looks around at the papers covering the island's top. "I don't want to set us behind. You've made so much progress on the interior pages, and I have another few paintings to do still. Plus, we need to revisit a reasonable amount for you to pay me. I don't like talking about money, but if we can make sure it's enough for me to leave, then—"

Reaching out, I lightly grip her upper arms, pulling myself close to her. "A million per haven works for me. A night away won't set us back, ma siréne, and you need this. Allow me to help, please? I'll bring work with me, if it makes you feel better." When she still looks worried, I grab her prosthetic. "Shall we put this back on and see how it feels?"

She sighs and takes the leg from me with a baleful look. "You don't take no for an answer, do you?"

I slip my hands into my pockets. "What do you think, darling?"

She sighs but rolls her eyes playfully. "Let's put this Thalassa-damned thing back on; otherwise, you'll have to carry me the whole way home."

Calling my shadow wings, I flare them wide. Open like this, they span the entire length of the kitchen island. I'm old, very old, and my wings are very, very powerful. "I'm ready for that. Excited, even."

She slaps me playfully on the chest. "You can't carry me everywhere. I need to take myself sometimes, you know."

"Actually, I *don't* know that. I'd be perfectly content delivering you right to the deep end of the lake so you could avoid a single moment on this ill-fitting prosthetic."

She blanches but laughs a little anyhow. "You're a true gentleman, Betmal. I didn't foresee this, but I'm deeply appreciative." She smiles at me as she straps the prosthetic over her knee. I don't miss the lines of pain around the corners of her eyes when she tightens the straps.

Oh, I'm not having that. "I'm carrying you," I demand. "Right to the lake. Grab your things, ma siréne."

She lets out another sigh. "Depths, don't let me get used to this, or I'll be totally depressed when this project is over."

No, I want to say. You won't. Because there won't ever be a time when I'm not there for you. And this project will never, ever be finished.

CHAPTER TEN
AMATHEIA

As Betmal carries me to the front of the house and out the double doors, I find myself confused and a little disjointed. He's…affectionate—flirtatious even. And when I asked if that's how vampires are, he said yes. Yet that hasn't been my experience with the Keeper or Pietro and Alessandro from Higher Grounds. Of course, they're all mated. But still.

I wish I could have asked Morgan while she was here. She seems so worldly, I bet she'd know. It was so nice to see her again in a more normal setting, although I regret getting so wrapped up in painting that we never ate her casserole. I feel like we could be friends, and I've never had one of those outside of Thatraeia.

In the kitchen, Betmal had every chance to kiss me, if that's what he wanted. And depths below, I would have welcomed it even though I swore to keep this project professional. Maybe it's just that nobody's ever shown interest in me like this. I know there *have* been interested mermen before, just like I know that my uncle shut them all down and scared them away, ensuring I'd never date until it was someone of his choosing.

And fuck me, that time is now, I guess. The idea of a suitor makes me want to barf. I *know* my parents wouldn't have forced me into this. We'd have discussed it. They'd have cared about my opinion.

But hearing how Malakat talked about Prince Stefan makes me certain *I'll* find him horrible. Her description of him doesn't inspire confidence. I suppose Caralorn telling me about the arrangement was the push I needed to finally take my future fully into my hands. Because, if I know one thing, it's that I won't be used as a political pawn. If Stefan has his way, he'll probably take me back to his kingdom, and I will never see Thatraeia again.

Absolutely fucking not.

Which brings me back to my current confounding state of affairs.

As Betmal and I fly over downtown, it occurs to me that I need to conduct more research about vampires. I don't know what I'm in for traveling with one, and I'd like to feel more prepared—I can always count on the Historical Society to have what I need. I suspect if I tell Betmal I'd like to go there, he'll take me, but then I'll be forced to explain what I need to research. That could be awkward, especially if his flirtatious style is just the way all single vampires are.

No, I'll go after he drops me off.

True to his word, he alights gracefully on the lake's edge, then stalks up to his knees in the water. He sets me carefully down and waits for me to unstrap my prosthetic and remove my clothing.

"I'll put these in the locker for you," he offers, holding out his hand.

When I set the leg in it, he tucks it over one shoulder and bends low, brushing his lips over my cheek. "Tomorrow, ma siréne. Come to me when you can. Comm me, and I'll swing by to get you."

"I will." I resist the urge to step onto my tippy-toes and kiss his cheek the way he does mine.

For a long moment, ruby-red eyes flicker with an unnamed emotion, but he stares right into my soul. Like always, I feel like Betmal understands me to my core in a way nobody else has ever taken the time to. If he looks hard enough, he'll read my plan to hobble up to the Historical Society, and he'll insist on taking me himself.

"Good night, Betmal," I say with a wink. "Try not to lose sleep thinking about my neck, alright?"

He barks out a laugh, looking off into the distance. When he looks back, the black pupil of his eye has eaten up the dark red iris. "If you only knew, ma siréne."

He spreads his wings wide and crouches down. When he bullets up into the sky and heads for the locker, depositing my stuff inside, I splash backward into the deeper water. Turning, he pushes easily off the beach and coasts over the water's surface to me, dragging one hand in the water. I follow playfully, reaching up to brush his fingers with mine. It occurs to me that it would be fun to grab his hand and yank him under. But I don't do it. I just play until we reach the far side of the lake.

He uncurls his fingers from mine and swoops off into the trees. I pull myself up onto a log and watch as he glides gracefully through the huge trunks and off into the darkness. I sit and stare for a long time after that, thinking about the dynamic between us, about how playful and sensual he is.

I could get used to it. I think I *have* gotten used to it, and too quickly.

Will that change when we leave Ever to see his friend?

I should go up to the Historical Society now, but since I'm meeting Betmal tomorrow, it would be just as easy to do it in the morning.

Somehow, I manage to get back home and into the suite I share with my cousins without anyone questioning me about where I've been. Since the Sea Julienne is one of my primary responsibilities—the one nobody else wants—it's easy to disappear for hours at a time. The only indication that anyone has noticed I've been gone is a surreptitious look from Thatraeia when I sink into my bed and pull the woven seaweed coverlet over my tail.

"You alright?" she mouths from the shell bed next to mine.

When I give her a thumbs-up, she harrumphs and flips over to face the wall.

Unsettled and hating being at odds with her for not sharing more, I turn the opposite way. The inlaid mother-of-pearl wall begins to flip around, all the triangular pieces spinning and turning until they form into a painted picture—my favorite picture—of my parents and me before they passed. Father floats behind Mother, his arm around her waist. They smile down at me as if I'm the pride of their life.

And I suppose I was before their death. But it's all been downhill since then. I miss them *so* much. Yet when I think about my prosthetic in the locker on shore, I know they wouldn't want this pain for me. In my heart of hearts, I realize I've been torturing myself over their deaths. I don't know if that'll ever stop, but for my sake, I have to try.

I stare at the painting, reaching out to touch the paint strokes in thanks to the castle for her kindness in showing me. Eventually, I drift off to sleep, cocooned by a faint, relaxing current.

∽

In the morning, I quietly pack a bag with an extra shell bra. All the land clothes I own are in the locker on the shore, but I can at least bring this with me. Grabbing a shell comb and my mother's pearl earrings, I slip quietly out of the suite.

Descending into depths of the city, I move through still-dark streets until I reach the very edge of the kingdom. I manage to make it up to the shore without seeing anyone else. I suppose it's a good thing the merfolk are more nocturnal than anything, although the city is technically never fully asleep.

On shore, I limp to the log and shake myself dry. Reaching into the locker, I grab my land clothing and stuff it in my wet bag. Then I apply Betmal's ointments to my stump. Today it doesn't hurt that badly, although I worry how it'll feel by the time I make it to the Historical Society downtown. It's a solid half hour of fast walking.

Strapping my leg on, I stand and test out the pain. It's slightly tender but the best it's felt in literal years. Feeling victorious, I throw my bag over my shoulder and head for town. Walking is easier than it's been in ages, but by the time I make it to Downtown Ever, painful stabs begin to jolt through my knee and up into my hip bone.

I sit at one of the picnic tables in front of Scoops Ice Cream. It's not open this early, and I don't think they'll mind if I borrow the seat for a moment. Unstrapping my prosthetic, I slather on more of the gel Betmal gave me, sighing with relief as it soaks into my skin. Closing my eyes, I lift my face to the sun, enjoying the warmth as its rays caress me.

"Good morning, Amatheia."

Startling, I jump and open my eyes, turning toward the direction the voice came from.

Abemet, Betmal's son, stands there with both hands slung in his pockets, looking for all the world like a younger version of his father. Unlike Betmal, Abemet's expression is more neutral. He glances down at my leg.

"Prosthetic still giving you trouble? Let's do something about that, shall we? I can have someone come to—"

"That's okay," I say quickly. I don't know if Betmal has told him about our impending trip, although I can't imagine he'd care. "I was just heading to the Historical Society to grab some books, but I needed a moment."

He reaches out and opens his hand. "Let me help, please."

Taking his hand, I allow him to pull me back onto my feet. My leg feels better now that Betmal's ointment has soaked in. I'll just need to remember to reapply it every quarter hour or so.

Abemet glances at the bag over my shoulder. "Taking a trip?"

I decide right then that secrets are not my way, and if Betmal needs to keep this trip one, then he needed to tell me that yesterday. Smiling, I opt for the truth.

"Betmal noticed how much my leg was bothering me and offered to take me to a friend who can quickly make me a better-fitting leg."

When Abemet's neutral expression becomes a smirk, I laugh nervously. "He was probably getting sick of me falling all over his house doing this project. I've knocked things over two or three times now."

"Mmm," is all he says.

"Anyways," I rush on, "I'm nervous about leaving Ever, but I can't wait to maybe get a better leg. It's long past time."

"You deserve to live pain-free," he says quietly. "I've told you so many times over the years."

"I know." I hold his arm tightly as we pass the movie theater, the Historical Society in view up ahead on the right. "I just...I knew it would cause a fight at the castle. This is going to cause one for *sure*, but my uncle's not the one living with this pain, and it gets worse every year. I just...I can't do it anymore."

Abemet is quiet the remainder of our walk, and I wonder if I've said too much about my uncle and the pain. Monsters don't always like to talk about it or obvious things like missing limbs. I think, sometimes, it makes them uncomfortable for someone to *look* like they need help. That's my theory, anyway. I've seen the sorrowful looks as I limp down the street. I've heard the occasional whisper. I'm not blind to how others see me. I just wish they saw me for more than my disability. I wish they saw the rest of me, because my limb difference is such a small part of Amatheia, the Female as a Whole.

When we pause, I realize we've arrived at the Historical Society. I was so lost in thought, I didn't notice. But friendly building that she is, she swings her doors wide for me, inviting me in.

Abemet nudges me forward gently. "See you later, Amatheia."

I bid him farewell and enter one of my most favorite places in the world. I love the Historical Society—the smell of the books, the quietness of it, the hidden worlds each tucked into neatly handbound tomes.

I get quickly lost in a section about vampiric history. Luckily, there's a small book entitled "Vampires for Humans: What You Need to Know." I grab that and a book of French words and find a seat.

Perfect. Because I know as much about my vampiric brethren as I do humans themselves, even though I've met a few. I'm not supposed to join Betmal for an hour, and it won't take me terribly long to get back to the forest. I've got time to read up on vampires.

Taking a seat in a quiet corner, I flip through the first pages of the book. The very first sentence fills me with existential dread—fear Betmal is the way any single vampire male would be around an unmated female monster.

In vampire culture, sex and blood are inextricably intertwined. The giving and taking of blood is by invitation only, and may happen between anyone at any time and in any location.

Thalassa below, he *has* mentioned biting me several times. Was he waiting for an invitation? Does that mean he wants to have sex with me? Concerned, I read on.

Vampires, of all monsters, are intensely sexual in nature, often taking multiple partners in days-long orgies that push the limits of sexual creativity. Highly renowned for their prowess in the bedroom, vampires are often sought by other monster species for the pleasures of their company.

A flush runs through me, thinking about Betmal buried beneath a pile of bodies. The image of it irritates me even as I wipe a bead of sweat from my forehead. Growling, I read through the first chapter to learn that, yeah, vampires are *really* into sex. Sex and blood, blood and sex—everything is about those two things.

I've heard whispers of some of this, and when I asked Betmal about vampires, he mentioned sex and blood so casually. Still, seeing it in black-and-white textbook form makes it seem far more real.

Eventually, I can't read anymore, because what I'm picking up is that vampires are insanely sensual monsters. Betmal would probably be flirtatious with anyone. And that's fine. That's his right. He was mated for a long time; he's probably missing his sex orgy days or…whatever.

Irritation sparking jealousy deep down inside me, I toss the book into my bag and head for the door. When I exit, I'm surprised to find Abemet sitting on a bench just outside.

He glances up at me with a half-smile. "All done, Amatheia?"

I gasp like a fish. "Were you waiting for me?"

He shrugs. "Something like that. I thought perhaps I'd accompany you to your next destination."

I gulp but this isn't a big deal unless I make it a big deal.

"Well," I begin with a laugh, "we'd be headed to the lake. That's where your father is picking me up."

Expression completely neutral, Abemet inclines his head as he lifts the blue comm watch on his wrist. "Call Betmal, please."

Moments later, Betmal's voice echoes out of the watch's surface, his name hologram floating over it. "Darling, how are you?"

Abemet's smile grows a little broader. "Hello, Father. I'm

well. I ran into Amatheia, who tells me you're taking a little trip. I'd love to accompany her to meet you at the portal station." He glances at me. "She looks ready to go."

There's momentary silence, and then, "Of course, my son. I'll see you both there."

Abemet drops his hand to his lap and stands, reaching for my bag. "I suspect I know what you came here to research, Amatheia. Would you like to discuss it?"

Oh, depths below. Am I that transparent?

He chuckles. "I've been around a long time, my friend. And I know my father well. What would you like to know?"

A blush heats my cheeks. If I had a collar to tug at, I'd be yanking on it right now.

"Well, I...I suppose I'm trying to understand what behavior is normal for a vampire male. We're headed out of town, and I want to make sure I don't do something inadvertently inappropriate or..." I run a hand through my hair. "I'm not sure. This is weird to talk about with you."

Abe's nostrils flare, and he pauses to glance at me. "What sort of behavior do you mean?" His voice is almost perfectly neutral.

"Well, Betmal's an excellent host," I say quickly. "I just...I don't know that much about vampires, being that you and the Higher Grounds guys are the only ones I've ever met."

He smiles, but it looks forced. "Well, I'm not the best example, given my Keeper training. It zapped me of, well, a lot of my personality, and so I'm not...normal." It seems hard for him to admit that aloud. He runs both hands through his blond hair. "Morgan says, if I say it, maybe one day I'll internalize it, and some of what I lost will come back, but that's not helpful to you in this moment."

He grabs my hand and loops it through his arm again. "How about a primer on vampires in general?"

Nodding, I focus on him even as the pain in my leg starts up again. As we walk toward downtown, he fills me in. "Do you know what a ziol is?"

When I nod, he seems relieved not to have to explain the bloodletting cross to me and moves on.

"Any mated male would hold off on flirting with you unless he knew his mates were looking for that sort of dalliance. If I flirted with you, for instance, you'd know that Morgan was into that." He gives me a quick look. "This is not me flirting; I'm just using myself as an example."

I think back to Betmal's nose against my neck and have to hold back a laugh that Abemet would think this was anything at all like flirting.

"Any unmated vampire would flirt with you *if* he was sexually interested. But sensual as vampires are, they still need some sort of connection. We're sexual by nature, but that doesn't mean we want to have sex with everyone we see. We're just more…open to it than other monsters."

I have questions. A lot of questions. But I can't ask Betmal's son questions about his father's sensuality. Depths, how awkward. So, I keep my mouth shut even though I want to ask him everything bouncing around in my mind. Instead, he keeps talking, and I zone out with the pain in my leg. By the time we've reached the portal station entrance, I'm holding back from gasping aloud.

Betmal appears out of nowhere and swoops me into his arms, kicking the portal station door open. He crosses the giant portal station room and sets me on a bench, unstrapping my prosthetic and setting it carefully aside. Abemet appears next to us, placing my bag next to me on the bench. Betmal says nothing but opens my bag and digs around for the ointments. I'm not sure who to stare at, him or Abemet, so I look between them as Betmal slathers both ointments over my knee and stump, careful to coat every inch.

Abemet watches his father with something like amused

satisfaction on his handsome features. As Betmal rubs the last of the ointment in, Abemet clears his throat.

"I think you've covered it, Father."

Betmal glances up, brows furrowed. He looks angry. "I was supposed to pick her up to avoid her walking and feeling worse."

Abemet frowns. "My apologies. We were talking, and she had applied it already. I didn't think she'd need it so soon again." He glances down at me. "I'm sorry I didn't ask, friend."

Thalassa below, this is getting weird. Grabbing the prosthetic, I strap it back on and stand, gritting my teeth against the pain.

"It's fine, and I appreciated the excellent conversation."

Abemet nods slowly, glancing between his father and me. "Well, I'm headed to Shifter Hollow to meet with pack leadership and the Keeper. I'm around if either of you need anything." He gives Betmal a look. "How about dinner when you return? I'd love to...catch up."

"Of course, darling," Betmal croons. "Call you when I'm home. Give Morgan my love."

We watch as Abemet sails away. He moves as elegantly as his father, although the similarities end with their physical looks.

Betmal turns to me, reaching out to place a hand on my hip. "I absolutely must insist on picking you up next time, ma siréne. This ointment is not a miracle worker."

"I know." I reach out to place my hand on his chest. His skin is the same temperature as mine. Cooler than most other monsters but still warmer than merfolk. "I promise to listen next time. Probably."

He lets out an irritated huff, then spins us to face into the room. "Moving on. That green glowing circle across the room is the portal. It's simple. We'll step in, walk through a tunnel, and reappear inside Hearth HQ's Grand Portal Station. Once there, we'll find the portal for Arcadia, and then we'll walk through another tunnel and appear in *their* portal station. Easy. Are you ready?"

"Your ointment's already working a miracle on my leg," I say with a laugh. "So, yeah, I'm ready." I stare at the glowing green door, marveling at how similar it is to my imagined drawings. That leads me to wondering how similar the portal station will look. Nerves and excitement fill me in equal measure.

"Good." He gives me a wicked grin. "Then let's go on an adventure."

CHAPTER ELEVEN
BETMAL

Amatheia's eyes light up as we near the portal. I keep one hand around her waist, my fingers digging into her soft skin, not that she seems to notice. At the portal, she pauses and stares in apparent wonder.

"I've never seen ours," she says softly. "It seemed a waste to walk all the way here just to see it, knowing I couldn't step through."

Spinning in place, I tickle her side. "Perhaps you simply needed someone to accompany you, a travel partner, as it were."

She smiles. "Perhaps. Now that you've opened this door, maybe I'll never be content to stay in one place again. Actually, I'm certain I would be that way if I had the money to disappear all the time." Her smile grows viciously broad. "Well, I suppose when you pay me a million dollars, I'll be able to go anywhere I want."

Little does she know we are going to address that topic ASAP. I resist the urge to offer to extend our trip. Gods know, I'd love to. I grin at her playful quip.

Instead of spoiling a surprise, I return her happy look. "Ma siréne, if this idea is successful, a little bit of travel is probably in our future, assuming you're willing to continue this journey with me."

I didn't think her eyes could light up any more, but I can see the idea take root in her mind. She looks positively delighted.

"Let's go," she chirps, clapping her hands together. Like every time she's excited, the wavy tips of her ears bend and twitch.

After guiding her up a few steps, we push through the portal's chilly green surface and into a long tunnel that leads to the new Grand Portal Station inside an old building at Hearth HQ. Amatheia stares around as we walk through, and when we emerge on the other side, she gasps aloud, spinning in place with her hands clasped to her chest.

"Gods, Betmal. Look at that! A gargoyle just above the door! That's exactly how I pictured it!" She turns before I can answer. "And yes! That's how I imagined the portals to be, all around the edge. But, oh, Thalassa below, I forgot Higher Grounds had a second location here. Look at it, it's just *beautiful*."

I can't pull my eyes from her as she absorbs the Grand Portal Station. Architecturally speaking, it's stunning with the green portals placed around the edges of a long, well-lit oval. Above us, the faux sky sparks and sputters with thunder and lightning, even though rays of sun peek through to shine into the station itself. The weather's different all the time. Gargoyle guardians stand quietly at their stations, there in case of any sort of attack on the portal.

"So," I begin, "the mate of Pietro and Alessandro from Higher Grounds, Alessandra, designed and pitched this station to Evenia. It only exists because she took a chance. The entire station actually sits within a small haven encased inside this building. At any moment, if there were a security incident, they could redirect this haven to Belcastle Prison and keep Hearth HQ safe."

Amatheia listens with rapt attention as I guide her across the black-and-white-checkered floor toward the center.

"Listen," I stop us both and move my hand to her waist, "would you like to sit here and draw for a while before we go to Arcadia?"

She nips her lip and looks around, eyes wide as she takes in the bustling portal station. Turning to me, she nods, looking thrilled. "I'd love that, actually. Just for a few moments, if it's alright?"

"Of course." I curl my fingers into her skin, rubbing soft circles as I stare into depthless, beautiful wide eyes. "Pick any seat you like. I'll grab us coffee and a little treat, and I'll find you in a minute."

She beams at me. "Alright, Betmal."

Leaving her to find a spot, I head to Higher Grounds' newest location and order a Type A latte for myself and a pumpkin cinnamon latte for her. After picking out a few baked treats that I've learned she likes, I pay and return to the center of the portal station.

Amatheia sits at a chunky wooden table with four chairs, legs crossed as she sketches in her notebook. I set our luggage down and slip into the seat next to hers, handing her the coffee. I place the muffins and scones in the center of the table, then reach into my sling bag to withdraw my notebook and pencils.

She reaches for a scone and takes a bite, watching me. When I sip my drink and begin to draw a beautifully potted money tree situated between several of the tables, she looks over with interest.

"I keep forgetting you're an artist too." She leans closer, watching as I sketch the base shapes of the tree first, then begin to layer on the more intricate details. "Thalassa below, you're good. Why aren't you doing the art for the book yourself?"

I smile. "I'll likely include a piece or two, but I want your work to be the highlight." I gesture at the troll female she started sketching in her notebook. "You capture emotion in your sketches. I want to bottle that sentiment up and imbue it into the welcome books. I don't draw in the same way."

She takes a sip of her latte and lets out a happy moan. "This is so good. Thank you, Betmal."

Unbidden, the mental image of her on her knees before me, thanking me for feeding her my cock, takes over rational thought. I grit my teeth to avoid turning and sinking my fangs into her throat. Emotion rampages through me, and I focus on allowing it to simply be. That need, that want, that intense desire to bite and fuck and claim.

It means something, something I've wondered about since the moment I first scented her and was so drawn to introduce myself. Something that's clear to me now.

She's my mate.

My partner.

Mine in every possible way.

And I know that because I was never like this—obsessive, possessive, inflamed—by Evenia or Aberen. It was all intense sexual promise with them, and as a younger male, I admired their ambition. I had it too, and we were so powerful together.

But Amatheia unleashes something in me that I barely keep restrained. It's as if my entire world focus shifted to her, and I will not be happy until I spend all day every day putting a blissful smile on her face.

She takes another sip, a happy hum leaving her plump lips as she begins drawing again, focused on the troll female seated at the table across from ours.

A smile tips my lips upward, joy coursing through me at realizing so completely what she is to me. I stare at her, watching the tips of her ears twitch happily as she sketches. She moves the pencil across the paper with confident, practiced slashes.

And I cannot stop staring.

She's beautiful inside and out, and I have the rest of my life to learn every intricate, intimate detail of her.

Mine.

Mine.

Mine.

I don't bother to hide the fact that I'm looking, and she says nothing, simply drawing and sketching as I watch. Eventually, she finishes the troll woman's likeness and turns to me. When she notices how I stare, she blushes but smiles.

"Everything okay, Betmal? Are you ready to go? I got lost in the drawing."

I sip my latte. "Okay, ma siréne? No. I am *fascinated*. It is absolutely delightful to watch you work." I lean closer, slinging an arm over the back of her chair. This near to her, the scent of her blood fills my senses, white hot swirls of heat building deep inside me.

I gaze at her work, admiring every gorgeous detail. After a few moments, I look at her, my mouth close to hers. "Your likeness of her is stunning. Well done, darling."

"Thank you," she whispers, eyes roaming my face as her heart rate kicks up.

I drop my focus to her lips, admiring how perfectly bow-shaped they are. Bringing my gaze back up, I lean a little closer, close enough that we're almost touching.

"Are you ready, my sweet?"

She seems to search my face for something, eyes flickering from my mouth upward and back down. Her chest heaves softly, blood rushing through her veins as her body reacts to mine.

"Mmm, ma siréne, you tempt me." I reach out and drag my knuckles along her angular jawline. "What an enchanting creature you are."

She leans into my touch, mouth dropped slightly open as she stares at my fangs.

I hold the moment for a second, then two, then three, enjoying the sight of my woman.

My woman.

At long last.

I'm going to tell her what she is to me on this trip. Now that I'm absolutely certain, I need her to know.

Leaning away from her, I stand and offer her my hand with a teasing smile.

"Shall we go, darling?"

She pauses for a moment, staring up at me, then takes my hand and allows me to pull her upright. When she rises, she steps forward enough to press her body to mine, glancing up with a deadpan look, though I can see she's holding back a smile.

"You're such a good business partner, ma vampire. So… attentive."

I roar out a laugh at the new moniker and she slaps my chest, grabbing my shirt and pulling me toward the wall of portals. I grab our things and guide her carefully through the throng of monsters toward Arcadia's portal door.

She turns to me before we step through. "I looked up the French word in a book at the historical society. French does feel nice on the tongue."

I resist the urge to comment about other things that feel nice on one's tongue.

She seems to understand because she blushes and tucks her hair behind her wavy ears. "You said Arcadia's different from Ever, right?"

I nod. "It's a kink-based haven. It's very common to see public sex on the street and in any of the restaurants and businesses. It's also a place of healers—troll healers, to be specific."

She snaps her fingers in apparent recognition. "Oh, I've read about that…" her voice trails off. "I learned you can come here to spend a week or two with a troll, engaging in, well, you know."

Uncharacteristic jealousy burns bright in my chest at the idea of her here, engaging in I-know-*exactly*-what.

"Ultimately," she says with a sigh, "I decided there was no use in fixing my pain if I had to put on the same prosthetic, so I never explored that path. Maybe I should have."

Gods, it takes every ounce of strength I have not to pull her to me and say no, I don't want a troll touching you. I don't want *anyone* touching you. Only me. We will heal this together, but the only hands on your body will be mine.

Instead, I focus on getting her through the portal and out the other side. The Arcadia portal station is beautiful, showcasing the mountains off in the distance. It's snowy and thundery here, and she seems to love that. Just as I thought, she's shocked when we leave the portal station to see trolls and giants leading one another around on leashes.

I enjoy her running commentary as we walk slowly through town, until we reach our street. "Come, ma siréne," I encourage, tugging her with me into a shadowy stone alleyway.

Her blue eyes go wide, but she nods and tucks her body closer to mine.

Sixty feet from the main road, I open a door. The sign above simply says Martin's.

Amatheia looks up at it, then hobbles carefully through the door and into the dimly lit shop. Inside, boxes are stacked to the ceiling, and dusty books cover every surface. Martin's never appears to be well organized, but he knows precisely where everything is.

On cue, a handsome vampire emerges from a back room with a hammer in one hand and a rag slung over his shoulder. Long black hair is pulled into a bun on top of his head, pieces of it framing a square face. As always, he wears a V-necked tee that exposes his family tattoos. He's been the black sheep of his house for centuries, and I think he loves showing off the family crest to prove he doesn't give a fuck what anyone thinks, least of all his purebred-loving vampire grandparents.

"Greetings, Betmal," he croons, slipping across the store toward us with a sensual grin.

When he winks into view right in front of Amatheia, she sinks against me. If he notices the move, he says nothing but smirks and glances at me as if to ask if she's mine.

The moment stretches long, as I shoot him a look. Eventually, he sighs. "Come to the back, beautiful one. Let's take a look at what you need."

Amatheia looks up at me.

"I'll be there the whole time, if you'd like," I confirm.

When she nods, I follow them to the back.

"Right there." Martin points to a chair. "Take your leg off and set it aside, please."

I help Amatheia into the chair as Martin sits on a spinning stool and wheels himself over to us. He looks up at her. "I'm going to handle your knee and leg. Please tell me honestly if anything hurts. My goal is to understand what's wrong with your prosthetic now, so I can craft one that fits you and your lifestyle."

For the next half hour, he examines every inch of her knee and what remains of her leg. He questions her about her level of activity and desired level, and what challenges she's experienced. Hearing her talk about her leg and how it's held her back crushes my soul. It's hard to remind myself that we're here to buy back the freedom to do what she wants, when she wants.

Examination concluded, Martin looks between us. "I can do this, but it'll take several weeks."

That won't do.

Summoning a power I possess but almost never use, I focus deeply on Martin's ruby eyes. "You can have it ready within a day, actually. That's what you told me before, remember?"

Amatheia watches the exchange with her head cocked to the side.

My power of influence isn't very obvious to anyone not under its sway. But from the outside looking in, I expect it appears...strange. I haven't needed to use it in hundreds of years. But this? This calls for an *encouraging*.

"I...suppose I could," Martin hedges, his eyelid twitching. "But I really—"

"Must complete this quickly," I remind him, pushing my influencer power into his mind, reworking his priorities so Amatheia fits at the very top of his to-do list. "It is imperative you complete your work for her within a day's time. You'll do that, Martin."

"Of course," he reassures us, looking somewhat stoned and confused. "Right away, of course."

I call my power back. I don't like to use it if the circumstances aren't dire. But I consider these to be so.

Amatheia says nothing, watching in silence as Martin confirms the details of where we're staying. She's equally quiet as we thank Martin and take our leave, heading toward the elegant hotel I booked for us.

As we near it, I realize she hasn't said a word. Glancing down, I scratch at her side. "What is it, ma siréne?"

She halts and looks up at me, dark aqua brows bunched together. "Did you do something to him?"

Surprised she noticed, I run a hand through my hair and straighten my shoulders. I won't lie to her, so I nod. "Yes, darling. I have the very rare power of influence. I can make anyone do anything I want, a shocking power, really. One I use infrequently, as you might imagine."

"But you did it right now, to get him to help us first. Didn't you?" She plants both hands on her hips.

Uncharacteristic nerves bubble my stomach. "I did."

"Why?"

"Because I'd do anything to fix this for you as quickly as possible, and he is always booked out far ahead of time."

"With monsters equally deserving of a pain-free life," she states, lifting her hands to cross her arms. "It's not right."

"It's not," I admit. "But I would give anything to spare you another moment of pain, even if it means putting everyone else after you on my list of priorities."

This is going mightily sideways, but when I reach for her, she steps back. Immediately, she hits a pile of boxes and is thrown off-balance. Before I can catch her, she falls to one side, landing on a pile of building supplies. I grab her, but not before a piece of metal gashes her thigh, opening a wound several inches long.

She gasps and yips as I hold her tightly. Blood drips from the wound down her thigh. The scent of it is a battering ram to my senses, smashing its way through rational thought as my fangs descend to poke my lower lip.

She watches, eyes going wide as a needy growl rumbles from my throat. I drop to a knee, focused on the blood. Forcing myself to remember that she's in pain, I look up from my spot at her feet.

"We need to get this cleaned up. I'm going to carry you to our rooms, and we'll talk when we get there."

A clipped nod is her only answer. In front of my face, blood drips from the wound. One lick is all it would take to close that gash up, but she won't understand if I don't explain more fully. And I have a lot of explaining to do, it turns out.

Standing, I pull her into my arms and slip through the streets until we reach Hotel Asara, a vampire property I've stayed at many times. I sail through the grand entryway, passing the check-in. I've been here so many times, I have my own key. The difference is that, this time, I've booked adjoining rooms and ensured that Evenia and Aberen no longer have access.

Moving swiftly to the top floor, I slide my key into the lock and swing the door open. I cross the room and deposit her at the foot of the bed, careful not to jostle her injured leg. Dropping her bag to the floor, I focus on her injury and not throwing myself on top of her like a madman to lap at the delicacy flowing from her thigh.

"Do you use that power on me?"

Her question catches me off guard, and I halt my perusal as I shake my head vehemently. "Never, ma siréne. I haven't used my gift in several hundred years. I don't use it unless it's life and death."

"My leg is not that."

"I don't agree." I point to the gash. "I can close that up and heal it, but it means I'll need to lick the wound. Would you allow me to do so?"

She narrows her eyes. "Why is everything you do sexual? Is anything ever just…normal? I need a Band-Aid."

"Normal?" I plant my hands on either side of her, backing her flat onto the bed. "No, ma siréne, I've never been accused of anything so boring as normal. Now, will you allow me to heal you?"

She sits up onto her elbows. "How is your tongue going to heal me?"

I slip down her body to her waist, eyeing her even as the blood scent is a near physical caress to my cock. "Trust me for a moment. I'll show you." Glancing up at her, I cock my head to the side, breathing over the wound.

She stiffens but nods.

Steeling my resolve, I lean down and bring my tongue flat to her thigh. I drag a slow, steady path along the cut. She hisses, but there's something else there. As the depthless taste of her caresses my senses, her scent deepens and blooms. She's ocean spray and swirling waves crashing against my mind. She's the tide, drowning me in pleasure as I lap at the wound, depositing my saliva. Her hips rock slowly, a soft moan pulling my focus to her.

When our eyes meet, she blushes and runs a hand through her hair, looking away from me.

"I'm sorry," she sputters, but I—"

Growling, I lick a harder path over her thigh, pulling a second needy moan from her.

"Goddess," she grits out. "Give me a second, Betmal."

When I lick again, an equally needy moan erupting from my throat, she shoves at my head. "Stop, please. Goddess, please, Betmal!"

Panting, I shift upright, her blood dripping from my fangs and down my chin. Need and lust and worry for her war within me, even though I know, when I look down, the wound will be closed. Amatheia lies beneath me on the bed, skin flushed, chest heaving as her thighs tremble.

It takes every ounce of control I have not to slip her miniskirt up and part her thighs.

She stares at me, eyes wide, mouth still open. Then, she glances down at her healed leg. Her mouth drops wide open at finding the wound gone. She stares at me.

"How? Why? I've never heard of this. I thought you were kidding!"

Now is the time for honesty.

"Because, ma siréne," I murmur, keeping my eyes locked to hers. "You are mine, my mate, and, so for you alone, the gods have blessed me with this gift."

CHAPTER TWELVE
AMATHEIA

My mind goes blank at Betmal's words. His *mate?* Thalassa below, he can't be serious. Can he? Shit, shit, shit, I haven't gotten to that part in my vampire book, and I don't even know what that entails.

"Explain," I manage to sputter, heart pounding like a drum in my chest.

I find him insanely attractive, and he's crazy flirtatious, but it's just because that's how single vampire males are…right? It's what the book said!!!

He stands between my thighs. Reaching out, he unstraps my leg and carefully sets it aside. Crossing the room, he grabs the tins of cream and begins to slather them on my skin, as carefully as ever.

Ruby eyes meet mine as he works. "When I first saw you at Higher Grounds, your blood sang to me, ma siréne. I had to *know* you, to introduce myself. For vampires, finding that soul-deep connection can feel like seeing a part of yourself finally. I suspected what you were to me then."

He rubs gentle circles over my knee, soothing away the pain from Martin's earlier ministrations, eyes locked onto mine.

"And I also knew I had a project that needed to be done. When I found out you were a painter, I knew I'd hire you for that project. A benefit to that is you being alone with me in my house, all the time. You are my mate, Amatheia, and that is why my mouth heals you. My saliva has no healing properties for anyone else. This," he gestures between us, "is irrefutable."

I sit fully upright, gobsmacked at this confession as shock courses through me in waves that make me feel like I'm suffocating. "So...you knew this whole time? And you hired me to get us alone together? And what about this trip?"

He shakes his head. "Non, ma siréne. I would have hired you for this project regardless of my feelings. It was lucky happenstance that you are who you are, and I am who I am, and I also needed an artist. Very, very lucky indeed." He caps both tins of ointment and sets them aside, then slides his hands in his pockets, looking for all the world like a sexy professor.

"You have questions, darling, I can see that. Ask me anything, anything at all. I am an open book."

I gasp like a fish out of water. I've never felt so unsteady or unmoored.

Except that, deep inside me, something that's always felt trapped at the bottom of the lake breaks free and rejoices at what he's saying. I *want* what he's suggesting, want it so badly, I can taste it. And he's standing right there in front of me.

But the entire reason I took this job was to finally gain my independence. And being mated feels like the farthest thing from independence I can possibly imagine. Isn't it?

"I...I'm not sure what to say," I admit.

Betmal's smile goes coy, his fangs poking at his lower lip. "Say you feel it too, that my words make sense because every time we're close, you wish we were closer. Say you want it, ma siréne."

He brings his hand to my throat and wraps his fingers around it, pulling me until my chest bumps against his. He feels so good pressed to me, and the sensations his proximity unleashes inside me have my doubts flying away on the tide.

He hovers those sinful lips above mine. "There is no one here to judge us, to see us, Amatheia. Allow me to kiss you. If you don't enjoy it, nobody ever has to know." His breath is warm against my mouth, and I open just to breathe him in.

"If you do not enjoy this, ma siréne, we shall never speak of it again. Deal?" Crimson eyes roam my face as I debate my answer.

What if I say yes?

What if I say no?

My heart pounds in my chest. He breathes in, eyes rolling back into his head.

"Your blood, ma siréne. The smell intoxicates me. Ask me to kiss you."

"What if I don't?" I lift a brow.

"Anywhere you like," he continues. "I didn't specify your mouth, darling."

Heat barrels through me with all the strength of a train. I've had so many thoughts like that, and never had the chance to act out any of them. I was a fool to think I could keep things professional with a male this sensual, a male who thinks he's mine. And if I'm honest with myself, I don't even want to. I'm terrified to say yes, but I'm more terrified to say no. If I tell him no, I'll regret it for the rest of my life.

Just one thing bothers me.

I'm upset he used his power to put me at the head of a line. I can't live with taking someone else's spot, knowing pain the way I do.

"Call that man and tell him to do my leg when he can. I don't want to be ahead of anyone. Do that, and perhaps I'll ask for a kiss."

Betmal's eyes narrow, and he removes his hand from my throat to cross his muscular arms. "No."

"Yes."

"Don't ask me to do that," he barks. "You'll be in pain for weeks, months, maybe. Don't ask me to watch that, knowing I could fix it."

I scoot all the way to the headboard, ensconcing myself in the pillows like a queen. "If you think I'm yours, then you should know I don't feel comfortable being the cause of someone else's pain. Call him, or I'll call him myself. But then I'll be mad at you."

I shoot him a ferocious look to demonstrate how very mad I can be when the occasion calls for it.

Betmal growls but crosses the room to the communication disk on the wall. He tosses it to the floor and directs it to call Martin. Martin's hologram appears, and in a very terse conversation, Betmal directs him to craft my new leg at whatever his normal time frame is. Martin seems confused by the conversation, but agrees he'll let us know when it can be done.

When the hologram disappears, Betmal remains across the room, rolling up the sleeves of his collared shirt. "It pained me to do that, Amatheia."

"Oh, my full first name. Well, consequences of your actions and all," I say lightly.

He's across the room and on top of me before I see him move. His lips are against mine, his breath warm as he grinds his hips against my body, shoving my miniskirt up to my hips. The heat and hardness of an obvious erection brush over my mound and stoke the embers of the fire burning there.

"I did what you demanded. Ask me. Now."

"Kiss my hand," I tease. "I don't know what I think about this whole 'you're mine thing,' and I might need to see you in action. I've never had a boyfriend, you know."

He sits up and grabs me by the wrist, his eyes never leaving mine. "I shall cherish being your first in all things, my darling."

I can't hold back a smirk. "And my suitor? Remember him?"

Betmal's chuckle has flames licking over my skin, raising the scales along the back of my neck. "That male will never touch you, ma siréne," he says quietly. The possessive, predatory way he says it tells me he would do anything to keep me from Stefan.

And thank Thalassa for that. I'd already decided Stefan was never going to be my future.

No...I'm staring at my future right here.

"Well, go on then," I say, my tone silky with lust.

Bringing my fingers to his lips, he nips first one, then the next, sending shards of desire through me. The smirk on his thin lips tells me he knows exactly what he's doing.

Next, he sucks my middle finger into his mouth, hollowing his cheeks around it as he swirls his tongue over the digit. Still, he doesn't look away. Not as he pulls my finger from his mouth with a pop. Dragging his tongue down my palm, he bites softly at the inside of my wrist, tongue dipping from between his teeth to tease my skin about all the ways Betmal knows how to be sensual.

He pauses, lips barely touching my skin. "Anywhere else need a kiss, ma siréne? Imagine this talented tongue somewhere more...intimate."

"You're serious about this." I stare up at him in wonder. "You really think we're mates? How? I'm merfolk. You know the males carry the children...right? There are incompatibility issues at play, Betmal, assuming children are part of your desire."

"I'm serious about this," he confirms. "I was in a relationship for so long, knowing it wasn't the right one. And I wasn't looking for you, yet there you were, right in front of me. Being with you is the easiest decision I've ever made." He shrugs. "As for children, I have a grown son who is the light of my life. If you want children of our own, I will find a way, darling. Whatever you want, I will make it happen for you. Perhaps there is some magical way to accomplish this, if you want me to carry our sons and daughters."

Something breaks inside me at his words. Something tender and needy. That huge part of my heart that always wanted someone of my own, someone who would put me first and be in my corner. Someone who would look at me the way Betmal's looking at me right now.

"Kiss me," I command.

He grins and drops down to one hand, leaning over me even as the weight of his body presses me hard into the mattress. I could get lost in him like this, in the feeling of being so completely possessed by another.

But when his lips brush mine, opening just enough to suck at my lower lip, my mind goes blank. Or maybe everything in my brain is burning up, because there's nothing but his mouth on mine. The first pass of his tongue along the seam of my lips is gentle, probing, tender. When I moan, he deepens the kiss and flips us so that I'm on top of him. Both of his hands come to the back of my head, carding through my hair as he explores my mouth with practiced skill.

But I want the version of him that's not so in control. Grinding my hips against his hardness, I preen at the way he groans into the kiss, parting from me for a moment.

"I will not turn that down if you offer it," he growls. "Think long and hard about that, ma siréne, because if that is on the table, I'm taking it. But today has been a day of revelations, my darling."

I cry out as his kiss moves to my chin and downward from there. He's all soft bites and deep growls as he nips and licks at my skin, until I'm rocking my hips against his hard cock and trying desperately to figure out what to do next. But he's got that figured out too, slipping his hands down the back of my skirt to play at the crack of my ass. He moves deftly, stroking and rubbing his fingers over my ass and down my cleft to my pussy. I'm the only one who has touched me there, and I'm embarrassed by how wet I am.

"Soaked," he growls into my mouth. "I could use my gift on you if you like. I could talk to you and rack this body with pleasure. What do you think about *that* use?"

I can't find an answer except to pant into our kiss as he explores my body with teasing, tantalizing fingers. That's when I realize the kind of access I have being on top of him. Sitting upright, I pull his shirt open to reveal a muscular chest covered in swirling red tattoos. Like always, a cluster of necklaces surrounds the ziol cross nestled between his pecs.

"It's yours," he says quietly. "Shall I show you how to use it?"

I'm so shocked at his offer, I pause and stare at him. "I've read about this. It's a ziol bloodletting cross, right? That's quite a gift, Betmal. Shouldn't we…wait and make sure we're compatible? Or go on a few dates, or…something?"

He grins at me, rocking his hips beneath mine as he drags my pussy over his cock. My skirt provides next to no barrier, and I'm wearing no underwear beneath it. His pants are soaked with my need.

"Of course we'll date, ma siréne. But compatibility is not going to be an issue." He glances down at his lap as if to prove his point.

"What are we doing?" My voice is soft, tentative as I stare at the male I thought was my friend. He *is* my friend, maybe my *best* friend. And he's so much more than that. When I examine the deepest, darkest places of my heart, I know he's right. I was drawn to him from the moment we met.

"I'm pursuing you romantically," he says as if it's the easiest thing in the world. "And if we want to take it easy, you can be my girlfriend for a time. But we both know that word scarcely encompasses what we are to one another. Don't you think?"

"I like it," I admit. "But when we're working on the project, we need to be in professional mode."

He laughs and rocks my hips harder against his cock. "I can't agree to that. Because when you paint, I find myself entranced. And I cannot agree that sometime I might not leap over the railing, tackle you to the sofa, and fuck you on top of a canvas. I am, after all, just a vampire male, the most sensual of creatures, obsessed with blood and sex. Or so the books would lead you to believe." He jerks his head toward my bag across the room. "Or have you not gotten to the chapters on sex yet?" When he grins, embarrassment fills me.

"I saw when I set your bag down, my darling."

I laugh. "I was just trying to learn a few things, you know. I was—"

"Already mine," he says. "Trying to figure out if I was yours. I was attempting to take it slowly, darling, but I should have known it wasn't possible with a connection like ours."

I lie down on his chest, folding my arms over his pecs. "So, what will it be like dating a vampire?"

He scoffs. "Any old vampire? Boring but lots of hot sex, probably. Dating me? That's another beast entirely." He sits up and kisses the tip of my nose. "Prepare to be pursued, fed, supported. Prepare to travel, to make love in every haven in the system. Prepare to have your senses delighted, my love. Because my sole purpose is to please you." He strokes chunky strands of my hair over my shoulder, eyes scanning hungrily over my face and neck. "When I met you, my world narrowed, ma siréne. You are at the very center of it."

"Is that so?" I laugh and pretend I'm thinking. "I suppose you'll have to learn what pleases me, then." It's so fun to play with him like this. It's such a natural extension of our easy companionship.

"Do you know?" he asks quietly. "Do you know what pleases you, Amatheia? Have you had a chance to explore pleasure for yourself?"

Shame fills me before I remember that I don't have to feel that with him.

"No." I pick at the tangled pile of necklaces resting against his chest. "My uncle's always planned a connection for me to some far-off kingdom. He chased off every merman who was ever interested. I was never allowed suitors, until Stefan."

"Over my dead body," Betmal growls. "Absolutely not."

"You're a touch possessive."

His eyes flash angrily. "If possession means being there for you always, yes. You've never had someone in your corner until you've had me at your back."

Momentary hesitation fills me. "What about your former mates?"

"What about them?"

"Is it a problem if we run into them?"

He sighs. "I can't say it would be a pleasant experience for you, but they really have nothing to say." He frowns. "I'll tell you anything you want to know, ma siréne, but they're in my past."

I finger the ziol around his neck. It's beautiful, a cross encrusted with swirling metalwork and inlaid red jewels.

"This was my mother's," he says softly. "Given to her by my father. The first ziol in our family line. It's very, very old, and I have carried it for a long time. In all the time I was mated, I never offered it to them."

He shifts forward and lifts the ziol over his neck, settling us upright in bed at the same time. My eyes are drawn to his chest and below, to abs clearly outlined and thick with muscle.

"Take this as a symbol of my utter adoration," he whispers, slipping the cross over my neck so it dangles between my breasts. "When you are ready, my darling, tell me, and I will show you how to use this to bring you great pleasure."

I pick up the cross, admiring the stunning inlaid red jewels. They're slotted between clear diamonds so it looks like blood dripping down the frame. Betmal remains silent as I set the necklace against my skin and nibble my lower lip, staring at his muscular chest.

"Touch me if you like." He reaches down and grabs his shirt, pulling it over his head and tossing it to the floor.

I'm overwhelmed by stacked shoulders and the strong lines of his neck. He reclines against the pillows with a self-satisfied smile.

I reach forward and rest my hands on his chest, feeling his strength. Dragging my hands down to his stomach, I explore the dips and curves of him. He's all male, all dominant strength and masculine intensity. And he remains quiet as I explore, touching and marveling. Because I can't stop myself. This was supposed to be a job. Make the money, hope it was enough to grant me at least some independence from the merkingdom, and that was that.

I didn't expect *him*.

He brings his fingers to my forearm and strokes, giving me a quizzical look. "What are you thinking about?"

I look deep into those ruby-red eyes.

"How unexpected this is. How attracted I was to you from that first moment, but how I didn't want to muddy the waters of a job that might allow me some independence. And now...this." I gesture to him, and he laughs.

"Ah, ma siréne, nothing worth having is ever wholly uncomplicated. Independence can still be had, darling." His hand drifts up my shoulder and around my upper body, his fingers carding into my hair as he pulls me flush with his chest. "You can do whatever you want, anywhere you want, Ama. I am not your master. I will be your lover, your partner. I am on call for snacks, my sweet. I have no desire to control you."

Tears spring to my eyes as I stare at him.

He smiles softly. "You asked what it would be like to date a vampire, ma siréne. What I just shared is what it will be like to be loved by *me*." His eyes flash with emotion. "Come here and kiss me again."

~

Later that afternoon, I watch Betmal as he gathers items from around the room and stuffs them into an elegant leather bag.

Is this real? Is this my real life? Because I've never been lucky, and I'm not fool enough to think Malakat and Caralorn won't raise the depths over this once they find out. The new leg is a big enough deal, but I could likely hide that for a while. Betmal, though? I can't hide him, and I would never want to.

The storm is coming, though, because the moment I decline Prince Stefan, Caralorn is going to lose his mind.

I can't think about that right now, however. We're going to get something to eat, and Betmal has already promised to show me around Arcadia.

I keep thinking I'm going to wake up to find myself in my shell bed, surrounded by my cousins and wishing I had a way out of my life. Part of me can't wait to get back and update Thatraeia. If she sees a *real* way out, I think she'll be on board to come with me.

I'll go back to the merkingdom. I have to. I can't just…disappear from the lake. But for the next day or two, I can pretend this is my life all the time, that I get to just travel and go places with Betmal.

As we cross the lobby, a shorthorn minotaur male at the front door swings it open for us with a deep bow. "Betmal of House Zeniphon. Good to see you, sir."

Betmal claps the male on the back as we pass. "You too, Belirius. Give your parents my love."

The minotaur smiles and nods as we exit onto the street. Outside, it's just as bustling as it was before, although, admittedly, I was focused on the gash on my thigh when Betmal swooped us through the lobby.

He slides an arm around my waist. "Alright, darling. There's a perfect place just around the corner where we can get a drink and have some peace and quiet. They've got standard Arcadian fare, lots of meat and vegetables. Does that sound alright with you?"

I nod. "I'm up for anything. I'm feeling like such an adventurer just being out of Ever."

He smiles and reaches up, tucking long strands of hair back behind my ears. "I can show you the world, ma siréne, if that's what you wish."

I want to say yes, show me everything, even as the reality of accepting Betmal as mine begins to set in. But something about him unlocked a side of me that's willing to go against the grain. Between our project and this trip, I'm taking more risks than I ever have. I'm less worried over that than I probably should be.

Betmal guides me carefully up the street. We swing a right at the corner and duck immediately into a glossy black doorway covered with flowering vines. Inside, the restaurant is just as stunning. Vines and flowers drip down from the ceiling, giving it an overgrown forest vibe. Huge tree trunks spring up from the ground. Some are hollowed out with tables set inside.

I'm busy admiring it as Betmal speaks with the hostess. She leads us to a two-person table set on a small platform in a front window. It's tucked into a little alcove with bookshelves on either side that soar all the way to the ceiling.

Betmal pulls out my chair as the waitress sets two menus on the table. I take a seat carefully, holding Betmal's hand as I lower myself. Even though we applied the ointment before we left, the usual pangs are back, sending shards of glass up into my hip.

How did I live with this for so long? I know why I did it, but now that I've had a taste of freedom, I can't imagine going back to the way things were.

I ignore all of that as Betmal sits across from me, crossing one leg elegantly over the other. He leans back in his chair and rests one arm along the back of it.

"Darling, I've been here many times. Would you like to peruse the menu, or shall I order for us and surprise you?"

Delighted he'd think to do that, I pick the second option. I love surprises.

A pixie waiter comes over and introduces himself as Jack, and he and Betmal hit it off right away. I watch as they joke and Betmal orders. I don't recognize the name of anything he asked Jack to bring us, but it's fun to watch them interact. Betmal has such an easy, natural way with everyone we've met. I suppose he's had quite a bit of practice over the last few thousand years.

Jack returns with a bottle of wine, pouring a glass for each of us. I stare at Betmal as he brings the glass to his nose and swirls the wine, sniffing delicately at it.

"Perfection, Jack," he croons. "Absolutely lovely."

I swear Jack's chest puffs up, but he bows to us both and leaves.

Hours later, I've eaten my fill, and we've drunk two bottles of wine. I'm tipsy as depths but having the time of my life. From our vantage point, we can see the entryway to the hotel across the street, and we've spent the last hour inventing stories about the people entering the hotel.

A giant troll male carries a handsome pixie male in his arms like a bride, seemingly oblivious to anyone staring at them.

"Hmm." Betmal rubs his chin as we stare out the front window, spying on the pair as they head across the street in our direction. "I think perhaps the pixie is here for medical intervention. They discovered they're perfectly suited to one another, and now he can't bear to set his mate down." He gives me a meaningful look.

I snort and take a sip of my wine. "That story sounds awfully self-serving."

Betmal winks. "It was worth a try, ma siréne."

"Oh, what about those two?" I gush, pointing to an elegant vampire couple striding toward the hotel's entryway. The woman walks stiffly, her chin held high, black hair pulled back into a harsh bun. But she's stunning. And the male by her side exudes confidence, wearing a black shirt open to his navel and tight black slacks.

Betmal freezes and makes an unhappy noise. "Ah. They're away on a weekend excursion to keep the romance alive. That one's easy. Those are my ex-mates."

My mouth drops open as I stare at the handsome couple, then back at Betmal. "Thalassa below, do you need to go say hello? Or should we hide? Or…what do you want to do?"

He narrows his eyes, watching as they near the hotel's entryway. Eventually, he looks over at me. "I had many years with them, Amatheia. I don't feel the need to chase them down to speak, but I also don't want you to think I'm hiding you from them."

"Of course not," I rush out. "We can take this slowly. We sort of said that might be an option, so I don't want to say hello if you don't."

"I don't." He grimaces. "It's unfortunate they're here, but let's not let them ruin our lovely lunch."

I glance out at the darkening sky with a laugh. "I think you mean dinner. The shift has already changed, and we're probably getting a new waiter soon." Glancing back out the window, I stare at the beautiful vampire couple who were part of Betmal's life for so long. It's hard to believe they're Abemet's parents too. I don't see anything of him in them.

When they disappear into the hotel, I turn to look at Betmal. But he's looking at me, lust obvious in his eyes.

I lean over the table and bring my chin to my palms. "What are you thinking?"

A soft growl is his answer. "That I booked us adjoining

rooms because I had every intention of being a gentleman. But now that the truth is out, I am going to find it exceedingly difficult not to perch at the foot of your bed and watch you sleep."

I sigh. "You make it sound so easy to be together."

He shrugs. "It can be, Amatheia, once you stop caring what others think, which is something I did a very long time ago." He lifts his chin. "For centuries, my only focus was Abemet and raising him. But now I get to think about what I want for myself." He waves at the hotel across the street. "I don't have to think about them or their wants or cares. I get to think about you and us and it *is* easy."

I nod, but inside I'm a turmoil of emotion.

"It's not going to be easy with my uncle," I whisper. "The new leg is one thing. The disappearing for a few days is another. I'm going to catch an earful for that because I've never been gone that long. But when Prince Stefan eventually arrives, all depths will break loose."

Betmal's nostrils flare. "I know this is the opposite of moving slowly, but you don't have to remain in the merkingdom if you don't want to. I want you with me, in our home. If that is uncomfortable for you, Catherine would gladly welcome you at the Annabelle Inn for as long as you want. They are excellent hostesses."

"I honestly think my uncle would send my cousin Malakat or the King's Guard to retrieve me if I did that." I frown over at him, swirling the dregs of my last glass of wine. "Not to mention I'd feel guilty leaving Thatraeia without me. She's more delicate. You should really think about if you're ready for a fight with Caralorn, because that's what this will be. I'm not sure I really absorbed that until we came here and I was away from Ever. I *left town*, and I told no one, Betmal."

His frown matches mine. "Your uncle doesn't frighten me, darling girl. I knew his father, and his father before him, all the way back to the beginning of your clan's line. I am *ancient* in comparison to him, over two thousand years old. There is nothing your uncle could do that would worry me, other than the way he treats you, and how that affects you."

I reach for his hand, stroking the back of it. He turns it over so that I'm touching his palm, his fingers curling underneath my wrist.

"I don't want to be the cause of a lot of drama in town," I admit. "I've flown under the radar for so long."

"Suffering to ease others' pain," he reminds me. "You don't deserve that, Amatheia."

We fall silent after that, because he's right. I know he's right. Yet I still dread returning to Ever and facing the music for choosing myself and my comfort for once. Every day that passes takes us a step closer to a big showdown, and I don't know if I'm ready for that.

∼

Eventually, we make our way back to the hotel and to our rooms. Betmal insists on rubbing his ointments on my leg again, but, honestly, it feels good. Maybe it's just knowing I'm almost done with this prosthetic. I feel lighter than I have in years. The usual guilt over my parents' deaths has even receded to the back of my mind.

When Betmal finishes with my leg, I stand and cross to my bag, grabbing the light pajamas I brought for the trip. He waits at the foot of my bed, one foot crossed over the other ankle as I pull my shirt up over my head. Red eyes narrow, his nostrils flaring as I shimmy out of my skirt next, revealing my fully nude figure.

He clears his throat, eyes roving up and down my body. "Darling, this hardly seems like taking it slowly. You're teasing me."

"Maybe a little," I admit, still feeling tipsy and delicious. "And maybe I'm just getting you back for what you did to Martin. Poor thing."

"Yes, poor Martin," he murmurs, crossing the room and stopping right in front of me. Reaching out, he drags the backs of his fingers along the underside of my left breast.

The nipple pebbles, gooseflesh covering my skin even as heat and need swirl through me.

"These need my mouth." He brings his fingers up to my nipple and pinches lightly, pulling until I arch into his touch with a small cry.

Why did I start this? What was I thinking?

Betmal steps closer, sliding his hand around my torso to rest between my shoulder blades. He brings his mouth just beneath my ear.

"You mentioned moving slowly for a time, ma siréne, so I'm going to retire to my room and work for a while. But if you should wake in the night and find yourself in need of anything, anything at all, I'm just in the next room." He nips hard, and my body jerks as adrenaline floods through me. I grasp at his shirt as he growls into my skin. "Goodnight, ma siréne, sleep well."

Releasing his hold on me, he presses a chaste kiss to the tip of my nose, then turns. He crosses the room with predatory ease, opening the far door as I stand, desperately trying to decide what the depths to do with myself.

He pauses in the doorway, flashing me a brilliant smile. "Anything, darling. I'll be waiting."

Fuck.

Oh fuckity fuck.

"Okay," I manage. "Goodnight, Betmal." *Mate?*

He sails through the door and closes it quietly. I grab my leg and shove it back on, then hobble across the room to plant my ear against the thick wooden door. Betmal pads quietly around the room. Moments later, the swish of clothes hitting the floor echoes softly. I clap a hand over my mouth to avoid making any noise at the idea of him naked in the room next to mine.

What would happen if I opened the door right now?

What would happen if I simply crawled into bed with him?

I turn and rest my back against the wood, closing my eyes as thoughts war in my mind. I want to go in there. But I don't want to start something I can't finish. Are we really doing this? Am I really going to start dating a thousands-of-years-old vampire? What does that mean for Thatraeia? What does it mean for my relationship with my family, if I can even call it that? And how do I feel about all of it?

Sighing, I hobble back toward my bed and fall into it, pulling a pillow between my thighs as I consider everything. I fall asleep thinking about him and dream about traveling the world with Betmal, seeing all the things I've never been able to.

In the morning, I wake to find him seated at the singular round table in my room, sipping an espresso as he speaks with Martin via the communication disk. Martin's hologram spins when I slip out of the bed, don my pajamas, and join them.

"Good morning, Amatheia," he says cheerfully. "I was just telling Betmal how I had you farther back on the schedule, but I really couldn't stop thinking about your case yesterday, so I worked through the night and completed your leg."

I give Betmal a warning look through the hologram, but he throws both hands up in a "not guilty" pose.

Martin smiles at me. "Come by the shop this morning if you can. We'll fit it, and I can make any final tweaks as needed."

Surprising emotion runs through me. Is this happening? Betmal wraps up the conversation with Martin and pulls me into his lap, tucking me against his chest. "Everything all right?"

I sniffle as tears fill my eyes. Pressing against him, I sit up and stare into his eyes. "The last day has been one shock after another, and I can't believe this is happening. For twenty years,

I've thought about this, and now, because of you, it's happening overnight. I just…is this real?"

Betmal's jaw goes tight, and he nods. "You'll never want for this sort of care again, ma siréne, not if I have anything to do with it. If your needs change, we'll fix the problem over and over. If it is within my power to do so, it will be done. You'll start believing me if I keep saying it." He smiles down at me. "How did you sleep?"

The first tear spills over as I stare up at this wondrous person who has so quickly invaded my thoughts and my heart. He's not asking why I didn't come to his room. He's not pressuring me for anything more than my company. What started as a relatively simple job has turned into…a whole thing. And honestly? I'm powerless against it. Betmal is an all-encompassing maelstrom, sweeping me up inside his power and holding me close.

I got used to this way too fast, and I worry that a day of reckoning is coming for us. But the idea that I could have a new prosthetic—today—is too exciting for me to worry. Last night's worries will keep for tomorrow.

We dress quickly, although Betmal insists on rubbing ointment on my leg before we leave the room.

I'm a bundle of nerves as we leave the hotel and walk the short distance to Martin's. When we enter the shop, he's up front, rubbing oil over a sleek metallic-looking leg the same shade and sheen as my natural leg in humanoid form. I step closer, shocked to see there's even the barest hint of aqua and rust scale pattern down the outside, just like my full leg.

The tears return as I stare at the top cup portion where I'll attach it. It's far more detailed with dips and grooves that look like they'll match up to my knee.

"Let's try it on, sweetheart," Martin says quietly, gesturing for us to come back.

We follow, Betmal a soothing presence at my back. I sit in

the same chair as before, Martin dropping onto the stool in front of me. He looks up with a serious expression.

"My prosthetics come with a bit of magic to them, so you won't need straps like before. Instead, the magic forms a sort of suction against your leg. To take it off, you just apply pressure to one side to break that suction. Here, try putting it on. All you need to do is bring it to your leg until the fit feels right."

Shocked, I take the limb with trembling hands. Betmal unhooks my current prosthetic and sets it aside, ruby eyes locked onto the new one. A smirk tilts his lips upward.

Nerves clanging in my chest, I pull the new leg to my knee and jump when it suctions tight like a second skin. Sparks fly up from the connection, and then a warm sensation spreads from the prosthetic up along my leg, pooling pleasantly in my knee.

"It auto-applies a healing spell, although it shouldn't be needed, assuming the fit is right. Let's have you stand and do a quick jump to see how you feel. If there's any pain at all, I'll tweak the leg, and then it's all yours."

A jump.

A jump?

I look up at Betmal. I haven't jumped anywhere since I was ten. The idea is unfathomable.

Betmal slings both hands in his pockets, giving me a confident smile. "Let's give it a try, shall we? You can hold my hand if it helps."

I grab for his hand the moment he suggests it, standing tentatively on the new leg. But...there's no pain. I take a step forward, then another as Betmal curls his fingers lightly around mine.

"Oh my depths," I whisper, spinning in place.

Without pain.

"Try the jump," suggests Martin, crossing his big arms with a broad grin on his handsome face.

I blow out a breath and look at Betmal, who's also smiling.

Then, I hop in place, grimacing as I wait for the sensation of glass slicing through my hip.

But it doesn't come. So, I hop a little more.

Nothing. No pain. No irritation. Nothing at all. It's as if the prosthetic was a true extension of my original leg.

The reality of it hits me like a ton of bricks, and tears flow from my eyes as I bring both hands to cover my mouth, staring at the men who are giving me back movement. Movement I haven't had since I was a child.

Martin stands and claps Betmal on the shoulder. "I'll give you two a moment." Then he turns to me with a smile. "This is wonderful, eh?" Without waiting for me to answer, he stalks from the room and disappears toward the front of the shop.

Betmal pulls me toward him, his smile as big as Martin's. "Ma siréne, talk to me."

I shake my head. I can't. I can't find the words to thank him for this gift. I can't find the words to say anything at all. So I bury my face in his neck and wrap my arms around him, sobbing into his skin as he croons and rubs my back, holding me close. His crisp, clean scent fills my senses as I cry and cry and cry. And the entire time, my leg is fine. There's no pain. I can just stand and hold him, and there's no worry about where the closest chair is or how far my destination is from me.

The tears fade, and heat replaces my overwhelm. Nuzzling against Betmal's neck, I lick a stripe to his ear then bite just beneath it.

A low grunt of pleasure is his answer, his hold on me tightening. He turns to look at me, lips brushing against mine.

"I have no shame, ma siréne, I will do this right here in the back of Martin's shop, but for your first time, I'd love a bit more romance."

Growling, I leap into his arms and wrap my legs around his trim waist. I attack him with my lips first, thrusting my tongue into his mouth as his responding groan goes guttural and ragged. He spins and presses me to the wall as he takes over, sucking my tongue between his lips as I imagine him doing the same thing much lower.

He growls and grabs my hair in both hands, guiding my neck back so he can drag his mouth up to my chin. "Ama, you smell delicious, my sweet."

Depths below, when he says my nickname like that, it's utterly sinful.

He nips my chin, then moves down, each bite harder and harder until he pierces the skin just above my collarbone. His groan of need has Martin clearing his throat from the front room.

Betmal parts just far enough to laugh, then wraps his hand around mine. "Come, darling, let's take this party elsewhere."

We swoop through the short hallway to the front of the store where Martin waits patiently, examining a speck of dust as if it's the most important thing in the world.

"Charge my card, Martin!" Betmal shouts as he pulls me toward the door.

I try my best to thank Martin as we rush from the store, but it's no use. We reach the street and nearly break into a run. When we round the corner, I crash into someone, stumbling backward into Betmal's arms.

The moment I catch my balance, I throw my hands up in apology, only to look into the narrowed, crimson eyes of Evenia, Betmal's former mate. Aberen gets in my face immediately, but before I can say anything, I find myself behind Betmal, who keeps one arm wrapped around me and the other by his side, his fist lightly balled.

My chest heaves, and my muscles tremble. It happened so quickly. I wasn't looking.

"Betmal," purrs the other male. "How unsurprising to see you down a dark alleyway. Whatever are you doing here?"

"And with whom?" the woman tacks on, peeking around him

to look at me. Her dark eyes are cruel, black hair pulled into the same harsh bun as yesterday.

I remind myself that these are the mates who didn't appreciate him. This is the woman he could have given his ziol to anytime over years of being together. But he didn't. So, I lift my chin and step out of his hold and around his side, smiling politely, although I don't offer my hand in greeting. "I'm Amatheia, hello."

The woman scoffs, shooting me a dismissive look. "So soon, Betmal? We've hardly signed separation papers." Her eyes drift to the ziol around my neck, and her frown deepens as the skin around her eyes tightens. She almost looks…upset.

Betmal ignores the comment and returns her smile, but I don't recognize this smile on him. It's cruel and calculated and utterly devoid of the joy I usually see on his face.

"Lovely as it is to see you both, I'm taking my female back to our room. Chat soon, I'm sure. She and I are working on a project that I'll need your stamp of approval on."

The woman looks me up and down, bringing one black-nailed hand to her chin as she smiles. "Is that so?"

Betmal matches the smile. "It is, and you'll stamp it the moment I ask. You owe me that much, and you know what will happen if you do not."

Her nostrils flare, and for a moment, I think she'll say something. But after a quick glance at me, she holds her tongue. Aberen, the male, says nothing and glares the entire time.

Betmal wraps his right arm around me. "I'm ready to go, ma siréne. Shall we?"

"Can't wait," I say brightly, placing my hand over his. We step around the other couple and head up the street, but Betmal's tense and silent by my side. By the time we reach the hotel, he's said nothing.

When we sail through the door, I stop him, shocked anew at

how totally fine my leg is but worried at how quiet he's being.

"Hey, are you alright?"

He shakes his head, running both hands through perfectly coiffed blond hair.

"No, ma siréne. I hate seeing them, and I hate wondering if you feel awkward because they're so obviously cruel. Today's joy should belong only to you. I don't want them to steal a minute of it."

"Okay, so…" I stretch onto my tiptoes and bring my mouth to his ear. "How about we go upstairs and make our own joy, forgetting completely about them and focusing on all the many ways you can teach me about filthy dirty things. I've never had a chance to do them, if you remember." I bat my lashes playfully.

His smile returns—the real one—and he whisks me into his arms with a chuckle. "Is this the taking-it-slowly track you spoke of yesterday?"

"Well…" I shrug. "We can still go a little slow, right?"

His feral grin suggests otherwise. "Perhaps, darling. I'll have food brought to the room, and we'll see how it goes."

I laugh as he slips up the stairs toward our room. "My leg feels great. You don't have to carry me, you know."

"Oh," he says, "I carry you because I want you in my arms. I'm not planning to stop doing so."

By the time we reach our room, we're laughing and panting together. He sets me down and backs me against the door, his hand wrapped around my throat as he kisses me so hard, I see stars. For long moments, we look at one another. And the entire time, the emotion from last night solidifies into a deep sense of knowing.

I want him.

I deserve to have him.

He's the best thing that's happened to me in my entire life. And while I think it's smart to take things slowly, I also want to dive into him and experience everything. I'm going to take this moment by moment and follow my gut.

He opens the door and carries me through. Ten minutes later, food is ordered, and he pulls me out onto the room's balcony. Outside, Arcadia is lit by winking lights and softly falling snow. It's chilly, but not so cold that I need a coat.

Betmal stands behind me, both hands on the railing as his slightly warmer body heats mine. "Look at this beautiful, magical place, ma siréne. I want us to experience everything there is to see here. And in every other haven. And one day, if you like, I can take you to the human world to experience that."

I gasp and spin in his arms. "Outside the haven system? You'd do that?"

He tucks my hair behind my ear, playing with the sensitive tip. "If you want it. You'd need a glamour, but that is easily crafted. I like to disappear into the human world from time to time, keeping up with important contacts and visiting some old friends."

A knock at the door breaks through my shock. Betmal spins and walks to the door, opening it and bringing in a rolling tray of food. The scents of stewed meat, fresh vegetables and something sugary waft into the room. My stomach rumbles.

Betmal rolls the tray all the way toward our table, then grabs my notebook from the tabletop. He comes outside and hands it to me. "Draw for a while, if you like. I'll get the food ready, darling."

Another chaste kiss on my cheek has me aching for more.

Oh gods, he took my "take it slowly" mandate very seriously. It's only been twelve hours, and I'm already regretting it.

What was I thinking?

CHAPTER THIRTEEN
BETMAL

This trip was meant to be about Amatheia's leg, and now that we've accomplished that goal, the rest of our time is about pleasure. Hers. Ours. I suspected, given the rigidity of her uncle's court, she wasn't well versed in the bedroom. But when she said she's never done what we're doing now—I shouldn't take pride in being the first to do it with her.

But I do.

Because I know I'll make it beautiful for her, like she deserves.

She stands on the balcony, sketching in her notebook as I arrange the food for us. That done, I join her, laying her glorious dark locks over her shoulder and planting a trail of less-than-chaste kisses up her spine. When I reach her shoulder again, I bite my way along it, swirling my tongue over her soft, cool skin.

A moan is her response, and she arches back, rubbing her ass against my front. Growling out my pleasure, I run a hand up her stomach to collar her throat, angling her head to one side as I make my way roughly up her neck.

"Ama," I manage. "The food is ready, darling. Come eat."

Her chest heaves beneath my forearm. The pencil falls from her hand, the notebook nearly toppling over the railing to fall below. I grab it with my free hand and laugh low in her ear. "Don't lose the art, ma siréne. We need that. Come."

She spins in my arms, blue eyes dropping to my lips. Her cheeks are flushed, her body rocking against mine.

Taking it slowly is for the fucking birds. But the best thing I can do is honor that request. I give her twenty-four hours before she scraps the idea and tackles me.

How fucking glorious.

Turning, I stand in the doorway, offering her my hand. She takes it, curling her fingers around mine. I pull her inside and sit next to her. As she drops into the seat, I pull a slip of silk from my pocket.

"Come here, darling." I crook a finger, holding it as I stare at her. "Do you trust me, Ama?"

"Yes." She lets out a ragged breath. "But what's that for?"

I grin. "I want to blindfold you and feed you, darling. Nothing further than that. Sexy but still slow."

Her mouth drops open.

Oh, my poor sweet mate.

Taking her silence and that heated look for consent, I lean forward and wrap the silk over her eyes and around her head, tying it off at the back. She halts, zipping her mouth closed.

"Stop me at any time if you're nervous," I murmur in her ear. "This is about finding out what you like, my sweet."

Grabbing a chocolate-covered strawberry from the rolling cart, I rub it over her lips, dragging the soft shell along her plump mouth.

"What do you think I picked first?" I wait for her to answer.

She licks her lips. "Food, I expect."

Brat.

I reach out and slap the side of her ass. The sound cracks

through the room as she yips, but she arches and moans at the same time.

"Try harder, darling."

She nips her lower lip. "I didn't see what the food was…but I think I smell chocolate?"

Grabbing the strawberry, I roll it down the column of her throat and along her collarbone, then back up to her mouth.

"Take a bite." I hold it still as her tongue peeks out to taste it.

When she bites, I join her and nip the berry, my tongue tangling with hers, teasing, just the hint of what I want to do. She moans soft and low, arching into me as she moves her tongue against mine.

"Let's try something else," I offer. I grab a bit of pineapple next, slipping it between her lips. "Suck, ma siréne. Gently now."

She hollows her cheeks around the length of pineapple, sucking hard enough for the juice to drip down her chin and into the divot at the base of her throat.

"When I teach you to suck me off," I say with a growl, "it'll be like this, Ama. Gently at first. Run your tongue around the tip, then flick it."

Her acquiescence has my cock throbbing in my pants, imagining those beautiful lips wrapped around my length. I cannot wait to teach her how to take me to the back of her throat and beyond. Another night, though. Because this night is all about her.

"Well done, my darling," I praise. "Now bite and swallow."

She bites a small chunk of the pineapple and chews. As she does, I bend forward and lick a stripe up her throat, capturing the juice that dripped there, cleaning her with my tongue.

Gods, "slowly" can be fun. I'd forgotten…it's been so long.

Amatheia moans as I bite softly under her chin.

"I want more," I whisper. "I want everything, ma siréne."

I ordered a beautiful coconut créme brûlée, and I dip my forefinger into it now. Bringing it to her lip, I coat it with the sugary confection, then slide my finger into her mouth. I hold back a groan when her tongue slicks a wet circle around my digit. Gods above, I cannot wait to fuck her mouth and teach her everything I've learned over thousands of years of oral.

"Perfect." I rub softly at her tongue before pulling my finger from her mouth. "Let's try something a little more filling, shall we? Open wide, darling."

She follows direction beautifully, opening her mouth even as her nostrils flare. The tips of her ears twitch as I cut a small bite of beef bourguignon, dredging it through mashed potatoes. When I lift it to her mouth, she sniffs delicately at it.

"I...don't recognize that scent."

"Take it into your mouth," I command, loving how dirty and sensual almost anything can sound when said in the right tone.

She moans softly, but nips at the edges of the beef. Seeming to decide she likes it, she takes a larger bite and eats the whole thing from my fingers, licking them clean.

When she's done, I grip the back of the chair and sink down onto her lap, holding myself steady as I rock my hips against hers. She gasps, which pulls a satisfied chuckle from me.

"If we weren't taking it slowly, ma siréne, I'd remove my clothing and rub you all over my body."

She cries out, curving against me as her hands come to my stomach and explore.

I bring my mouth just below her ear. "I'd tease you for hours with this big cock, and when I finally filled you, you'd shatter with me, Ama."

She pants, her body rolling beneath mine as she runs her hands all over my torso. I grab one and guide it down my stomach to my rigid length, brushing her fingertips over it.

"This belongs to you and no one else. Never again, unless you want us to explore others."

She sits up and rips the blindfold off, her expression fierce.

"Never." Her voice is all ferocious growl, her tiny fangs glinting in the low light of the room.

"I love how possessive you are, now that you know the truth." I brush my lips over hers. "I aim to be worthy of your possession, Ama."

She sits back, eyes roving my body, her gaze nearly a physical touch. An appreciative smile pulls tiny wrinkles to the corner of her lips.

"Eat, ma siréne," I croon. "You must always be fed before anything else."

She brings her eyes back to mine, brows curving mischievously as she opens her mouth.

I laugh and feed her until her belly's full and the scent of her arousal is thick in the room. When dinner's done, I bid her goodnight the same way I did yesterday. My darling looks ready to combust, but like before, she allows me to leave.

Not for much longer, ma siréne, I think to myself. Because soon you won't be able to hold back.

Soon, the heat will burn you alive.

CHAPTER FOURTEEN
AMATHEIA

I wake in the morning and stretch long in the sumptuous sheets, marveling at how much less stiff my knee and leg feel after hours on the new one. After Betmal teased me and left me, I lay there for a long while, thinking through everything that's happened on this trip. All that thinking led me to a determination.

I want him.

I want us.

I want to live in this magical bubble where I get to be with him all the time, and where painting is my real-life job, and where my uncle isn't going to freak out and do something drastic once he finds out what's going on.

But I know Caralorn well, and I know he'll do everything in his power to put a stop to this. He'll threaten Betmal with the King's Guard. I don't want Betmal embroiled in that kind of drama. If we could easily pick up and leave Ever, it would be one thing. But he has the house and his family. Not to mention I could never leave Thatraeia behind.

I'm quiet as we walk toward the Arcadian portal station. After a few minutes of silence, Betmal slips his arm around my waist and tickles my stomach. "Talk to me, darling. Whatever has you looking so troubled is surely something we can tackle together."

And that's the crux of what I love so much about him. He thinks anything is solvable if we do it as a team. Can he be right? Is there a world where I get to choose my happiness?

Sighing, I wrap my arm around his waist and lean into him. For a moment, I marvel that I'm able to do it, and that my leg isn't a problem. There's no pain at all. I can't believe it. Then I remember what he asked me.

"I dread returning." I look up. "This trip was full of surprises and fun, and it's the best time I've ever had in my life. But when we get back, it's business as usual, which means I need to go home. I probably won't be able to get away for a few days. I just…dread that."

He remains silent for a moment, jaw grit tightly as he seems to consider my words. As the portal station comes into view, he glances down at me. "And you won't consider moving in with me or going to the Annabelle?"

Gods, living full-time at Betmal's place sounds amazing. But I truly don't think my uncle would allow it.

He squeezes me again. "You're worried about your uncle, or perhaps your cousins?"

"Yes." The singular word comes out as a whisper. "You make it sound so simple to not care what others think. And it's not that I really care what my uncle thinks, not after how callous he's always been. But I worry for Thatraeia and what he'll do. Not to mention the Stefan issue."

Betmal's jaw muscles tighten, but he jerks his head toward an alleyway off the street next to the station. "I have something for you that might change how you feel, ma siréne. Come."

Curious, I follow as he guides me down the narrow space. Threading my fingers through his, I giggle, trying to bring some of this trip's happiness back into my heart. "Betmal, why are you always leading me into dark alleyways? Aberen did mention that yesterday. Do you have a habit of hanging out in dangerous seeming places?"

He spins and presses me against the bricks, hovering his gorgeous mouth above mine. "My darling, the things I want to do to you in dark alleyways are absolute filth. But if you tempt me now, we will never make it to our final destination." He turns and points to a simple black sign with gold lettering.

Bank of Arcadia.

I stare at him, trying to process why we'd be here.

Betmal smiles and pulls me toward a glossy navy door. From the outside, the bank entry is understated elegance. But all of that disappears once we enter.

The bank is one cavernous room with cube-like structures lining the walls. No two cube-shaped rooms are alike. To my right, the first cube room has flowers dripping from every possible surface. A banker sits with a client with tea service perched atop a mushroom table. The cube next to that is set inside the base of an enormous tree, just like the ones in Shifter Hollow back home.

I glance up at Betmal in wonder. "I could paint this place for *hours*, Betmal. This is incredible!"

He winks. "Wait until we meet with our banker, my darling. Let's go." He wraps his hand around mine and guides me down the long room to the last cube on the left.

I blink as I try to understand. It's entirely encased in glass bricks with water and tiny fish in them. Clownfish zip between the rectangles, so there must be tubes of some sort. Corals and jellyfish and sea urchins complete the picture—every wall is a mini ocean of sorts.

My heart stutters in my chest.

Betmal pulls me through the cube's arched doorway. Behind the desk, a handsome merman sits in human form, his wavy ear tips giving him away. He smiles when we enter, reaching a hand out to shake Betmal's. Then he grips mine in both of his. "Miss Amatheia, what an absolute pleasure it is to meet you."

"Okay," I manage, wondering how he knows me in the first place.

"Sit down, please." He waves at two chairs in front of his aqua-green coral desk.

Betmal holds the back of my chair as I drop into it, shocked anew at the absence of pain. I try not to let the tears come right here in front of others, but I can't believe I put up with it for so long. I should have—

"Ama, darling," Betmal says quietly. "Are you alright?"

I look over at him, my eyes watery. "Yes. That was just…" My voice trails off. I don't want to talk about my leg in front of a merman.

The banker clears his throat. "My name is Kadriel, and I am so pleased you're with us today." He spreads several sheets of paper out on the desk between us. "Miss Amatheia, these documents outline the details of your newly opened account and the current balance. I need to grab the card attached to the account so you have that, but while I run to do so, please review the documents and sign. If you've any questions, I'll answer as soon as I return."

My mouth drops open as he rises and grins at us both. Then, he spins in place and heads out of an arched doorway on the back side of the cube.

I turn to Betmal. "You did this? You opened an account for me?"

He shifts forward, both elbows on his knees as he takes one of my hands in his.

"I had to deposit your payment somewhere, darling, and I wanted to ensure it was somewhere only you have access to. Kadriel already has instructions to remove me from the account for any purposes other than deposits. I wanted you to have money that's *entirely* yours."

Gobsmacked, I turn to the pages and pick them up, fingers trembling.

Account total: $2,000,000.

I gasp and look at him again.

"Two million dollars?! Even one million was excessive, Betmal. I thought you were kidding about *that*."

He smirks and sits back in his chair, crossing one leg elegantly over the other. "I promised you a tip, my darling. So if we extrapolate this out over fifty havens, you'll be quite a rich woman in no time."

I try to close my mouth, but I can't as I read through the documents to find that Betmal's right—this account is only in my name. No one else has access, and there's a singular card for it…also in my name.

My first thought is Thatraeia and how I can get her out of the merkingdom with this money. The second thought that comes is worry over how we'll deal with Caralorn. But the third? The third is beautiful. Because my third thought is about how Betmal and I will figure this out together.

I open my mouth to say something, but Kadriel swoops back in and lays a glittering turquoise credit card on the table. My name is printed in gold on the front with the Bank of Arcadia logo.

For the next few minutes, he explains where the bank has branches and how I can contact them if needed.

Kadriel and Betmal both watch as I sign my name at the bottom of the paperwork. When I do, Kadriel stands and runs the pages through a small copy machine on top of his desk. He keeps the originals and slips the rest into a manila envelope for me, along with the credit card.

"Here, Miss Amatheia. We're all done, but call me at any time with questions, alright?"

I nod, still shocked and silent as Betmal offers me a hand. I rise from the chair and thank Kadriel. Betmal holds my hand as we walk toward the door. But by the time I'm there, reality has set in, and I pull him to a stop.

"I'm a multimillionaire," I whisper-hiss. "What in the depths is happening?"

Betmal grins at me. "You did a job, ma siréne, and you did so well at that job that I felt it necessary to tip you." His expression grows serious. "And what I did is not because of who you are to me. I would have paid anyone this way."

I narrow my eyes, trying to decide if he's serious.

He brings my hands to his chest. "I swear to you I am not exaggerating. By the time we do books for all of the havens, you will be an incredibly wealthy female in your own right, by your own hand."

I'm so shocked, I honestly can't find anything to say, but I cling to Betmal as we leave the bank. We head for the portal station, and it's not until he steps forward and opens the door that I find my voice.

Halting just inside the doorway, I look up into his glittering ruby eyes. "This is a gift beyond measure, Betmal."

"Not gift, ma siréne. Payment for services." He winks and dips down, brushing his lips along my cheekbone.

I straighten. "Trouble is coming for us when we return home. I've been gone for two and a half days, and Prince Stefan is due next week. I don't know how to navigate the near future. Will you help me?"

His playful smile falls, and he tucks my hair over my shoulder as a hand slips up my back and hauls me close. "Always, my darling." The ferocious look on his face softens. "Having me in your corner is the equivalent of an army. You will *have* the future you want, Ama. I swear that much to you."

Smiling, I press my forehead to his chest and breathe in his crisp scent. I don't know how we're going to do this and protect Thatraeia at the same time, but I have to do it, to gain her freedom along with mine.

"Let's go, darling," he urges. "I'm not anxious to part from you, but to your point, we will need to deal with Caralorn soon."

I nod and turn for the portal. Betmal follows, a comforting presence at my back.

The next quarter hour is a blur while we pass through the portal to Hearth HQ, and then the second portal to Ever. I feel nothing but dread when we appear in the Ever portal station, and I half expect to find Malakat and the King's Guard standing there waiting for me. They do whatever Caralorn says. If he tells them to find me and drag me home, they absolutely will.

Thankfully, there are no merfolk when we arrive. Which is good, because when I imagine Malakat finding the glittering turquoise credit card in my name, I almost shudder.

Betmal turns to me with a smile. "Shall we go home and eat something, darling? Would you like to paint?"

Sorrow spears through me.

"I need to go back to the lake, Betmal." I can barely choke out the words. I despise the idea of going home. The only good thing there is Thatraeia, and to some degree, the castle herself.

He smiles, pulling me into his arms and running both hands up my back underneath my tee. "When can you come to me again?"

"I...don't know. Probably two or three days. Let's make it two. I'll find a way."

"Perfect," he murmurs, rubbing my back with slow, measured strokes. "Morgan had the brilliant idea of having you paint monster portraits. If you're up for it, I'll arrange it on the second afternoon. You can sit at Higher Grounds and paint. What do you think?"

Excitement and sadness war within me.

"I love that idea." I've never wanted to stay on land so badly in my entire life.

"I'll walk you to the lake," he says quietly. "Want me to keep your bag? Or would you like to attempt to stuff it into your locker?"

I laugh at the idea of that. "Take it home, please."

His fingers dig into my back as a low growl rumbles from his throat. "You called my place home, Ama."

"It is," I admit. "I've never fit in in my original home. The place I feel the best is with you."

He grins. "Perhaps you believe what I told you on this trip, then? That you belong to me, and I to you."

Heat curls needy and hot in my belly.

"I do," I manage.

His lips brush mine, featherlight even as he nips my lower lip with a soft growl.

"After you paint, two days from now, we're going home, and we're going to spend some time exploring your pleasure, ma siréne. Don't bother bringing extra clothing with you, because we won't be leaving the bedroom."

Oh depths. My pussy clenches on nothing as I gasp against his sinful mouth. This tease is too much. I was an idiot for thinking I could take things slowly with him.

"I take back what I said about going slow," I blurt out.

His low laugh tells me he already knows what I just said. "We did take it slowly, darling. But we're done with that, Ama. Two days from now, when you return to me, I'm tasting every inch of you—thoroughly. And then I'm going to teach you how I like to be pleased. And when all of that is done, we'll discover how you like to be fucked."

I snarl against his mouth, feeling for all the world like a rabid animal. I want to throw myself on top of him and take everything he's offering.

But not here. Not in the Ever portal station where anyone we know could happen upon us.

On the way to the lake, we talk about who I'd like to paint a portrait of for the welcome book. We settle on the guardian gargoyle Alo and his adorable son, Ignatius. I love how Iggy will bring humor to Alo's normally stoic expression. Maybe we'll even get Shepherd in there with his brother and nephew. I'd like to paint Catherine and the Annabelle Inn, too, because they're both so iconic, and because she was one of the very first land monsters to befriend me. I'm also thinking Herschel, from Herschel's Fine Dining on Main Street.

By the time we reach the lake, I'm a bundle of excitement. My new leg feels *amazing,* and I'm so grateful. But as we walk along the trail, and the lake and locker log come into view, all of that dies a swift death. I turn and bury my face in Betmal's chest.

"I don't want to go," I moan into his pecs, slipping my hands inside his shirt.

He's quiet, wrapping his arms around me and laying his cheek on top of my head. We stand like that for a minute, maybe two before he speaks. "When you come back to me in two days, we're formulating a plan, darling. I won't allow us to continue like this, not with you miserable about returning home. Think on it while you're gone. I'll do the same. When we come together, we'll decide how to proceed."

When I look up at him, he smiles that same confident smile as the first day we met.

"Things are going to be just fine, ma siréne, I promise." He bends down to kiss the tip of my nose. "You'll see."

Pulling his ziol necklace off, I slip it over his head and nestle it against his chest with a smile. "Keep this safe for me, ma vampíre?"

He rests his hand over mine, white flashing over his crimson irises. "Always, ma siréne…when you return to me, I'll give it back."

∾

I manage to make it back to my shared suite just in time for dinner. Thatraeia swims up to me, concern evident on her face.

She grabs me by the upper arm and drags me to the corner, away from the hustle and bustle of our cousins getting ready for dinner. Several of them look over at us with suspicion. Thank Thalassa, Malakat lives in the barracks with the King's Guard, so she's not here.

"Where have you been?" Thatraeia hisses, ear fins flaring wide as she stares me down. "Malakat was looking for you all morning. Prince Stefan is arriving in three days."

I sigh despite the immediate dread, unwrapping Thatraeia's fingers from my upper arm. "I was out of town, remember?"

She sucks in a deep breath of water, gills fluttering wildly. "Right." Her brows knit together as her mouth drops open. "It's just...Father was raging about where you were. He wanted to prepare for Stefan's arrival or something. And the Guard questioned me, and how are you going to explain your absence, Ama? I can't say you were at the Julienne fields!"

"I'm not planning to explain it." I float in front of her, anger reminding me just why I want to leave this place. "I don't owe anyone an explanation of where I've been, Thatraeia. The Sea Julienne won't wilt in a day, and neither will Stefan. I'm one of a dozen of us who technically have responsibility to it and everything else Caralorn and the King's Guard ask us to do." I plant both hands on my hips. "Don't you ever get tired of gardening and doing busy work?"

She crosses her arms, looking unsure. "Right, but..."

I feel sick, bile rising in my throat. "Wait. What did you tell your father?"

She straightens and looks around surreptitiously, as if there might be King's Guards hiding around the seaweed-encrusted pilings that hold up our suite.

"I said I didn't know, alright? And then I burst into tears, and Father was horrified and commanded me out of his suite. You know he hates it when I cry, so thank Thalassa I can do it on command. But I don't know what to say when Malakat asks me to find you for something."

I suck in a breath, the cool water flowing through my gills as I attempt to calm myself. Reaching out, I place my palms on either side of her round cheeks, forcing her to look deeply into my eyes.

"Cousin, I love you to the ends of this world and beyond. But when Malakat asks you for me, it is sufficient to tell her you don't know where I am. You are not my keeper."

She sputters. "But—"

"But nothing." I give her a stern look. "I've been paid for the paintings, sweet cousin, and it's enough money for both of us to leave this place very soon. You don't love it here any more than I do. A storm is brewing, but you'll come with me when I leave, right? I can pay for us both, and we can travel the world!"

She pulls close, slipping both arms around my waist. "I think I'd like that, Ama, but Father and Malakat would never let it happen."

"They will," I promise her, pulling her in close for a hug. "If you want out too, I will find a way. Betmal will help us."

"Okay," she says softly. "Can you trust a vampire, Ama?"

I resist the urge to shake her. But she's been under Caralorn's thumb so long, she's too terrified to remember there's a whole world outside the lake. If I'm honest with myself, I was like that too before Betmal.

Thatraeia and I should be free to come and go if we wish. The lake is not a prison, however much it feels like one some days.

No more.

I'm done.

I level her with the most serious stare I can muster. "I trust him with my life, Cousin. He's in our corner, okay?"

She nods, then slips into my arms, resting her head against my chest. Her hair floats in long coral waves around us. I reach out to stroke the cylindrical strands as I think about my mate.

My mate.

Thinking of him steels my resolve. Betmal's there for me in a way nobody ever has been. I need his help. But with it, I'll figure out how to get free of this place.

CHAPTER FIFTEEN
BETMAL

"Father, you're quiet, what's wrong?" Abemet looks over Morgan's head at me, blond brows furrowed as he scans my face.

Morgan slips her arm through mine, laying her hand over my forearm. "Go on and spit it out. You know we'll question you until you do."

Abe snorts, and she glances over at him. Returning her focus to me, she beams. "Well, you know *I* will needle you until you do. Abe would probably do something insane like give you your privacy."

I laugh and glance at the joys of my life. "Darlings, Amatheia is my mate, and I told her on the trip. Dropping her off at the lake, knowing she's returning to Caralorn's kingdom is eating me alive."

Morgan turns and grabs her mate's hand, looking utterly unsurprised. "You were right."

He winks down at her. "You owe me. You can pay up later."

She blushes but looks back at me. "She hates going home, huh?"

I growl as we walk along Main Street toward Herschel's Fine

Dining for a late dinner reservation. "He's found a suitor for her, who is arriving the day after tomorrow, I believe. Obviously, she doesn't want him, but she has responsibilities at home. All I want is her out of the lake and happy, but the situation is complicated."

Abemet crosses his arms as we walk. "It's not really *that* complicated, Father. Bring her home to your place and keep him away from you both. Haven leadership will get involved to keep everyone safe."

I shake my head. "It's more of an internal struggle, my darling. She's very connected with her youngest cousin and also worried about bringing drama to Ever." I glance at them both. "Fortunately, the house and I spent some time this morning coming up with a plan and several backup plans. Amatheia returns tomorrow to paint portraits downtown, and then I'll speak with her about it."

Abemet's expression is calculated and cold as he drops his arms, grabs the handle, and opens the door to Herschel's. "Don't forget we have a blue witch, Father. Lou would move heaven and earth to keep Amatheia safe. You're not without options."

I sail through the door with my daughter-in-law on my arm. Abemet's right, of course. There are plenty of threatening, violent solutions. But I'd rather not *start* there, if only for Ama's sake. If it were up to me, I'd simply remove the king's head for the pain he's put her through over the years. But I know in my heart of hearts that would gut her, and I'm not willing to do that.

For *her*, I can put on a cloak of civility. But only ever for her peace of mind. The moment she tells me she's through being civil, I will stain the lake with Caralorn's blood.

A smile comes to my face as Herschel guides us to a lovely corner table. I hold a chair for Morgan, and she drops into it with a thankful smile.

Dinner's as lovely as ever, the restaurant filled with familiar faces and plenty of new ones. Clearly tourism is on the rise. By the time we leave, Herschel's has a line out the door, and the restauranteur himself is rushing around shouting orders.

We head across Main to Miriam's Sweets. Miriam and Iggy are behind the checkout counter, whispering about something. When we enter, Iggy's dark brows lift in surprise. He whoops and zips over the counter toward us. The moment he's close enough, he wraps himself around Morgan's head like a scarf, slinging his tail around her neck.

"Morrrgannnn!" he draws her name out long. "I just saw Lou and her mates, and she was showing me how she can make a spear with her blue magic, and it was so cool, and do you think I could do it one day? I'd really like to, and it would be good because I could protect everyone like Dad and Uncle Shepherd! They'd be so proud, right?!"

His hellhound, Minnie, lumbers out from behind the checkout counter, her pregnant belly swaying. She flops down in front of the register and watches us with Iggy.

Abemet looks at me. "Remarkable, isn't it? That he bonded with a hellhound?"

I stare in wonder as Morgan unwraps Iggy, beaming at him. "Ig, what has your dad said about suffocating friends with your hugs?"

He flaps slowly in front of her face, crossing his arms and scowling. "To be more gentle because sometimes I'm overly exbuberent?"

Miriam laughs at the mispronunciation.

Morgan grabs him and drags him to her chest, squeezing him tightly. "Hugs we can do, suffocation not so much."

He sighs and slips his tail around to rest it over her heart. Like all gargoyle children, he's fascinated with heartbeats. He won't have one until he meets his mate one day. Sweet boy.

Morgan carries Iggy back to Miriam, Minnie the hellhound watching them with glittering red eyes. She looks exhausted and pregnant, but she's ready for action if Iggy's in any danger at all.

As Morgan picks out candies with Iggy and Miriam's help, my thoughts drift to my Ama, wondering how she's doing in the merkingdom. It's a struggle not to go to her, but the last thing I want to do is make things worse.

For now.

In my mind, there's a plan. But I need to discuss it with her before I do anything that might set violent events into motion. Ever doesn't deserve that, either.

But at the end of the day, it's like I told Ama in Arcadia—she is my priority, and *everything* else comes second.

CHAPTER SIXTEEN
AMATHEIA

I daydream about returning to Betmal and my art as I float toward the door of my suite. Formal dinner starts in half an hour, and if the rumors are to be believed, Stefan will be there.

He arrived early. Great.

This morning, I pleaded with Caralorn not to put me in this position. I told him I wasn't interested in being sold off to the highest bidder. He didn't care. So, I appealed to his love for my mother. That only incensed him. Finally, I promised to simply disappear and become someone else's problem. I held back from mentioning Betmal *only* because I didn't want Caralorn to immediately leave the lake and cause drama in Downtown Ever.

I know he would.

After I told him I'd disappear, Caralorn roared at me to go farm the Sea Julienne fields and never gave me an answer of any sort.

I'm mad now, though. I'm not a prize broodmare to be auctioned off. I'll be polite tonight only because I don't want to cause a scene in front of the entire kingdom. Technically, Caralorn is not only within his rights but also doing what my parents might have wanted by arranging a suitable marriage for me.

Technically.

I just don't want it. None of it. Especially after being out of town with Betmal and getting a taste of freedom. And the freedom isn't even the best part. *Betmal* is, and I want it so badly, I will risk anything to get it. But I need to do so in a way that keeps him safe.

So, I'll be polite tonight, but I'll make sure I'm not alone with Stefan and I'm noncommittal if he references our… arrangement.

When I open the door to my suite and glide through, I swim right into a bare chest. Sucking in water, I jolt backwards and throw up my hands, glancing up into the handsome face of a gold and rust-colored merman. Eyes the color of amber facets wrinkle at the corners as he smiles at me.

Malakat hovers behind him, staring daggers at me as she holds her spear, her fins stiff. "Prince Stefan insisted on meeting you privately ahead of tonight's meal, Cousin," she says in a simperingly sweet tone.

Oh Thalassa. Oh *depths*. This is him, the suitor.

I force a polite smile as I look at the muscular merman floating in front of me. "I wasn't expecting to meet you so soon." It's all I can manage. How the depths am I going to get out of this situation?

Stefan smiles, but even though it looks genuine, I flutter my hip fins and move slightly away from him. His smile falters as he looks down at me.

"I know this isn't traditional in the slightest, to see you before tonight's meal, but I thought perhaps it would be nice to chat before everyone gets…" he grins, "tense and weird and formal."

Behind him, Malakat lets out an irritated snort.

Stefan glances over his shoulder. "Mala, why don't you give me a little space, alright?"

Her emerald eyes move to him, and for a moment she looks stricken. But she flips in place and zooms along the corridor, disappearing from view.

His smile falls when he looks back at me. Amber eyes drift down to my missing fin then back up. "I thought perhaps we could take a little swim and chat, but I don't want to put you in pain. I've...heard about the attack."

Shock courses through me. Did Mala tell him when she arranged this on Caralorn's orders?

He *cares* if I'm in pain?

I gulp. "That is an unexpected kindness, Prince Stefan, but I'd be happy to take a quick swim, if you like."

He smiles again and offers me an arm.

Cautious, I slip my hand through the crook of his elbow, careful to keep my body as far away from his as I can.

He guides us through the suite and out the giant archway into the city, toward the Sea Julienne fields. After a few minutes of silence, during which I can't think of a thing to say, he glances down at me.

"Although it's customary for our people to arrange marriages like this, I hope you'll find me a pleasant enough husband. I thought perhaps if we went away from everyone for a few minutes, we might get to know one another and find common ground."

Goddess, I can't do this. I can't pretend this is fine in order to save face at tonight's dinner.

"I'm in love with someone else," I blurt out, dropping his arm and halting mid-glide.

His mouth drops open in surprise, amber eyes wide. His shoulders slump as he grits his jaw and glances away from me. When he looks back again, a deep, watery sigh comes from his throat. "As am I, Wife, but we have a duty to fill, do we not?"

I snort. "I suppose we do, and yet I cannot find it in my heart to agree to this, no matter what my uncle wishes or what he promised my parents."

Stefan runs both hands through long, golden-yellow hair. "We cannot simply say no, Amatheia."

I ball my fists. "Why can't we? Why can't we be the first to come to another agreement? If you love someone else, why shouldn't you have her?"

His expression goes resigned. "She is not the first in line of her house," he whispers. "Were she, I'd have taken her already."

"Fuck that," I growl. "Now that I've blurted out my thoughts on this topic, I find myself unable to stay quiet on this topic. I have begged and pleaded with Caralorn not to follow through with this. I have offered to disappear and never return to this place. Do you truly wish to take a wife who will be miserable? I would never see my cousin Thatraeia again. I would—"

He throws his hands up. "Wait, wait one second. Are you saying, if you come with me, you think I would keep you from your family?"

I halt. "Err, Caralorn has always said that is how it would be."

Stefan barks out a laugh. "I have only been in Caralorn's clan for a few hours, Amatheia, but I can tell you he runs this place far differently than my father runs my clan. And when I become king, I will make further changes still." His eyes narrow. "I would never seek to keep you from coming or going or traveling, or whatever you would like to do. My goal is to be a good partner for you."

"I don't want any of it," I manage. "I want the man I love, the man who is, as we speak, waiting for me to come to him. I can't do this, Stefan. I *refuse* to do this."

His next sigh is softer. "I don't know how to make that happen, Amatheia. Our kings brokered this deal, and there is much on the line." He looks off into the dark depths of the merkingdom. "We do not need to figure this out right now. Let us return and make our appearances. I will think on it. But honestly," his expression grows sorrowful, "it's entirely possible that the only way out of this is war."

He pushes through the water and brings a finger underneath my chin. "Would you bring war to your kingdom and mine simply to be away from me?"

Sorrow and understanding fill me in equal measure as I stare up into his handsome face. "Would you not fight for your love, Stefan? Would you not raze this city to the ground to have her?"

He drops his hold of my chin and spins slowly, looking over his shoulder at me. "Let's go, Princess. Dinner is beginning."

I watch as he heads toward the city, golden fins seeming to cast light into the darkness as he sluices gracefully through the water.

Thalassa below, help me figure this out.

CHAPTER SEVENTEEN
BETMAL

Two days without my female have been abysmal. Abemet and Morgan took me to Herschel's last night for a delightful meal, but the moment I was alone in the house, the sorrow nearly ate me alive. The house is covered in flowers, the fridge is stocked with Ama's favorite seaweed kimchi and a salted cheese I think she might like. There's more fruit cut and ready to go.

Everything is ready, but I pace anxiously. I've always trusted my gut, and my gut tells me a showdown with Caralorn is coming soon. I need to speak with Amatheia about it today. I'm ready to put an end to her worries over this.

She should be available this afternoon—assuming nothing has happened in the last two days—so we'll get a chance to talk about it. I'm going to ensure she has time to paint, and then we'll come home and discuss what's next.

As if my thoughts summoned her, my comm watch rings, her name rising above it in hologram form. Excitement and relief shatter me in equal measure. I can't *wait* to see her.

Directing the comm watch to answer her, I greet her with all the excitement I feel.

"Darling, how are you?" My voice sounds husky and needful to my ears.

"Hi!" She sounds breathless and excited. "I just left the lake, and I'm on my way to your place. Can we talk for a minute before we get to work? Things have…happened."

"Of course," I purr, calling my wings and heading for the back door. "I'm on my way."

"I'd love to walk," she continues as I bullet up into the sky.

I catch a current and zip toward the lake. "I'll walk with you then. Please, darling. I'm desperate to see you."

She laughs. "Of course, Betmal. Come find me."

And just like that, I'm hard. Hard and aching, because the idea of playing sexy hide and seek in our house does things to me. We hang up, and I reach down to adjust my cock. It throbs with the need to take things further with her, to play in a way we haven't gotten to yet.

But after our trip, after all of that teasing, after so much want and need…now is our time.

Catching a current, I relish the sunshine on my face as I bullet over Downtown Ever and toward Shifter Hollow. I swoop around a corner to find her jogging toward me—jogging!—looking for all the world like she never had a single issue with her leg.

When I alight in the middle of the road and stop, allowing myself to peruse her beautiful figure, she laughs.

"Way to make a female feel sexy, all that intense ogling." She shrugs, looking at me with a smirk. "Must be that vampire male sex and blood thing, hmm?"

Gods, the teasing. I love the teasing.

Stalking toward her, I don't stop until my chest hits hers. She reaches for me, grabbing the lapels of my shirt. I grasp her throat in one hand, sliding the other up the back of her neck and into all that glorious dark hair. Guiding her slightly backward, I arc her body against mine and bury my nose in the hollow at the base of her throat.

I breathe in deeply, her caramel and crisp sea scent filling my nostrils. It brings me peace, soothing the jittery places inside me that feel hollowed out when she's not around.

I drag my tongue up the side of her neck and bite her earlobe softly. "I missed you," I murmur. "So much, ma siréne. I was in utter misery without you."

She rubs her head against me, dragging her jawline along my mouth, teasing me with luscious, soft skin. "I missed you too. But we've got a problem." Dark eyes flick to mine. "Stefan arrived, and Caralorn hosted a formal dinner. I told my uncle I wanted no part of it, but he would not budge. We have to do something, Betmal."

I stand straighter, pressing a soft kiss to her plump lips. "That arrangement is not your future, darling. I've got a plan, but everything is ready for you to paint today at Higher Grounds. Why don't we tackle that first so your day begins with fun, and once you're done, we'll go home and talk about handling this once and for all, hmm?"

She leans into me, sliding long arms around my neck. Nuzzling the tip of my nose with hers, she teases me with a mouth so sinful, I can't stop dreaming about it.

"I'd like that. They won't notice I'm gone until tomorrow."

"Deal." I nip at her lower lip as a needy groan rips from me. My cock throbs against my thigh, desperate to finally, *finally* take things further with her.

Amatheia looks into my eyes, her lips pulling into a sensual smirk. Standing on her tiptoes, she brings her mouth to my ear, her lips brushing along my sensitive skin. I shudder, holding her body tighter to mine.

"After we deal with this," she whispers, "I want you to teach me what makes you feel good. I can't stop thinking about it,

Betmal. I want to know what it sounds like when you lose control."

A guttural groan rips from my throat, followed by a growl that pulls goosebumps to her skin. I reach up and grip her hair, holding her taut against me.

"I'll teach you everything I know, ma siréne. I cannot wait. Watching you paint all afternoon will be a delicious tease."

"Mmm." She slides a hand down between us, running her fingers over the length of my hard shaft. "Delicious, indeed."

"Fuuuuck..." I can't hold back the groan as she slowly jacks me right in the middle of the street. I rock into her grip, heat and need spiraling inside me as the bloodlust begins to take over, my fangs descending and filling with venom. I snarl, yanking her head back to bare her neck to me. "Need to bury my teeth in your throat. Now."

With a laugh, she pushes out of my arms and walks backward toward Downtown Ever, a devilish glint in her eyes. "Well, we can't do it right this very moment, *darling*. What is it you told me in Arcadia? Something about how taking it slowly was exactly what we needed? I believe you agreed with the sentiment at the time..."

"We did that for several days," I say. "I'm done with slow." I wink at her. "Not to mention, you told me you were done with it as well."

She spins around and glances over her shoulder at me. "Perhaps after we work and plan, you can show me just how fast you'd prefer to go, when given free rein."

Snarling, I watch as my mate walks away from me, hips sashaying, long legs disappearing up into a ruffled jean miniskirt that barely covers her ass. I stare as the barest hint of cheek peeks out from underneath the tiny slip of fabric.

"I do believe you shortened that skirt," I mutter, more to myself than anything.

A laugh echoes back from in front of me.

Jogging to catch up with her, I slide my arm around her waist and walk with her in companionable silence to Higher Grounds. Earlier today, I dropped off her easel, paints and paintbrushes. Alé promised to set them up in a sunny corner, and her first subjects should arrive in the next half hour or so.

It's a risk to take this time to paint, but I'll stand watch in case Caralorn figures out where Ama disappeared to. I'd rather get to him first, but she and I need to discuss that plan so we can enact it quickly. I won't have him ruining her time with me.

When we arrive at Higher Grounds, the coffee shop swings the door open for us, the front bell dinging to announce our arrival. Alé looks up from behind the countertop, smiling as we approach. He waves at Amatheia's favorite table next to the pickup counter.

"Everything's ready for you there. The shop has been so excited all morning, wiggling the floorboards at anyone who came too close to your things." He rubs the countertop lovingly.

Overhead, the ceiling tiles flutter and fan out from a chandelier in the center.

Amatheia pats the counter next to Alé's hand, looking up at the ceiling. "Thank you, beautiful girl, for protecting my spot. Are you ready for a bit of fun?"

I don't miss the joy in how she looks at the coffee shop, or the free way she moves. Alé smiles at her new prosthetic, seeming to note how easily she's getting around. There's a visible weight off my mate's shoulders. She hasn't looked this happy since I first showed her our backyard cottage.

Now, she smiles at Alé and me. "Thank you both." She steps closer and goes up on her tippytoes to brush her lips against my cheek. "You staying to watch?"

"Always," I whisper, closing my eyes to fully relish the feel of her mouth on my skin. "Always and forever, ma siréne."

CHAPTER EIGHTEEN
AMATHEIA

Is it possible to feel a lover's gaze on your body like actual hands? I swear the way Betmal stares at me has phantom fingers running over my skin. His eyes are slightly narrowed, pupils dilated as his nostrils flare. His chest rises and falls with quick, light breaths. He's a predator ready to take its prey.

That's me.

And I couldn't be happier about it, despite what's happening in the merkingdom. Away from it, it's easier to lose myself in how much I love downtown.

As excited as I am to paint today—and I've been dreaming of it for two days—I'm even more excited to get him home and touch him. Now that I've met Stefan and I know he's *also* not excited about our joining, I'm even more determined to figure out how to get out of it. Why should we suffer for our families' sake?

Sliding my hands down Betmal's chest, I turn and walk to my usual table. I clasp my hands together at the joy of seeing all my supplies set up and ready to go. Turning to Alé and Betmal, I smile. "Thank you both, again. This is wonderful."

Betmal returns my expression of joy and leans against the counter, crossing a foot over his ankle. I take a moment to admire him, really *admire* him. He's all masculine lines and focused intent.

But then something hits me in the head, and I topple to one side, suffocated by the sudden presence of a body wrapped around my face. Laughing, I right myself even as I sense a much larger presence, hands grasping for the tiny person who just attacked me.

"Ignatius Zion, what on earth?" Alo the gargoyle grabs his son around the waist as I try to peel Iggy off me. "We literally *just* talked about this!"

The gargoyle child laughs hysterically and wraps his tail around my head, the spade at the very tip slapping over one of my eyes. I can't hold back a laugh, but that seems to egg him on as he scratches at his father's hands and reaches for me.

"Just. Wanted. A. Hug!" he screeches loudly as Alo begins to look incredibly flustered.

Behind him, Betmal watches us with amusement evident on his face.

"Ignatius." Alo's stern tone brooks no argument.

Iggy goes limp as a noodle in his father's arms, allowing Alo to toss him up onto his shoulder, where Iggy perches with a dismayed-sounding growl. They both look at me, and I bark out a laugh at seeing the exact same expression on both of their faces.

"Hi, Iggy, Alo." I clear my throat to hold back ferocious laughter as Iggy crosses his arms, his tail lashing from side to side. He looks beyond irritated at being pulled off my head.

Alo glances at his son. "Ig, what have I said about this?"

Iggy rolls his eyes, dropping his hands by his sides and balling his fists. "That I can't just hug monsters without checking if it's okay, and that we have to be careful with Amatheia because of her bad leg."

I blanch, and Alo groans, slapping a hand over his face in apparent exasperation. He parts his fingers, looking at me from between them. "So sorry, Amatheia, that part was not for public consumption. I didn't mean to—"

"It's fine," I reassure him, lifting my leg to show them both the new one. "New leg, new me. It feels awesome, and it doesn't hurt anymore."

Iggy zooms off his father's shoulder and drops to the floor, rapping his knuckles on the long part of my new prosthetic. "Oh my gods, Dad, look! Her other leg was wood, but this one is different wood like metal, and"—he looks up at me—"does it get cold?"

Alo clears his throat and smiles down at his child. "Hey, Ig, why don't we stop touching Amatheia's leg, and sit down so she can paint us? That's our job today, remember?"

Iggy giggles and removes his hand. "Oops! Sorry, Amatheia! Dad literally just reminded me not to touch monsters, and I touched you."

I sit in my chair and pat my lap. "You can sit with me for a moment, if you like. I need to get my paints ready."

He hops closer to me, then flaps his wings and alights on my knee. Alo sits across from us, wincing as Iggy tries to steady himself, one foot gripping my leg.

"It's fine," I mouth, waving away his concern.

And it *is* fine. I feel amazing. The difference in my leg, even in my posture, is shocking. I walked the entire way to Higher Grounds, and I didn't have to think about every step. The freedom in that is unbelievable.

I grab a brush and put it sideways in my mouth.

Iggy grabs a bunch of my hair in his hand to steady himself, blue eyes flicking to the brush and then my hand as I grab the white paint. "What are you doing?"

I reach around him and take the brush from my mouth, sticking it in a jar of water Alé must have put there for me. "Just picking my brush. Now I need to outline your dad while he sits across from us. You can sit with me while I do that. But once I outline him, I want you to go sit on his shoulder and look very fierce. Can you do that for me?"

Iggy nods, grinning to reveal a gap where one of his front fangs should be.

I feign shock at his huge smile. "You been losing teeth, Iggy?"

He nods and hops up and down. "Yeah, and Auntie Wren taught me all about the tooth fairy, and it's so weird 'cause she comes into your house when you're asleep." He shudders. "I don't really like that because it makes me feel like I'm not a good guardian if I don't notice a fairy in my house. Buuuut, she brings me money every time I lose a tooth."

"Well," I say sagely, "if there was truly anything to worry about, your dad would notice, right?"

"Yeah." Iggy smiles over at his father. "He keeps us safe, so that's why I don't worry about fairies too much. Besides, we don't even have any fairies who live in Ever. Just pixies. And Miriam would definitely know if there were other pixies sneaking into our house."

Alo smiles softly, staring at his adorable son.

The next three hours pass in a blur. Alo and Iggy are my first appointment. When I'm nearly done with them, Herschel from Herschel's Fine Dining comes by. He sits elegantly, and his portrait goes by quickly. After that is Wren Hector, Ever's resident green witch. She brings a tiny plant and grows it right there at the table. For her portrait, I paint the vine wrapping around her arm. She's wearing her "Fat and Fabulous" tee, and I make sure to include that too. I love her wonderful shirts.

My last appointment is Catherine. She sits in the chair and smiles at me. "You're glowing, my friend."

I can't help the matching smile on my face. "I'm having the time of my life, Catherine, truly."

Gray eyes move across the room. To Betmal, I'd bet. He's

been drinking coffee and watching me this entire time, and I don't think anything could be more delicious than that.

Catherine smirks, and when I direct her to hold that look, she does, for the better part of forty minutes. Painting her comes easily, and by the time I'm putting the finishing touches on it, my brain goes sated and blissfully blank. Catherine rises from her chair, and Betmal joins her to look as I add a bit of white to her wispy, elegant waves.

"Marvelous," Catherine murmurs. "You have such talent, Amatheia. I'm so thrilled to see you putting it to good use. What a wonderful project to be part of." She turns to Betmal. "Thank you for asking me to join in, old friend."

He takes her hand and lifts it to his lips, placing a chaste kiss on the back. "Of course, darling. It wouldn't be an Ever welcome packet without you in it."

Catherine smiles at him and then me. "Well, once you're done with that portrait, I'd love to buy the actual painting from you to hang in the Annabelle. I think she'll love it. She's always nudging me to paint myself, but I've never felt inspired to. I could easily hang more of your work in the Inn, though."

"It's yours," I say, gesturing to Betmal. "As soon as he's done what he needs to do."

Movement behind Catherine draws my eye. Shades of pink and coral appear at her back. My mouth drops open as Catherine spins, revealing Thatraeia in human form, standing just behind her.

My cousin's coral eyes flick between Catherine, Betmal and me as she nips at her lip, playing with the hem of her shirt.

Betmal shifts from one foot to the other, bringing his body closer to mine. Catherine looks between us and says her goodbyes, leaving Betmal and me standing there, staring at Thatraeia in surprise.

He's across the room in a moment, his expression fiercely concerned. "What's wrong?"

"And wh—what are you doing here?" I can barely manage the words as her gaze moves to Betmal. Her lashes flutter against pink skin, and she drops her eyes before looking back up at me.

"Has Caralorn figured out where I went? I'm not due at any events until tomorrow."

She shakes her head. "No, nothing like that. Can we talk for a minute, Ama?"

Betmal brings his lips to my cheek, kissing me lightly. "I'll give you a moment, ma siréne, but I'm here if you need me." He nods at Thatraeia then stalks across Higher Grounds to his table, dropping into his seat and focusing on an open sketchbook.

Thatraeia watches him go, and once he seems oblivious to us, she looks at me. "Ama, I just…I had to see what you were doing that was so important that you'd really, *really* talk about leaving the lake. I heard you told Father you'd even disappear, if he wanted you to." She glances at the stack of paintings propped against the wall behind my table. "Is this it? Is this worth everything you're doing?"

I nod and wave at my new prosthetic. "It is. And this. Cousin, all of these things are part of me, part of the life I *want* for myself. I'm so happy when I'm here, and when I return to the merkingdom, the only good thing is you."

She blushes, her cheeks going scarlet as she eyes my paintings. "Would you show me, Ama? I want to understand. I always sort of thought you were joking about leaving, but lately you seem so determined, and I just…I *don't* understand. I want to, though. I'd like to know more about this world."

Love for my baby cousin wells hard in my chest, and I pull her into my arms, squeezing her tight. "Thank you for coming here," I whisper into her ear. "It means the world to me."

She sniffles, wrapping her arms around my neck. "Love you too, Ama. Now show me what you've been working on before I get overwhelmed and start crying. I'm already nervous to be up here."

Laughing, I pull away from her but grab her hand and drag her to the first painting. We go through them all, and I tell her stories about every monster. Who they are to Ever and why they were chosen for portraits for the welcome book. She's particularly fascinated by Wren and the vine wrapping around the human witch's forearm.

Thatraeia slips her hand into mine, twining our fingers together as she looks up at me with a thoughtful smile. "Your work is beautiful, Ama. I never realized…"

Betmal appears by my side, and Thatraeia jolts a little, squeezing my hand tightly.

"Apologies, darling," he croons, smiling at my cousin before looking at me. "Ama, what do you think about inviting your cousin to dinner with us this evening? I put a coq au vin in the oven before I left, and there will be plenty of food."

I look at him, and in that moment, I know I've fallen in love. Nobody's ever had my back like Betmal does, and despite our earlier tease about what tonight could be, he sees how important this is, winning Thatraeia over.

Pulling her close, I give her a reassuring look. "How about it, Cousin? We'd love for you to join us."

She nips at the edge of her thumb. "Well, I don't know. I need to get back to—"

"The Sea Julienne will be there in a few hours." I tickle her side. "Come on. The art is just a part of why I love being up here." I look at Betmal, emotion welling inside me. "But he's the rest."

Betmal's smile is blindingly gorgeous. He turns that radiance on Thatraeia. "Not to mention, sweet girl, we were planning to discuss how to handle your father. I would love to include you in that, if you like."

Thatraeia's expression morphs into something a teeny bit

devilish, the corners of her mouth turning up. I can almost see the fullness of her personality, no matter how much Caralorn has tried to crush it over the years.

"Deal," she says, the smile growing bigger. "I don't know how you're going to pull off a miracle, but I'd like to know."

Betmal grabs her hand and mine. "Excellent. Let's go, my sweets. I'll feed you, and then we will scheme."

"I love it," I murmur, brushing my cheek against his.

And I love you. The words are on the tip of my tongue.

CHAPTER NINETEEN
BETMAL

I'm desperate to respond to Ama's comment and tell her I love her. That from the moment I realized who she was to me, I've been hers. But when I'm clutching her cousin's hand is not the right time.

Thatraeia looks up at me inquisitively, ears twitching at the tips just like Amatheia's do when she's interested in something. Her being here is huge for my mate, because it's the first time she's been even remotely supportive of the time Ama spends up here.

With me.

Thatraeia rubs at the back of her elbow, glancing toward her cousin as she drops my hand. "Malakat will wonder where we are if I don't come home soon, so I won't stay too terribly long."

Alé joins us, smiling at the females. "I'll keep an eye on your paintings while they dry. Once I can move them, I'll store them upstairs so they don't get jostled or knocked into."

"Thanks." Amatheia looks over at me. "Shall we go home?"

I smile. "Of course, darling. Would you like to walk? If not, I'll grab the car."

She laughs. "Walk, for sure. I love walking now."

Thatraeia glances at Ama's leg and gasps. "Goddess, I didn't notice at first. Ama, your leg! It's new, right?"

Amatheia smiles and bends down, knocking at the new prosthetic. "I refused one for so long because of the guilt, but he convinced me to do this and it's been amazing—the pain is gone. It's *so freeing,* Cousin." She looks over at me. "And he did that."

Thatraeia takes Ama's hand and brings it to her heart. "I'm worried about all of this working out, but I'm happy for you, Ama. I never wanted that pain for you. You don't deserve it. You're the best person in the entire world."

"Agreed," I tack on. "Shall we go?"

When I reach the door, I open it for the girls. My love holds her cousin's hand as they walk through together, but the smile she directs at me lights me up from the inside out.

Our walk home is quiet but peaceful. Ama gives Thatraeia a verbal tour of the Annabelle Inn and the Community Garden. We pass those landmarks and walk in companionable silence along Sycamore Street until we reach our driveway.

Ama grabs her cousin's shoulders and spins her to face the house. "This is Betmal's place. It's beautiful, Cousin. I can't wait to show you."

Thatraeia gasps and starts forward, walking along the crushed shell driveway as the cottage swings her front doors open wide. As the younger mermaid walks away from us, I come behind Amatheia and slide my arm around her waist, slipping my fingers into the top of her skirt. I press myself against the crack of her ass, bringing my lips to her ear.

"There's a surprise for you in the backyard, darling. The house and I have been working on a little something for the last two days. Morgan and Abe came over last night to help me put the finishing touches on it. I had grand plans of unveiling it to you in a very sensual way, but I think, perhaps, you two should discover it together."

Ama grinds her ass against me, covering my hand with both of hers. She looks up and back at me. "I promise we'll find time alone tonight. We need it, don't you think?"

Smiling, I press my lips to hers. "I do," I breathe into her mouth.

She grabs my hand and pulls me forward as we follow Thatraeia toward the house.

The girls bound toward the back, giggling over something. I smile as Ama drags her cousin through the back door. "Come, Thatraeia. You absolutely must see the cottage where I've been painting this whole time. Well, except for today."

I planned to give them space, but I want to see my woman's reaction when she sees the project that's occupied most of the last two days.

A gasp is the first sign she's seen it.

Ama stops dead in her tracks, still holding her cousin's hand. In front of the women, there's now a glittering pond with a smooth rock shore reminiscent of their lake. Large boulders surround it on one side, and I cut the branches off the trees to let light in to shine directly on that spot. The small body of water takes up nearly all of the space between the back of the house and the workshop.

Amatheia turns from side to side, then steps forward and dips her toes into the first few inches of the lake. She spins to face me, eyes wide and mouth dropped open.

"Is this heated? You…made a heated lake in your backyard?"

Thatraeia is silent, looking between us as I nod.

"Yes, ma siréne. When you are not in *the* lake, I still want you to be able to be in your merfolk form if you wish. This is a spot for you to relax, to—"

She silences me by dashing across the scant space between us and throwing herself into my arms. Pressing her lips to mine, she kisses me nearly senseless. When we part, it's a struggle to remind myself that we have an audience.

I card the fingers of one hand through her hair, holding her close as she wraps long legs around my waist. A tear slides down her cheek. "It's perfect, Betmal, absolutely perfect. I can't believe you did this for me. You're amazing."

"I would do anything for you," I remind her. "Anything at all, my darling."

If her cousin was not standing just to the side, this would be the perfect time to carry my woman to the closest rock, lay her down on it and start teaching her about all the things we've only begun to hint at.

Patience, Betmal, I tell myself. Later tonight, once Thatraeia is gone and our plan is finalized, I'll have that chance.

I set Ama down, resisting the urge to run both hands over the lush curves of her hips and thighs.

Thatraeia joins us, wrapping her arms protectively around her torso. "This is, ermm, really cool. I've never seen something like this, but it looks like a lot of fun."

I smile. "You called me dangerous once, dear girl, and you were right. I can be. But I can also be quite romantic when the occasion calls for it."

She laughs a little, nervously, coral eyes moving back to the small lake. "I can see that. I just…when Father or Malakat find out about this, all depths will break loose."

The formerly happy moment grows tense, Ama freezing in my arms as she tucks her hair nervously behind one long ear. "We know," she whispers. "Part of tonight was us figuring out a plan."

I hold back the growl that threatens to rumble from my throat. Caralorn will be a problem indeed.

Slipping an arm around my mate's waist, I focus on her cousin. "It continues to amaze me how everyone seems to think they have a say at all in what Amatheia does with her life. Now that she has me in her corner, know this—I will fight tooth and nail for her to decide how she wants to live every moment of every day."

Thatraeia blanches. "It's just that Father *will* fight this."

"Let him fight, then," I manage. "I welcome it. I'd like to try talking with him first, but when he is not amenable to this," I gesture between Ama and me, "I will become physical if I have to."

"It won't come to that," Amatheia says quietly, looking between us as she straightens tall. "I've already decided I'm simply telling him I'm leaving the lake." She looks at me. "If you're truly fine with me coming here, I will, but I'd be happy to go to the Annabelle if—"

"Here," I demand. "Absolutely here unless you don't feel comfortable, ma siréne. And when you go to tell Caralorn, I'll be coming with you. I've quietly prepared Haven leadership, and they are ready to back us and protect downtown if Caralorn brings the fight up here."

Thatraeia gasps. "Depths, is this really happening? I've always dreamed of leaving with Ama, but now the net is closing around us, and this is terrifying." She throws a trembling hand over her mouth, glancing between us as she shifts from one foot to the other.

"Come with us," I offer. "You're welcome here or at the Annabelle Inn, if you want to leave." When she shoots me an incredulous look, I nod. "You're Amatheia's cousin; my duty is just as much to care for you as it is her. We can keep you safe, my sweet, I promise."

"But…why?" Her voice is small as she wraps her arms more tightly around her upper body again. I'm sensing it's a nervous habit and I hate that she feels the need to do so.

I hold back for just a moment, not sure how much Amatheia's ready to reveal.

She pulls her cousin in close for a hug. "He's my mate,

Thatraeia. I won't allow Malakat or Caralorn or even Stefan to keep us apart. Not when I've been compliant and complacent for so long. It's my time. I get to pick myself, finally, and I would encourage you to do the same. This won't be easy, but it *will* be worth it."

Thatraeia looks up at me from Ama's embrace, and I sense we've broken through her fear to some degree. "What would you recommend I do?"

I smile at the lovely mermaid. "Let's have dinner, shall we?" I wave at the house, who opens and shuts all the kitchen windows in rapid succession to call us inside. "We'll talk through some details about our plan and go from there."

The girls follow me back inside. Ama directs her cousin to the dining room table, then comes to help me in the kitchen.

Dinner is a quiet affair, Thatraeia more silent than I'd like, despite Amatheia's urging that she ask questions or share her thoughts. We do manage to get through some detail about how to proceed with Caralorn, but it's clear Thatraeia is as uncomfortable as she is tentatively excited.

Eventually, the younger female grows agitated, looking at her comm watch and biting at her lip.

"Darling, I can drive you back to the lake, if you like." I gesture toward the front of the house.

Thatraeia looks from me to Amatheia. "Are you coming home too? Or not?"

Amatheia shakes her head, and I expect her to seem anxious, but all I read from her is confident peacefulness.

"No, Cousin, I'm not coming home tonight. Tonight is about Betmal and me. But tomorrow, we'll come back and talk to your father. That's the plan."

"It's going to be fine," I reassure the timid mermaid.

It takes us all of a quarter hour to return Thatraeia to the lake. Amatheia walks her cousin up the path, disappearing into the forest. They're gone for a short time, and I wait patiently, knowing she's coming back to me. That this day has been long and gone a little sideways.

Tomorrow probably won't be any better.

But once we get home... Gods above and below, once we get home, she is *mine*.

CHAPTER TWENTY
AMATHEIA

Tomorrow's going to be a shitshow. But the benefit of being out of the lake is that I can compartmentalize my worry, to a degree. Tomorrow, I can agonize over a plan. Nobody's going to miss me tonight—I'm supposed to be working in the Sea Julienne fields and then preparing for yet another dinner in the evening. Unless Stefan shows up at my suite again and finds me gone—and cares enough to do something about it—I'm confident it'll be okay.

Tonight is all about Betmal.

He's silent on the car ride home, but tension simmers between us, my body wound tight like a string waiting to be plucked. He rests a hand on my knee, stroking light circles on the inside of it but focused on the road ahead. That wayward bit of blond hair waves in the breeze, making him look so carefree.

But I know better.

Because there's a tense set to his jaw, a hardness to the way he's focused on the road ahead. He's a predator waiting for his moment, and the closer we get to the house, the more desperate I become. By the time he pulls down the driveway and parks under the carport, my breath comes in short, rapid pants. I can't pull air into my lungs fast enough.

This is it.

Betmal slips the car in park and hops out. After rounding the front, he opens my door, offering me his hand. I take it, allowing him to pull me up out of the car. The minute I'm upright, he lunges forward and grabs me by the throat. He spins and lifts me onto the hood of the car, planting himself between my thighs. He yanks me to the edge of the hard, warm surface and growls into my lips.

"Mine."

He closes his lips over mine and sucks at my tongue with soft, teasing passes, hinting at what it might feel like elsewhere—lower, much lower, in that place that throbs in anticipation of him.

The next slant of his mouth over mine is rougher, needier. Giant black shadow wings flare out behind him, cloaking us in darkness as he kisses my mouth, my chin, my jawline, kisses turning to nips and then hard bites that have me crying out for more.

He pauses, wiping his mouth with the back of his hand, and takes a step back. Where his eyes are normally red, they're completely white now. I read about this in the later chapters of the book from the Historical Society. The second eyelid protects vampires from their prey, but it's also a sign his emotions are high.

That he's losing control.

That he's ready to strike.

I'm inexperienced, but I know I want this. I want all of it, whatever he's holding back right now with that ridiculous amount of control he possesses.

Sliding back on the hood, I step my feet out just enough to tease him with the view beneath my very, very short skirt. Fully white eyes drop to the juncture of my thighs, and he lets out a ragged growl that has me soaking the car hood with need.

I rub my knees together, and the move rubs my clit against my pussy lips, sending heat rushing through me as Betmal watches in silence.

He rolls his shirt sleeves up slowly, eyes never leaving my pussy. "We have been the slowest of burns, ma siréne." Pure white eyes flick up and lock onto mine. "Are you ready to catch fire?"

I spread my thighs wider, showing him just how ready I am. "See for yourself," I whisper. "I was ready ages ago, Betmal. I've missed you."

He steps forward. "I haven't eaten what I want to eat, Ama. On your knees, cheek flat against the car hood. Do it now."

Commands? Oh depths, yessssss! I'm certain I can get on board with that.

I flip quickly over, ass up in the air and my cheek on the hood as directed. Cool hands come to my hips and pull them backward. I know what's coming next, but I'm still not ready for the warm swipe of Betmal's tongue from my clit all the way to my ass. Scorching heat follows in its wake. And when he slides it back down my slit to swirl a soft circle over that most sensitive spot, I cry out and scramble to grab something, anything to tether me back to earth.

There's nobody around for miles, no one to see this lascivious thing we're doing right out in the open.

Betmal runs a hand up the back of my thigh, gripping my ass and spreading me wide to spear his tongue inside, curling it and sucking at the same time. He probes with leisurely, rhythmic thrusts as I pant and claw at the hood of the car. Soft growls vibrate against my skin, dragging pleasure from me as tension builds between my thighs. They tremble as I rock back to meet him. I need more of him, thicker, deeper, touching that spot inside me that aches for his attention. The tiny cilia that line my channel grab his tongue, trying to pull him deeper.

"I need more," I manage with a gasp. "I want to see youuu-uu..." the word ends in a howl as he slips long fingers into my pussy and curls them, stroking until I see stars. He rubs and licks until I can't see, can't hear, and there's nothing at all but the sensations he pulls so easily from my poor, overwhelmed body.

I barely notice him grabbing me and flipping me carefully onto my back. Not until he snarls and attacks my clit with fervor, sucking rhythmically as one hand presses flat on my stomach, holding me against the warm car hood.

My thighs tremble as I try desperately to clamp them around his head. But I can't move; I can't do anything but allow pleasure to build and rush through me as Betmal eats me out with practiced ease.

Sudden jealousy spears through me, knowing he's done this before. That somewhere, sometime in his very long past, others benefitted from his sensual nature.

When I let out a warning growl, he stands and licks his lips, staring at me with a heated look. "Now, now, ma siréne, why the frustrated sounds? Do you need to come more quickly? Or is it something else?"

I sit up and grab the lapels of his shirt, yanking them until the fabric tears. After ripping it over his shoulders, I shove it down until I can toss the torn clothing away. Shifting up onto both knees, I pull my shirt over my head and throw it with his. Then I press our upper bodies together and growl as I inch closer to him, so close we're breathing the same air.

Reaching down, I rub at the hard cock straining the front of his pants. "This is mine," I say simply. "Never again will it belong to anyone else."

He cants his head to the side, running both hands up my

front to pinch softly at my nipples. "Only yours," he promises me. "Yours to touch, to taste, to tease. Yours to do whatever the *fuck* you want with, Ama. So, pretty girl," he smirks at me, "what will you do with it, hmm?"

CHAPTER TWENTY-ONE
BETMAL

Amatheia slides into my arms, winding hers around my neck as she brushes her lips against mine. "Take me to bed, mate." Her expression goes tentative. "I haven't done this but I'm *so* ready to."

Groaning, I take her mouth, my kiss desperate as I turn toward the house. The cottage swings the side entry door open and I stalk toward my bedroom. Inside, I pace to the bed and toss my mate in.

I had planned to introduce her to my bedroom through a very sexy tour, but we're too lost to the heat. She doesn't even look around, just rises from the bed like a fucking queen and points me toward it.

I'd prepped the room with the curtains drawn and candles on the side tables. It's darkly sumptuous but she's past the point of noticing those small details.

"Sit."

I spin to face her, unable to hold back a smile.

She pushes me toward the bed with a little laugh, but I hold my ground, hauling her against me as I run both hands over the firm globes of her perfect ass.

"You called me *mate*."

One dark brow lifts, her self-satisfied smile matching mine. "And so?"

I slide a hand up between her breasts, curling my fingers around her throat.

"And so, it's an admission, ma siréne, that you know I'm right. We belong together; we have *always* belonged together."

"Yes," she whispers, her lips curling back to reveal her tiny upper fangs. "And I want to taste what belongs to me, Betmal."

That *confidence* is such an aphrodisiac, and I want to blow oxygen into the flames of that fire.

"It turns me on when you talk to me like that," I murmur. "Keep going, my sweet." Reaching down, I slide her skirt off her hips, pushing it toward the ground so she stands before me in all her glorious nudity. Tiny scales run down her sides, accentuating the lines of her abdominal muscles. The same scale pattern runs up the sides of her thighs and around dark aqua nipples, pebbled in anticipation of me.

Tossing my ripped shirt aside, I stare at her. But she's staring back, eyes eating me up as they move over my chest and shoulders, down my stomach to my waist.

Chuckling, I unbutton my slacks and let them fall. My cock bobs hard against my thigh, dripping seed from our earlier play on the car hood.

"Touch me," I command. "Ma siréne, I need to feel your hands on me. Tell me what you're thinking."

"So swollen," she whispers, reaching out to gather the seed from my slit. "Will you always be like this for me? Does it ache, Betmal?"

As she drags her finger over the opening, I groan, and my cock kicks into her touch. She brings her cum-soaked finger to her mouth, slipping it between her lips. As she hollows her cheeks around the digit and sucks, I forget to breathe. I forget everything but instinctive bloodlust that demands I sate the need clawing at me.

"Ama," I growl out. "Yes, I will. And yes, it does."

She smiles and jerks her head toward the bed behind us. "Lie down, Betmal."

I hadn't expected dominance from her, not this first time. Still, I drop dutifully to the edge and spread my thighs wide.

Ama goes to her knees, but I don't love that. I'm worried it might bother her. So I grab her around the core and haul her on top of me, flipping us both into the middle of the bed. She makes a displeased little sound as I manhandle and turn her, so she's facing my cock and I have the most perfect view of the treasure between her thighs.

"Better." I run a hand up the back of one toned leg, gripping her ass as I spread her wide. Her pussy's smooth, the tiny pebble of her clit nestled at the top. I run my fingers along the seams of her channel, marveling at the tiny cilia that line the inside. They stretch toward my fingertips as I rub my way along her slick opening. I can't wait to feel them on other parts of me.

She lurches off me, crouching down near my cock to hover her mouth just above it, shooting me a saucy look.

Right back where she started.

Gods, that view. Those *lips*.

"Teach me what you like," she whispers, her expression the slightest bit tentative. "I haven't done this before."

That shouldn't please me so deeply. A female's first time isn't a war to win, it's not a *thing* to conquer, it is not something to *possess*.

Yet knowing I'll be her first turns me on in a way that has me sliding a hand into her hair and wrapping it tightly around my fist. "Explore me, ma siréne," I whisper. "With your lips and teeth. I am a great lover of your darling little fangs."

She looks confused, dark brows furrowing in the middle. "That won't hurt?"

"Oh, yes," I say with a laugh. "It'll be the most beautiful of pains. And for a vampire male, pain is often pleasure."

She moves lower, low enough for her lips to brush my sopping cock head. "I don't think I'd like pain, but I guess I don't really know."

"We can play with that another time." I roll my hips, pushing my spongy tip against her teeth, begging for entry into that wet heat. The slightest hint of her mouth has me dripping all over her.

Ama's pupils widen, overtaking her dark irises as she opens wide. Leaning forward, she places a sucking kiss on my skin. I jolt and hiss at shards of pleasure that streak up my length and fan out from my core. Her scent explodes in the room, her heart rate kicking into overdrive.

This is turning her on. She bends lower and licks a stripe up the underside of my cock. I tighten my fingers in her hair.

"Ma siréne, that tongue is *magnificent*. More of that."

She licks in big long strokes, two, three, then four times as I resist the urge to guide her down deep. I want to hit the back of her throat and keep going, to feel myself fully enveloped inside her. I want her to suck on me, to wrap that cool tongue around my dick and pull.

But the tease of her licking is the most perfect edging. She bends lower and laps at my sack, making a wet, sticky exploration of first one ball, then the other.

"Suck on them," I direct, opening my thighs wider to give her access.

Warm lips close around my sack, sucking softly as her tongue swirls, featherlight, over my sensitive, puckered skin. I groan as I watch her move from one to the other, eyes closed as she explores me. She takes her time, teasing me until I pant, my mouth dropping open as I all but beg her to rise and pay attention to the rest of my cock.

Her scent saturates the room, drowning me in need as she

presses sloppy kisses up the side of my dick. When she reaches the crown, she closes her mouth around it and locks her eyes with mine. Hollowing her cheeks, she sucks hard, and my body jerks in response to the pressure.

I arch my back to avoid fucking her throat and traumatizing her. Releasing my hold on her hair, I grip the sheets and force myself to breathe. But she fucking does it again, sucking on just the tip, soft tongue swirling around it. Oral has never felt this good, this all-consuming.

Because it was never her.

I'm going to explode in half a second if she keeps going.

She wraps her lips around me and leans down, taking me far enough to hit the back of her throat. Reaching down, I tuck her hair to one side so I can view every moment. She pulls back and repeats the move. When my tip hits a stopping point, she chokes and backs off me with a concerned look.

"Breathe through your nose, darling," I offer, grabbing my cock and rubbing the tip over her swollen lower lip. "Deep throating is an art and it takes practice."

She bends over me again, nostrils flaring as she takes me to the back of her mouth and then, there! An inch further, and a second inch after that. My eyes roll into my head as I clench my thighs, desperate to hold back an impending orgasm that threatens to obliterate my sanity.

"Stop," I whisper. "Ama, stop."

She pops off me and scratches at my thighs. "Oh gods, did I do it wrong? Are you okay?"

Huffing out a laugh, I pull her on top of me then flip us so she's beneath me.

"Wrong? No, ma siréne. Too terribly right. I was moments from coming and we cannot have that, not this first time. Your pleasure is first, my sweet, every time."

Her eyes are wide as she scans my face, nipping at her lower lip.

I smile down at her. "What?"

She drags the fingertips of one hand up my forearm and over my biceps, along my shoulder to the ziol hanging between us.

"Do you think we'll ever come together? I've heard that can happen, but…well, I don't know what I don't know."

Oh, ma siréne, I think to myself.

"We will sometimes," I say. "And sometimes we won't. And the orgasm isn't necessarily the destination, my sweet. The journey is most of the fun and coming is the cherry on top, so to speak."

Dark brows scrunch together. "Your goal isn't to come?"

I shake my head. "Non, ma siréne. The goal is to have fun, to enjoy every moment. Coming is simply one way to do that. So as we play, don't focus on achieving that, don't chase it. Just enjoy each moment."

She glances down at my cock where it rests along her thigh, then looks up at me.

"Are you finally going to give me that today? You've been teasing me for a long time, Betmal."

I notch my hips against her channel and stroke my cockhead along her opening. The tiny cilia reach for me, suctioning onto the very tip of my cock and pulling softly. I grunt and angle back.

She shifts onto her elbows. "Perhaps an anatomy lesson, ma vampíre? You look…unsure."

Laughing, I roll us again so she's on top.

"Non, darling. I know what treasure awaits me." Nestling her spread around me, I guide her hips along my length, my cock dragging through her pussy lips. With each pass, her cilia suction onto me, popping off as she rocks her hips. It's like thousands of tiny mouths sucking and letting go and it takes every ounce of my considerable restraint not to fill her in one fell swoop.

But no, her pleasure is the goal. Mine will happen when hers does.

Ama rests her hands on my chest, over my ziol as I guide her forward and back over my length. Soft pants morph into slightly louder cries until every pass of her pussy over my cock soaks me with honey.

She gives me a desperate look. "I want more than this, Betmal. Can we go into the lake? I want to feel you inside me. I want you there, please?"

Heat consumes me from the inside out until I'm nothing but need and desire and want. Shifting forward, I spread my wings and pull her into my arms. I stalk across the room as the house opens the double doors leading into the backyard. Grabbing a bottle of lube from a nearby table, I cup it in one hand, then jump out of the window. I don't stop until we hit water.

Ama shifts the moment a toe touches the pond. She grows heavier in my arms as her legs morph into a tail, splashing the long, gorgeous limb as she wriggles against me.

I push us through the water until we can rest halfway on her rock. She's on her back, arms above her head as she arches and stretches like a cat, a half smile on her turquoise lips.

"Better, ma siréne?" I dip and capture a nipple between my lips, pulling it taut.

She clears her throat. "I'm a little nervous."

"We'll go as fast or slow as you like," I say, reaching down to slide two fingers along either side of her opening, shifting the scales to access her channel.

Dark lashes flutter against her cheeks as she lets out a soft moan that has my balls tightening.

"It is my job to banish those nerves, ma siréne." I stroke slightly inside, her tiny cilia prodding and sucking at my fingers in rhythmic waves. "Think about the pleasure, my sweet."

"I...oh goddess. Stop, give me a second. *Fuck*, that feels good."

But I don't stop, because I want her bliss. As I move my fingers rhythmically inside, her mouth drops open and her head falls back. All the signs of impending bliss are there and watching her build to ecstasy has me ready to strike and unleash her.

Removing my fingers, I rest on my knees and uncap the bottle of lube. I drip it onto my length, running it over the veined thickness, taking extra care to fully coat my cockhead.

Ama watches, eyes hooded as she nibbles at her lower lip.

Reaching down, I nestle the tip of my cock against her slit and press. Immediately, the cilia latch onto me and try to pull me inside, and she jolts, stiffening. When she clutches at the rock surface, I grab my cock and rub it along her slit, barely teasing myself inside her.

She relaxes, and I feed another inch into her, rolling my hips in a slow rhythm until she's rocking hers to meet me. Her pussy grips me like a glove, trying to get more of me, all of me.

"Slowly, ma siréne," I tease as heat flares along my neck, cum pooling in my balls.

She shifts onto her elbows and watches as I fill her slightly fuller, thrusting until nearly half my length is buried inside.

"Betmal." She's breathless, mouth open and brows furrowed. "You feel incredible. But please."

Gods, the way she says that makes me think I could go faster, perhaps a little rougher.

Rolling my hips again, I push deeper, her pussy clamping around my cock and pulling. I bark out a curse and halt, because if I slam home, it might hurt her.

"Mooooore," she moans, thrusting up.

Her channel clenches around me and pulls hard, and it's everything I can do not to unleash. The way her pussy kisses my cock, those thousands of tiny suctioned tips, it's more than I can take.

"I said slowly," I remind her when she claws at my forearms.

She lifts up and bares tiny fangs at me, pupils blown wide as her nostrils flare.

"No, Betmal. Give me more."

When she reaches up and fists my ziol around her tiny hand, twisting it until she clutches the metal cross, I lose control.

Pistoning my hips, I slide deeper, deeper, deeper until I'm fully seated inside her.

Ama gasps and arches her back, dragging me forward by the ziol's long chain.

Her pussy clamps and clutches and sucks at me as the tiny tendrils begin attaching themselves to my sack, pulling more of me inside her.

I sputter out something unintelligible as Ama grunts in my arms and then wails, clawing at the rock beneath her.

"Oh gods*damn*," I roar hoarsely. My muscles lock up tight as her pussy squeezes and strokes until I'm seeing stars. I thought this first time I'd teach her, but her body is *taking* what it wants from me. I'm a passenger to her pleasure.

"More," she growls, looking up at me, her eyes glittering with need. "I need more, Betmal. Fill me again."

Pulling out of her, I moan at how good it feels for all those tiny suction points to pop off my skin. Growling, I slam home and she screams, back arching as she presses her breasts up toward my eager mouth.

I bend down and plunge inside her again as I close my lips over one dark, peaked nipple, sucking until it forms a hard point.

Her channel drags and pulls at my sack, pulsing until I'm a blubbering mess of precum. It roils inside me as her pussy milks my cock and balls. She brings her forehead to mine. "Bite me. Please. I need to know what it's like."

I strike before I make a fool of myself and come without her. Bliss erupts like a volcano inside me as pleasure overtakes us simultaneously. She writhes in my arms, her channel locking tight so I can't even move. Her pussy is a thousand pinpoints of pleasure. Screaming into the bite, I soak the tiny punctures with my venom.

Ama wails and claws at my back as I fill her with seed, cock kicking deep inside her as she pleasures every thick inch of me.

I lose all sense of space and time. There is nothing but the taste of her blood—rich and depthless and crisp. And below that, a lingering, niggling *knowing* curls around the edges of our bliss.

Our bond, beginning to form. I can't fully bond her without a conversation, but I can *feel* it already, that sense of her. My mate. My Ama.

Ecstasy recedes as slow as the tide, washing away until I'm left a dried-out husk, Ama trembling in my arms as I pull carefully out of her.

She looks up at me with eyes full of heat and wonder. "That was…indescribable, Betmal." She bats her lashes, the moment drawing long as she nibbles the edge of her lower lip. "Can we do it again?"

I growl and swim us toward the shallow end of the lake where I can get on top and take command.

"Yes, ma siréne," I murmur. "Always."

∼

The following morning, I stand at the kitchen's long, low bookcase, staring at my mate as she splashes in the water behind the house. The workshop waves its doors at her, asking for her to come work. With a laugh, she springs from the water onto a rock and grabs her new prosthetic.

I watch with joy in my heart as she attaches it and stands, naked, to walk around the lake and toward the workshop. She disappears inside, and I let out a contented sigh.

This is what life is about. This easy bliss.

Thinking of bliss reminds me that my mate is naked in the workshop right now, and if I head over there, I might be able to knock out a few more bedroom lessons before she gets deep into painting mode.

Just as I reach down to adjust my aching cock, the house shimmies around me.

Twitching an ear, I listen.

Rapid footsteps echo from the driveway.

Stalking toward the front door, I focus.

Heavy breathing, soft pants. A woman.

I step out the front doors just as Thatraeia rounds the bend in the driveway and halts. When she sees me, she takes off running again, heading toward me as if a hells' worth of devils nip at her heels.

I'm down the stairs in a flash, meeting her halfway up the driveway. She slides to a stop in front of me, and I grip her upper arms, scanning her face.

Peachy-pink eyes are wide, her ears twitching as her heart races in her chest.

"F-father," she blurts out, "he knows. *Somehow,* he knows about you and Ama. The King's Guard is coming for her. You don't have much time."

Straightening, I lift my chin. "We won't run from them, darling. We planned to visit him today anyhow, so this timing is fine."

"Excellent idea, *Vampire.*"

A deeper, deadly voice echoes up the driveway as a second mer female comes into view. She looks so much like Ama and Thatraeia, but she's taller, more muscular, her skin a pale green while her hair is the color of a glittering emerald.

Inky leather crisscrosses her naked chest, a black miniskirt the only thing covering any of her. In one hand, she holds a tall spear with a pointed blade at the end.

Thatraeia gasps and steps behind me, holding on to the back of my shirt. Her hands quiver against my skin. "Malakat," she whispers. "My sister. She's head of the King's Guard."

I slide my hands into my pockets, shooting the sister a wicked, confident smile as the other woman stalks like a predator toward us.

She stops ten feet in front of me, gripping the spear loosely with a practiced hand. Eyes the color of pine needles drop down my body and back up, her gaze casual and dismissive. She waves at my body with her free hand.

"So you're the vampire my cousin keeps sneaking up here to see." She shrugs, picking at her teeth. "Somehow, I thought there'd be more to you. Stefan could take you in a moment and, goddess, how I'd love to see him remove your head."

Gods, I love the way monsters posture when they *think* they have the upper hand in a situation.

I don't respond to her comment, instead jerking my head toward the house. "Ama's out back, enjoying the lake I built for her. We'd planned to visit Caralorn after breakfast. Would you like to come in? Now seems like a good time for us to chat, all together."

Malakat looks around me toward the house, eyes flicking from side to side.

I sigh. "There is no danger here, mermaid, apart from what you bring yourself."

She chuckles, low and deadly. "Lead the way, bloodsucker."

Laughing, I turn and pull Thatraeia's slim hand through my arm, settling it at my elbow. Glancing down at her, I wink. "This is going to be fine, my sweet, don't worry."

"She *should* worry," Malakat hisses from behind us. "When Father finds out she helped Am—"

"No one helped anyone except for me," I cast over my shoulder, guiding Thatraeia up the steps and through the front door. I let her go, waving her toward the kitchen as I spin to face

Malakat. Off in the distance behind her, other guards come into view, surrounding the house from the front. I almost laugh, but I suspect that will just inflame the already furious-looking mermaid.

"There's no need to bring your guard here," I state simply. "We can talk like adults."

"Right," she says with a sneer. "Because Amatheia did so much talking when she decided to leave her responsibilities behind to—what was it you said she was doing?" She makes air quotes. "Swimming in your backyard lake?"

I'd love to snatch the smirk off her face, but instead I smile. Sometimes, it's the best weapon there is.

"Come on through, then." I spin on my heel and stalk down the hall toward the kitchen. Thatraeia must have already gone out back, because the kitchen is empty.

The house opens the back doors wide, and as I exit with Malakat behind me, I find Ama with Thatraeia behind her, glaring as we appear in the doorway.

"What are you doing here?" she snarls at her cousin, tightening her arm around Thatraeia.

Malakat veers widely around me, moving her spear to the arm closest to me. I could almost laugh at how predictable she is. She's been taught in the classic way as a warrior. I haven't had the occasion in many centuries to fight, but when I do, I fight dirty.

"Darling," I stare at my beautiful mate, "it seems your cousin and uncle have concerns about our relationship. I think we should pay the king a visit together. What do you think?"

Before she can respond, Malakat growls, "We don't need you, Vampire. I came to retrieve Amatheia, and that is all. There is an introduction ceremony tonight where she will be formally presented as Stefan's betrothed." She chokes out the last word like it's stuck in her throat.

I smile at the three women, although I know, like this, I look every bit the predator I can be. "Unfortunately, that doesn't work for Amatheia and me." I glance over at Malakat. "Her happiness means more to me than every ounce of gold in your glitter coffers. I will fight for her to keep it, although I'd like to avoid that, if possible. I've already mentioned we're happy to come address the king this morning."

Malakat's mouth drops open, but she quickly zips it shut at my mention of their lake hoard. It's merely a guess on my part, but merfolk are great collectors of shiny objects, rivaling dragons in their adoration of it.

Amatheia rounds the lake as the workshop clatters all the windows and doors, visibly distressed at what's transpiring in the backyard.

I turn to my mate and smile. "I can hold my breath for quite a while, darling. It'll be fine. This is good. We have a chance to clear the air, as it were. We knew this was coming, Ama. Let us deal with Caralorn once and for all." I narrow my eyes and give her a look. "This fits our plan, remember?"

Figures appear to the left and right of us—more of the King's Guard, if I had to guess.

I shoot Malakat a look. "Tell your guard to stand down. We'll go peacefully."

Malakat lifts her chin. "It's a good idea for you not to fight, bloodsucker. This backyard is pretty, and blood would really ruin the ambiance."

I reach for Amatheia once she's close enough to touch.

"I don't know, mermaid," I whisper, flashing my second eyelid over my eyes in warning. "Sometimes, a splash of blood is exactly what's needed."

CHAPTER TWENTY-TWO
AMATHEIA

This is a disaster. I thought I had another hour or two to gird my proverbial loins before we went to see Caralorn.

We walk down Sycamore Street toward the lake, Thatraeia stiff and silent to my left. She grips my hand so tightly, I can't feel the tips of my fingers. To my right, Betmal saunters as if he doesn't have a care in the world. He keeps one arm slung low around my waist, his fingers curled through the belt loops of my short skirt.

Malakat leads the King's Guard who walk in a stiff, awkward circle around us.

As we pass over Main Street, our group catches the attention of monsters frequenting the businesses at our crossroads. I see Morgan and Abemet sitting in front of Higher Grounds, two drinks on the table between them. Morgan's gray eyes flash to mine and widen in concern.

I want to sink into the ground and die of embarrassment.

Abemet rises from the table and walks toward us as we pass. "Father, need a little help?"

Betmal shakes his head. "Not unless I comm you, darling. Dinner soon?"

Abemet watches us go, eyes narrowed to slits as he observes the guard surrounding us. Whispers and hushed murmurings echo around us as my cheeks heat. I keep my head lifted high. I won't allow the King's Guard to get me down, no matter how mortified I am inside.

I can't fathom how this is going to go with Betmal joining us in the lake, but I have to trust that if he thinks it'll be fine, it'll be fine. This was his initial plan, after all.

But by the time we reach the lakeshore, I'm a bundle of nerves. Even if he *can* go without breathing for a long time, what if that's only a few minutes? What if Caralorn locks him up, and he drowns? What if—

"Ma siréne." He slides his fingers along my jawline and pulls me to face him. "This is good. One way or another, everything will be out in the open. I'll be by your side the entire time. This will go our way. You'll see."

"It's not my side I'm worried about." I cradle his hand with mine, rubbing my cheek against his palm. "This is a risk, Betmal, no matter how confident you may feel."

He gives me a surprised look even though his lips curve into a wicked smile. "You wound me, darling." He kicks off his shoes and strides into the lake, holding on to my hand. "Shall we?"

I notice he doesn't call me mate, and I wonder if it's because he thinks I don't want to tell my cousins or the guards.

But fuck this.

They aren't in charge of my life.

"After you, *mate*," I say loudly, clearly.

Malakat swings around from her position ahead of us, nostrils flared as the tips of her ears twitch in fury. She says nothing but schools her face back to neutral and spins, morphing into merfolk form and disappearing beneath the lake's surface.

Thatraeia follows her, along with the guards in front of us. Several still stand at our back as I come to Betmal's side and smile up at him.

"That was a nice touch," he whispers, pressing a kiss to my forehead. "Shall we go ruffle more fins, darling?"

"Let's," I say simply, pulling him farther into the water.

As the water reaches his thighs, he starts to breathe in deeply. Then, he smiles at me and dives gracefully into the water. Shocked anew at his confidence, I take my prosthetic off and set it on the beach before I dive after him, transitioning my legs into a tail.

Betmal waits below the surface for me, hovering in the water. I reach for him, holding his hand. He allows me to pull him along into the lake. I can't resist checking on him every few minutes, but he seems absolutely fine, focused on Malakat and the guard, barely visible ahead of us. Thatraeia glides cautiously by his side.

We swim quickly toward the lake's center, then down toward the city. Betmal's fine.

He's fine.

I keep telling myself that as we pass two hundred feet and most of the light emanates from the city itself.

It shocks me how I don't feel like I'm home despite the pretty pink castle off in the distance. I feel like I'm visiting a prison.

That sentiment settles in deep as we approach the city but bypass the main swimming lanes and head deep into the catacombs. They link to my uncle's chambers. I stress about the idea of Betmal swimming in closed spaces, but he doesn't slow as we enter the rounded stone gate and head into the depths of the castle's belly.

Ten minutes later, he still seems comfortable as we rise out of the catacombs and glide along empty shell-encrusted hallways toward Caralorn's personal meeting room.

That can be the only place they're taking us to. I thought he wanted to publicly humiliate me, but it seems a private humiliation is plenty to start with. In a way, that's good, because it means we don't have to fight in front of the entire clan.

Two King's Guards swim ahead and grab the big doors that separate Caralorn's private suite from the rest of the castle. We enter, and my blood runs cold at seeing my uncle seated on his suite throne, both muscular forearms resting on the chair as he looks at us with a completely neutral expression.

"Out, everyone," Mala commands, waving her spear toward the door.

Thatraeia whimpers as she glances between me and Malakat. "I want to stay with you," she whispers.

Betmal wraps an arm around both of us, his fingers resting lightly on my cousin's shoulder. She gives no sign she notices other than pressing closer to me and sucking in a deep gulp of water. The guards leave but Mala doesn't force Thatraeia to join them.

My eldest cousin bows deeply. "Father, Amatheia, as requested. Unfortunately, we—"

"Silence," Caralorn hisses without looking at her.

Although she says nothing, I notice how the fins along the back of Malakat's tail stiffen and stand in frustration.

"Uncle," I begin, swimming slightly forward. "I—"

"I said silence!" he roars, rising from his throne and balling both fists at his sides.

Malakat swims to her father's side and matches his furious glare.

Caralorn glances at the three of us, eyes narrowing on Betmal as he bares his fangs. "I don't know what possessed you to come down here. I ordered Malakat to retrieve Amatheia." He shoots Malakat a withering look. "It seems she was unable to complete even that simple task." Dark eyes move back to us.

"Whatever it is you think you've been doing with my charge, it stops right now."

Not niece, *charge*.

Because that's all I am to him—a burden, a responsibility.

Balling my fists, I glare back.

Betmal chuckles, the sound watery. "That doesn't work for Ama and me, Caralorn." He stands confidently as I marvel that he's able to speak underwater. Tiny air bubbles leave his nose and burble toward the ceiling. I'll question him about that later, assuming we make it out of here in one piece.

"He's my mate," I add. "He's my *mate*, Uncle, something I never could have expected, but it's true. I begged and pleaded with you to let me go, and this is why."

"He isn't," Caralorn growls. "I made *her* a promise, and I will not see you wed to a vampire."

Hearing him speak of his promise to my mother shreds my heart. She wouldn't have cared what Betmal was. She'd have *loved* him. I know that.

Betmal takes a step forward. "While you've been primarily concerned with how to crush Ama under the weight of your power and this so-called promise, I've been focused on loving her the way she deserves. I do that because she's mine, and I hers, and there is not a force in this world that can stop us, not you or the arcane laws you cling to like long dead fish bones."

Caralorn's nostrils flare, and he's across the room in a second, halting just before Betmal.

Betmal doesn't bother to move, smiling at my uncle as a chuckle leaves his throat. "I'm going to say this once and only once. What Amatheia wants, I will ensure she gets, up to and including freedom from you and this entire kingdom, if that is what she wishes. Do not come to my home again and threaten her or anyone else, or I can promise you will regret it."

Love for Betmal wells inside me. It could only ever have gone like this. It was always going to be a fight, and I think that's why I avoided this topic for so long, keeping Betmal hidden like a little secret. But he doesn't deserve that, and I don't either.

I float in front of my uncle, offering a half smile as I raise my hands. "Uncle, I don't want to be a reject from this kingdom. I want to come and go, to visit Thatraeia and see my people. I'd like to still spend time at the Sovereign Sip. I'd like to be of occasional service. But I cannot live here any longer. I want something different for my life. Can you understand that? You can be free of me."

Malakat sneaks slowly and quietly off the dais, spear pointed toward Betmal.

"You've got precisely three seconds to get out of my face, Caralorn," Betmal says quietly, bringing a hand up to examine his nails. Crimson eyes flick to my uncle. "If you do not back up and acquiesce to Ama's request that you stop ruling over her like a little lordling, I will *take* her freedom from you. And then I will stain this lake red with your blood and take her back home anyhow." His smile grows sinister, reminding me of the way he looked at his former mates in Arcadia. "Two seconds."

Malakat moves first, sluicing through the air toward us with her spear raised. Thatraeia shrieks and grabs my hand as I lurch toward her sister.

Everything happens in a blur as Betmal shoots through the water toward Malakat. He grabs the tip of her spear and yanks her to him, executes a flip and snatches her by the braids, hauling her against his chest.

Before I can warn him about the knife she keeps at her waist, pain lances down my spine. Caralorn drags me into his arms, sharp nails pressed to the front of my neck.

Thatraeia screams, and then everything goes still as Caralorn digs his claws into my flesh, the tips pricking through the sensitive skin beneath my chin.

Eyes wide, I stare at Betmal. I don't recognize the male I see.

He wears a bored expression as he grips both of Malakat's hands in one of his, his other around the front of her neck.

"Let go of my mate," he says evenly. "Or I will take her from you."

I scratch at Caralorn's hands, struggling against his grip. "Uncle, please! We just want—"

"I do not care," he hisses, squeezing tighter. "Stefan is here in this castle promising treasure and support and we will have it. Not to mention I'd be fulfilling your mother's dying wish. Two birds, one stone and all of that."

The pain from his nails pulls a whimper from my throat, blood wafting from the wound. It's nothing to the fresh pain from my uncle's words. To him, I'm a pawn and nothing more. Not a person deserving of love whose opinion should be heard.

Across from us, Betmal's eyes narrow.

"You're hurting her," he says coolly. His second eyelid flashes white, and he shoves Malakat, floating slowly away from her even as he eyes my uncle. "Let go of my mate, Caralorn." His tone is strange, flat and neutral.

I've heard that tone before, when he used his power of influence in Arcadia.

Caralorn's fingers loosen on my throat, and I use that moment to flit away from him to Betmal's side.

"Behind me, darling," he says quietly.

In front of us, Caralorn's eyes spring wide as the skin underneath them twitches. The corners of his mouth pull up into a sneer, like he's trying to move but can't.

Malakat is frozen watching her father claw at his throat as if he's desperate to speak but can't do that either. Her hair floats wide around her, her green eyes flashing between Betmal and Caralorn.

Betmal turns to her and cocks his head to one side, utterly focused on my cousin.

"Kill him," Betmal commands.

I gasp, scratching at the back of his shirt. "Betmal, no, please."

But he doesn't respond, except to pull my hand around to his stomach, laying his over mine.

"Kill your father," he commands Malakat again. "Stick that blade into his gills and watch him bleed out. Now."

Malakat screams but moves slowly across the space between her and Caralorn. She growls as she lifts the spear, muscles trembling as she seemingly tries to hold back.

"Nooo," Caralorn wails. "St-stop it this instant!"

Malakat lifts the spear higher, chest heaving.

I scream when she slices down through the water.

"Stop," Betmal commands.

The point of Malakat's spear stops at the very edges of her father's neck gills. She flashes us a desperate look. "Please," she pleads.

I scratch at Betmal's stomach. "Mate, please!"

He squeezes my fingers, never looking away from my cousin and uncle.

"We can do this easily, or we can do this *very* easily," he croons. "I can kill you now, although I'd prefer not to have quite that much blood on my hands. Or you can let us go and stop this nonsense with Amatheia. You've just gotten the barest taste of my power. I will decimate this kingdom for her if I need to. Ama is *not* your property. Are we clear?"

Caralorn's eyes narrow, but he says nothing.

"Stay where you are, both of you," Betmal commands, moving my hand aside and gently pushing me toward Thatraeia. My cousin floats wordlessly near the dais, eyes wide as she stares at the unfolding scene.

Betmal glides to my uncle and cousin and grabs Malakat's knife from the holster around her thigh. Thalassa below, I don't want him to kill Caralorn. That's not how this should have gone down, but if I know anything about Betmal, it's that he *would* kill for me.

I never want him to have to.

"Betmal." I start toward him, one hand lifted.

He moves to Caralorn, and in one swift move, slips Malakat's knife deep into the outer section of my uncle's tail.

Caralorn screams, and Malakat shouts to the guard for help.

Thatraeia is frozen, and even I halt in place, shocked that Betmal stabbed him.

"That's for her leg," he growls. "For letting her be in pain for fucking *years*. For not helping her when that's all you should have done...had the decency to be kind to a child." He yanks the knife out, and Caralorn whimpers, grabbing Malakat's shoulder and squeezing.

She grunts, seemingly unable to lift a hand to help him.

Betmal drops the knife, my uncle's blood wafting away in the slight current. "I'm taking my mate and Thatraeia, and we are leaving now. Do not attempt to stop us and do not follow us. In fact, do not come *near* us. If I see you again, I will take this further. Are we clear?"

When Caralorn does nothing but glare, struggling to bring his free hand down to cover his wound, Betmal growls and gets in his face, snapping his fangs at Caralorn's neck. "Are. We. Clear?" He bites out each word like it's another stab of the knife.

A clipped nod is my uncle's only answer.

Betmal floats backward, reaching for me and putting an arm around Thatraeia.

"In ten minutes, you will have bodily control again. We will be long gone. Remember that we tried to speak with you as adults. Remember that all we asked for was kindness. And then *remember* my warning because I will not hesitate to harm you in the future."

I'm quiet as we head for the door. Caralorn roars behind us, but neither he nor my cousin make any movement in our direction when I look.

At the door, the King's Guard float, frozen in the water.

Betmal looks at them. "In ten minutes, you will be free to assist your king. He's bleeding from a wound I gave him, but he'll be fine."

The guard closest to us tries to say something but chokes around the words, brows furrowed in apparent anger.

As we move up the hall, Betmal's jaw goes tight.

"He needs air," Thatraeia says.

"I'll...be fine," Betmal insists, even as his movements slow.

Terror overtakes me. "Thatraeia, help me!"

She takes one hand, and I take the other as we power through the corridors and out of the nearest exit.

"Ama," Betmal moans. Then his head lolls forward and bubbles exit his nose.

I scream as Thatraeia and I bullet through the city as fast as we can, heading for the surface.

The moment we break it, I shove him as high toward the sky as I can, shaking him. He splashes back into the water, falling against Thatraeia and me.

"Drag him to shore!" she shouts. "We've got to get out of the water in case they come for us."

Ten minutes. We had ten minutes. If they're going to follow us, we've only got a few minutes to get him up and moving. Oh Thalassa, bless us please. Don't let him die now.

CHAPTER TWENTY-THREE
BETMAL

I blink, gasping for breath as I struggle to fill my lungs.

"Oh depths!" Ama moans, hovering over my face, eyes wide. Her cousin sits beside her, glancing nervously between us.

When I roll to my side and choke out lake water, they clap my back to assist the water's exit. Once it's out, I sit up and wrap my arms around both girls. "My darlings, thank you. Speaking underwater and using my power like I did are…tiresome. I underestimated the toll they would take."

"You scared me to death!" Ama shouts, throwing her arms around my neck.

Thatraeia shakes my shoulders. "And you stabbed Father! If you think he won't come after you for that, you are crazy! Goddess, I think you might be crazy anyhow!" She flops onto her back and puts both hands over her eyes. "Thalassa help me process this." A nervous giggle erupts from her.

"I thought you were really going to make Malakat kill him," Ama whispers in my ear. "It was terrifying seeing you like that."

"Apologies, my love," I say. "We should have talked about that when we discussed the plan. I should have foreseen he'd be that unreasonable. Although, if I'm being honest, him allowing you to suffer was reason alone for me to consider slicing his entire tail off."

She squeezes me tighter.

"Now what?" Thatraeia sits up and hugs her knees. "The reality of what we did just hit me. I don't know if I can even go back down there. Oh goddess, what have I done? Should I have stayed and helped?"

Ama lets go of me and grasps her cousin's hand, pulling her closer to us. "Come home with us, sweet Cousin. We will protect you until we figure this out, alright?"

She looks at Betmal. "I've never seen anyone control others like you did."

"My power of influence is quite strong." I give her an encouraging smile. "I will protect you, darling girl."

Her frown doesn't lessen. "You can't be with us all of the time, Betmal. Father won't let it go. He'll figure out a weakness somewhere." She glances at Ama. "That's likely to be one of us."

I lift my wrist and comm Abemet, asking him and Morgan to come to my house. Next I comm Arkan with the same request.

The girls are silent while I make the calls. When I'm finished, Ama's frowning as much as her cousin. "I never wanted to cause drama for the landers, and here we are."

I rest back on my hands, my soaked clothing clinging uncomfortably to me. "We were perhaps foolish to think Caralorn would see reason, especially with Stefan in the mix. I'm sure your uncle is eyeing Stefan's coffers and thinking how close money is. He did mention that…"

"He's broke," Thatraeia whispers. "Completely."

Ama gasps. "What? How do you know?"

Her cousin sighs. "I was sneaking past his quarters one day to go through the catacombs. I was…well, he was on his comm disk speaking with someone, shouting, and I overheard him say the kingdom is broke. There's barely any money left, only your dowry, Ama. I'd bet that's why Stefan's gifts for your marriage are so important. The rest of us have no dowries at all unless he gets Stefan's traditional jewels."

"Broke," Ama whispers. She glances at me. "He always told me my dowry was meager but maybe it's not. In any case, it was always inaccessible until my marriage. What do you wanna bet he's planned on giving just part of it to Stefan and keeping the rest for himself?"

Anger rushes through me as I consider the political wheeling and dealing the king is likely attempting here. Ama's money is hers alone, a gift from her parents—Thalassa rest their souls—and I will not see it pawned off like this.

"Let's go home," I say. "We'll discuss next steps with Abemet, Morgan, and Arkan. I need to consider this. For now, you're both safe with me, and that's all that matters."

Ama says nothing the entire walk home, and I don't push her. This day went sideways quickly, and I suspect the worst is not behind us. I embarrassed her uncle, albeit privately, and he will want recompense for that. I don't give two shits about the suitor, Stefan, but Thatraeia was right when she said I can't be with both girls twenty-four hours a day.

Perhaps Catherine could paint the lake into its own haven within ours so we can control the comings and goings. Hmm, that's too prisonlike, and that is not our way. No, we've got to find an amenable solution that doesn't lead to war within Ever.

I cast those thoughts aside as we arrive home. Ama sits at the kitchen island, rubbing long fingers over the black marble, lost in thought until her cousin takes a seat next to her. The girls lean against one another, brushing their cheeks together.

Ama looks at me, opening her mouth to say something, when the front doors swing noisily open and Abemet calls my name. I glance backward through the archway toward the front. "In here, my darling!"

Smiling at the girls, I point toward our bedroom. "I've stocked the closet with clothes in Ama's size, if you like."

Ama glances down at her naked chest and laughs. "Oh, depths, I was so lost in thought I didn't grab anything."

Thatraeia arranges her long peach hair over her chest. "I forget landers are fussier about boobs."

I grin as the girls rise, Ama taking her cousin's hand and heading for our bedroom. She mouths a quick thank you as they head away from me.

Abemet and Morgan arrive with Arkan clip-clopping behind them. Coming into the kitchen, Morgan looks around. "Where's Ama? What happened?"

I quickly fill them in on our trip before the girls emerge from the bedroom.

Morgan rushes to Ama and slings her arms around my love's neck. "Ama, oh my gods, that sounds harrowing!" She steps back, eyes scanning Ama's face. "Are you okay?"

Ama smiles softly, although the strain is clear in the wrinkle between her dark brows. "It went about how I expected." She glances at Thatraeia, who stands just behind her with a hand on her elbow, rubbing at the skin there. "This is my cousin, Thatraeia. She was there when it all happened."

Morgan smiles softly at the younger mermaid. "I imagine you don't feel super comfy being home right now, huh?"

Thatraeia shakes her head. "I've always wanted to leave if Ama did, but now…I'm just not sure. I don't think either of us can ever go back there."

My muscles quiver from the adrenaline dump of everything that happened today. "I imagine Caralorn will hold a grudge, and, earlier, Thatraeia made the excellent point that I cannot be with both girls all day and night. If Caralorn *does* attempt retribution, it's unlikely he'll come for me, not with my power. But he'd perhaps come for the girls."

Morgan grits her jaw tightly. "The hells he will."

Arkan clears his throat. "Listen, as Keeper, there are a number of legal options we can take here. But what I don't want to do is make the entire lake community suffer for Caralorn's bullshit. For now, I can deliver him a notice that he's unwelcome in downtown unless he comes in peace. There's a magical component to that, which will make it...difficult for him to become violent."

Ama's brows lift. "Magical restraints? What about the King's Guard, though, and Malakat?"

Arkan sighs. "It's not a perfect system. It's meant to be protective, so it's not a very strong magic. While it'll apply most stringently to your uncle, the power lessens down the reporting line. Malakat, as head of the guard, will be slightly less constrained. The King's Guard even less so. It's more of a formal reminder than anything."

He crosses muscular arms over his chest. "It's not perfect, but it's a clear notice that the town of Ever is on your side. Plus, let's not forget our resident blue witch, Lou Hector." He shakes his head. "But just like you, Betmal, she can't be everywhere all the time."

Morgan wags a finger as if an idea's coming to her. "You know what? That's a good point. She's at my place a lot." She glances at Thatraeia and Ama. "Why don't you come stay with us until this blows over?"

Ama presses into my arms. "I want to be with Betmal, but maybe when he's busy, we can come your way?"

"Of course." Morgan's expression softens. "What about you, Thatraeia? We're pretty fun, and we can keep you busy. Plus, your dad will never know where you are. And if for some reason he figures it out, Abe can fly, so we can keep you safe. It's probably a good idea for you and Ama to be in different places to divide his focus."

Ama sighs, and I feel her worry straight to the center of my chest. "I hate this. I never wanted to bring Caralorn's nonsense to your doorstep. I'm so sorry."

Arkan clip-clops around the island, dropping slowly to his front knees so his face is closer to hers. He takes Ama's hands and brings them over his heart. "Amatheia, your safety and happiness are our primary concern. If Caralorn brings the fight to us, it is he who will be in the wrong. We're here for you, okay?" He glances at Thatraeia. "Both of you."

Thatraeia comes close and shoves her way into Ama's arms. I bring my hand up and place it on her shoulder, reminding her I'm there as well. She looks over at Morgan. "I'd love to come with you, if you're certain I won't be in the way."

Morgan laughs. "Naw, girl, there are people at our house all the time. In fact, Alba's nephew Taylor is coming over with some friends tonight to play poker. I'll teach you, and we can team up against the dudes."

Thatraeia sighs. "That sounds nice. It sounds...normal." She spins and looks up at Ama. "I think they're right that splitting up will make it harder for Father to do something rash. Will you be okay with that?"

Ama presses her palm to her cousin's cheek, leaning slightly away from me. "Go see a little bit of this beautiful world, Cousin. I will be fine here, and Morgan and Abe will take care of you. I trust them; they've been good friends to me."

Abemet steps closer to us. "I will guard you with my life, Thatraeia. It's a promise."

The next quarter hour is a blur as Arkan and Abemet make calls from our house. Ama and Morgan help Thatraeia pack a bag, pilfering things I stocked in our closet.

Arkan leaves first, Morgan, Abemet and Thatraeia shortly after. She embraces Ama, but if I'm honest, she appears excited to be going with my son and his mate. There's a glint in her eye despite today's nonsense. I suspect when she lies down tonight, it will all hit her, and we may get a late night call. But I'll worry about that later.

They go, and Ama turns to me, burying her face in my chest. She breathes quietly while I slide my hands up her back. We stand until everyone's gone from view, then she looks up at me, elegant nostrils flared.

"Take me to bed, mate. I need to forget about today, if only for a little while."

"Done," I whisper as I bend to kiss her forehead. "I've got plenty of ideas on how to best keep you busy, ma siréne."

We head into the kitchen, and I lean over the island onto my forearms, reaching for her hand with one of mine. When she glances up at me, I curl my fingers around hers.

"Darling, we can play this one of two ways, now that everyone's gone. First, we can have a lovely dinner and an easy, relaxed night. Or—"

"I want to *forget*, Betmal" she repeats, sliding onto the island top and crawling to me. "For a few hours, at least. This problem with Caralorn will still be here tomorrow, hanging over our heads."

"Indeed it will," I confirm, pulling her lithe body tightly to mine. "Then let us cast aside that topic, and instead discuss something more fun." I grip her throat, running my thumb along her sharp jawline. "I want to hunt you, ma siréne, like the dangerous predator I am. I want you to run and hide, and I want to find you. And when I do…" I roll my second eyelid over my eyes as she smiles at me. "When I do, darling, I want to take you harder than I've done yet."

She presses forward, nipping at my upper lip. "Betmal, have you been holding back on me?"

I growl and drag her head back, exposing the long column of her throat to my hungry gaze. "Not holding back, darling. Beginning with care. Teaching the basics. But tonight, we take that further."

"Good," she whispers, sighing as I lick a warm path up the front of her throat.

I bite just under her chin, teasing her with the barest hint of fang. As she should, she relaxes and sinks against me, head falling heavily into my hands.

I release the slight hold and pull her upright so I can look deep into her eyes. Pulling her to the edge of the counter, I kiss her hard, groaning as she opens for me. When we part, we're both breathless. We need to connect deeply after a shit day.

I slide her miniskirt up. "I'm going to count to a hundred, ma siréne, and then I will hunt you. It's time to flee, my little prey."

She hops off the countertop and casts me a sultry look before taking off at a run down the hallway toward the guest rooms.

Calling on an age-old technique for concentration, I lean against the counter and close my eyes. I focus on muffling my hearing, my sense of smell, even my intuitive gift. I don't want to know where she is before I begin. Instead, I focus on the sensations building inside me—bloodlust, the desire to hunt, to spread my wings and swoop down on my prey, to take, to claim, to fuck.

Dick straining against the front of my pants, I open my eyes and look around the room. Flaring my nostrils, I scent for her, but her sea spray perfume is stale in this room. I push off the countertop with a growl and stalk through the living room, twitching my sensitive ears to listen for her heartbeat.

Stalking from room to room, I hunt my mate.

She's nowhere.

In my bedroom, I look into the backyard and smile. Perhaps she's in the lake or the workshop. Pushing my double doors to the outside wide open, I call my wings and rise above the lake, high enough to see the entirety of its depths.

No Ama to be seen.

With a smile, I swoop to the workshop doors. Darling girl

that the workshop is, she opens them for me, and I sail through, alighting in the main room where Ama usually paints.

She's not here, but her scent is stronger. Bingo. I walk around the kitchen, but her scent stales toward the back of the workshop. Humming, I glance up at the ceiling.

I ascend the stairs slowly, anticipation tightening my sack as my dick throbs against my thigh. At the landing, I pause.

Ama sits on my desk, one long leg crossed over the other as she leans back on her hands. A tiny smirk tilts her lips up. Lips I've had wrapped around my cock. Lips I need on it again.

"Hello, Betmal," she murmurs, her voice husky with need.

I stalk around the table, eyeing her as I do. She turns her head, following with the same smirky smile.

"Hello, ma siréne." I flare my wings wide and cocoon us within them, effectively blotting out the light so we're cloaked in darkness. I lean over the desk from behind her, mouth at her neck. "Do you know how hot it makes me to look for you? To hunt you? Next time, I want you to—"

She bursts off the desk with surprising speed, across the room before I process the fact that she's running.

She's fucking running from me.

Gods, yesssssss.

I slip over the desk with zip past her, stopping on the first step. She slams into my body and grunts, falling back.

I've already got an arm around her waist to keep her from landing on the ground.

"I will *always* catch you," I purr, fangs descending, throbbing with venom as she brings her head up and stares at me like a queen.

"Want to know why I came to this particular spot, Betmal?" She rights herself and trails a finger seductively down my chest.

"Tell me," I manage, dipping down to capture her lower lip with my teeth.

She moans as I suck on her plump bow of a mouth. When

we part, she gives me a devious look. "This room needs some red, mate, don't you think?"

Pushing off the landing, I soar across the room with Ama in my arms. I don't stop until we hit the bookshelf. Shoving her high around my waist, I grab her wrists in one hand and slowly place them above her head.

"Leave them there," I command, my voice ragged with need.

"Yes, sir," she whispers, and those words from her lips send my lust soaring.

With one hand, I shove my pants down. I notch my cock between her legs and drag the spongy head over her clit and through her folds.

Ama moans, letting her head fall to one side as she bats her lashes playfully at me. "I need that bite, Betmal. I want to feel you in my chest like the last time you bit me."

"The beginnings of our mate bond," I murmur. "If I bite you with full intention, and you accept me with full intention, we'll feel one anothers' emotions in that bond. Just like that sensation in your chest, but stronger."

Ama cocks her head sideways. "And so? I've read about it in the book and I want it, mate. Or is that not what you are to me?" She shoots me a devious, feral look.

"Patience, darling." I'm dripping precum like a faucet, so I deposit it all over her slick channel, teasing her with the tip of my cock. She tries to rock her hips to get me inside, but she can't move pressed to the bookshelves.

A little growl is the first sign of her frustration. She curls her lips back and snarls at me as I rub my cockhead along her slit, teasing the first inch or so inside her.

With a quick, violent jerk of her hips, she manages to take another inch of me into her sweet, hot pussy. The cilia take over and drag my cock and sack inside, kneading and sucking at my skin as I bark out a stream of inelegant curses.

"Naughty girl," I caution. "Running from your mate,

disobeying my orders. What's next? You'll move those hands from where I told you to keep them?"

On cue, she drops them from their spot against the wall and wraps them around my neck, leaning forward as I continue to tease her. "I think I'm learning that I like disobeying, Betmal. I like it when you get all 'let me teach you a lesson, ma siréne.'"

Growling, I shift backward with her in my arms. I settle onto my desk with her straddling my lap as I kick my pants fully off. I move my hands to the swell of her ass and part her, guiding her onto my cock. She sinks down with a needy moan, pussy clenching around me as her inner walls stroke and tease my thick length.

"Ahhh, my little mate," I say with a groan. "This pussy is perfection."

CHAPTER TWENTY-FOUR
AMATHEIA

Betmal's rigid, throbbing length tickles the tiny cilia inside of me, sending streaks of pleasure like miniature lightning bolts radiating out from between my thighs. Heat streaks down the back of my neck as I prop myself up on my knees and encourage him farther back to give me space to *ride*.

Giant wings hold steady behind him, flared as I gaze in awe at this male who's made me feel so incredibly complete, so cared for.

Cherished.

That's the word for how I feel with him. Like I'm the center of someone's universe.

Rising off him, I hold his fierce look as I sink back down onto his cock. It kicks inside me, teasing my inner walls as he hisses in a breath and bites his lower lip.

"You enchant me, my darling," he murmurs, pulling me forward to nip at my throat. His lips and tongue trace a lazy, hot trail along my jawline and down the front of my neck. Every touch of his mouth has me clenching tighter, heat coiling deep inside me as my skin flushes.

Sweat beads at the base of my spine as he runs a hand up my back. I let my head fall into his palm as he explores my neck and shoulders and the top of my chest, teasing me with the barest hint of his teeth.

"Please," I beg. "Please, Betmal. I'm so close."

A satisfied-sounding chuckle is his only answer, followed by a low, needy groan when I tighten around him.

He bites a spot on the side of my neck, another groan following the first. "Here," he says quietly. "Here's where I want you, ma siréne."

"Take me." I rise faster on and off him, thighs trembling as he begins to piston his hips to sink deeper. "Bite me, claim me. I want to *feel* you."

"Not up and down," he corrects, gripping my hips and rocking me forward and backward. "Like this, my sweet. Every pass will drag my cock against your G spot. More pleasure to be had."

The change of direction sends instant heat through my pussy and I can't stop clenching down *hard*.

He brushes his lips softly over my neck as he strokes deeper, our breath becoming short, desperate pants as we chase that bliss that's so close, so…close…

With a growl, Betmal flips us and slams me onto my back. He falls forward on top of me, catching himself at the last moment. With one hand, he grips my left knee and pushes my thigh out to the side. Snarling, he sinks fully inside, second eyelid rolling over his crimson irises as he lets out a growl that shakes the desk.

His free hand comes to the middle of my back, and he arches me up so he can bend down and suck one of my nipples between his lips. His mouth is rough, needy, and every pass of his tongue over my sensitive, puckered skin has me mewling and scratching at the desk surface.

My entire body is a series of sensations as emotion overwhelms me. Love for him. Love for what we have. Love for the perfect, intense way he loves me.

He must sense I'm almost there because he strikes like a viper. A sudden pinch at my neck is all the warning I get before he floods the bite with venom, and bliss erupts, pleasure rocking my system like a tidal wave.

I scream and beg and shout, clawing at every inch of him I can reach as sound and vision muffle. There's nothing, nothing at all but a *sense* of Betmal, of the intense pleasure he's feeling. It's a *knowing* in a way I can barely absorb. He's all dark emotion —desire, covetousness, devotion, love.

Our bond. There. *There!*

"Betmallll!" I wail his name as he fills me in every sense, our combined pleasure pushing me higher, higher until stars burst behind my eyelids and everything fades but my mate's teeth buried in my neck.

I think I come for hours. It *seems* that long, my orgasm drawn out by his venom and the feel of his perfect cock buried deep inside.

Eventually, he releases the bite. I gasp; I could cry from the loss of that contact. I want to get lost in that bliss.

"Mine," he growls into my lips. "You're mine now, my sweet."

I reach up and rub his chest beneath the ziol.

"That means you're mine, too." I grin as a sense of satisfaction fills the bright bond between us.

He dips down and licks over the spot he just bit. "I will heal you, ma siréne, but a claiming bite like that will scar."

"Good," I manage between ragged breaths. "Can we do it again?"

He laughs with me. "Needy little darling. Shall we go for a swim and then retire to our bedroom? We can do that as many times as you like."

"Take me." I reach for him with a smile. "Ma vampire."

~

"**M**organ just left the kitchen," Thatraeia hiss-whispers, her voice slightly muffled through the comm watch. "Lou, the blue witch, is here too, and they're so *cool*, I don't know how to act!"

I laugh even as my heart pangs. It'll be good for my youngest cousin to spend time around nice, normal women and see more of the world outside of the lake.

"What have you been doing all morning?" I keep my tone light, even though I'm worried about what Caralorn might be planning. Despite how completely Betmal controlled yesterday's situation, I know Caralorn's a petty, conniving sea slug, and he'll want vengeance for all of it, especially once he realizes Thatraeia came with us.

"I was nervous, but the girls took me to the Galloping Green Bean for breakfast, and I got to meet Alba and see Taylor again." She falls silent for a moment. "Ama, Ever is so different from what I imagined. And Lou and Morgan, depths, they're so nice and funny. Is this what it feels like to have friends?"

It takes everything in me not to burst into tears at her innocent question. "Yes," I manage. "And there's so much more we can show you, sweet Cousin."

"I saw the Keeper, Arkan, at the diner." She sighs. "He made a point to tell me he sent Father that notice or whatever. I'm so anxious about that."

I nod in agreement, although she can't see me. "Yeah, he called to let us know too." I gather my thoughts for a moment. "I suppose I'm not really worried about some physical attack, you know? I just want all of this to be resolved. I want Caralorn to stop acting like he's the only one who can make important decisions for us."

MAKING OUT WITH MERMAIDS

"Yeah," my cousin says. "I miss home, though, the castle especially. I'd like to be able to come and go."

I can't think of anything to say to that. I have no desire to go back to the place that's home for her. It never felt like home to me, even though the castle herself was always kind.

Someone calls Thatraeia's name, and she rushes off the comm watch, promising to check in later.

I'm sitting at the bar, musing about how quickly my cousin seemed to take to Ever living when there's a slight thud, and the house swings the front door open.

Sliding off the barstool, I marvel at how good my leg feels as I stride easily up the hall. The house swings the front doors fully open to reveal a small package on the porch.

Nerves clang through me. I wonder if this is some nonsense from Caralorn. Surely the house wouldn't lead me astray, though...

Peeking around, I look for signs of anything amiss. But when the house shimmies the welcome mat, tossing the box in my direction, I laugh.

"Alright, alright," I say, chuckling. "We'll take this inside, shall we?"

Hands come around my body, and I jump in place, but realizing it's Betmal, I sink against him. He slides his fingers down between my thighs, peppering kisses along my shoulder blades and the side of my neck.

"This is for you, darling," he murmurs, his voice husky. "Come to the kitchen. I'm in desperate need of an espresso, and we can open it there."

Intrigued, I turn and reach between us, stroking his rigid length as his head falls back. I love it when he exposes his neck to me. It makes me feel like a vampire. Surging onto my tiptoes, I bite his throat, my tiny fangs sinking into his skin as I lap at it.

He jolts against me, groaning, his hips jerking as he thrusts into my hand. "Or we can fuck on the front porch," he says on a growl. "I'd welcome that, too. Gods*damn*, your teeth feel good at my throat."

I release the bite and nip and lick at his skin, teasing him before I skirt around him and head for the kitchen. He's at my back, all predatory intensity as we enter the kitchen. I hop up onto the bar, and he turns to the espresso machine, setting it up. That done, he spins in place and hands me a knife.

I take it with a smile and slice the edges of the box. When I open it, shock courses through me, my muscles trembling. I pull out a large, heavy square encased in bubble wrap. But through the translucent puffy bubbles, I can already see the book's cover. And its title.

Welcome to Ever: A Guide.

"Betmal…" I look up at him with tears in my eyes. "How did you get it so fast? We *just* finished the paintings yesterday!! I just…oh depths. I can barely believe this."

He crosses the space between the counter and island, covering my hands with his.

"Believe it, ma siréne. I worked on this after you fell asleep and called in a favor to have a sample overnighted. We have worked hard, and now you get to see the book for the first time." He pats the hard surface, lifting a dark brow as he smiles. "Shall we, darling?"

Emotion wells up inside me, and I set the book down. Wrapping my legs around him, I pull him close and slide my hands up his abs to rest them over his heart.

"I want to say something first." I clear my throat, nerves joining the excitement barreling around inside of me. Looking up into eyes the color of garnets, I let everything I feel for him show on my face. "I love you," I say, my voice wavering. "I know it's fast, but—"

Betmal draws in a ragged breath, one hand carding into my hair as he holds me close. "That singular word cannot possibly encompass how I feel about you, ma siréne. I love you too. I cherish you. I adore you. I want to possess you in every way it's possible for a male to claim his mate. I am yours, Ama, until the very end of our days."

Tears stream down my face as he leans down, closing his mouth over mine. He eats up the first sob, and then the next, until we're clawing at one another. I can't get close enough. I need *everything*.

When we part, he grits his jaw, nostrils flaring as his second eyelids flash over his red irises. "Back to bed, darling? Or shall we open the book...?"

I glance at the still packaged book, debating.

Betmal laughs and picks it up, holding it between us. "I know that look, my love. Book it is."

Hands trembling, I pull carefully at the puffy packaging until I can slide the welcome book from its protective sheath. The house opens the cabinet with the trash can in it, and Betmal tosses the packaging inside.

The book is absolutely stunning. The cover features my painting of town hall, and the title and everything else is done in a gold foil that accentuates the artwork. And Thalassa below, my art looks amazing printed on the glossy surface.

Betmal takes it and flips the book, examining the spine and then the back. I'm overwhelmed by how my art wraps around. The blurb on the back is actually the town's usual welcome letter, repurposed to fit human and monster newcomers alike.

"Stunning," Betmal murmurs. "This exceeds even my high expectations. Open it, darling. Let's have a look at the inside." He sets the book on my lap and turns for his espresso. I open the cover, marveling at the end papers inside that are another of my paintings, this time of Main Street, full of monsters. Everyone looks so joyful, I can hardly believe it.

Betmal returns with a tiny cup of espresso for him and a

latte for me. He sets my drink on the counter and joins me, looking over my shoulder as we flip through the book.

The art is amazing. The typography is stunning. Every page is chock-full of helpful details about Ever's locations and inhabitants. Plus, the book is big, nearly twelve inches tall and wide. It'll be beautiful on a coffee table.

"So," Betmal drags his fingertips up my thigh, "a few things need to happen now. I'll need official approval from Evenia."

I scrunch up my nose at the mention of that rude-ass bitch.

"I know." His expression matches mine. "She *will* give it, though. In conjunction with that, I'd like to plan a launch party. Morgan and Abe can help us. What do you think?"

My immediate excitement dims as I think of Caralorn and the sense of unfinished business I have about him.

Betmal reads me like a book.

"But your cousin will be there," he says. "You know she'll want to support you, and I'll work with haven leadership to ensure nothing ruins your night."

I pull in a deep, steadying breath, forcing a smile. "We can't ask them to protect us forever. In the meantime, I love your idea. Let's invite everyone to dinner and see if they'd like to help."

"Done," Betmal says. "I'll call Abemet in a moment. Then I'll comm Evenia to get that out of the way." He gives me a wry look. "Would you like to be here for that?"

I laugh and shake my head. "If you want me there for backup, I'm there, mate. But if you don't care either way, I think I'll go sun myself for a while."

"Alright, darling." He leans down and licks a stripe along my collarbone, biting my shoulder as he reaches it. A low moan rumbles from his throat. "I'll be out shortly, my love." He rubs my shoulders softly. "If Caralorn's going to make a move, it'll be soon. And if he doesn't, then great."

Except I think we both know something will happen. It's not a matter of if, just a matter of when.

~

"Give me the book, Ama; I have to see it right now!" Morgan shouts up the hallway as she, Thatraeia, and Abemet arrive for dinner. The house waves them through from the front, and I stand there dressed, ready, and maybe even a little nervous.

But I'm giddy by the time Morgan appears in the arched doorway to the kitchen, Abe at her back with his typically neutral expression. She crosses to me in a rush, and I hand the book to her as Thatraeia slips into my arms and beams up at me.

"It's so beautiful," I say quietly. "It arrived this morning, and I'm pretty sure I spent the entire day looking at it."

Morgan sets the book down next to me on the counter, stroking the front cover as her mouth drops open. She looks up at Abe, who joins us and wraps an arm possessively around her waist.

"Look how fucking beautiful this is, Abe. Swear to God, if I open this book and find out our welcome packets were missing even more information, I'm gonna slap you."

He chuckles. "Is this a good time to remind you that I was never in charge of the welcome packets?"

She shrugs. "No, because you were in *charge* charge, so it still counts. Being a leader is rough, huh?"

He smirks as she returns her focus to the book, flipping it open to reveal the first end papers.

Betmal appears out of the bedroom as Morgan's flipping through, oohing and ahhing over every page.

"Darlings!" Betmal pulls Morgan in for a quick hug, kissing her cheek. Then he hugs Abe the same way, and I have to do a weird double take at seeing them together. They could be twins, except Betmal's got gray at his temples and far more extravagant taste in clothing.

Abe wears jeans, a dark V-necked tee and Chuck Taylors while Betmal's wearing fitted black slacks, a billowy knitted sweater and a million necklaces draped around his neck. He could be a human fashion model.

Morgan grins at Thatraeia and then me. "We had a great afternoon messing around with Lou. She's really getting a handle on her blue magic. If Caralorn tries anything, he's gonna get bitch-slapped right down."

Thatraeia brings a hand to her mouth as I sigh. "Part of me hopes he does something just so this can be done. The suspense is killing me."

Betmal plants a kiss on my exposed shoulder. "I've already promised to forcefully remove him as a problem, my sweet. You said I wasn't allowed."

"Not everybody hates him," I grumble, glancing at my cousin.

Abe looks between his father and me. "This book is remarkable. You've both done a wonderful job."

Betmal smiles. "I simply made the formatting beautiful. The highlight is Ama's art. Which is why I want this launch party to be perfect. Food, drinks, a true celebration of the culmination of this project. And perhaps a tiny sneak peek of what's to come."

Morgan's eyes go wide. "So you got approval from Evenia to do the other havens?"

Betmal shrugs and shoots us a wicked look, his eyes glittering with malice. "I did."

"Well done, Father," Abe says. "I don't know how you managed that, but good for you."

Betmal rounds everyone and comes behind me, wrapping both arms around my waist as he rests his chin on my shoulder.

"When I want something," he croons, "I get it eventually." He winks at me.

I laugh as Betmal kisses my neck.

Hours later, we're laughing as my mate opens a third bottle of wine, offering it to me first, and then our guests.

Morgan stares at the enormous sheet of paper Betmal covered the dining room table with. We've got notes scribbled all the way to the edges in parts. She's an absolute whiz at event planning, it turns out.

She claps her hands together. "Okay, so we'll have a red carpet up the front steps of Town Hall. We shou—oh, ewww." She turns to Betmal. "Since Evenia had to rubber-stamp this project, do we technically need to invite her? 'Cause I feel like she'd show up for no other reason than to be shitty."

I scrunch my nose and look at Betmal, who shakes his head and frowns.

"No, my darlings. That won't be necessary. This night is all about a new age for the welcome books. We want it to be a celebration. Neither Evenia nor Aberen will be invited."

"Okay, thank gods," Morgan says in a huffy tone. She gives me a sour look. "I really hate that woman. I wish I could snap my fingers and replace her with Abe." She winks at me. "Or maybe me."

"I ran into her once. Literally," I offer. I look at Betmal with a chuckle. "Or did I technically run them both over?"

Morgan slow claps for me. "Whichever you did, good for you. I hope they fell."

Thatraeia looks between us, brows knit together in confusion. "Who is this again?" She rolls her eyes. "I don't get out much."

I snort out a laugh as Abe and Betmal share a look.

Morgan waves a dismissive hand in the air. "Abe's mother, honey. She runs the whole haven system, but she is truly the worst being I know. So we aren't gonna invite her to this amazing party." She reaches over the table to squeeze my hand. "I can't wait to help you with this. Come to Herschel's with Thatraeia and me tomorrow to take a look at his specialty menus?"

"Deal," I say to my new friend.

Thatraeia beams at me and lifts her glass of wine to her lips.

I can't believe this is my life. I just hope I get to keep it.

CHAPTER TWENTY-FIVE
BETMAL

The following afternoon, Ama's at Herschel's with Morgan and her cousin, and I'm alone at home. The house is quiet without her here, but her scent saturates every surface. The house and workshop are happy; they love having her here too.

But I'm not fool enough to think the issue with Caralorn is over. My primary concern is that not having *some* sort of resolution means my mate remains anxious.

We can't have that, and we can't travel full-time just to steer clear of him.

I spent the morning in the workshop, organizing some of the party details assigned to me by Morgan. The plans for the launch party are coming along brilliantly. I also ordered Ama a little present that I pray shows up in time.

I sit on her rock for a while, staring at her pond and considering all the possible ways this could play out with the king. Truthfully, it's not that I'm worried he and his guard could best me in a fight. There's really no chance they could decimate anything in Downtown Ever.

It's the effect such an event would have on Ama that worries me.

The hurt would ripple through her, affecting her and Thatraeia, and I'm not willing for that to be the outcome.

I dress and head deep into my closet to a small chest where I keep family gems and jewels. I pick through the gold and silver until I find what I'm looking for, then I slip it into my pocket.

Half an hour later, I stand at the lake's edge, drawing oxygen into my lungs to saturate them before I enter the water. I've got a plan. I can only hope it works.

Saying a prayer to the old gods, I dive into the water.

Without Ama's quicker swimming, it takes me the better part of a half hour to reach the merkingdom. But by the time I near the borders, guards appear from the murky depths to surround me.

I don't see Malakat, but I stop in the water to address the guard who appears to be leading the group. I recognize him from our earlier run-in with Caralorn.

"I'm here to request an audience with the king. I'd like to settle our differences, if it's possible."

The guard cocks his head to the side and stares at me. He swims closer, glittering onyx eyes dropping down my body as he takes in my soaked, billowing clothes.

"So...you must really believe Amatheia to be your mate? I can't imagine you'd have come down here otherwise."

I nod. "She is, and I do. This situation with her uncle is gutting her. She misses her cousins and her people. I don't want that to be how this ends. I'd like to speak with him. Please."

The male swims closer still, a spear in one hand, long black hair waving in the water behind him. He sneers at me.

"I hope you're right, Vampire. That you *will* love and cherish her for all of her days. Because Amatheia is the gentlest, the kindest of our people. I can't imagine how she feels being caught between two worlds like this. You better be worth it."

Oh.

Oh.

I wonder if Ama even knows the guard views her in this way? That he sees her for who she is, and perhaps not for what her uncle wishes she was.

"Then why did you never help her?" I grit out. "You must all have known she was in pain for decades, yet you didn't lift a fin to make it better."

His expression darkens, but he doesn't respond to my accusation. "Come," he barks, turning and swimming for the city.

I follow dutifully, refusing to start a fight despite my frustration. We glide through the beautiful, shell-encrusted towers of the merkingdom until we reach the palace and enter through arched coral front gates.

The lead guard spins to face me. "His Majesty is holding public court today. It's a chance for any merfolks to bring grievances to be settled. This is a good time and place for you to make whatever request you came here to make." He grins wickedly. "You'll have to wait your turn, though."

Great.

Perhaps he thinks I'll run out of air and give up.

And when I see the line of merfolk waiting to speak to their king, I understand why he mentioned it. Dozens of beings are ahead of me.

The guard drops me at the back of the line, flits toward the king and bends to his ear, whispering. Caralorn stiffens and glances toward me, frowning as he looks down the long line of merfolk waiting to be heard.

The only advantage I may have here is that we're in public. The king's response will have to be more diplomatic than if we were in private with just his guard. As I wait for my turn, I take the chance to observe the room.

Amatheia's cousins swim around, offering sustenance to those waiting in line. They're greeted with deferential nods and quiet murmurs of thanks. Eventually, the green one—Malakat—joins her father on the dais, glaring at me.

Forty or so minutes later, I swim to the bottom of the dais and stare up at my mate's uncle.

King Caralorn glares at me, eyes narrowed and both fists balled, even though his arms rest casually on his throne. "How dare you return here, bloodsucker." The king's voice echoes underwater. I can almost feel the entire room freeze under his wrath.

I smile. "I'd rather not have the threat of your retribution hanging over Ama's head like a dark cloud. She has been working on a project with me to create a book for our haven, a welcome book to replace the former packets. She's worked incredibly hard, and we're throwing a launch party for the first book next week. I'd like to invite you, and her cousins, of course, a formal goodbye from you to her, if you will."

The king sneers, "Painting? Launch parties? Take a look around, Vampire. We have more important things to do than attend your lander events. She's due to be married, you know. She is not free to be with you. Or have you forgotten?"

I swim up the first few steps. Malakat and the guard come closer, spears pointed in my direction.

Sighing, I look the king in the eyes. "I thought you might say something like that, so I'll offer you a bit of advice, and a gift."

The king growls, rising from his throne to swim to the step above me. When I glance down at his tail, there's still an obvious gash, knitted together with crude stitches.

"Get out," he hisses.

"I will, in a moment." I reach into my pocket and withdraw a flat golden amulet. The etching on the front features a merking in a chariot, holding a whip as he roars at the horses that carry the chariot forward. I offer the amulet to the king, who snatches it from my hands with a mighty roar.

"The amulet of Osayrus! How came you by this?"

I smile at the king. "I knew Osayrus well. We were friends when he was alive, your great-grandfather and I. Perhaps you weren't aware that, after the great battle for which this amulet was created, I was the one who ordered its creation. Osayrus spoke of the amulet in his now-famous writings, but it always remained with me. He felt it important for something of his fame to remain on land, where he led his army to victory. I'd like for your kingdom to have it."

The king sneers, "What other mertreasures do you hold? Hmm?"

"Just your niece," I say with a smile. "Although 'hold' isn't the right word. She blesses me daily with her presence. Which is why I'd like, again, to invite you to the launch party, so you can give her your blessing. It will be a night to remember, a celebration of her skill and hard work. And I know it would mean the world to her if you came." I glance up at Malakat. "All of you."

Dark lashes flutter against Malakat's green skin, and her emerald eyes flick to her father. "Father, should—"

"Silence," he hisses, clutching the amulet until his knuckles turn white. "Get out, vampire."

I dip my head to him, then take another step up until our chests nearly brush together. "I'm a father too," I whisper. "I know how difficult it can be, and you raised far more children than I did. That takes its own kind of bravery." I stare hard at him. "But the ultimate bravery is in letting go when your children want to travel a different path than that which you wanted for them. Please come."

A vein pops in the king's temple as he flares both nostrils, gills flapping wildly as his ears twitch at the tips. "Get out!" he roars again, shoving me toward the bottom of the dais.

His words ring in my ears as I give him a last, sorrowful look, then turn to swim out of the room.

The guards follow me all the way to shore, watching as I drag myself onto the black stone beach and suck in great lungfuls of air. Even for me, more than an hour underwater is almost too much. Stripping my wet clothes off, I call my shadow wings and bullet up into the sky, leaving the lake behind.

That experience was…frustrating. But I hope the king will consider the gift and my words and choose to do what's right. Amatheia is worth it. She deserves it. I had to try, for her sake.

Hours later, I stand in the kitchen, plating a charcuterie board with all the things I now know are her favorites—seaweed kimchi, local honey from the Community Garden, rice crackers, brie cheese, big chunks of salted sausage. She comes in the door with a laugh, speaking quietly to the house as she paces through the hallway toward me.

When she arrives in the kitchen, I sink against the countertop and stare, eating her up with my eyes. "Gods, you are so fucking beautiful," I murmur.

A blush tinges her cheeks, and she walks across the kitchen, jumping up into my arms. I kiss her as I set her on the countertop, wrapping both arms around her and sliding my hands into her hair.

On cue, her head falls back into my waiting palms, and she exposes her mating bite to me. Hungry, I dip and suck at the tiny pinhole scars at the base of her throat.

"Need you," I growl. "I missed you all day, ma siréne."

"Then have me," she commands. "I missed you too."

I reach down and swirl my fingers over her knee. "How's the leg? You've been walking a lot this week. Do we need to visit Martin for any tweaks?"

"There's no pain, which is still a little unbelievable to me." She grips my throat and bares her tiny fangs to me. "But my thighs burn from being suddenly used so," she bats her lashes at me, "vigorously."

And just like that, I'm hard as a rock, needy, aching and desperate to be deep inside her. With a growl, I yank her skirt up with one hand and shove my pants down with the other. I pull her to the edge of the counter and off it just enough to enter her with a single, deep thrust.

Ama moans, head falling back as she braces herself on the countertop.

Sweet, tight heat envelops my cock as my protective eyelid rolls over my irises.

"Gods*damn*," I grunt.

She tightens around me, the cilia inside her pussy stroking my length like a thousand tiny fists. I let my head fall back to simply *feel* her for a moment, but when she lurches forward, snapping at my neck and latching on, I jolt inside her.

She gasps, releasing the bite, but that desperately needy sound unleashes me.

Rolling my hips, I thrust in and out with steady, deep moves. Ama mewls and pants, eyes rolling into her head as her mouth drops open. The dark blush along her cheeks spreads to the tips of her ears and down to her chest. Satisfaction blooms hot and heavy, orgasm building fast between my thighs.

Sometimes the burn is slow, and we get hours together to play before we come.

But sometimes the burn is fast, and a hot, dirty, three-minute fuck is exactly what we need.

Snarling, I lift her ass off the counter just enough to hold her steady as I pound into her. My hips snap against her thighs as I slide one hand up her leg to grip the back of her knee. Using that leverage, I spread her wider, fucking harder, deeper as she strokes me off.

Pleasure rages through me as she tightens, rocking her hips to meet mine, her pants rising into needy cries for release.

"Betmal, oh goddess, oh fuck, yes, please!" Her voice goes ragged as she begs, and that sends me spiraling to the edge of bliss.

One hand at her throat, I yank her upper body to mine and strike, sinking my fangs into my claiming bite. Cum rushes down my shaft, cock throbbing as I unload inside her, bellowing into the hold.

Her pussy clamps around me, pulsing in rhythmic waves that tighten every muscle in my body until I'm nothing but rock-hard ecstasy. Her orgasm fades, but as I bite harder, growling into the pinch, need fills our bond, and a second lightning strike of pleasure hits us both. My cock kicks inside her, spurting seed deep into her channel as I howl, releasing the bite and screaming into the kitchen.

Rapture batters me until I'm a senseless, trembling mess. Ama goes limp in my arms, sagging down onto the countertop and throwing an arm over her face.

"Oh goddess," she whispers, her voice hoarse, "is it just me or is the pleasure getting stronger? Because I swear I saw the depths on that one." She rubs her chest. "And I feel you in *here*, Betmal."

I chuckle and lean over her on the counter, resting my hand above her heart. It beats like a wounded bird, fluttering wildly in her chest as satisfaction fills me.

"That was exceptional, ma siréne," I whisper, shoving up onto my forearms as my cock slips out of her channel, well used, sated and dripping. I stand and grip the backs of both her knees, spreading her wide so I can see the evidence of what we just did.

Her pussy lips are swollen and covered in cum and her honey. My seed drips in sticky strings from her channel, which still clenches in slow waves.

"Look at that mess," I croon. "You're so full, darling."

"Mmm." She looks down between her thighs, then shoots me a wicked grin. "I'm not done, Betmal. Take me to the lake so we can do it again."

A huge smile splits my face as I toss her over my shoulder and stalk for the pond in the backyard. I slap her ass on the way there, loving how her soft skin goes bright blue in the shape of my handprint. Walking into the lake, I hiss as the warm water massages my skin.

Ama shifts into her merform and splashes playfully out of my arms.

"Come and get me, mate!" she singsongs as she heads for the deeper water.

"Always, darling," I whisper as I dive in after her.

∼

A handful of peaceful days pass in a whir of planning and food. Morgan, Abemet and Thatraeia join us a half-dozen times to work on the plans for the launch party. In that time, I keep an eye and ear out for any sign that Caralorn might consider joining us. The lake is suspiciously quiet despite multiple attempts by Arkan to reach out to the king.

It concerns me how Caralorn mentioned Stefan despite my warnings to him.

The night before the party, Ama's in town with Morgan doing a final taste test of the menu they picked. I stayed behind solely to wait for a package. The tracking says it'll arrive today, and I'm anxious for that to be the case.

As the sun starts to dip behind the trees, casting shadows through the kitchen, I hear the slow clip-clop of hooves on my driveway. There are only a handful of centaurs or pegasi in this haven who would come to my home without calling first.

Concern bristles through me, and I stalk to the front of the house. Gracious girl that she is, she throws the front doors open wide.

Outside, Arkan clops to the base of the stairs and ascends them with his front half. He hands me the package.

"The driver was just dropping this off in your mailbox, trying to stuff it in there, but to be honest, whatever's in here didn't look like it was going to fit. I offered to personally deliver it."

"Keeper." I greet the male who took over the keeping position from Abemet when my son retired. "Your presence here does not bode well for my evening's peace."

He shrugs. "I could simply be out for a walk and happen upon this beautiful home."

I cross my arms and lean into the doorway. "As much as I love a guest, I'd like you to tell me what's wrong."

He sighs and crosses both muscular arms over his broad chest. He's wearing a shirt that says "Sorry, This Centaur's Taken by the Perfect Female." Normally, I'd laugh, but the half-serious look on his face has me stone-cold sober.

"You're right that I don't come bearing the best of news." He glances around me. "Is Amatheia home?"

I bristle. "She's in town. What's *wrong*, Arkan?" Without thinking, I call my wings and flare them wide, ready to bullet toward downtown and get my woman.

He runs both hands over his black braided hair. "I'm hearing whispers of the merking planning…something, perhaps some sort of," he casts around for the right word, "uprising feels too strong." He gives me a wry look. "I know you've been to see him since you stabbed him, and that it didn't go particularly well."

Now *that* is curious. He must have insight directly into the merfolk through one of their own.

I wonder who. My thoughts stray to the guard who seemed to hold affection for Ama.

Arkan continues on. "Obviously, everyone in town is excited for the launch party tomorrow, and it could be nothing, but it wouldn't surprise me if Caralorn plans to ruin it somehow."

I pull in a steadying breath, looking for calm, although I feel nothing but storm inside.

Arkan uncrosses his arms and swishes his tail, rubbing both sides of the horse half of his powerful body. "The shifters are keeping an eye on the lake, and the protector team will be ready for anything. It's going to be fine, but I wanted to make you and Ama aware. Ever's behind you a thousand percent. We'll make sure Ama's night is absolutely perfect."

He smiles. "I've been working with Abe on that surprise, per your request. It's going to be gorgeous."

Pride fills me. Of the havens I've had a chance to visit, Ever has the best community feeling.

"Thank you," I manage, tucking the package under my arm. "I can't wait to see what she thinks of it."

"Alright, so," Arkan steps down the stairs and winks, "we'll meet you at the intersection of Sycamore and Main tomorrow at six p.m., right?"

I confirm and thank him, watching as the young Keeper walks gracefully up the driveway. He's observant, looking around and seeming to notice everything. My son was an incredible Keeper, but Arkan is part of the new guard, something different than Abe was. It's a good change, in my opinion.

And tomorrow is going to be amazing.

So long as the merking doesn't fuck it up.

CHAPTER TWENTY-SIX
AMATHEIA

Morgan hugs me in front of Herschel's Fine Dining, and then Herschel comes out of the front door to hug me as well.

"We cannot wait for tomorrow, lovely girl," he says kindly, folding his hands over his plump belly. "It is going to be amazing! It's been so long since we've had a haven-wide party!"

"Oh, don't forget Halloween," Morgan says with a laugh. "That'll be coming around again in a few months, and you *know* Miriam won't let us forget it. I think she's taken to human holidays even more than us humans do." She turns to look at Thatraeia. "Halloween is so weird and cool, and it's the best time. You're gonna love it."

"Awww," I whine with a laugh. "I missed it last year, but I heard about it at Higher Grounds the next day. I can't wait to see it this year. I heard the pumpkins chased people, and Miriam had candy scorpions and exploding pumpkins in her front window display."

"It was amazing," Morgan gushes. She gives me a soft smile and pulls me in for another hug. "You'll be here to see it. Shit, maybe the goddess Thalassa herself will knock some sense into your family, and Malakat and your other cousins will come."

I snort. "Malakat celebrating a human holiday? The lake will freeze over before that happens."

"Well," Morgan says, "I'm holding out hope for them not to be douchebags."

We laugh together as we walk toward the corner of Sycamore and Main. Main looks so beautiful at night, all flickering lights and colorful flowers. It's almost busier than the daytime. Couples and groups cross the street and frequent every business. As usual, Higher Grounds has a line out the door.

I smile when I see a handsome dark elf with giant sweeping horns walking down the line, offering monsters sample sizes of some sort of drink.

Morgan nudges me. "That's Diavolo. I heard he's living with the Higher Grounds guys and Valentina now. He's so nice; I met him last week at the shop. He's mostly running their Grand Portal Station location."

We watch as the handsome male gives out the last of the drinks. He twirls his round tray expertly in one hand before stalking toward the front door and through it, smiling at the patrons as he goes.

"I can't imagine three mates," I muse as we pause on the street corner.

Morgan laughs. "I'm telling you, when you're ready, come with Abe and me to the kink clubs in some of the other havens. You don't have to do anything if you don't want. You can just watch. Sometimes that's the most fun."

"I'll go," Thatraeia says, slipping her hands into her back pockets.

Morgan and I spin on a swivel.

Thatraeia's eyes spring wide. "What?! I'm just saying, I've heard a couple stories, and I'm curious…"

I stare at her in shock, this woman who seems to have suddenly fit into Ever as easily as if she's lived downtown her whole life.

"I'm in awe of you," I admit, pulling my cousin into a hug. "You're so brave to defy your father and remain up here."

"Don't be," she whispers, taking my hand and squeezing it. "I'm in awe of *you*, Ama. And I can't wait to share your gift with all of Ever tomorrow." She pulls me in for a quick hug. "I love that we're getting to be friends and family all at the same time. Tomorrow's going to be amazing, *dahling*."

We both laugh as she pronounces the moniker Betmal calls all of us, complete with his elegant accent.

"You dork," I say with a laugh, slapping her on the side.

"Dorks for life." She winks at me. "Night, Ama."

As I walk home, I'm equal parts excited for tomorrow's event and full of dread over Caralorn potentially causing drama. It was bad enough what happened beneath the lake's surface, but up here? With the downtown Evertons I've quickly come to love?

I just want him to leave me alone. But if I know one thing for certain, it's that he won't.

∼

The following evening, I'm a bundle of nerves thinking about tonight's launch party. I rush around the house making sure I have everything I need to bring with me.

Pens to sign copies of the book for any Evertons who want one.

A clean paintbrush in case anyone wants me to sign with that.

Paints. A plate to put paint on in case I need it.

"Ama, darling, it's time to get dressed," Betmal calls to me from deep in his bedroom. No, *our* bedroom.

It's *our* bedroom.

Nerves that have been shattering inside me all day decide now is the time to bash around in full force. I can't stop thinking about Caralorn and hoping he doesn't somehow fuck tonight up for us. But I'm also torn because, despite everything that's happened, I don't wish ill upon my uncle, even though he doesn't deserve my respect.

That familial connection is a real bitch to logic around when your relative kinda sucks.

Shoving the negative train of thought aside, I join Betmal in the closet. He stands at the back, leaning against the wall with a large box in his hands.

He crooks two fingers at me. "Come, ma siréne, open your gift."

I'm into the closet in a moment, taking the box from his hands. "Betmal! You did *not* have to get anything." I slap his chest. "I didn't buy you anything! Do we need to have a discussion about presents and when they're acceptable?"

He laughs. "I'll never agree not to buy things for you. Please remember that I spent thousands of years wishing for you, darling, and I'm a billionaire many times over. I could never spend all the money I've made. So, no, I will never agree to forgo the gifts."

"Good," I say with a laugh. "Because I didn't *buy* you anything, but I did make you something." I set the box down. "Let's come back to that because something tells me it's gonna be sexy, and I want to show you mine first."

"You have me intrigued, darling." He laughs. "Show me."

I drag him out of the closet and across the kitchen. We don't stop until we reach the workshop.

"Go on upstairs!" I push him ahead of me. The workshop and I messed with this earlier, and I can't wait to show him something I've been working on in secret for the last week or so.

Betmal laughs until we reach the top of the stairs. There, hung above his desk on the wall, is a giant portrait of us. I've got my back to his chest but I'm looking up over my shoulder with a smile. He's smiling down at me with one hand wrapped loosely around my throat. His mating bite is evident in the twin pinpricks just above my shoulder.

"I think it's some of my best work," I admit, wrapping my arm around his waist.

He stares at the giant portrait, at the way he's holding me close, staring at me with love in his eyes. And I'm equally obsessed, based on the look on my face. Rather than painting us in full color, I opted for shades of black, gray, and red.

"Ama." His voice breaks as he pulls my back to his front, encircling me with both arms. "It's the most stunning work you've done yet. I'm…I have no words, ma siréne."

I turn in his arms. "I love you, Betmal of House Zeniphon. And even though we've faced our challenges, I've always taken comfort in knowing you're by my side. We can do anything if we're together, right?"

His eyes shine glossy with tears as he bends and presses his lips to my mouth. "We can," he murmurs. "I love you, Amatheia."

Our kiss is tender, gentle, his tongue making a thorough exploration of my mouth as tears slide down his cheeks. When we part, he stares over my head at the painting, his extra lid slipping over his crimson irises.

"You really do like it, don't you?" I stroke his smooth jawline.

"I adore it," he whispers. "It's perfect, you sneaky female. When did you even make time to do this?"

I laugh. "I *was* sneaky. I want to open my present now, but I'll tell you all about it on the way back to the house, if you want." Around us, the wallpaper pulls off the walls in sheets that unroll and reroll with excitement. The workshop has been waiting to unveil this.

"We did it!" I reach for the wall and rub it gently. "Thanks for your help, my love."

The wallpaper stills, and the floorboards rumble under our feet.

"She's overcome with emotion." Betmal glances at the home around us. "You are a wonder, Ama."

I take his hand as he leads me out of the workshop and back to our closet. He strides to the back as I stare at his ass, admiring how freaking gorgeous and round and muscular it is.

"I can feel you staring, ma siréne," he says from the far end of the closet.

"Just admiring what's mine." I join him, slipping my arms around his waist, up his shirt to rest on his muscular pecs. "Maybe we should reveal the gift later. And right now, we should be naughty. What do you think?"

He spins, handing me the box again. "This may be the only time in our entire life I turn you down when you offer that, darling, but there's no time. We've got to be at the juncture of Sycamore and Main in half an hour, and you are not dressed."

"Oh fuck," I snap, turning to the outfit I laid out.

Betmal stays my hand. "No, Ama. Present first." He hands me the box and takes the top off.

Inside is a pile of sequin-covered fabric.

I glance up at Betmal. "Is this…?"

He smiles. "Custom-made to fit you for tonight's event. Try it on, please."

He holds the bottom of the box as I take the pile of fabric out.

When it falls long, I gasp. It's a dress, but not just any dress. A slinky, fully sequined dress with a slit almost up to the damn neckline.

"Betmal, my lady bits are gonna hang out of this!" I shoot him an accusatory look. "Or is that what you had in mind?"

"Just put it on." He laughs.

Shucking my clothes off, I step into the dress and pull the halter top up over my head. The slit actually goes all the way up my prosthetic leg, so when I walk, my leg will be visible to anyone who sees.

Betmal spins me to the mirror on the other side of the closet, bringing his lips to my ear. "I wrote you a poem, my darling. Would you like to hear it?"

His eyes meet mine in the mirror as I nod. Soft lips come to my ear, his focus never leaving my eyes.

"The moon forever gazes upon the sea without ever knowing the kiss of its waves. Daughter of the salt, I have unraveled the secret, why gods envy mere mortals. Do you know it? For each time we meet, I am reborn. A lifetime gifted with the span of your company. It is in this which lies the answer: amour."

My mouth drops open as he grins and presses a less-than-chaste kiss at the base of my neck. "You made that *up*?!"

"Yes, ma siréne. Poetry is a favorite pastime of mine, and you are my favorite topic."

I laugh and shimmy deeper into his arms. "Does that mean there are more poems about me?"

His answering chuckle sends heat flushing through me. "Perhaps, darling. When we come home tonight, I can share more, if you like."

"I love it, and I love you," I manage.

He grabs my hand and spins me slowly in front of the mirror. "You are absolutely ravishing in this dress. And if we didn't have somewhere to be, I'd pull it off you inch by inch with my teeth to show you exactly how much I love it. But we have a date, darling."

"Oh, I am definitely wearing this dress," I murmur. "This is incredible, mate." I spin in his arms. "Thank you, Betmal."

He grins and nips at my lower lip. "Thank me with your tongue later, ma siréne."

We make it out of the house with minimal shenanigans. The house waves all her shutters at us as we go, and regret fills me that we can't shrink her and take her with us to experience tonight's event.

We walk hand in hand toward Main Street. As we round the final bend near the Community Garden, I'm shocked to see what feels like all of Ever crowded at the intersection.

Abe and Morgan walk up the street toward us. Morgan wears a gorgeous crimson sheath dress that's tight around her waist and flares long. Her triplet sisters, Wren and Thea, join us, all dressed to the nines. Thatraeia walks next to Wren, and next to her is Taylor, Alba the centaur's nephew. He wears a vest cut to show off his muscular chest, smiling down at Thatraeia as she grins at me.

"Oh my goddess, you all look so beautiful!" I clasp my hands together as I stare at the gorgeous sisters. Morgan loops my hand through her arm and turns us to face Main Street.

"Look at all of this, Ama. This is all for you and Betmal. The whole town can't wait to celebrate with you."

Betmal joins us, taking my free hand. "Leave me out of it. This is a celebration of Ama's gift. I don't need any attention, thank you."

We laugh and head for the intersection. I notice Arkan standing in front of the gathered crowd, his hands clasped in front of his waist and his beautiful wife, Hana, by his side. When he sees Betmal and me, he nods and raises both arms high.

"Evertons! If I could have your attention, please!"

A hush falls over the crowd as we stare at our mayor of sorts. I turn to Betmal. "I don't remember this being part of the plan. I thought we were meeting at Town Hall. Wanna fill me in on your sneaky plan? Because this has you written all over it."

Morgan pats my hand. "Don't forget your sneaky friend-slash…shit…what am I to you, relationally speaking? I think you're my step-mother-in-law? That sounds fucking weird. Anyways, Arkan, Betmal and I did this. You're welcome in advance."

When I glance at Thatraeia, she simply laughs and throws both hands up. "I was sworn to secrecy. Sorry, but not really?"

I gasp as I look between them, unable to do anything but snort at how schemy they are. Turning to the front, I smile as Betmal squeezes my hand tighter, love filling the mate bond in my chest.

Arkan continues speaking, "Prepared to be dazzled, Ever. I present a night of celebration for the town of Ever and everything it represents. A place where ever-y-one is welcome, right?"

The crowd snickers, but he raises his arms higher. "Prepare yourselves!"

He drops his hands, and sparkles rain down from the sky in great sheets, cloaking Main Street. I've never seen the town's glamour in person, although I know it exists and can be edited by the Keeper depending on Ever's needs.

But as the sparkly wave overtakes every building and falls over the crowd, my mouth drops open in shock. Paintings—my paintings—are overlaid in front of every building, forming a hallway all the way down the street and culminating at Town Hall.

A virtual red carpet rolls down the middle of the street, disappearing into Town Hall at the far end.

Tears spring into my eyes as the Evertons start forward, marveling over the art and talking amongst themselves. I watch as they reach out and touch my brushstrokes.

There's the portrait of Iggy and Alo, and next to that, Wren.

Farther down is an up-close view of just the vine wrapping around her arm. All of Main Street looks like one giant painting.

"Come on, *dahling*," Morgan says, clicking at me like I'm a horse being ridden. "Let's go!"

As we make our way down Main, I'm more and more overwhelmed by how beautiful my art looks like this. Betmal is a silent, comfortable presence in my mind, filling me with love as we walk.

We reach the end of the street before I'm ready, but the red carpet runs all the way over the lawn and into Town Hall, where red streamers hang from every window, her doors flung wide open. In the long hallway that leads to the auditorium at the back, lights are strung in a haphazard crisscrossed fashion, looking like stars to light our way.

"Come." Betmal pulls me toward the front doors, glancing around almost like he's looking for something. Slight hesitation fills our bond, and I push concern back.

"What is it?" I whisper.

"I just can't wait to see it," he lies.

"Betmal," I warn with a growl. But the crowd pushes us up the stairs, through the doors, and down the long hall into the auditorium.

I was in here earlier to help set everything up. A table full of books sits on the stage with two chairs so Betmal and I can sit and sign books for the Evertons. My original artwork is placed at different stations throughout the room.

But I don't recognize anything past that. This'll be Morgan and Betmal's doing. Those sneaky sneaks.

String lights hang down from the ceiling, giving the entire room a timeless, ethereal glow. Floating, flickering candles hover just below that. Herschel's waitstaff glide around the room with trays of hand snacks, greeting our guests. But they don't look like themselves. No, they're glamoured to look like *painted* versions of themselves.

It is *awesome!*

I drag Betmal and Morgan in front of me. "Did you two?"

"Oh yeah," Morgan crows with a satisfied smile. "Yeah, we did." She pushes Betmal and me toward the front of the room. "Now go enjoy yourselves!"

Looking up at my mate, I smile. "Thank you, my love."

He bends down to breathe against my lips. "My only goal is making you happy, darling. Mission accomplished, judging by the smile on this beautiful mouth."

"Mission accomplished." I press my lips to his, forgetting about the milling crowd around us. When we part, I jerk my head toward the front. "Shall we sign some books, ma vampíre?"

He quirks a brow upward. "I love the French, my sweet." He brings his mouth to my ear. "But if you have time to learn French and paint secret portraits, perhaps I'm not keeping you busy enough in the bedroom. I'll remember that, ma siréne…"

A chill snakes down my spine, followed by a flush of heat outward from my core.

I lift my chin defiantly, knowing my eyes glimmer with need. "Maybe, Betmal. Maybe you need to work a little *harder*. Perhaps teach me a few new lessons?"

He places a finger under my chin, lifting until I stare into his gorgeous eyes. "I will remember this impudence when we return home." He brings his lips to my ear again. "We haven't explored all the kinks related to bondage and submission, but tonight seems a good time to begin your lessons in those."

I stare at him, this shocking male who pulled me from a humdrum life and gave me a chance to chase my dreams.

He must see all the thoughts running through my head, or read them with his gift, or feel them in our bond, because he smiles. "I know, darling. Come, let's enjoy this night, shall we?"

The next two hours fly by. Betmal and I visit every painting and talk to Evertons as they swing by to ask questions. Iggy and Alo stand with their portrait, and Iggy tells everyone all about it in a voice seven decibels too loud.

It's adorable.

Eventually, Betmal and I take the stage, and the Evertons line up to have free copies of the welcome book signed. I write my name carefully, whereas he signs with giant, carefree swooshes of the gold permanent marker. I laugh watching him; it's like he does everything—exactly the way he meant to without a thought about anyone else's opinion.

When he bristles, rising from the chair, I freeze with sudden concern. He calls his enormous wings and leaps over the signing table, landing gracefully in the center of the room. The crowd parts around him as I stand, heart thudding rapidly as he stalks to the auditorium door.

And there, oh goddess, there in the door stands Caralorn, Malakat hovering by his side. At his right stands Prince Stefan, and behind him, filling the hallway, is the entire King's Guard.

CHAPTER TWENTY-SEVEN
BETMAL

I stalk to the king, pushing reassurance through my bond with Ama. Her concern fills it, overwhelming every other sensation. Behind me, the sounds of her scrambling to rush off the stage echo throughout the room.

The auditorium is busy, still full of monsters eating and drinking and enjoying the new welcome book and all the displays. Iggy zips past my face, shouting at someone to come see his portrait.

But my eyes remain locked on the king. To my right, Arkan and Abemet join us, along with most of the rest of Ever's leadership. The other monsters stand in a half circle around me as I halt in front of Ama's uncle.

I lift my chin in defiance of whatever he's planning. Balling my fists, I spread my shadow wings wide enough to cover any view of the room from him. Just behind Malakat stands a merman I haven't seen yet. His stance and the way he looks around the room tells me he's royal, and probably a warrior too.

This must be the suitor.

I glare at them all. "If you are here to ruin this night for her in any capacity, I will *strike you down*. That is a promise," I hiss.

The King's Guard starts forward, spears raised, but the king lifts a hand to stop them. Eyes the color of emeralds narrow, and he sighs. "I know what this looks like, given how I—"

"Uncle!" Ama slides under my left wing and steps in front of me. "Please don't cause a scene."

He sputters, "I did not come for that, Amatheia." He gestures at the room behind us. "Malakat convinced me to come and see your work, and that is all we are here to do."

Thatraeia joins us, glaring at her father. "Father, this is—"

"Show me your work, please." The king waves at the full auditorium as he takes it in. When he offers Ama his elbow, glancing at her leg then quickly into her eyes, I bristle further.

Nothing is right about this. I can't imagine he's had a change of heart, given that the suitor stands just behind his daughter. When I look at the other male, he's not looking at me—surprising because I'm the closest threat. But, no, his eyes are firmly on Amatheia in a way that has me ready to rip his wavy amber ears bodily from him.

I glance at Arkan, but he's staring at Caralorn with a suspicious expression, the same sentiment in my gut. If the king wanted to start a fight, this would be the perfect place to do so. I keep my fists loosely balled, scanning Malakat and the guard behind her. Caralorn would have to be an idiot to fight us in such a public way. Especially with me here.

Thankfully, no one else seems to notice anything amiss.

The shifters spread out along the perimeter. Another half dozen are outside waiting to respond if needed.

Arkan clip-clops forward. "Thrilled to have you, Your Majesty. Perhaps you wouldn't mind leaving the guard in the hallway so we don't frighten your lander neighbors?"

The king looks at Malakat. "You may come, if you wish, but leave the rest behind." He turns and looks at Ama as Malakat barks orders at her men. She shoos them toward the door but remains just behind her father.

Fuck me, she looks...curious?

Ama loops Thatraeia's arm through hers, declining Caralorn's elbow, but looks at Malakat and the other male. "If you'd like to join me, I'd be more than happy to show you around the room and explain what my mate and I have been working so hard on."

The tall, muscular merman blanches but recovers quickly. Malakat's frown twitches as emerald green eyes flicker between her father, Stefan, and me.

"After you," Caralorn murmurs, gesturing for Ama to lead the way.

Arkan pauses beside me. "I'll stand here if you want to accompany her. We've got this, friend."

Still on edge, I trail behind Ama and the other merfolk as she starts on one side of the room.

A quarter hour later, they listen raptly as she explains Wren's green witch power, and the vine crawling up her forearm in that particular portrait.

Ama is in her element like this. It's not lost on me how much the discord between her and her uncle weighed her down. I still find myself glancing at the door every few moments, but Arkan and his wife stand there. Around the edges of the room, the protector team is fanned out, eyeing the crowd and ready for anything that might come at us. So far, Caralorn hasn't tried anything.

By the time we get to the stack of books on stage, there are just a few left.

Ama rounds the table and hands a book to her uncle, then each of her cousins. "You can see inside that Betmal married my paintings and sketches with the core of the welcome data. The typography is perfect, and it beautifully fits his desire to make the welcome packet something *more*...something *better*." She smiles tentatively at Caralorn. "And this version is printed on waterproof paper, so it'll be accessible for anyone in the lake, if they want one."

Caralorn takes the book and hands it to Stefan, then picks up another for himself.

I notice how the supposed suitor barely glances through it before setting it aside on an empty table.

Malakat flips through her book until she lands on a page with a painted view of the black stone beach and the lake. Ama added Thatraeia's head popping out of the lake, a smile on her sweet face as she looks at the viewer on shore. Malakat looks at her youngest sister. "Did you pose for this painting, or…"

Thatraeia shakes her head and takes the book, smiling at Ama. "I didn't. How did you do this, Ama?"

My mate smiles with pleasure. "From memory, Cousin. You're in my heart, always. I could paint you with my eyes closed."

Malakat stiffens, but Thatraeia rounds the table and slings an arm around Ama's waist. "Will you sign this for me?"

The green mermaid barks out a laugh. "What will you do with it, Sister? You already know all about this haven."

"I don't, actually," Thatraeia snaps back. "Because I was never encouraged to come take part in the community outside of the lake."

I glance at the king, who purses his lips, nostrils flaring as he looks off into the distance. If he's surprised to see this sudden confidence in his daughter, he barely seems to acknowledge it.

Perhaps that's because this is the moment he chooses to unleash on us. I'm ready for it, if so.

But the moment passes, and he looks at Ama as she tucks her hair over her shoulder. Her claiming bite is clear, two pinpoints that are still healing.

He turns to me with a ferocious look, stalking until his chest hits mine. "Claimed? She is claimed?"

Ama shoves her way between us as I glare at the puffed-up merking.

"Uncle, yes, I am," she says, her tone pleading. "Happily. And this is what I've been trying to tell you this whole time. I've always been different. I've never wanted to stay in the lake. I need something different to be happy. And that's…okay. It's more than okay."

He glares at her, then me, then back at her. After a tense moment where I resist the urge to call my wings back, he visibly slumps. "You're like her, you know, your mother. She was always torn between the land and the sea. She always worried about how dangerous the sea could be, and she was right to. It killed her, in the end. But she always loved the land, just like you. She would have loved this." He waves at the busy auditorium around us.

Ama, Thatraeia and Malakat all stare at Caralorn in apparent shock.

The suitor stands quietly next to Malakat, but his muscles bunch and stiffen.

My intuitive gift pings, sensing darkness in the king just as all hells break loose.

Caralorn tosses a small disk to the ground, Malakat lurching toward Ama at the same time.

I shove Ama out of the way as I leap for the younger merman, my biggest threat. Caralorn sidesteps around the disk on the ground just as it lets out a great cracking noise and a small green surface appears in the floor.

Oh gods. It's a fucking portal.

Time slows for me as multiple things occur simultaneously. The younger merman lurches toward Caralorn, whose eyes spring wide in shock. Thatraeia reaches for Ama even as Malakat drags them toward the shimmering green hole in the floor. Ama flails and struggles, but Malakat's got a hold on her neck.

Intuition tells me the males remain my biggest problem, even as the portal expands until it's big enough for someone to go through. Not a male.

But a female.

One Ama's size.

Realization courses through me as I burst over it and knock into the males. At the edges of my vision, I sense Arkan, Abe and the others rushing toward the fray.

Ama screams for me, and I leap up to see Malakat shoving her toward the portal. Thatraeia scratches and tears at her sister's arms and hair.

Caralorn roars in triumph until I leap for Ama, knocking all three girls to the floor. I rip my mate from Malakat's arms and swoop halfway across the room, setting her down near the door. The room is in chaos, screams echoing and shouting off the ceiling as Evertons flee the scene.

I focus as Malakat, Caralorn and the other merman stand in a line on the opposite side of the portal. Caralorn and the bigger male stare daggers at one another.

"What the depths are you doing, Stefan?" Caralorn barks, even as the shifters form a half circle around him.

Malakat comes quietly behind her father, swinging her spear and pressing the pointed tip to the base of his spine.

He growls and spins, reaching for it, but is halted by Stefan's arms around his throat, yanking him away from his daughter.

"Your reign is done, Caralorn," Stefan snarls.

In my arms, Ama gasps and pushes free, running toward Thatraeia.

I swoop behind her, slinging an arm around her waist as I watch the scene unfold. The merfolk are surrounded. My woman is safe.

"You're done, Father," Malakat announces loudly. "This nonsense with Amatheia stops now."

Caralorn sputters, the sound choked off as Stefan's arm

tightens around the king's neck. The bigger merman kicks the back of the king's knees, dropping him quickly to the ground. "Not to mention I think Hearth HQ will be very interested in your possession of this bit of portal tech. Possession of anything related to the portal system is illegal, but I suppose you knew that, didn't you?"

Caralorn glares at Malakat and Stefan. "You were in on this plan. You're no more innocent than I!"

Malakat shakes her head and takes a step back, glancing at Amatheia. "No, Father. We went along with it only to put an end to this. Oh, and to seat Stefan on your throne, of course." She grins at the younger man.

Caralorn sputters and attempts to rise, but can't when Stefan backhands him across the face.

"You do not deserve the beautiful kingdom you have," Stefan growls. "So I will be relieving you of it and taking your throne, in partnership with my queen."

I snarl as I pull Ama into my arms, daring the other male to even think of taking her from me.

"Not Amatheia," Stefan says with a glittering, triumphant smile. Bright amber eyes flick to Malakat. "My vicious, perfect princess."

Ama and Thatraeia let out matching gasps as murmurs float through the gathered crowd.

Malakat looks at Arkan, who appears by my side. "Can you house my father somewhere until we're able to file a formal report with Hearth HQ?"

Arkan nods as he stares at the merfolk. "We'll need to fill out quite a bit of paperwork." He waves at Caralorn who's still crouched on the ground on his knees. "This is all quite unexpected."

Malakat grins, the look sinister on her. "I imagine so, Keeper. Let me assure you that Stefan and I plan to usher in a new age between the merfolk and Downtown Ever. You'll remove the magical bindings, naturally. We won't be needing those."

Arkan harrumphs. "As long as you don't plan any further bullshit like what your father did to Amatheia, you'll have a partner in me."

Stefan grips Caralorn by the braids and drags him around the portal as it slowly begins to close. He shoves the king at Ama's feet and smiles at us.

"No. My own clan is constantly at war with others in our region. I don't want that in my future. I want peace and stability. Mala and I will work hard alongside you."

Ama surprises me by pulling out of my arms and joining Malakat and Stefan. She takes their hands in her own. "Thank you both. Truly, I cannot thank you enough for putting a stop to all of this." She eyes Caralorn warily. "Although to be honest, I never imagined it might go down like this."

Stefan's smile is wry. "I knew when I met you that I couldn't allow the farce of our marriage to continue. You were as trapped as I felt, Princess. Once Mala learned of Caralorn's plan, it was easy enough to figure out how to subvert him."

"The portal was engineered to take you directly to Stefan's kingdom," Malakat says quietly. "You and I have never been... close. But I know what it feels like to love someone you can't have. I couldn't be party to what he was doing any longer."

"That's surprising, Malakat," Ama says, her tone slightly less friendly. "To say we aren't close is the understatement of a century."

Malakat blanches, cheeks blushing a darker shade of green. "You're right, Cousin. I can't change what I did in the past, but I hope you'll give me the chance to learn and grow. I want to be a good queen, now that I have a chance to."

Thatraeia rushes forward into Ama's arms. "Then Ama can come home whenever she wants to, right?"

Malakat smiles, and this smile finally appears genuine. "Anytime she wants, Little Sister." Her focus moves to Ama once more. "Any time you want, Cousin. I'm serious."

I've been watching this little scene play out, wondering how the chips would fall. But I step forward now, staring at Malakat. "I trust you do not hold your father's desire to keep Ama from me, and this issue is now *fully* resolved?"

She lifts her chin. "Yes, Vampire. Distasteful as I find it for Ama to pick a bloodsucker, you're welcome in the merkingdom as well."

"Depths, Malakat," Thatraeia barks. "That was crazy rude."

Malakat lifts both hands. "Whaaaaaat?"

I sigh. Hopefully Ama won't want to spend too much time with her blunt, discourteous cousin. Perhaps I should plan to keep my mate too busy traveling to have any time to spend with Malakat in the lake.

Arkan claps me on the shoulder. "Well, Betmal, looks like things turned out fine in the end, my friend." He glances at Caralorn. "Mostly fine."

I glare down at Caralorn in a grumbly, crumpled heap on the floor. "Oh, if only you'd let me deal directly with this, it *would* be delightful, Arkan."

The big keeper laughs. "No murdering today, Betmal. Sorry. I'm not sure even *you* could get out of that one."

Sighing, I spin my woman in my arms and bring my lips to hers. "Mine," I murmur.

She smiles up at me, dragging me into the beautiful depths of those dark azure eyes.

"And now nobody will ever part us, Betmal."

CHAPTER TWENTY-EIGHT
AMATHEIA

Somehow, Morgan and her sisters manage to get the party back on track as Arkan and the shifters remove Caralorn and the portal disk. Catherine followed them out to inspect it because apparently she has theories about how my uncle even got it in the first place.

I'll have plenty of questions once I absorb the crap that just happened, but for now, I want to enjoy the tattered shreds of the launch event.

Despite the Hector triplets' best efforts, the party naturally winds down, and Betmal and I sign more books. Eventually, Morgan and Abe bring over two stacked plates of food and force us to eat something.

"Don't be like humans at a wedding where you forget to eat," she says as she sets the plate down in front of me. "Who knows what a hangry mermaid looks like."

I laugh as I pick up a piece of kimchi flatbread that Herschel outdid himself with. Shoving it in my mouth, I laugh around a piece that was too big. "It's not, mmph, good," I manage, nearly choking on the kimchi as I struggle to swallow. "We get a little crazy."

Betmal pulls me to his side. "If you wanted to choke on something, ma siréne, I have better ideas than food."

"Okay!" Morgan claps her hands together, eyes springing wide. "I was just coming to check on you two, but I think you're fine, and that's all I really need to hear about that." She leans in close to me. "But also, get it, girl, because he is really so fine."

I laugh as she dances away from me and into Abe's arms. The big vampire twirls her across the floor and toward the door, casting us a quick salute as he leaves.

We look around, but the auditorium is nearly empty at this point. Arkan and his wife walk over to us, looking tired but happy.

Hana reaches down and places a hand on my shoulder. "This evening was incredible. We're so thrilled for the both of you. Arkan tells me you've actually got approval from Evenia to begin stocking the welcome books, is that right?"

Betmal nods. "Correct. I'll order a small stockpile on Evenia's credit card and have them sent to Town Hall, if you like."

"Perfect," she says, smiling at her mate. "I didn't realize how much this project was needed until I saw your vision, and I'm blown away by how gorgeous it is. What's the best way for us to update it as things change?" She winces. "Not that we're expecting change, I just wanted to ask."

Betmal laughs and pinches my side. "See what I meant in the very beginning, darling? This project is not going to end for a very, very long time. I've already deposited payment for the second haven into your account."

We laugh as one while we head for the door. But already, my mind is spinning around Ever's growth and how we might incorporate new businesses into the welcome books. At the exit, I pat Town Hall's front doors, glancing up at the beautifully etched ceiling. "Thank you, friend. You were the perfect hostess for tonight's festivities. I'm sorry things went a little bit sideways."

The entire hall's worth of wallpaper peels from the walls and dances around joyfully. Overhead, the ceiling tiles clap in waves up and down the hall.

"She's thrilled." Arkan lays his hand on his wife's withers. "And so are we. I'm glad this all worked out."

"Oh yeah." I smile up at Betmal. "Yeah, it did." Even so, part of my heart hurts for Caralorn. He lost something when my mother died, and even though I don't agree with his behavior, he's been in pain since her death. I hope one day he figures out how to deal with that, but for now, it's not looking good for him.

Betmal returns my smile with a feral, wicked look as the centaurs carefully descend the front steps and trot toward downtown. Somewhere ahead on Main, it sounds like the party rages on. I don't recall that being part of our plans either.

Sneaky, *sneaky* friends and mate.

Thatraeia comes to say goodbye, announcing that she and Taylor are headed to Herschel's for a late dinner.

Oh my gods, is this a *date*?!

Betmal spreads his shadow wings wide, curling one around me. His feathers tickle my side and leg. "Darling, would you like to go enjoy downtown a bit more? It seems the party might carry on for a while, and I know there's always dancing behind the movie theater. In fact, Abemet and Morgan are probably there now."

I shake my head, wrapping both arms around my big vampire. "I'm all monstered out, my love. Take me home? I believe there was a lesson in obedience promised to me, and I want it."

Betmal laughs and picks me up bridal style, cradling me to his muscular chest. "I can do that, ma siréne. Having you on your knees before me has always been a particularly thrilling fantasy of mine. But on the way, I have one last gift. Reach into my pocket, if you will."

I snort. "I've heard that one before, ma vampíre."

He winks at me. "You might find that, too, but you'll also find a folded sheet of paper."

Curious, I slide my hand into one pocket to find it empty. Reaching around his other side, I retrieve a folded sheet of paper.

I stare up at him in confusion. "It's a flier for a musical in another haven." My mouth drops open. "Are we going? Is that our next assignment?!" I almost kick my legs in joy. I pause for a moment, worried that it'll hurt. Then I remember that I don't have to worry about that anymore, because I finally have a prosthetic that fits.

He *did that* for me.

"We have tickets to that musical," he says as he pushes off the ground and swoops up into the sky. We catch a current near the magical ward ceiling that protects all of Ever. "It's an underwater musical in the New York City haven, Rainbow. Most of the performers are merfolk. I thought that might make an excellent next adventure, ma siréne." He drops a kiss to my forehead. "We can stay for a few weeks and work, if you like. I have carte blanche from Evenia to work on this project in whatever order I want."

"Oh, I bet you do," I say with a giddy laugh. "I can't wait, Betmal." I nip at my lip. "When do you want to go?"

He smiles at me, hugging me tight as we soar over downtown and toward our home. "Tomorrow, ma siréne? Or the next day or the next? Anytime. Anywhere. As long as we're together."

I tuck my head beneath his chin and sigh with happiness.

CHAPTER TWENTY-NINE
BETMAL

I stand knee-deep in the water on the lakeshore with Arkan and Abe by my side. The new merking, Stefan, stands opposite us with Malakat. In the week since they ousted Caralorn, we've discovered them to be brutally efficient but highly pragmatic.

A step above their predecessor.

Still, I don't think I'll ever forgive Malakat for her role prior to what happened with Caralorn, or her inaction over decades while Ama was in pain. But Ama begrudgingly thinks of them as her family, and so dropping Malakat into a deep crevasse isn't an option.

Stefan gets straight to the point. "Caralorn?"

Arkan's nod is clipped. "Removed from Ever by Hearth HQ and rehomed elsewhere, per your and Amatheia's requests."

Malakat sucks in a quick breath, relief splashing across her features.

"He'll be fine, my love," Stefan says quietly.

She nods but says nothing.

Stefan lifts his chin. "I've notified the merfolk High Council about Caralorn's actions and the subsequent need for me to take over to prevent the collapse of his kingdom. The Council was… grateful." His smile grows feral. "Apparently, Caralorn was not well liked among his peers."

I snort. "I suspect that to be the understatement of the century."

He continues, "You will find me to be a peaceful king with a vicious streak only if absolutely necessary. That said, I'd like my people to experience Downtown Ever more fully. There is a beautiful world outside our lake."

Arkan smiles. "Ever welcomes that, King Stefan. I'd love to meet with you and discuss any accessibility accommodations that might have worked for you in your prior haven." He smiles at me. "The waterproof welcome book is a nice start, but I'm sure there's more to be done."

He dips his head respectfully. "Of course, Keeper." Glancing at me, his smile softens. "I'd like to visit Amatheia very soon to discuss the return of her dowry. It seemed appropriate to tell you now rather than show up unannounced."

I hold back a sigh, but I know this is important to her. "Of course. Let me know when, and I'll cook you some of her favorites."

Stefan nods and reaches for Malakat's hand. She looks up at him, and it's easy to see a softer side of her. She's in love; that much is clear. I just hope their union *does* usher in a new order for the lake, one where Ama can come and go if she wants to. I honestly think the things she'll miss the most are the castle herself and Sovereign Sip, the bar.

Speaking of which, I need to plan a cocktail hour down there. She swears she makes a mean martini, but I bet her that mine's superior. I'm eager to win and enjoy collecting on that bet.

Arkan looks at me. "I need a few minutes with the king and queen, Betmal. Tell Ama hi for me?"

It's a clear dismissal, but I don't care. Ama didn't want to come to this meeting, preferring to splash around in the pond at home. She and the house are cooking something up, I just know it.

Abemet joins me as we leave the lake behind, walking through peaceful, quiet forest toward my convertible. When we get there, he slips into the passenger seat.

"Thatraeia moved into the Annabelle Inn this morning. Sounds like Catherine refused to charge her, but Ama insisted on paying, or perhaps you did?"

I shrug. "My mate is a wealthy woman, darling. She does what she wants with her money."

Abe laughs, the sound like a purr. I haven't heard him laugh in centuries. Not until Morgan.

I turn and smile at my son. "Where shall I drop you, darling?"

He grins, waving at the street in front of us. "Diner, please. Morgan's working on shoring up the foundation beneath it today. Apparently, she felt some weakness last time we were there."

That pulls a laugh from me. "I call bullshit. I think your mate wants to flex her powers, Abemet. Perhaps a few adventures outside of Ever would be good for her."

He grins. "She bores easily—well, of everything but me. Why do you think I take her on so many vacations? She's keeping me young." He laughs. "Well, young at heart. Now that this issue with Caralorn has ended, we're going to Rainbow for a rock concert."

I smile as we pull into the street and head toward downtown.

A quarter hour later, after I've dropped him at the diner, I park the car under the carport. Splashing sounds echo from around the back of the house. I slip my hands into my pockets and walk the path, leaning against an arched trellis. In front of me, Ama splashes and plays in the pond, laughing as the workshop tosses paintbrushes and closed jars of paint at her.

"My darlings, are you playing tag?"

Ama jolts upright, shocked expression morphing into a wicked grin. "Something like that, ma vampíre. The water's nice. Want to come in and tell me how things went?"

Pulling my shirt over my head, I toss it aside. Ama's dark aqua eyes follow as I shove my pants down and step out of them. I'm naked before her, and like always, the way she scans my whole body and then beams up at me fills me with need.

"Darling," I purr. "Let's discuss meetings later, shall we? For now, I want to talk about our next assignment."

She grins at me. "Evenia called while you were gone. As you might imagine, I did not answer."

I laugh at that as I stalk into the lake until I'm close enough to pull her into my arms. "My naughty girl, did you leave her wondering what we were up to?"

Ama joins me in laughter. "Oh, I know she *knows* what we're up to, and I bet Thalassa she's jealous as hells because I get to keep you."

"That's right," I whisper into her mouth. Capturing her lower lip, I suck and wrap her lithe legs around my waist.

We kiss until we're breathless, and when we part, she puts a finger beneath my chin. "Betmal, I got notification of a new deposit into my account today. That's the third one, and we haven't even planned the second book. Getting a little ahead of yourself, aren't you?"

My prideful chuckle is all the answer she needs.

I remove her finger from beneath my chin and nip my way along it until I reach her palm. "What did I tell you in the very beginning, my darling? You've never known support until you've had *me* in your corner. Do you remember?"

Aqua eyes flash and narrow as she watches my tongue. "Yes."

I bite her thumb. "Yes, what?"

"Yes, mate," she whispers.

Smiling, I push us across the pond until I can lay her on the beach closest to the workshop. "Shall I show you just how much I love you, Amatheia?"

She flutters dark lashes at me. "Perhaps."

I frown down at her as she slides out from between my arms, attaching her prosthetic to her leg.

"You'll have to catch me first," she screeches as she takes off into the forest, crashing through the undergrowth.

Laughing, I close my eyes.

Salt. Sand. Caramel.

Blinking my eyes open, I call my senses, narrowing them as I start toward the trees. Time to hunt, and when that hunt is over, time to love. I smile as I power through the forest, following the sounds of my mate, giggling as she flees.

Happily ever after isn't so far away, after all.

THE END

++

Are you ready for the final Haven Ever After romance?!
Catherine gets her happily ever after...
Preorder Misbehaving with Minotaurs now!
(And read on for the first two chapters)

BONUS CONTENT:
Want to follow along as Betmal and Ama take the Big Apple (and a royal merman)? Sign up for my newsletter to access the steamy epilogue!

CHAPTER ONE - CATHERINE

"Annabelle," I admonish as the black cat kitchen timer swivels on its base and meows at me. The countertop ripples, slinging the salt shaker toward the pan of vegetables I just started sauteeing. Rolling my eyes upward, I chuckle as the inn's ceiling tiles ripple playfully, clacking like piano keys.

"No more salt." I grab the shaker and shove it in the cabinet above the stove. "Guests can add it as needed, but there's no need for us to go salt crazy."

The cat timer spins to face away from me as the ceiling tiles still, the kitchen going utterly silent except for the sound of the vegetables in the pan.

"Don't be irritated, my love." Reaching out, I rub the tiles behind the stovetop.

One of the kitchen windows opens and slams angrily shut.

Sighing, I open the cabinet, withdraw the salt, and toss a dash on the vegetables.

For whatever reason, my home has a very strong preference on salt content and this is not the hill I want to die on today. Last time I disagreed with her about salting the breakfast foods, she locked my bedroom door for twenty minutes until I apologized profusely.

It's funny what topics Annabelle feels strongly about. She and I are usually in lock step about *everything*, but occasionally she surprises me in her preferences.

The salt, for instance.

And her refusal to let me touch up the white paint on her shutters.

The tiny cat timer executes a darling series of flips along the countertop, popping onto the back of the stove, its kitty features curling into a smile.

We fall into an easy silence as I finish the vegetables for the breakfast buffet. All of our rooms are full but one, and I'm expecting a guest any mo—

The ding of a bell echoes down the hallway, interrupting my thoughts. Annabelle ripples the backsplash tile to warn me that there's someone up front. I laugh and stroke the tile again.

"Thank you, my darling."

The cat timer meows as the front bell dings a second time.

Leaving the kitchen, I hurry along the skinny hallway to find a handsome young pixie male standing in the inn's front entryway. He holds a suitcase in one hand, a long garment draped over his other forearm. Translucent blue wings flutter lightly at his back, the tips of his pointed ears twitching slightly.

"Welcome to the Annabelle Inn." I slide behind the tall wooden check in desk and smile. "You must be Gilbert Sintjan?"

His blue lips pull into a half smile. "That's me. I presume you're Catherine, the Annabelle Inn's famous proprietress?"

I laugh. "I do believe you made up that word, Gilbert, but yes, that's me."

The edges of his lips turn down. "You don't happen to still have breakfast available, do you? I had heard the Galloping Green Bean diner makes a to die for burger, and I was actually going to have that for breakfast, but they were *quite* busy."

When I give him a surprised look, he laughs.

"I know, it's weird. I don't like breakfast food. But anyhow, the line was out the door and the very terse centaur hostess told me in no uncertain terms that it would be two hours at least before she could seat me."

I sigh, shooting him an understanding look. "Alba is direct on the best of days but you're right that the burger is absolutely fantastic there. You're in luck, though, I was just about to replenish the breakfast buffet. It runs from eight to ten a.m. each morning except on the weekends."

He winks. "You don't happen to have burgers though, do you?"

We laugh together as I shake my head. "No burgers, but I was just sauteing vegetables and there's plenty of variety. I'm so busy these days it's easier to justify a wide selection of offerings." I return his wink. "And don't worry, it's not all traditional breakfast food."

I take Gilbert's credit card and hand him a key for his room—the mermaid themed room upstairs. We head for the second floor where I drop him off at his door and offer to give him a tour of Ever at any point, if he'd like one.

Remembering the vegetables, I rush back to the kitchen. The pan swirls slowly on the stove, the veggies sizzling and snapping.

"Thank you Annabelle," I manage, grabbing the pan and tossing the perfectly cooked veggies in a bowl. The black cat timer turns to watch me as I carry the veggies through a small butler's pantry and into the formal dining room. My guests are beginning to arrive, and I greet each monster, answering a few questions as they begin to dig into the buffet.

The breakfast hours are a blur as I constantly refill the buffet and clean up as monsters make a bit of a mess. It's not until the last guest leaves that I return to the kitchen and sit at the island for a moment.

Around me, the Annabelle feels happy. I sense her the way I always have—she's like a warm hug, constantly there, a friend by my side. I've often wondered if this is how shifter mate bonds feel, that innate and deep sense of *knowing* about another being. Because I swear I can think something and Annabelle seems to know.

I glance up at the beautiful coffered ceiling. "I'm headed to a meeting with town leadership, darling. Arkan thinks it's time to expand downtown Ever. Most of the businesses are stretched past capacity, as are we. Wouldn't you agree?"

Annabelle groans her assent, the floorboards creaking beneath my feet.

I rise and go to the fridge, grabbing a filtered water bottle. "I suppose we'd have to expand into the rose garden because I don't really want to stack a bunch more stories on top of you."

Around me, she stills. The only sound is the steady tick-tock of the wall clock. I look around the kitchen while Annabelle thinks. We'd need to bump out this space to give it more industrial size, and we'd cut into the rose garden a bit. But it's an easy enough fix. Now, if we wanted more rooms we'd have to add on another story, because there's not enough space in my backyard to expand that way. Although to be honest, I'm already a bit busier than I'd like to be. If anything, I want less rooms, not more.

The cat timer hops around the back of the stove and to the far end of the countertop. Scrunching down, it executes a leap onto the window ledge, spinning to face the backyard rose garden. Like always, it's a perfect sixty-five degrees outside—a weather pattern I chose when I designed Ever all those centuries ago—and the rose bushes sway gently, their blooms beautifully vibrant year round.

The timer spins slowly to face me as the window behind it opens, allowing the breeze in. It brushes over my face, rustling pale gray waves over my eyes. Shoving my hair out of the way, I stare at the gorgeous rose garden behind the inn, musing about what it would be like to finally grow the Annabelle Inn...and if I even want that.

Realistically, the Annabelle might be my heart building and best friend, but she was always meant to be my retirement hobby. I'm already busier than I'd like to be, but I haven't been willing to hire a helper just yet. It hasn't felt like the right time... although as two separate guests appear in the doorway, I consider that it might be the time now.

Smiling broadly, I greet the guests.

No rest for the weary.

~

"So, thrall attacks and warlocks and revenants don't seem to be deterring anyone from moving to Ever. Have you all noticed?"

Ever's Keeper, Arkan, crosses his muscular arms over his chest as he swishes his tail lazily against his black-coated sides. He looks around at us with glittering blue eyes. The rest of us are seated, but the handsome young centaur prefers to remain standing during haven leadership meetings. He walks circles around our table sometimes and it's very distracting to me, but he's an excellent Keeper. Much like a human mayor, if monsters have such a thing.

Alo Rygold, one of two gargoyles from the town's protector team, leans back with a wry look on his handsome, angular features. "Hopefully Ever's many *charms* are the main draw? Although to be honest, having a blue witch living in town is probably pulling monsters here, too."

Arkan nods, making eye contact with each of us in turn. I'd almost laugh at how focused he is—young people can be so intense—but we need that excitement.

"Since the opening of the Grand Portal Station at Hearth HQ

haven, we're drawing in an average of twenty new residents per month. The wraith motel and Annabelle Inn are constantly full. Homes keep popping up to accommodate the new Evertons. I've got five requests to call humans here from the outside world via the town map. And our businesses are...well..." he glances at Ohken Stonesmith, the troll owner of our singular General Store and Fleur, the flower shop. "Ohken, you're busy. Too busy. Tell me I'm wrong."

Ohken sighs around the big tusks that stick up from his lower jaw. "I never thought the day would come when I'd need more help or have to consider expanding the General Store, but I am. Wren and I talked about hiring an architect to design a second floor, but I haven't bitten the bullet yet. I'm not getting nearly enough time at home with her, and that's a problem for me."

I smile. I had the privilege of watching him fall in love with Wren Hector. And I watched her triplet sisters and their young aunt, the blue witch, all fall in love, too. Ever's been awash with love stories in these last few months.

That almost makes my smile fall. I've been working on my own love story.

It's not going well.

I risk a glance at Arkan's father, Vikand, who rests comfortably on a long centaur bench by his son's side. Like always, the brilliant centaur appears lost in thought, arms crossed over his broad chest and pale eyes glazed. Arkan says something, but Vikand looks across the table at me. A soft smile tips his lips upward.

Even from here, my succubus' senses are strong enough to pick up a wash of pheromones from him. He's always found me attractive, but he's quiet, shy, bookish to the extreme. I've been pursuing him slowly, certain he'll never make the first move. I return the half smile. After this meeting, I'm asking him out.

When he glances away from me and up at his son, who's still

talking, I shove that thought away. I need to focus because this meeting is important to Ever's future.

Arkan barrels on, seemingly oblivious to my temporary inattention.

"I want to get ahead of the growth, because I believe what we've seen so far is just a trickle. Since the opening of the headquarters portal station, we've been slammed. Now that it's easier to come to Ever, I predict our tourism to grow by leaps and bounds. We need more restaurants and inns. Actually…" his voice trails off as he sinks down onto his forelegs, pointing at a rolled up tube of paper on the giant round table in front of us. "This is a set of old plans from a very long time ago when Ever was created. It wasn't the final design, obviously, but some elements could be reused now. Town Hall provided these to me when I spoke with her earlier this evening about potential expansion." He looks around the table with a smile. "She's on board, by the way, excited even."

I've seen these plans. I know what he's going to show us before he unrolls them. I was there when the various options were originally designed. But it's still fun when he rolls the paper flat and sets paperweights at each corner.

"There," he says, pointing to a street at the far end of Main, just before the Historical Society and Town Hall. "The reason there's currently the grassy area between the last shops on either side of Main and Town Hall is because there was always meant to be another cross street there. We need it now. And I need to be courting business folks from other havens to open locations here. Restaurants, coffee shops, gift shops." He glances at me. "Probably inns, too."

"Let's take a step back for a second. Do we *want* to grow Ever?" A handsome shifter male with white-flecked black hair stands and points at the edge of town. "I'm not saying we don't, I'm just asking if we're all in agreement that we *do*. All the new homes springing up are beginning to encroach on Shifter

Hollow territory and my people are getting antsy. Which again, is fine if that's what we want. But we'll need to expand Shifter Hollow, too. The shifters, centaur and pegasi need more space." He stares at the old plans before looking up at Arkan. "My population is growing."

Arkan nods. "Don't I know it. These old plans don't account for that, but I think it'd be easy enough to expand the ward and grow Shifter Hollow's surface area too." He glances over at me. "Can you see any complications with that, Catherine?"

It sounds like he's just asking my opinion as a member of Ever's leadership team, but he and I know the question goes deeper than that. I'm involved in haven creation in a way few monsters know about. Not even everyone in this room is aware. But Ohken looks over at me, his expression neutral. He's been there when I've used my power. He's seen what I'm capable of.

I smile up at Arkan. "We're not close to any human towns. There's only forest around us for a hundred miles in every direction...plenty of space to expand into. It's wise to think about this growth now." I look around to the gathered monsters, wonderful beings I've known, some for centuries. "Our growth rate is only going to increase and as Arkan mentioned, tourism is on the rise thanks to the new portal station. We never had much tourism before since it was such a pain to travel between havens, but now?" I run my fingers over the slightly curled old plans. "We thought this might happen one day, that's how these plans came to be. I'm in agreement that we need to have these conversations sooner than later."

Arkan barks out a laugh. "Oh, I'm not done with my suggestions, either." He opens his hands wide, grinning at the gathered group. "We have a shiny new skyball stadium and a team that never practices. Even so, we almost won last year's skyball championship. I want to put a bigger focus on our team. I'd like to attract regular games and court some rising stars.

There's big money in skyball, and we don't really get a piece of that pie now."

Ohken lets out an uncharacteristic growl. "I don't want to take *more* time away from Wren, even though I'm technically on the Ever team. You know most of us who play are part time at best. I assume you'd want regular practices? We don't do that now and I don't want to start."

"I know we don't." Arkan crosses his arms again. "But we should. Again, with the new portal station it's a rock solid investment for us to do this. It'll bring tourism, and tourism will be good for everyone in this room." He shoots Ohken a pointed look. "I'm not suggesting you have to become a full time skyball player, friend, just that we should consider investing in a professional team."

"He's right," I offer.

"Catherine, care to expand on that thought?" Shepherd, Alo's younger brother, smiles at me from across the table. "Ever's got such a wonderful small town feel. Are we talking about losing that if we bring skyball here?"

I toss my long gray waves over my shoulder as I pull my thoughts quickly together. "During last year's skyball tournament, Ever was packed and busy, but it was the best weekend on record for sales at many of our shops and restaurants. Money doesn't buy happiness, but it can buy freedom. I'm in favor of creating that opportunity for our friends and neighbors."

I look around at the group of monsters I've come to admire so highly over the years. "I have friends I haven't seen in years because interhaven travel was previously such a pain. That's already changing because of the new Grand Portal Station. Getting busier is going to happen whether we're ready for it or not. The pinch we're feeling now is nothing compared to what's coming. I'm in favor of being ready."

"Exactly," Arkan says, looking around the room as the others chat quietly. "We need more infrastructure to support the growth. And selfishly, I'd like to see us get a skyball coach, seeing as how we've never had one. I have two candidates in mind and I'd love to bring them both to Ever on a trial basis."

"Moving fast, aren't you?" Alo frowns at Arkan from his spot across the table.

Arkan's tail stops swishing. "Part of the reason I came to Ever was to usher in an era of growth. This haven hasn't grown meaningfully in about two centuries. That was fine for a time. But Catherine's point about growth happening either way is spot on. We can be ready for it and provide everyone with a good experience. Or we can ignore it and deal with being too busy and the pains that'll bring."

Ohken sinks back into his chair with a sigh, scratching at his stubble with the fingers of one big green hand. After a long moment, he nods. "I'm in favor of exploring this. At the end of the day, I want more time with my mate. Let's keep Ever functioning like a well oiled machine."

Arkan beams, white teeth flashing in the fluorescent light from Town Hall's auditorium ceiling. "I'm glad you're all in agreement, because I have a call with Manorin Longhorn tomorrow about coming to Ever for a trial period."

Oh my gods.

Manorin Longhorn.

I clasp my hands in my lap as I try to gather the thoughts that dash around my mind at that name.

Alo snorts. "Manorin Longhorn? Are you shitting me? He's a fucking skyball legend."

Arkan's smile grows impossibly broad, stretching across his handsome face. "He coached me when I was going through the Protector Academy. I tried to recruit him for my last haven but he had no interest in leaving Hearth Headquarters or the Hellions. He agreed to take my call tomorrow, though, so I'm hopeful things are changing for him. I'll keep you posted." He sighs. "I know it seems like I'm suggesting we move quickly, but if we can get Manorin Longhorn to come here and build a team, wow. That would really be something. And I don't see why we can't do that and plan expansion all at the same time. The stadium's just sitting there unused..." His voice drifts off as he looks around the table.

I glance at Vikand, curious to see what he thinks. To my surprise, he's holding a tiny book in one hand, glasses perched on the tip of his nose as he reads. He's not listening. At all.

A delicious scent curls across my consciousness and my nostrils flare to pull in more of that delectable smell.

Across the table from me, Vikand glances up from his book, appearing lost in thought. I'd bet a million dollars he's thinking about something sensual, because he smells so damn good like fresh hay and pine needles. My sensual nature rises as I watch him cock his head to one side. After a moment, he looks back down at the book, shifting on his bench.

Arkan closes the meeting, and when Vikand rises from the centaur bench, I round the table and approach him, marveling at how much taller he is than me. Not that that would be a problem between us. I'm a succubus. I can handle literally anything in *that* department.

Vikand's dark coat shines with health, his form still fit despite his age. He's got to be nearly as old as I am—many, many centuries—and I love that.

"Hello, Vikand." I smile brightly up at the handsome centaur.

He jolts slightly, having been lost in thought. Just as quickly, he tucks the tiny book into a pocket in his vest and smiles down at me, adjusting the glasses perched on the tip of his nose. He and Arkan could be twins with the same dark skin and long braided hair, but Vikand's age is evident in the creased lines at the edges of his eyes and mouth. Gods above, he's handsome with those high cheekbones and brilliant blue eyes.

"H-hello, Catherine." He clears his throat, slipping a thumb into the pocket of his fitted navy vest. "You look lovely this evening."

I glance down at the figure hugging emerald wrap dress I picked out. I've always had a full, buxom figure—most succubi do—but this particular dress really shows off my curves.

"Thank you." I beam up at him. "Listen, would you like to have a picnic with me one afternoon next week? There's a great little spot I know, I think you'd really enjoy it."

Vikand stares for a long moment, then clears his throat again as sensual pheromones saturate the air between us. My power means I can read everyone's pheromones. It's an ability that helps me read those around me more easily. It's how I always know which monsters will end up together, because I can literally smell attraction the moment I see them together.

It's how I know *now* that Vikand is sincere in his compliment. I take another step forward, knowing my proximity's having an effect on him as the scent of pine needles takes on a bright, lemony edge. His mouth drops slightly open, his nostrils flaring as his pupils blow wide.

"I...yes, sure. I'd like that. Just let me know when and where."

I knew I'd have to make the first move. Vikand is many, many enticing things, but forward in the romance department is not one of them. And honestly? I'm good with that. I was once mated to a male who could charm the pants off of anyone and it ended poorly. I've had enough of that sort of monster to last a million lifetimes.

"How about next Wednesday. Pick me up at the Annabelle and we'll walk together, alright?" I reach up and rest a hand on his upper stomach, curling my fingers gently into the fabric of his vest.

He shudders and shifts from one foot to the other, his voice quiet when he speaks. "Alright, Catherine. Would lunchtime work for you?"

I try to shove disappointment away. Lunchtime feels like a business meeting. But still…it's a start.

"Lunchtime sounds lovely, Vikand. I'll pack us a picnic."

"I'm not a picky eater," he says with a smile.

Errr…okay.

Dropping my hand, I wink at him as I turn and flip my hair over my shoulder. "See you Wednesday for lunch, Vikand."

I sashay toward the exit. My neighbor Alo stands at the door, a wry smile on his face.

"Not a word," I chirp as he holds his elbow out for me.

Alo snorts out a laugh. "Oh my gorgeous friend, you already know my thoughts on this topic."

"So I do." I wave those thoughts away as I slip a hand through his elbow. "Remember how you ignored me for five years while I suggested you ask Miriam out? I'm going to ignore you like you did me and it's going to be just fine, Alo. Now, can we talk about something more fun on the way back home or are you going to give me love advice?"

He rests his free hand over mine as he guides me along the long hall to the exit.

"I don't need to give advice that's gonna fall on deaf ears, Cath. You're a grown ass woman. Do what you want. For the record, I did eventually ask her out."

I grin up at him. "I will, thank you. And I'm glad it only took you five years to realize your best friend was your soul mate."

He smiles down at me. "Point taken. Moving on. What do you make of this Manorin Longhorn news? I'm pretty excited about that, honestly, although I don't wanna play full time either. I'd do part time though."

Something deep inside me heats at Manorin's name.

"I dated him back in the day," I whisper, not willing that secret to go any farther than Alo's ears.

"Get the hells outta here." He scoffs, dark horns flexing as his amethyst eyes go wide. "Seriously?"

I nod. "It was pretty serious at the time, but we were younger. It was before he coached skyball at the headquarters haven. And before you-know-who."

Alo waggles both black brows at me. "Well, Catherine. I must say, this is an interesting development."

"Is it?" I feign innocence, then I scowl up at one of my favorite monsters in Ever. "Keep that to yourself. At this point, Manorin and I are nothing but old friends."

"Certainly would give him a leg up in this coach search Arkan's got going on."

I shake my head. "Nah. Our ancient history will have absolutely no bearing on that. You know I love skyball so I'm fully on board with Arkan's plan to bring it here. I want the best coach we can possibly get."

"Mhm, okay." Alo's tone is agreeable, but I suspect it's not the last I'll hear on this subject. Just like he keeps promising not to insert himself into my pursuit of Vikand the centaur. Yet even so, he's regular and loud with his opinions on the topic.

Not that it matters. I will do whatever, and whoever, the hells I want.

CHAPTER TWO - MANORIN

I glance out of the window in my first floor office, admiring how peaceful and quiet the skyball field looks this early in the morning. In a half hour, the perfectly manicured field will be bustling with the Protector Academy *and* pro skyball teams—intramurals start today.

A reminder pings from the blue leather watch strapped around my wrist. I've got an important call starting in two minutes. I've been working at my computer for hours, planning the primary and secondary lineups for the upcoming season, and my back hurts from hunching so far over the desk. Standing, I roll my broad shoulders, grimacing at how my long horns scrape the ceiling if I stand up too straight.

This office wasn't made for a minotaur of my size, much less a longhorn minotaur. I've been the head coach of the Hearth HQ Hellions for a very long time. The coach before me was a gargoyle.

A lot shorter.

And a lot less strict with his players, if the old stories are to be believed.

I probably should've had the office renovated, but it never seemed to be top of mind.

The Hearth HQ skyball team was a damn mess when I got hired, but I've whipped them into shape over the last two centuries. Many seasons' worth of players have come and gone during that time, but I've turned out a solid string of superstars, many of whom have gone on to have long, illustrious pro careers. Glancing out the door of my office, I smile at the paintings of famous skyball players lining the hallway. Ninety percent of those were cultivated during my tenure here.

I smile bigger as I consider that. A ping breaks through the thought, the communication disk on my wall flashing blue. A name hologram rises above the tech's circular surface.

Ever Keeper.

Of course, I always knew him as Arkan Canterbury, a centaur who was a star player while studying at the academy. Now he goes by his title—Keeper—of the monster haven of Ever, in America.

Massachusetts state, I think.

I grab the comm disk and set it carefully on my desk, directing it to answer Arkan's call.

A life-sized hologram figure rises up from the disk, and my former player smiles, the grin splitting his handsome dark features.

I cross my arms over my chest. "You don't look a day older, Arkan. Or should I say "Keeper"?"

He waves away the comment. "The Evertons call me both. It was hard for me to give up my name for the title, even though that's traditional for a keeper."

I consider that for a moment. I could no sooner give up the Longhorn name than chop off an arm. It's a point of pride for other longhorn minotaurs to cherish our shared last name.

"So," Arkan says, "I'll get straight to the point. I wanted to recruit you in my last haven, but it wasn't the right time for that community or you. I'm pretty sure you know why I'm calling this time, and you took the call, so what's changed?"

I suck at my teeth as I think about his question. What *has* changed in the decades since Arkan last tried to steal me from my position as head coach?

"To be honest," I begin, "I've accomplished a lot for the Hellions. I've run this program for almost two hundred years. My brain keeps going into build mode, but the Hellions program is a well-oiled machine at this point." I shrug and glance out the window at the skyball pitch again. After a moment, I return my focus to the black-coated centaur male. "I'm looking for something messy that I can fix up and make shine."

Arkan grins and crosses his arms, matching my stance. "Well, Coach, it just so happens that the Ever team is messy as hells, full of part-timers with no coach at *all*. In fact, one of my players threatened to quit last night if I made him attend a *practice*. The team made it all the way to the finals last year, as you know, despite that. But there's zero recruiting and literally no program to speak of. We have an empty stadium that I don't think anyone's set foot in since the finals. Ever wouldn't be something messy, it would be starting from the basement and working from the ground up. How does that sound?"

Part of me aches as he talks. That's exactly what I want. But another part of me longs for the open ranges and clear skies of my home haven, Pine Gulch. My dream job would take me there. Unfortunately for me, the Pine Gulch coach has held his role for six centuries with no signs of slowing down. I don't think that job'll ever open up, not unless the gods and goddesses themselves descend to drag Rip Shorthorn outta that job.

"I need more information." I uncross my arms and tuck my hands into the pockets of my too-tight jeans. "I'm interested, though. What's your evaluation process look like? Who else are you looking at? What are your next steps?"

Arkan grins. "I hoped you'd say that, Manorin. I'm also looking at a younger coach from a remote haven in Brazil...Gil Stoneswallow. As for eval, I'd like you to come here for a trial period once your intramurals end and before the season starts. He'll be doing the same thing, although you won't overlap. You've got a couple weeks off coming up, if memory serves?" He winks. I may technically have that time off, but he knows I've never taken it once in my entire career.

"I'll manage," I grit out. This is important. It's time for me to consider moving on.

"I'll start making arrangements," Arkan says with a huge smile. "Would you prefer to stay at our local wraith motel or up at the Annabelle Inn? The inn's closer to downtown and the skyball stadium. The wraith motel is like most others—opulent beyond belief with an incredible kitchen."

A smile turns my lips upward, the ring in my nose shimmying. "Catherine Evrien still run the Annabelle Inn?"

Arkan returns my feral look. "She does."

"Book me there, then. She and I are old friends."

Friends isn't the right word, but I don't need to get into that with Arkan.

"Done," Arkan says. "I'll email you later with all the details. I'm crazy excited about this, Manorin. I've got the one other candidate because I promised the haven leadership team that I'd do my due diligence. But the reality is that if you'll have us, I want you for Ever."

"You always were my favorite, but don't be a suckup," I say with a snort.

He beams and tosses long black braids over his shoulder. "My mate is calling me for dinner, but I'll email those details soon. Goodbye, old friend."

I swat at his hologram and he ducks out of the way. "It's still Coach to you, kid."

He laughs and signs off.

For a long time after he's gone, I stare at the communication disk. Eventually, I set it back on the wall as I consider our conversation. Am I really pursuing this? A team with no coach and no program to speak of? It's a dream come true, something I haven't done yet. The Hellions were a mess when I took them over, but there was the semblance of a program and there *was* a head coach before me, even if he was shitty.

Ever's a blank slate, and I love that for me.

Voices drift up the hall, followed by the thwap of wings and clipclop of hooves. The academy players are arriving for practice. Turning to the locker in my office, I unbutton my shirt along one shoulder and down one side so I can pull it off without yanking it up over my horns. I toss it aside and check out my reflection in the mirror. I might be approaching my eighth century—minotaurs are long-lived—but I'm still built like most of my players. The only hint that I'm older is a bit of salt dusting the oaky brown fur at my temples.

I grab a Hellions tee and button it over my broad chest. Kicking my way out of my jeans, I grab a pair of red and black athletic shorts. When I pull them up, they hug my thighs and sack, accentuating the bulge between my legs. I used to think it was ridiculous that athletic shorts aren't made in sizes that fit athletes. Then I realized that's on purpose.

The industry *wants* to tease its fans and onlookers with our bodies. Hot players in tight shirts and dick-hugging shorts are what the fans want. Cock outlines sell tickets. Actual erections are even better.

Adjusting my sack around the tight fabric, I mutter about the shorts issue and grab my whistle. I unclip it and reclip it around my neck. I'm so broad it barely hangs down into the hollow at the base of my throat. Maybe it's time for a longer string.

When I leave my office a shorthorn minotaur jogs up the hallway and stops in front of me with a big smile. "You ready for intramurals, coach? We're gonna kick some ass out there today!"

"Hells yeah we are," I say, my tone pure gravel. "Those pro assholes won't know what hit 'em, right player?" It's all bluster, I coach both Hearth's academy and pro teams, but we're split right now to prep for intramurals.

"Fuck yes," he hisses, clapping me on the shoulder. "I'm ready, Coach."

Good. I am too.

Ready to kick ass, take names, and maybe start something new.

~

The following Wednesday morning, I walk across the new Grand Portal Station, locating the glowing green portal that'll take me from Hearth HQ to Ever, all the way across the world. To the left of the Ever portal is a fabulous coffee shop called Higher Grounds. I consider stopping in for a latte, but it's actually their second location. The original is in downtown Ever.

I'd like to try the location I'd regularly go to, if this move works out. Smiling, I sling my duffel bag over my shoulder and step through the portal into a short hallway filled with luminescent green light. When I reach the end, the portal opens into Ever's portal station, a cavernous tiled room with a view of the forest beyond.

My goal for today is to get to the stadium as quickly as possible. I'm due to meet Arkan there in an hour, but I'd like to see it alone first…without outside perspective. It's Arkan's job to sell me on this monster haven and the position, but I like to form my own opinions irrespective of the sales pitch.

As I stalk across the big open portal station building toward the door, whispers follow me. My size is enough to garner attention on a good day, but couple that with my reputation as a skyball coach and you've got a recipe for lots of attention.

Not that I mind. I *live* for the attention. But I told no one at HQ about this trip and I don't plan to make a big fuss out of my presence here. For all the Evertons know, I'm here on vacation for now.

Grinning, I sail through the door and into a beautifully forested area. A singular road leads toward the main drag, according to the map I studied before my trip. It's crisp here. Ever's one of a few havens with the same weather pattern year round. I'm sure on the one hand that's nice, but it makes me think of how Pine Gulch simply follows Montana's natural weather patterns. I fucking love the snow there.

It's a quarter hour walk through beautiful quiet forest to downtown Ever. The first business I see apart from a doctor's cottage is the original Higher Grounds location, a two story brick thing with a cute red and white striped awning. I'm desperate for a latte, so I stop in. It's packed full on the inside, coffee dripping and popping and machines sputtering as the vampires behind the bar craft their famous monster-specific concoctions.

It takes nearly another quarter hour to order, and a few minutes after that to get my simple order. Twenty minutes to get a coffee is absurd.

Arkan mentioned that Ever's growing, and it's easy to see it's true. The vampires behind the counter hustled the entire time I was there…it's just crazy busy here. Hearth HQ has faced similar growing pains since the portal station opened, although not to the degree of other havens.

I consider the line out the door a good sign, actually. Smaller havens don't usually opt into the skyball program because it requires a certain amount of investment, and Ever's on the smaller size for a monster haven. Growth brings money and money makes developing a skyball program a whole lot easier.

Heading for the door, I take my first sip of the Azuro dark roast and groan in satisfaction. There's nothing like Azuro coffee beans and these are roasted to perfection. Even though the shop's busy, whispers follow me here, too. A few furtive glances and finger points later and I'm pretty sure I'm gonna end up signing at least one autograph before I get out the door.

Coffee in one hand and my bag in the other, I shoulder my way out of the shop without being stopped and head up the cross street, Sycamore, toward the skyball stadium. The Community Garden is on my left as I walk, and Catherine's beautiful Annabelle Inn sits across from it.

The Annabelle's pink siding and ornate gingerbread trim make me think of my old flame, Catherine, its owner. Memories from my younger years flood back. She and I dated pretty seriously for a while. It came to an unfortunate end—she was the one who got away—but it's been a long time since that.

Catherine was the hottest sex of my life, if I'm honest, and I've taken plenty of lovers since then.

My cock hardens in my sheath, threatening to make an inappropriate display as I rein in my errant thoughts. Now isn't the time to think about the succubus who stole my heart and shattered it when she left. No, that was a long time ago.

I sip my latte as I continue up Sycamore and past rows of adorable cottages. Ever really is quaint to the max—a polar opposite of the cold, dark, and snowy haven that's been my home these last few centuries.

Rounding a corner, I find the skyball stadium off in the distance across a giant field. I'm guessing the field is for parking. Ever hosted the skyball finals last year, but hasn't hosted a game since. As I walk across the field, it's clear that no one has parked here in a long time...grass grows in the tire tracks. It's a missed opportunity. Hosted games mean money and advertising, both of which are good for local businesses, assuming the haven wants to grow.

Of course, not every haven wants that. Many of them don't even have a skyball team. There are twenty-four teams at this point, though, so a solid half of the monster haven system has opted into the skyball program. But again, it takes money and commitment from haven leadership to produce a skyball program that's any good. Not to mention the haven itself has to be well designed to attract and keep star players.

That could be a problem in Ever. The downtown's pretty small and there aren't a ton of businesses to accommodate a growing population of monsters.

The stadium soars high above me, all dark stone with giant curved archway entries every twenty feet or so. Green and gold flags announce the home team as the Ever Misfits. I leave my bag by one of the doors and head into the stadium's interior.

It's brand new, built last year for the finals. It's got a troll's touch in the way the stone seems hewn directly out of a mountainside. I'd wager a troll worked with this haven's former Keeper to build this place. I run my fingers along the beautiful stone as I walk around the outer hallway where most of the concessions usually are.

By the time I reach the far side, I've got to give it to this stadium's designer. It's gorgeous and well thought out. There's plenty of access to the concession locations and the hallway itself is nice and wide and tall—which is important for winged monsters who often prefer to fly versus walk.

The clipclop of hooves announces Arkan's arrival. I turn to find the tall centaur walking up the hallway toward me. He grins as he reaches a hand out to shake mine.

His colorful shirt catches my eye.

I squint to read it, then snort with laughter as I shake his hand.

He grabs at the shirt and holds the fabric wide as if to help me see it better. "'*I'm a Fucking Delight*'. Wren Hector, our resident green witch, gave this to me and said it suited my cheerful disposition." He winks. "Imagine if she'd have met me before I became Ever's Keeper."

My smile goes softer at that. It's well known that the haven Keeper training strips keepers of most of their emotion, leaving them with an intense focus on rational, logical thought processes to help them make decisions more effectively. Despite that formal training for his role, Arkan's always remained more sunny and positive than the average monster.

"So," he continues, waving at the stadium around us, "this is the stadium. It was built last year by Ohken Stonesmith and the former Keeper, both of whom are casual players on the team. I was planning to give you a tour, but you've seen this much of it. Let's take a peek at the war room and locker rooms and what would be your office." He nudges me in the side. "It's extra tall. Your horns won't even hit the ceiling. That would be a nice change, eh?"

I snort in agreement and he continues on.

"I've got the team coming to meet us in half an hour. You mentioned wanting to see a short practice, and they're excited to meet you."

"Lead the way, kid."

He snorts and swishes his tail at me. "Not a kid anymore. Not hardly."

I shrug. "You'll always be a snarky, better than he should be for the effort he puts in player to me."

Arkan laughs. "I'll admit I was distracted on the best of days. I pulled through during the games, thank fuck."

We share a laugh at that, walking toward one end of the stadium. Arkan badges us into a private hallway that leads to the first locker room.

And it…is…amazing.

One entire wall is one-way glass, allowing the players to see the field without ticketholders seeing in. The view is incredible, the entire field visible from inside. The war room's even better, sitting at ground level but with a crazy screen showing the entire field from above. It's ideally suited for the type of planning I like to do.

Of course, Arkan already knows this. I suspect this part of the war room is an addition meant to entice me.

And it fucking does.

What doesn't thrill me is half an hour later when I meet the team. I know most of them—it's my job to know even those players who aren't full time—but there's not a single monster on this team who's full time or even *wants* to be. Not only that, but a vast majority of them seem almost skeptical about having me here for a trial period.

I plant both hands on my hips as I stare at the row of centaurs, gargoyles, and a big green troll who eyes me with his arms crossed.

The only one who looks excited to be here is Hana Canterbury, Arkan's beautiful centaur mate. She was a kickass player at the academy, too. She didn't go pro but she could have. My wheels start spinning, wondering if it's possible to get her to *consider* full time now. I'm not sure how much extra responsibility she takes on as the Keeper's mate.

"I'd like to see what you're capable of." I count the players out. "Split into two teams and let's play a quarter. Even though most of you aren't full timers, you're what I'd have to work with in the beginning. Let's see what you're made of."

Arkan stands by my side as a few muttered grumblings reach us. I glance up at him.

"This whole team needs to be rebuilt."

Arkan frowns, sucking at his teeth. "I did tell you we didn't have any pros, Manorin. I was serious."

I match his expression, lifting my whistle and biting it between my teeth.

Arkan holds a skyball under one arm. Cantering to the center of the field, he winks at his wife before tossing the skyball in the air. The flurry of activity happens fast, the bridge troll executing a perfect flip as he snatches the ball off the ground.

Damnit, he's good and of course he doesn't want to be full time.

As I watch the team play, it's clear there's a lot of talent despite the fact that, to my amazement, they haven't practiced since last year's skyball finals. I decide right then and there not to bother with any other practices while I'm here. There's no point to piss off the locals considering not a one of them would remain on the team if I get this job and accept it.

One thing is clear—building a skyball program in Ever would be a ton of fucking work.

BOOKS BY ANNA FURY (MY OTHER PEN NAME)

DARK FANTASY SHIFTER OMEGAVERSE

Temple Maze Series

NOIRE | JET | TENEBRIS

DYSTOPIAN OMEGAVERSE

Alpha Compound Series

THE ALPHA AWAKENS | WAKE UP, ALPHA | WIDE AWAKE | SLEEPWALK | AWAKE AT LAST

Northern Rejects Series

ROCK HARD REJECT | HEARTLESS HEATHEN | PRETTY LITTLE SINNER

Scan the QR code to access all my books, socials, current deals and more!

@annafuryauthor
liinks.co/annafuryauthor

ABOUT THE AUTHOR

Hazel Mack is the sweet alter-ego of Anna Fury, a North Carolina native fluent in snark and sarcasm, tiki decor, and an aficionado of phallic plants. Visit her on Instagram for a glimpse of the sexiest wiener wallpaper you've ever seen. #ifyouknowyouknow

She writes any time she has a free minute—walking the dogs, in the shower, ON THE TOILET. The voices in her head wait for no one. When she's not furiously hen-pecking at her computer, she loves to hike and bike and get out in nature.

She currently lives in Raleigh, North Carolina, with her Mr. Right, a tiny tornado, and two sassy dogs. Hazel LOVES to connect with readers, so visit her on social or email her at author@annafury.com.

Printed in Great Britain
by Amazon